Kings of the Earth

Kings of the Earth

Everything, Volume Two

STEVEN DELAY

RESOURCE *Publications* · Eugene, Oregon

KINGS OF THE EARTH
Everything, Volume Two

Resource Publications
An Imprint of Wipf and Stock Publishers
199 W. 8th Ave., Suite 3
Eugene, OR 97401

www.wipfandstock.com

PAPERBACK ISBN: 978-1-6667-4012-7
HARDCOVER ISBN: 978-1-6667-4013-4
EBOOK ISBN: 978-1-6667-4014-1

APRIL 25, 2022 12:06 PM

As always,
to Gabriella

ONE

I F the street lying below the window to his second-story room was socked in by thick mist, the burl of haze slowly untangling itself as it meandered past the streetlamps, corralled by the surrounding expanse of great limestone walls, he himself felt entirely translucent, as if he were emptied within of all shadow of turning. He had felt this way before, although he couldn't recall when or where exactly. It was an attunement to night at once as familiar as it was rare. He felt as still as the night itself, satisfied with that reflective contentment which delights in the sureness of its own serenity. In reverie, he looked down at the windowsill. He couldn't recall precisely how many cigarettes he had smoked, but judging by the pile of ashes, he realized he must have been where he was for nearly an hour now, sitting on top of his desk, his hand dangling outside the frame. A little while ago, according to nightly tradition, the college's bell tower had rung out one hundred and one times, and everything had been quiet since. Though he had always disliked the expression, perched here at his apartment window with a view to the whole street, the college's main front entrance to his left, its side gardens directly across the way, the back entrance looming in the distance, and the adjoining meadow too, he understood what people meant when they spoke of being in the catbird's seat. It had only been a few weeks since arriving to Oxford, but this was a place, he well already understood, that could easily enkindle an individual's pride—the City of Dreaming Spires. He searched his memory for the explanation behind the origin of the city's nickname. Relishing the scene outside his window embodying the verse itself, the line from Arnold's poem *Thyrsis* entered his thought:

> And that sweet City with her dreaming spires . . . Lovely all times she lies, lovely to-night.

It made manifest sense to him why someone might well even liken this place itself to a piece of poetry, or to an enchantment, to a dream, that invariably gives birth to rhyme.

Moving to a new place, he knew, could prematurely invite overly rosy impressions, but if there were any place in the world that might be suited to call forth inspired thinking, and writing, it appeared to him this would be it. The atmosphere was capacious, the halls, cafés, restaurants, shops, museums, and parks infused with a palpable aura of possibility and exploration. The contentment shifted to exhilaration thinking about it, and he felt stirred to leave the room, and to take a walk. It was late, to be sure, after midnight in fact, but he had nowhere to be tomorrow. His doctoral supervisor, Klaus Carman, who lived in London, was not in Oxford most days except when teaching at the college. This had delayed their first meeting, but he was so preoccupied getting to know the city and establishing a routine, that he hardly noticed it had been two weeks here already. In any case, they were due to meet the coming Wednesday at his supervisor's office, where they'd then walk over for lunch at the faculty dining room. What mattered at this hour was not any of the philosophical work he had come to do, but simply the fact that he was free tonight to do as he pleased. To him, the night beckoned.

Even now in his late twenties, he occasionally would still experience the sudden rush of freedom washing over him in moments like these, times when he would brim with an overwhelming feeling of appreciation for being able to set his own bedtime and go wherever he wished. Nobody could tell him when to go to bed like when he was a child, and he didn't have to be at work in the morning like so many of his old friends he had known from childhood did today. He himself had worked enough day jobs over the years to know the misery of dreading the night before having to go to the drudgery of work in the morning. He put on a coat, and walked down the stairs. When, then, he stepped through the gate onto the street, it was with a sense of immense gratitude. He was free to go wherever the night led him.

The city was a walking town, where one could get anywhere easily by foot, or, if really necessary when on a tight schedule, a short bike ride. There was considerable bus and taxi traffic in the city center throughout the day, but very few residents drove. Outside the gate to his building, he debated which way to take. Right would lead away from the town center, where the road would shortly reach an access path leading along the river Isis. Left would lead past the front gate of the college and then onto the High St. From there, any of the town's major attractions would be within minutes. A compromise presented itself. Head right toward the river, take the path on the near shore paralleling the edge of the college's meadow, and cut through the gardens to then emerge on the other side of the college. That would put him only a block from the High St. It was the sort of impromptu decision that demonstrated a growing command of the town's layout, a satisfying indicator that he was beginning to settle into the new place. This was still not home, but he was feeling more assured each day that soon it would be.

As he began walking, he immediately felt good about his decision to head right, which would allow him to see the meadow and river under the moonlight. He would be able to enjoy the solitude, but without wandering too far from the main sites still waiting to be seen in the town center. He had not yet seen many things at night without the tourists swarming them during the day. In a way, tonight's walk would be seeing things for the first time.

The corner Tesco was closed. Down the way in the near distance, he looked and saw the mist hovering over the surface of the river. The location was renowned for its beautiful swans, but he had not yet seen one since arriving. He scanned the water beneath Folly Bridge to see whether there were any out tonight, as he walked along the path with the meadow beside him. The cows were all put away, the birds were asleep, and so aside from the river itself, things were perfectly still.

A number of boathouses were tethered to the shore. A light flickered on, and a young man, probably a student from the college, came outside for a smoke. The man lit his cigarette and waved from the boat, "Hey, mate."

The man looked tipsy, and in the mood to chat with somebody, but he didn't feel like stopping, so he continued walking.

"Hi," he said, as he passed by the boat. He could feel the man watching him as he walked on, but he didn't turn to look back.

He cut over onto the meadow trail and proceeded toward the gardens. The meadow had recently been cut, which meant there was no brush obscuring the view of the college in the distance. In the night light, the college's silhouette surged up from the soil, alit with its golden lights, shrouded underneath the crystal moon. The college's cathedral spire and front tower were both even more impressive at night than in the day, he saw. Tom Tower was what they called the latter. Designed in the seventeenth century by Sir Christopher Wren, the Gothic gatehouse was one of the city's most iconic structures. The tower's grand dome loomed over Tom Quad, the largest among all of Oxford's quadrangles. Situated on Tom were a number of residences for senior college and Cathedral officials, including the Dean, along with the Great Hall, which in recent years had become famous for having served as the inspiration for Harry Potter's Hogwarts. He had never liked the book franchise, and he had never seen any of the movies. The college gift shop, which sold all sorts of trinkets associated with the story, attracted half a million tourists a year, clogging the college's walkways and cloisters, and blocking its entryways with gawkers. Many members of the college detested the crowds, viewing them as a personal inconvenience, but he didn't mind the bustle. In time, he conceded, perhaps the crowds would begin to irritate him. But not now. What troubled him about the tourism, if anything, was the fact that it was a sign of society's general decline, that the august college would today be best recognized by most people for having served as a movie set. And yet, although the reputation of the grandest Oxford college was no longer immune to the influences of commercialization, the buildings themselves were as beautiful here tonight as they were four or five hundred years ago. So many thinkers, writers, scientists, and statesmen had walked these grounds, he thought. The names entered his mind in rapid succession: John Wesley, W. H. Auden, Albert Einstein, and Lewis Carroll. He could not recall their names, but thirteen British prime ministers had been educated at the college. Queen Elizabeth I was the Visitor—he did not know what that meant exactly, but it was something everyone always mentioned. And, of course, there was the college's legacy of philosophers, boasting as it did John Locke, John Rawls, A. J. Ayer, and Gilbert Ryle. His thought drifted back to the protruding tower spiraling to the stars. It occurred to him that the architect, Wren, was rumored to have been a Mason. He thought of the bar in Houston and its checkerboard wall. He hoped Alison, who was still in Houston, was keeping her promise not to go there anymore. But there was no way to know.

Passing between the cricket fields and a cloistered garden, he reached the gate to enter the street, but finding it locked, he hopped the wrought iron fence. He looked over his shoulder to peer over the garden wall, and gazed up at the Cathedral. The Cathedral served as the Anglican diocese of Oxford, and it still held regular services. On the couple occasions on which he had visited it in his first weeks here, it hadn't felt like a house of God to him, more so just a place of empty ceremony and ritual. The choir, though, he thought, was absolutely beautiful.

As he strode through the series of narrow side streets on route to the High St, his thought turned to what he might want to write in the dissertation. Ultimately, of course, that was what he was here to do, and although there currently weren't any formal deadlines drawing near, he already felt an internal pressure to organize his thoughts on the matter. An oddity struck him. He had flown thousands of miles across the Atlantic to leave what had been home, to come here, only to do what, in a way, he could do anywhere. Thinking was thinking, he thought. And yet, at the same time, there was something to be said for the suggestion that one's surroundings shaped one's thinking. Beauty, for one, could inspire, and this was certainly a beautiful place. On the other hand, he quickly conceded, producing good work was still a matter of resolve, and no amount of inspiration could overcome laziness or frivolity. In fact, at a place such as this, it seemed to him that there was a danger in expecting the work to get itself done simply because it was the sort of place renowned for its history of producing great work. Nothing wrote itself, he decided. To not lose his way, he would have to remain mindful of that fundamental truth.

Considering the matter further, he concluded that his own intellectual itinerary had thus far been proof of the fact that thinking could always transcend its conditions. Among other things, that had meant exceeding institutional expectations. In California, for instance, he had attended a state school for his undergraduate studies. Originally, he had planned to study statistics with an eye to a career in polling or political consultancy, but after souring on politics and taking a philosophy course one summer, he was hooked, so he switched his major to philosophy. At the time, he had been a fervent atheist, a materialist, someone who thought that all the world's ills and injustices could be cured if everyone would be more rational. His thought turned briefly to the night of his conversion, the night, at least, when he came to believe there was a God in the face of his indisputable presence. It had been a solitary, starry night much like this one. As he had read later, from what Pascal wrote, evidently the Frenchman had known such an experience too: "From about half past ten at night until about half past midnight, FIRE. GOD of Abraham, GOD of Isaac, GOD of Jacob, not of the philosophers and of the learned. Certitude. Certitude. Feeling. Joy. Peace . . . Joy, joy, joy, tears of joy."

By the time he finished his undergraduate program, his worldview had changed completely, and continuing on to graduate school had become a realistic academic option. He laughed as he brought to mind the time that he and his mother had visited Chicago. The university there was one of his top choices. They picked a terrible day for a visit. The campus was cold and snowy, which made his mother grumpy. Even worse, it was over an academic holiday, so the department was deserted. Just as he reached the stairwell to leave, the department chair, who had been in his office, saw him and invited him in for a chat.

"Take a seat," the professor said.

"Thanks for your time," he said. They exchanged names.

The professor stared through his glasses, his eyes shifting slightly. "So, what brings you here?"

He briefly recounted his academic background, stating his intention to apply to the graduate program. The professor paused very delicately, letting it be known that he was trying to avoid saying anything potentially offensive or demeaning.

"I see. Well, do you know anyone affiliated with the department?"

At the time of the conversation, he hadn't understood the professor must have already known the answer to his own question. But years later, here now at Oxford, with the benefit of hindsight, it was clear to him that the professor must have known what he would go on to say in response. The professor's motivation for asking the question, then, must simply have been curiosity, to see whether the answer from this hapless student who had shown up cluelessly at his office might at least provide some amusing gossip.

"Oh, yes. I know Klaus. Klaus Carman. He taught at my school for a little while before taking a job at Oxford. He did his graduate studies here."

The professor, who of course knew Klaus had studied there, changed the subject.

"Oh, yes, I remember him. Well, coming from a state school as you are, to be honest, I don't think you'll have much of a chance of admission to our program, which is very competitive. But you can always apply."

They chatted for a few more minutes, after which he excused himself from the professor's office politely. When he got outside, his mother was waiting.

"How did it go?"

He recounted the conversation.

He could tell she didn't want to tell him what she must know he already knew also, that the professor had gone out of his way to tell him he was not cut out for the program. He remembered thinking it was strange for the chair of a philosophy department to reach that sort of conclusion so hastily, apparently based solely on the school he attended, which didn't seem to him to be something necessarily decisive as to whether or not he had the potential to be a good philosophy student. He understood well that elitism was part of the world, and academia was no exception, but he found it odd coming from a man who conceived of himself as being a philosopher. Or maybe the man he had just spoken to wasn't a philosopher, just a philosophy professor. There was a difference, of course, although it was hard to express precisely in what the difference consisted. Maybe for the man it was a job only, something he had been motivated to pursue because, though less lucrative, socially it would be about as impressive as being able to tell those he knew that he was a lawyer or a doctor. As vulgar and superficial as that would be, he recognized it was a mentality in academia more prevalent than he wished it were.

A year after the disheartening visit to Chicago, he received rejections from every single doctoral program to which he'd applied but one. Without ever expecting it, then, he found himself headed to Texas. Klaus, who by then was already settling in at Oxford, assured him the program would be a good fit for his particular budding philosophical interests, because Carrell, whom Klaus had known personally for a number of years, was among the top scholars in the field. As for the program in Chicago, he consoled himself by remembering the one time that Klaus a couple years before had mentioned how it was a place full of head cases. Ultimately, perhaps he had dodged a bullet by not being accepted. In any case, coming from a state school had evidently hurt his admission chances everywhere else just as badly, as the department chair at Chicago had predicted it would.

Initially, Klaus appeared to be right about Texas. Carrell took him under his wing, helping him chart an intellectual course. In a meeting on one sunny summer afternoon not long after arriving to Texas, Carrell looked at him seriously and said, "Good writing comes from finding a voice. You need to find yours. Read as much as you can."

It had been good advice which experience had borne out. The trouble, however, was that the more he cultivated a voice of his own, the more Carrell himself became critical of the resulting work. It had all culminated with the independent reading leading to the B+ on the term paper. A few months after the ridiculous grade, the paper had appeared in print in a flagship journal in the field. It was his first publication. He did not have to mention anything to Carrell about it, because it was clear the paper had been vindicated, and that it hadn't deserved the grade it had received. After triangulating his own experience with those of others in the program such as Karl Roybal and James Dulas, he came to confirm, as he had suspected, that Carrell had ulterior motivations for treating the work as he was. Whatever those true reasons were, they had nothing strictly to do with philosophy. Seeing the writing on the wall, the transfer to Oxford was arranged. To his credit, Carrell had supplied a letter of recommendation. But the two of them never talked about why he was really leaving, nor did Carrell ever address the fate of the paper. He felt like Carrell had deceived him, by telling him to find his own voice, only to punish him when he did. For his own part, Carrell, he could tell, felt betrayed that he was taking his philosophical views in a direction critical of Carrell's own. As for Klaus, they never discussed Carrell explicitly, but he assumed Klaus must understand that he would not be desiring to leave Texas, unless the supervision with Carrell had been unsatisfying. He wondered whether Carrell and Klaus ever discussed the matter. Almost certainly they would have, although there was no way to know what either one had said to the other. As he now walked past the Rhodes statue outside Oriel College, he momentarily envisioned Carrell's screaming red face at the coffee house. He let out a relieved sigh, content to know he made the right decision to leave for here.

Inwardly cataloguing the events responsible for having led him to tonight's walk continued. Shortly before departing overseas, as he remembered, he had come home to California in order to see his parents. He wanted to see his old friends as well, but none of them were able to get away from work. His old undergraduate mentor, Phil Horowitz, however, sent him an email, offering to have lunch. He had not heard from Horowitz in a few years. Now that he was heading to Oxford, Horowitz probably was curious to see how he had managed to do it. Horowitz must have known Klaus had helped in some way. Perhaps Horowitz was interested in exploring the possibility of whether Klaus might help him make a similar move.

His old teacher had a reputation among students and colleagues for being egotistical, and perhaps it was not entirely unfounded, but he himself had always seen Horowitz as well-intentioned. Whatever arrogance there was about him, he thought, stemmed from a frustration Horowitz felt with those around him at the state school. The students tended to be lazy and only interested in partying and grades, indifferent to the ideas themselves. As for his colleagues, the vast majority of them had no serious research agenda, they weren't active in scholarly discussions, and they saw the job as a means to pay the bills, while they put their efforts into personal hobbies and other things outside philosophy. Horowitz, understandably, was starved for intellectual stimulation, and his egoism was a way of preserving his intellectual dignity despite his surroundings. It was somewhat vein, but it was not incomprehensible. When, then, Klaus had taken the job alongside Horowitz, the two of them naturally became fast friends, discussing all the ideas Horowitz couldn't discuss with anyone else. When Klaus later left for Oxford so shortly after having taken the job in California, Horowitz was devastated and felt abandoned. Being slighted that way made him further disillusioned, since, in his view, Klaus was off to greener pastures, while he remained behind to languish in the same intellectual backwater, in which he had been stuck for decades.

To Horowitz, then, he represented a bridge to Klaus, a way for his old teacher still to punch his own ticket elsewhere, maybe even to Oxford. He understood this was Horowitz's main reason for desiring to reconnect with him. He wished the relationship were founded on more than career ambitions, but so it was.

By the time Horowitz showed up to pick him up for lunch, he was beginning to feel uneasy about the whole thing. If Horowitz really thought his accepting the lunch offer was an implicit signal that he stood a chance of helping Horowitz make a move to Oxford through Klaus, he didn't want to give Horowitz false hope. Frankly, he had been surprised by his own acceptance to Oxford, and he had no institutional pull there at all. Klaus did, perhaps, but he wasn't in any position to tell Klaus to go to bat for Horowitz. He wondered if Horowitz and Klaus were themselves in touch, but he didn't want to ask, because that might offend Horowitz, since it would show he knew Horowitz was trying to find out whether there was a way through Klaus to get to Oxford. He sighed about how strange it all was, how so much of life with others was avoiding saying what everyone knew, or saying things in a way that avoided having to admit what others knew but for whatever reason didn't want to acknowledge. Language, he thought, should disclose things, but so often it instead was used to avoid or cloak reality, even distort it. In some way he would have to think through more fully later, reality itself could not be wholly linguistic. There must be something primal beneath it, otherwise language wouldn't be so effective at concealing and distorting the truth.

He heard a honk outside the window. He went to the door, opened it, and saw Horowitz idling the convertible outside, the top down, a big grin on his face, his hand waving. Despite it being a few years since seeing each other in person, his old teacher looked the same. He was tan, with a thick silver beard, and salt and pepper hair. As usual, he wore an expensive black button-down, and had sunglasses on.

"Phil," he said, approaching the car. "Very good to see you."

It truly was good to see him, even if he felt uncomfortable with the context motivating Horowitz to see him. He had experienced this before. Sometimes there could be trepidation toward someone or over a situation, but the moment he saw the person in the flesh, there was no feeling of negativity at all, and he would be surprised at the natural feelings of good will swirling inside him. He had always liked Horowitz, so the uneasiness he was feeling while waiting inside evaporated. As he walked to the car, his mind turned to the vignette someone had once told him that was meant to distill competing views about human nature. According to Hobbes, two strangers passing one another would stop to fight. According to Locke, they would introduce themselves and make fast friends. And according to Rousseau, they would pass by one another silently, each eyeing the other suspiciously. Even though so much of everyday human experience suggested otherwise, he believed that man was ultimately good. That was what made all of the world's terrible evils so appalling and unacceptable. Standing here in the California sun opening the convertible door, he looked at Phil's face, and he felt completely unguarded, totally unconcerned with whatever his old teacher's true motivations were for being here. As far as he was concerned, he was pleased to be an open book.

"It's been a while!" Phil said excitedly. His teacher threw the car in gear and sped off. "Is that your parents' house?"

"For now. They're just renting. They have a house in town which is being re-modelled. They should be moving in soon."

"Where?"

"Actually, not too far from the university. It's in that little neighborhood called Pineapple Hill."

"Oh, right, that's right down the street from campus," Phil said. Phil paused for a moment. "Well, congratulations on the extraordinary news. You must be thrilled." Phil kept his eyes on the road as he said it.

"Yes, I'm very excited. Thanks. Hard to believe. I wasn't expecting it."

"Neither was I! It's quite a move. I haven't heard of anything like it. I had assumed you were happily squared away in Texas. To all of a sudden end up at Oxford is very unusual. Have you talked to Klaus?" He decided whether he should get into it now with Phil, or wait till they got to the restaurant.

The moment of hesitation provided Phil time to decide to table it for later. Phil must have been worried that he had appeared overeager. "Oh, you know, never mind. We'll have time to catch up. Let's wait till we get to the restaurant," his teacher said.

"Where are we going?"

"Miguel's. It's a Mexican spot not far from my place." Phil lived outside town in the hills. It was stunning country, with wonderful vistas of the coastline. "You don't mind Mexican food, do you?"

"Oh, don't worry. I love it. Sounds good."

Phil sped up again, hugging the turn on the dirt country lane, as he changed lanes to get on the asphalt onramp for the freeway. "This thing handles really well," Phil said with a smile. It was hard to keep talking with the wind blowing from the top being down, so they both decided to be quiet till they reached the restaurant.

Inside, they snacked on chips, as they waited on the main dishes.

The waitress came to check on them. "Margarita, gentlemen?"

"No, no thanks. Just a water," he said.

"I'll take one, please. With salt," Horowitz said.

His teacher threw his arms up on top of the booth and leaned his head back. After staring at the ceiling for a moment, Horowitz turned his head. "So, have you talked to Klaus?"

"Yeah, I heard from him on the day of the decision. That was a few months ago. He said he'd see me when I get to Oxford. After receiving the news, which I heard here in California on a previous visit, I went back to Texas to organize my things, and we haven't talked since. I'm sure he's busy."

"I still don't understand how Klaus landed the job. He was up against some very impressive senior scholars." Phil shook his head bewilderedly. "Anyway, when do you leave?"

"Next month."

"Do you have a place?"

"Yeah, college accommodation. It's on St Aldates, right down the street from the college. It should be nice, because it will let me meet other international graduate students."

"Scholarship?"

"No, not yet. I may be eligible for some sort of award later."

Phil raised an eyebrow. It was typical, Phil knew, for the top students to be awarded scholarships along with their offer of admission. The fact his former student hadn't received one was potentially telling in a number of ways. He waited for Phil to decide what avenue he'd like to explore.

"What did Klaus say about the lack of a scholarship?"

"He asked me whether or not it would affect my decision to accept the offer. I told him it wouldn't. I can afford it."

"That's good," Phil said absent-mindedly, as he thought about what he really wanted to ask, but hadn't.

He couldn't be sure, but he surmised Phil wanted to ask whether he was offended by Klaus's expecting him to accept the offer without a scholarship. There was also the possibility that not receiving a scholarship was a polite way of saying the offer of admission wasn't to be taken seriously. He was aware of these possibilities, but he chose to take things at face value. He had been offered a place, and he would take it. When he got there, he would focus on the work, and show he was capable. Scholarships and finances were secondary to him.

Phil must have read his face. "Well, the main thing is you were accepted. What a fabulous opportunity. I hope you make the most of it."

"Me too," he said.

"You know, I don't know if I ever mentioned it, but before I came here years ago, I almost ended up where you are in Texas. The department there offered me a postdoctoral position. I was torn, but ultimately I declined, and came here instead." Phil was quiet, as he stared at the wall, taking a sip of his margarita which had just come. It was clear he meant to imply he regretted the decision not to have taken the postdoc.

"Well, things worked out well, I think. It's beautiful here," he said, trying to console Phil. He didn't mean to be rude by defending the decision in terms of the area's natural beauty, rather than the university itself, but since he knew that Phil loathed the university anyway, he figured he would highlight something positive about the choice.

"True, yes, it is beautiful here," Phil muttered. "You know," his teacher continued, "when I was studying with Paul Ricœur, I did an intensive study of beauty's role in answering the problem of evil." His teacher knew that he was a theist, which was a curiosity to Phil, since Phil thought belief in God was foolish. He knew, for Phil, it was an irony to have his most successful student turn out to be a theist. He didn't like arguing about God with others, since in his time in Houston, he had found it led to nothing but rancor. But if Phil wanted to go there, he figured he would.

"When people think of beauty, today most of them think of natural beauty. But I've always been drawn to music. I heard it said somewhere that the best argument for the existence of God was Bach," Phil said, waiting for him to reply.

"I've never listened to Bach much, I'm afraid." He had no issue confessing his lack of refinement in such matters. In any case, admitting his ignorance could serve as an invitation for Phil to further expand upon what precisely made Bach's music divine. But instead, Phil made a slightly different point.

"Of course, there is something ultimately compelling about Kant's claim, that sublimity and beauty are mysterious, that we can't see what lies behind them, to know what, if anything, has caused them," Phil said. He thought about mentioning the verse from Romans to Phil, that God is understood through his creation, but because he didn't want to have an argument over the validity of natural theology in the wake of Kant's critique of metaphysics, he paused in order to think of what else to say.

The waitress set their plates down. "Enjoy," she said.

"I think you'll like it. Sonia and I have been coming here for years."

"How is she?"

"Oh, you know. She's fine. Daniel moved away for college, and now he's out in New York working as an artist, so we're on our own." It was a vague answer, but it was clear enough that it wasn't a topic to delve further into here over tacos. He wished Phil hadn't mentioned his wife and son, because there was something he had been meaning to mention also. His good news might seem cruel.

"I hadn't told you, but I'm engaged."

Phil's eyes brightened. "Wow, I did not know. Congratulations! What's her name?"

"Alison." He told Phil about her.

"Marrying an artist could be good for you," Phil said.

"I think so too."

They talked about other things, finished lunch, and then Phil drove him to the rental. They said goodbye, and made plans to keep in touch.

"Tell Klaus I say hi, when you see him in Oxford."

"Will do."

He stood on the sidewalk as Horowitz drove away. The car pulled up to the stop sign, his teacher waved a hand out the window, and then he was gone.

When he had finished recollecting the conversation and related events, his attention returned to his immediate surroundings, where he was stunned to register just how much ground he'd covered walking. The night stretch had taken him the length of the High St, reaching the Deer Park at Magdalen. He chuckled to himself. One of the first common mistakes he'd made upon arriving was mispronouncing the college's name.

"It's Maud-lin," someone had corrected him.

He still had not yet seen the deer. Another thing to add to his list, he thought. Tourists adored the spot, because of its associations with C.S. Lewis. He had also walked by New College, one of the city's oldest, a true Medieval treasure founded in 1379. It would be a place he might get to know somewhat, he thought, owing to the fact one of the experts in his field, Thomas Quiller, was there. He had not yet met Quiller, though he was eager to do so. The other graduate students spoke of Quiller reverently in hushed voices, since the senior don had a reputation for being a towering intellect, and somebody very impressive in seminar. Quiller took on only the very best of students, it was known, so it was an honor to be able to say he was one's supervisor. Klaus and Quiller were close, although Klaus never mentioned anything about him during the application process. After passing by New College, he then passed by the Radcliffe Camera, finally wandering to the gate of All Souls College. In the summers, he heard, there was a gorgeous Almond tree in bloom down the street in front of St Mary's Church. He must have just missed it. Next year, he thought. After peering into All Souls, he made his way down the High St toward his college. He dodged one of those famous red buses, darting down a side alley past an open bar that was a favorite with the townies. Winding through the alleys, he came out on St Aldates, right next door to the college.

At Tom Gate, he used his fob to open the thick, heavy wooden doors. The quad was exquisite under the moonlight, the grounds still, the sound of the fountain barely audible. Nobody was there and all the lights of the rooms on the quad were off, except for the porter's lodge, where the night porter sat reading a paper at his desk. He checked for any important mail in his pidge, but there was nothing but statements from different local banks recruiting new students to open accounts.

"Goodnight," he said to porter.

"Same to you," the man said.

He crossed the street, opened the gate to his building, went up the stairs, opened the door to his room, and walked back to the window. He lit a cigarette, took a seat on the table, and looked outside. He was getting sleepy, so after finishing his cigarette, he went to bed.

In the morning, he awoke to the sound of voices and traffic coming through the window from the street below. Bells were chiming, and birds were chirping. He checked the time, and realized that the college choir and others at the Cathedral would be entering for a service, everyone in their white and red robes. He looked out the open window, to find a huge double rainbow arching high above the college. After a heavy downpour earlier in the morning, the sun was now out, which was a rarity for this time of year. He took a photo of the picturesque scene, the majestic double-rainbow hanging high above the gardens, the Great Hall, the tower, and the spire. Excitedly, he sent it off in an email to his whole family back home.

Sitting in his room alone that evening, he was disappointed when nobody had yet replied. He didn't understand why they wouldn't. For so many years, as far back as he could recall, really, everyone had said that life was all about family and friends, about everyone supporting each other and taking delight in one another's adventures. He sighed, and decided to do some nighttime reading.

Two

T HE next day, he awoke to a message. "I love you. I'll text you after the show."

That afternoon in Houston, Alison would be showing her art at a university exhibit. She was characteristically nervous. Although she was incredibly talented, she had self-confidence issues that made her incessantly question the quality of her work, sometimes even when everyone else so obviously highly esteemed it. This was a difference between them, he had been coming to appreciate. He was confident in his philosophical work. On more than one occasion, she had mentioned how she envied that about him. To her, seeing him have basic trust in his own creative capacities was a marvel. He sometimes wondered what she actually saw when she looked at her own art, to be so dubious of it. Did she simply not see what others saw? Or, did she see it, but something within herself prevented her from identifying with its value, as other artists did theirs?

Lying in bed, his mind turned to a scene from earlier that year, to a moment across the Atlantic in Alison's high school bedroom. His own parents had been in town for a visit to meet her family. In the living room before lunch, his mother, Regina, said something about wanting to see Alison's work, and the room got tense. Alison's parents pretended not to hear his mother, but rather than taking the hint that it was a touchy subject they'd prefer not to address, his mother pressed blithely on. Finally, by her third or fourth question to Alison about the artwork, Alison's father relented.

"Isn't some of your work upstairs, Alison?"

"Yes," she said quietly.

"Well! Let's go see it. I'd love to see it," his mother said.

16

Alison glanced at her parents, then waved to her future in-laws. "I'll show you."

They went upstairs, and waited as she pulled out a portfolio of paintings from under the bed and in the closet. She placed them delicately on the bed so as not to bend any of the works' corners, and began showing each one.

"Oh, these are just lovely," his mother said. Regina's own mother had been an artist herself, so his mother had a longstanding appreciation for watercolors because of his grandmother.

"Thank you," Alison said with a furtive smile.

"You know, Alison, we can't store all your art here forever. You'll have to take it eventually," her father said.

The man, Stuart Gicker, was tall and lanky, with graying red hair and slouching shoulders. He would never say it to anyone, but the man looked to him a bit like the puppet Howdy Doody. Stuart was arrogant and proud, aloof with those whom he deemed didn't matter. He had taken a doctorate in physics at M.I.T. in the eighties, and ever since, everything had been handed to him. He had a handsome salary, extensive travel paid for by the university, and a quaint family life he was free to ignore while off at work immersed in his research. Despite his snobbishness over his academic credentials, he was rather uncultured, the typical modern American man, who cared for little else besides personal pleasure and institutional esteem from those he knew. On a few occasions over dinner, he had tried talking with his soon to be father-in-law about history, or literature, or art, or philosophy, or politics, but to no avail. It bothered him to see how Stuart ignored Alison, but evidently it had been that way for years, and perhaps there was nothing to be done about it.

"That's the way it is," Alison had once said after coming home from one of those family trips that always left her exhausted.

"Why don't you talk about what's bothering you with them?" he asked.

"We don't do that," she explained.

"You're all living a lie," he said.

"I know. They like it that way," she said.

In his bed in Oxford, he recalled the room in her family's house, and the silent pause.

"Oh, let me help you put all this away," Alison's mother had fumbled.

The mother, Linda Garcia, was socially conventional, polite and even sometimes bubbly. But her big brown eyes were filled with immense dread, and the way she dyed her hair and dressed showed she was one of those women who, despite almost turning sixty, still couldn't accept the reality of aging. Or, perhaps more to the point, she couldn't accept her mortality. He thought this was a very odd thing about her, since Linda was a professed Christian. It was one thing to be worldly in ways a believer shouldn't be, another thing to so obviously loathe the very idea of dying, he thought. This was a woman who clung to the earth, and to secular society's opinions of what in life mattered. Her religion was a mere accoutrement that didn't fit. Her husband, after all, just as one might imagine, was himself a superficial atheist, the type who pretended he would never die, and that there was no God, so life was better spent gratifying one's desires, and simply hoping for the best regarding whatever might come after death. Life's big questions would be reserved for the death bed. This probably was why the question of God didn't cause any friction between the couple. Stuart knew Linda's faith was a sham, and Linda knew Stuart knew it too, so she never challenged his unapologetic godlessness. They had an understanding and hence a truce.

Linda leaned over to collect her daughter's drawings, her big gold necklace with a crucifix clanking against and then wrapping around the bedpost. She untangled it without saying a word, and then placed the paintings in the closet where they belonged. "Well, it's time for lunch, isn't it?" Linda motioned to the door and headed down the stairs. Everyone shuffled out of the room, including Alison.

He stood alone there for a few minutes. When he and Alison had a family, he would never treat their children this way, he told himself. As for her family, from what he could tell, the problems had begun many years ago, well before Alison was even born, with the fact that Linda had not taken Stuart's last name. Now, decades later, it was the sort of decision that somebody might try to explain in terms of an ideological critique of patriarchy, or heteronormativity, or whatever. But at the time when Linda made the decision in the seventies, it was simply a trendy thing to do among educated women who were looking to make their way in corporate America. It had been branding for her career. As for Stuart, he derived a perverse pride in it, since even though he was manipulative and highly controlling, it suggested to others that he was the opposite, a confident, progressive type, who had better things to do than worry about trivialities like whether or not his wife took his name. It was part of the mystique he cultivated, that of the absent-minded, detached scientist who had his mind set on grand things, and was thus too lost in the mysteries of the cosmos to be concerned with all the small things occupying others here on Earth.

"Of course, I'll take your name," Alison had said when they got engaged.

He had been relieved to hear it, since he worried that she might want to follow her mother's example. Alison mentioned that her parents were not enthusiastic about her decision to do so, but they never said anything overtly critical of it to him. Still, silence could be telling, and the fact that they never spoke about it was a way of telegraphing they didn't approve it. Stuart, of course, would never say anything about it to him directly, since having that sort of man-to-man conversation would be to lower himself to his future son-in-law's level, and because Stuart wanted to maintain a sense of noble indifference to his daughter's affairs, it had not come up, and it never would. That he was attending Oxford, and that Alison had plans to take his name, he knew, were two strikes against him in Stuart's eyes. The first socially inoculated him against Stuart's criticism, since it wouldn't be plausible for Stuart to claim he was a loser. The latter threatened to make Stuart look jealous, since his daughter was so clearly in love. He wondered what the third strike against him in Stuart's eyes would be. By this point, he was beginning to appreciate the reasons for all those in-law jokes he had never understood when growing up. When they were married, and Alison was with him in Oxford, hopefully whatever dysfunction he was seeing here at her home would be rendered moot. They could move on with their own life together, free from whatever unhealthy dominion she had been living under before meeting him.

As he walked down the stairs to catch up with the group for lunch, he suddenly was struck with the realization that the third strike had probably already occurred, though he hadn't registered it till now. His mind turned to an episode months before, to a revealing conversation in Stuart's university office. He had gone to campus, not precisely asking for Stuart's permission to marry Alison, since Alison had told him she would marry him no matter how her parents felt about it. And, in any case, there was something theatrical about going through such a traditional ritual, when Stuart himself, after all, wasn't the sort who should care anyway, since Linda hadn't even taken his own name. But out of respect, and to demonstrate his sincerity, he had decided to pay Stuart a visit.

Stuart had sat down across the desk in his corner office. The sun was shining through the window. He could see students mingling in the courtyard below. There was a long silence. When it was apparent Stuart wasn't going to say anything, he did.

"I'm here to say that I intend to marry your daughter. I hope that is okay."

Stuart stared at him, then stared out the window. Then he looked at him again. "This is all a little quick, don't you think?"

"Yes, but Alison and I are confident in each other. I've had a long relationship in the past that never led to marriage, so I know the difference. I want to marry her."

He thought back to the kind face of the Pilot, the man who so enthusiastically had commented on the love between Alison and him. He looked at the petulant smirk across from him here in the office, and he realized that he was dealing with a liar, somebody not worth taking seriously. Stuart didn't have his daughter's best interests at heart.

"Well, why don't you two wait a year," Stuart proposed. It had the tone of a command, rather than a suggestion.

"If that is what you want, I am fine with that."

Stuart was momentarily stunned. He could tell that the father had thought imposing a timetable would have led to an outburst, which then could have been used as a pretext to accuse him of being uncooperative or inconsiderate. By so readily agreeing to what Stuart anticipated was something to which he wouldn't, the professor was flummoxed. Experience had taught him how unexpected compliance could starve a schemer's plans of any oxygen. That appeared to be the case here.

The father's eyes narrowed, as he shifted into a different posture. Rather than appear to be the protective father who was doing his best to avert his daughter's making a rash decision contrary to her own interests, instead he became familiar, almost chummy, as if they were two buddies down at the bar or in the locker room.

"You know Alison has a condition? I wouldn't marry her, if I were you."

"It doesn't affect our decision." He wondered why the father was so reluctant to see her married.

Thinking about it here in Oxford now, he remembered how, when walking down the stairs from Alison's room to have lunch with the family, he had felt he had gained more insight since that conversation in Stuart's office. Later that day after the office visit, Alison and he had come to the house. Linda had bought champagne. They all made a toast in the kitchen. His mind recalled the scene.

"What was your reaction when he came to your office today, Stu?" Linda asked. Alison started laughing.

"I wanted to reach across the desk and kill him," Stuart said.

The two women laughed, finding it cute. But there wasn't anything particularly jovial about Stuart's tone, he thought. The "father-of-the-bride" act wasn't very compelling, especially after seeing what Stuart had said privately to him about Alison in the office. Obviously, the comment here in the kitchen was meant to taunt him, since if he told Linda and Alison what had really been said between them earlier in the office, he would be accused of spoiling the celebratory atmosphere. Stuart might even lie and deny he ever had said it. In any case, it would hurt Alison to hear what her father had said, which is precisely what made his saying what he said now about wanting to kill him so appalling. This was not a man interested in protecting his daughter. It was something entirely else. Perhaps he was dealing with a sadist, he thought. He bit his tongue.

"Game will be on soon," Stuart said, motioning to the television in the living room. It had been years since he watched any professional sports himself, though he had an appreciation for the athleticism. He had played sports when he was younger, and he respected the mastery it took to operate at the level elite athletes did. Linda turned to Alison and him.

"Oh, speaking of the game. That reminds me! I never told you two the funniest story," she said. "It's about the time Daddy went out for football."

Stuart stiffened. He could see Stuart wanted to tell Linda to stop, but there was no way to do so.

"He went out for football practice his freshman year. Can you imagine that? Stu playing football! He got hit so hard he was knocked unconscious on the field. After coming to, he walked off and that was it."

Linda and Alison chuckled naively, while Stuart smarted in silence.

Sensing the story hadn't produced the lighthearted effect she intended, Linda attempted to recover, whispering, "Oh, that's okay, dear. You went on to do more important things."

As it happened, the mother's comment about her husband's experience at football practice only rubbed salt in a fresh wound. Earlier that month, the four of them had all walked to the local park across the street from the house with a basketball. Alison took a few shots, and laughed when she missed them all. Stuart took one from the free-throw line that barely grazed the rim. Alison gathered the ball, and walked up to him. "You try."

As a youth, he had played organized basketball, and he had played pick-up in college. It had been a few years, though. He stepped behind the three-point line. The ball swished through the net. He was as surprised as they were. Alison passed him the ball. Again, the ball swished through the net. He shrugged his shoulders and started laughing. Alison passed him the ball a third time. Once again, the ball swished through the net. By now, he was in the zone, and wanted to see how many he could hit in a row. Alison was about to pass him the ball, when Stuart interrupted.

"C'mon, let's go. We'll be late to dinner." The three of them walked off the court.

Stuart's reaction was nothing new. He had seen others jealous at his athletic success. When he was twelve, for example, he played one season of Little League Baseball. His neighborhood friend, Johno, would go to the batting cage with him and play catch outside in the yard. When draft day came, his friend's father, Rick, picked him for the team Rick was coaching. Initially, he was ecstatic to be playing alongside his friend. But as the season wore on, he started thinking his friend's father wasn't giving him the chance to play. Everyone knew he was a good pitcher, but he hadn't yet pitched a single inning. Then about half way through the season, when he had already given up any hope of pitching, they were playing their team's rival. It was the final inning of the game, and they were hanging on to a one run lead. The opposing team had the bases loaded with no outs, with the heart of the line-up on deck. The opposition appeared to have it. Anything, a deep fly ball, a walk, or even a bunt, would be enough. It looked like they were going to lose. He was sitting on the bench, watching the events unfold, assuming he'd sit there as usual. But then, there was an unexpected break in the action, as his friend's father pulled the pitcher, and walked over to the dugout.

"You're in," Rick said pointing to him.

He grabbed his mitt and stepped onto the field, his knees trembling with nerves. He threw a few warm-up pitches, with all the parents and friends watching. His hand was so sweaty, he was afraid he wouldn't be able to grip the ball. Some of the other kids had been taught to throw curveballs and sliders. He only had a fastball. His father had told him that it reminded him of Koufax's: "I've never seen anything like it anywhere else. That movement! Incredible. It rises as it crosses the plate."

The first batter came to the plate. The pitch went right down the middle for a strike. The second pitch was low and away, as the batter swung and missed. Strike two. He wound up again, and threw a fastball belt high. The batter swung again as it sizzled into the catcher's mitt. Strike three. The same happened with the clean-up man. And then the third batter, too. With the game won, the entire time sprinted out from the dugout, swarming him on the mound. As everyone celebrated wildly, he glanced to the dugout, to see that Johno and Rick were walking off the field, their heads hanging down. He didn't understand why they would be, but they looked devastated. He never got to pitch again the rest of the season, after which he quit baseball.

Years later, he learned that his childhood neighbor had gone on to play four years of varsity at college. He wondered how far he could have played, but the question was now moot. All he knew standing here today with his parents and Alison was that Stuart resented him. He hoped the resentment wouldn't worsen into malice. But if it did, he took comfort in the thought that there would be nothing Stuart could do to interfere with their life. He was at Oxford, so the future was bright.

When the flood of episodes slowly ebbed to a trickle and then withdrew from his consciousness completely, he looked out his window. It was getting dark. He grabbed some dinner from the kebab van McCoys at the corner, and then began reading. There was work to do. For Alison and their future.

THREE

HE awoke later than he would like to have awoken. Before drifting off to sleep in the night, he had told himself he would be up with the sun filling the room in the morning, but the day proved cloudy, and there was no sun to serve as an alarm, so he had been detained by the dark, awaiting a light that had not come.

When he sat up in bed, he looked at the wall, where the telephone cord was plugged in. He didn't know the phone number to his room. It was doubtful anyone would ever call it, anyway. A pit in his stomach was eating away at him, and his heart ached. For the first time since relocating, he realized how homesick he was.

Rather than straining to avoid it, he let the thought that had been stalking him for the last two weeks assume full shape in his consciousness. He was tired of denying how badly he wished he could be in the States with her. The thought, which had been successfully relegated to the periphery of his attention until now, overtook him completely, so overcoming him with yearning that he forgot where he was. Then, in an instant, there was just sadness over being here, rather than there, and nothing else. Exiled from her and hence home, space was dislocated. As it turned out, it no longer felt to be the case that he had slept too late. In fact, to the contrary, maybe he had not slept long enough, since waking up at all was merely to be reminded that he was somewhere other than there with her.

Owing to the errands he had been running since moving here, finding distractions had been easy. But with the busyness that had come with organizing his basic living arrangements now over, there was nothing left to divert him from the reality that he was here, without her, and with only the pain he felt because of it to keep him company. He shuddered, a cringe welling up inside him, as he called to mind the famous quip from Sartre, which stung him, because it seemed more pertinent than he would like to admit: "If you're lonely when you're alone, you're in bad company." He snickered. It was one of those thoughts possessing an air of profoundness to it. And it did convey its element of truth. Ultimately, though, it missed the mark. Sartre very well could have meant what he had said sincerely, but to have said it only betrayed an unfamiliarity with the most fundamental of human experiences. Sartre, in short, must never truly have been in love. Of course, Sartre himself argued repeatedly, almost obsessively actually, that there really was no such thing as true love, but that, it seemed to him, was itself a confirmation of his own suspicion not to bother taking Sartre's argument seriously. Yes, in the last analysis, Sartre's position was one that only somebody who had not understood love could have argued for.

As he was about to approach the precipice of despairing to the point of going back to bed, a jolt of relief shot through him. There was, after all, one more errand still to run, which meant something to do, which meant not having to feel Alison's absence so acutely. Forgoing a cigarette at the desk window, as had become the custom, he threw on his clothes and hurried down the stairs, where he lit up as soon as he stepped outside to a bitingly cold afternoon. The street was draped in gray, but it was not damp, which was something to be grateful for. The road's pavement was glistening in the traffic lights from what must have been a morning drizzle earlier, so he was careful not to slip, as he darted through the taxis and buses. Across the street, the porters at the college recognized him. He nodded politely to them, walking through Tom Gate. He went to his pidge, retrieved the bank form, and popped onto the street.

Inside the Cornmarket branch, there was a long queue of students all of whom were looking to set up their own accounts. He thought about returning later, but since there was nothing else to do, and really the entire point of coming was to distract himself, he decided to stay. A pretty, young woman working with the bank hurried over to him.

She smiled widely, and fluttered her lashes. "Good afternoon. May I help you?"

Her body language said more than her words. He ignored the opening to talk to her personally, and instead kept things mundane.

"Yes, I'm new to town, and I'm looking to open a checking account."

Because of his accent, he knew she knew he was an international student. "Of course, we would be happy to assist you. Please take a place in the queue, and we'll be with you as soon as possible." She turned to leave, then hesitated momentarily, walked away, and then looked back at him briefly.

He raised his voice slightly before she was out of earshot. "Sorry. But I'm just curious . . . "

She spun around to hear what he had to say.

"How long do you expect the wait to be?"

She smiled, refreshed by his American bluntness, as evidently it wasn't the sort of question an Oxonian or Londoner would ask. "Good question. I could go check, if you like, but I imagine it will be an hour." He nodded pleasantly, and she walked away.

A half hour later, he was halfway up the stairs to the first floor, where the bankers were seeing new clients. At this rate, it would be much longer than an hour. He sighed gently. The automatic doors opened, and in walked a man in his late twenties, with an olive complexion, a full beard, and a shaved head that failed to disguise his premature balding. The same young woman who had approached him greeted the man.

"Hello, sir. How may we help you today?"

"Hi, I'm here to open an account. I'm from overseas." It was a fellow American, perhaps from New York, judging by the accent. He stared at the man. As he was about to look away, he realized he recognized the man from the apartment complex. They had not met yet, but he had seen the man there. A fellow international student at the college, he thought. The man was surveying the line, when the two made eye contact. The man pointed at him.

"Hey, how's it going? I see you're here to do the same thing!" Evidently, the man recognized him from the apartment as well.

"Yeah, I figured now was the time to do it. Long line, though."

"I'm sure it will move fast," the man said. His eyes widened, "Did you see the invitation to Friday's Freshers' GCR party?"

The man's local lingo was forced. Anyone coming to Oxford discovered quickly that being here meant learning all of the place's idiosyncratic terms for what felt like everything. In order to let others see that one was making fast progress toward belonging, all the new students were peppering every social interaction with the local lexicon in conversation. As a result of everyone doing so, it only ended up achieving the opposite of what was intended. Instead of casually appearing to be an Oxfordian, it made for a dead giveaway that one was new to town, just another somebody among the latest batch of annual awkward arrivals straining to prove they deserved to be here. The insecure, awestruck Fresher, an

Oxford fixture for nearly a thousand years, he thought. He considered all the students through the centuries who were all dead, and it made him realize that so many of the things that seemed to matter in life actually didn't. The dead before them had thought it all mattered—connections, parties, dining clubs, careers, and so on. Five hundred years on from today, two young men just like them on Cornmarket would be having an identical conversation as this one here, myopically concerned with a situation that to them would feel so unique upon arriving in Oxford, but really wasn't.

"Yeah, I saw that."

After formal dinner at Hall on Friday, the newly elected Graduate Common Room committee was hosting a welcoming event. There would be a wine reception for all of the incoming graduate students, followed by a pub crawl in town. He didn't enjoy organized events like these, but there would be nothing else to do, so he had been contemplating going.

"A few of us will be pre-drinking before formal at Michaela's room. You're invited," the man smiled. He did not know Michaela, but he could tell the man assumed he did.

It was generous of him to extend the invitation, but frankly the idea of attending repulsed him. In the first few weeks here, he was noticing that many of the other graduate students, most of whom were in their late twenties, were reverting to behavior reminiscent of what he had seen in California as a freshman when others had been rushing a fraternity or sorority. There were already cliques forming in the graduate housing, with the biggest social butterflies establishing themselves as the voice of the cohort. Coming to the bank today had apparently led him into stumbling into the middle of the inner circle of one such group. Being invited to the room before dinner, he realized, was the man's way of bestowing him a social favor, since the others in the building weren't invited. He wondered why they had decided to choose him. What he had been seeing at the complex had the feeling of something one would expect to see at a summer camp for teenagers. If he didn't go, they would be offended, and he didn't want to be rude, so he decided he would stop in before the dinner briefly, as much as he really didn't want to. That it was a girl hosting the get-together only further complicated things. Alison understandably would be nervous about it, even if she didn't say so. In a way, the encounter here at the bank was a disaster, worse than being alone. Go to the party, and one will regret it; don't go to the party, and one will regret it. Either way, one will regret it.

"I'm Craig, by the way," the man said. He gave his name.

"We'll have to swap numbers, when we're finished with this," Craig said.

"Sounds good," he nodded.

Two hours later, his account set up, he stepped onto the street to light a cigarette. Craig would be out shortly. He watched the tourists streaming by in the twilight, people from all around the world who had come to experience what for the foreseeable future would be his home. He sighed again at the thought of Alison not being here. Just as the pit in his stomach began churning again, Craig slapped him on the shoulder.

"Well, it's good to have that out of the way," his new friend said. "Let me get your number."

"Sure." He had to open his phone to look, since he hadn't yet memorized it.

"What do you study?"

"Medicine," Craig said. "You?"

"Philosophy."

"Philosophy? Interesting." He could tell Craig didn't mean it, so he didn't bother saying anything further.

"Where are you from?" Craig asked.

"Originally, California. But I was in Texas."

"Never been to Texas. I like California, though. I'm from New York."

"The city?"

"No, upstate. You know, Friday will be good for you. The others are Americans, too."

There was a pause.

"Okay, anyway, I should be off. I have to pick up supplies for my place. I'll see you Friday!" They shook hands, and Craig vanished into the sea of pedestrians.

He wondered whether the other American was homesick too. Perhaps the carefree, affable demeanor was all simply a façade. If it was an act, he wondered why Craig felt like he had to put it on, to hide the fact he was struggling to adjust to a new place. He had heard how foreigners thought Americans were too happy. He was starting to understand what they meant. It wasn't that they, or we, he reminded himself, were too happy, but that they pretended to be. There was something unnerving about the performance, something almost inhuman. After all, just as it was only natural to feel unsettled by moving, so it was equally unnatural to feign otherwise. Then again, he should be fair. Perhaps Craig was being entirely sincere, and he really was at ease in his new surroundings. But that was a possibility itself disconcerting for a different reason, since evidently Craig was reliving his college days in order to make himself comfortable, treating the graduate housing like it were the old dorm from years ago. Unless there were another possible interpretation he was overlooking, his new acquaintance's carefreeness was either a false veneer, or else genuinely stunted.

When he got to his room, he looked out the window to the Hall. In thinking more about it, he didn't know how exactly to feel about Friday. Before running the errand, he had been convinced it was awful having nowhere to be and nothing to do. With Friday's festivities looming now, however, he was beginning to worry that he had been mistaken. Something strange inside him said this turn of events might be worse. Whatever the case, he knew he didn't want to be here. He felt like sobbing, but instead he went to sleep early.

FOUR

HE time, at last, had come. It was Wednesday, and in fifteen minutes he was due to meet Klaus at the college. Normally, he would be wearing a white t-shirt, but today he had put on a white button-down. There was a coffee stain on the right cuff that he rolled up the sleeves to cover. It was sunny and mild enough, which meant he would make do without a jacket, he decided. He walked across the street.

"Hello," the porter said, as he passed through the rope barriers to the entrance.

One of the tourists glared, assuming he was cutting the line, only to realize that he was a member. He understood how, if one were sufficiently shallow, it would be very easy for college routine to induce one into thinking one was elite and important. It was a thought that made him twinge with revulsion, but there was no denying that there had to be a number of dons at the college, and maybe even fellow students too, who derived an immense satisfaction in being waved in by the porters while being seen by the frenzied, impatient tourists. He had to get around finally to reading Rousseau on *amour-propre*.

He walked to the center of Tom. Anyone who was not a member was forbidden from the fountain and the surrounding area. Visitors were relegated to the quad's perimeter. On extremely busy days, every few minutes a porter would have to shoo away tourists attempting to take photos where they were not allowed. It dawned on him that navigating the college's grounds was like peeling an onion, each ring leading to a more tightly controlled, and presumably more exclusive and mysterious, layer. The college's configuration, he now saw, was designed as if to allow those who were barred access to be able to see those who had it. He didn't like being watched by the tourists, so standing at the fountain made him uncomfortable. He tried clearing his mind by looking at the koi. They were difficult to spot beneath the floating lily pads, but they were there, he knew. He kneeled down at the edge, placing a hand above the surface of the water. Three large koi emerged from below, their open mouths pulsating above the waterline. He laughed and took a photo, since he knew Alison, who loved animals, would like to see. Someone, he couldn't remember whom, had told him that the koi were gifts from the Empress of Japan.

He glanced up at the bronze and lead statue of Mercury, Hermes to the Greeks. The same figure as the fountain in the park outside the bar in Texas, he thought. Of all the persons from mythic history, it was a perplexing choice. Why this particular pagan god, rather than some other? Or, better yet, why a Greek at all, and not a Christian saint or an English hero? These, presumably, were the sorts of minutiae answered on one of the guided tours.

He stood up from Mercury fountain and its koi pond, and began walking to the archway that would lead to where he was going. As he climbed the stairs from the sunken level of the quad, Klaus came through the archway. He was immediately recognizable, with the same thick, curly hair he remembered, the broad face, and sharp green eyes. It had been a few years since seeing one another in person, but Klaus didn't look to have aged at all.

His supervisor waved, "There's the scholar!"

They shook hands. Klaus was smiling, but then his face turned serious.

"Are you settling in? Need anything? Sorry it's taken too long to meet. I've been tied up in London."

"No, I think I'm good. There's some form I think you'll have to sign for me soon, but that's it."

"Okay, right. Well, leave it for me in my pidge, and I can take care of it. What's it for?"

"A college scholarship. The American Friends of Christ Church."

"I see. Well, I'll be happy to support any application of yours. I thought, though, you said money wasn't an issue for your family?"

"Oh, it isn't. The sum of the scholarship itself isn't much. But it's a pretty competitive award, so although it's a small thing monetarily, I figured it might be worth listing on the CV, assuming I get it."

"Ah, yes, of course. Okay. I have to pick up something from my office. C'mon."

They walked by the Deanery, then by the south side of the library. Peckwater Quadrangle, where the undergraduate students lived, lay right ahead, but before reaching it, Klaus led them to an imposing blue door on the left, which evidently was a side entryway to Kilcannon. Inside on the ground floor of the building was an ornate wooden staircase. They climbed their way to the top floor. At the landing, they walked by an office to their right belonging to a don, Landry Simpson, then by an unmarked room on the left, before stopping in front of a set of dark blue double doors. Klaus gestured toward the office behind them.

"You'll meet Landry later. He's a philosopher and your college advisor."

There was a sign above the buzzer at the blue doors: "Klaus Carman, Official Student and Tutor in Philosophy." His old teacher must have read the confusion on his face.

"That's just college-speak for Professor. At the other colleges, the dons are called Fellows, but here we're called Students. Don't ask me why. It's confusing, I know."

Klaus turned the key to the door, which opened unto a sprawling office, the largest he'd ever seen in person. Klaus looked at him gleefully.

"There's a second room in addition to this one, the one over there on the left. It's a living quarter. I rarely ever use it myself, because I'm in London, but it's nice to have a spare."

A white bookcase lining the whole left wall held hundreds of volumes. Across the room, on the opposite wall, were beautiful paneled white windows overlooking a garden. The sun was shining on the mahogany desk, the crimson leather sofa, and three matching chairs.

Resting a hand on one of the chairs, his old teacher said, "This is where I hold tutorials. Have a seat."

He followed Klaus, stepping onto the oriental floor rug, self-conscious that the soles of his shoes might be dirty.

"I can get you a coffee in the SCR after lunch. Have a seat when I fetch something."

Klaus walked to the shelf, fingering the books. After a minute of searching, he turned toward the windows, rubbing his chin, struggling to recall where he'd placed whatever it was that he was looking for.

"Aha!" He walked over to the desk, shuffled some papers around, and grabbed an item.

"It's the newest issue," Klaus said, handing it to him.

He read aloud the title, *"Philosophy Today in Europe,"* as he began flipping through the front pages.

Klaus took a seat in one of the chairs across from the sofa. "Yes, it's a lot of work. I don't really like all the editorial work, but the college relieves me of my teaching duties because of it, which is good." Klaus didn't attempt to reconcile his comment about believing relieved of teaching with what he had just said about holding his tutorials here in the office. It was a white lie, but it was slightly disconcerting that he'd lied so casually, because it suggested that lying was a habit of his.

"How long have you been editing the journal?"

"Almost a year now. I'm seeking a graduate assistant to help. Someone to liaise with authors, and to answer emails. Let me know if you're interested. It pays pretty well." He knew Klaus had other graduate students besides him, so the offer was not insignificant. He'd been selected.

"I've never done anything like that before," he said. It wasn't that he was hoping not to appear too overeager; he was genuinely worried he might not be up to the task.

"Don't worry. It's easy."

"Okay, well, I'd be happy to do it. Thank you for the opportunity."

"So, you're getting married, I understand."

He was temporarily disoriented by the question, before realizing that he had indeed mentioned Alison to Klaus the day he received his acceptance letter.

"Yep!"

"Do you have a date?"

"This coming August."

"That's a long way off. What? Ten months." He thought about mentioning the role his father-in-law, Stuart, had in that, about the concession he'd made regarding the length of the engagement. He decided not to say anything.

Klaus continued, "What's her name? April?"

"Alison."

"Oh, yes, sorry."

"You'll get to meet her very soon. She's coming for a visit next month."

"Next month?"

"Yeah, for Thanksgiving. We miss each other, and this seemed like a good excuse for a visit."

"How's being apart?"

He decided there was no reason to lie. If he had come all this way to study under Klaus, he should be able to be honest about something as important in his life as his engagement.

"Honestly, it's been really hard for us. I miss her a lot. I wish she was able to be here now, but she's finishing her degree."

"Yes, long distance can be challenging." Klaus glanced out the garden window.

"I'm not the jealous type, at least not usually, but it's been hard not to wonder whether she might be cheating on me," he said. He chided himself for having said more than he had intended to divulge, but before he could regret the mishap, he saw a look of titillation sweep across Klaus's face. His supervisor was no longer emotionally withdrawn, but captivated.

"What makes you think that? Do you have any evidence? Or is it just a hunch?"

The ice was breaking, and they were resurrecting the rapport he remembered having in California. It occurred to him that the subject of relationships would strike a chord with Klaus. His memory turned to the time when they were leaving Klaus's office after discussing a paper Klaus was working on for a conference. They were in some spirited exchange over the relation between self-knowledge and intersubjectivity, when, in order to drive home his point, Klaus had said, "You know that feeling you get when your friend finds out you've had sex with his girlfriend?"

Klaus's example had been meant to underscore the implausibility of Cartesian solipsism. The experience of shame presupposed the existence of actual others outside one's own mind. At the time, he had been shocked by the comment, and hadn't known how to respond. He himself had never cheated with a friend's girlfriend before, so he was surprised to learn that Klaus thought it was a common enough experience to simply assume he had. He remembered for a split-second noticing embarrassment flooding his teacher's face, when Klaus registered the fact that he didn't know the feeling. The two had said nothing further about it, and they segued into some other issue raised in the paper. Sitting here now in the office in Oxford, he wondered whether Klaus remembered that previous exchange.

"No, nothing definitive. Just a feeling, I guess. It's not even her fault. I think it's the nerves of moving. But sometimes I worry that she's lying to me. I wish there was a way to know."

"What does your gut say?"

"I don't know about that. It's not in my gut. It's more so a pain. Like a sliver in the soul."

"In situations such as these, I find faces misleading. If I want to tell whether somebody's lying, I listen to the voice," he said. It was intriguing advice, but he wasn't sure what exactly Klaus listened to in another's voice. He thought about asking for clarification, but before he could, his supervisor lowered his own voice almost to a hush.

"Listen, can you be trusted, if I tell you something?"

It was an odd question, of course, since nobody would say he couldn't be trusted to keep a secret. But he understood it was Klaus's way of working himself up to saying something he wanted to disclose.

"Of course." He shifted on the sofa, waiting for Klaus to continue. The situation in the room took on the mood of a confessional.

"There's someone I'm seeing. You'll meet her eventually. She's here at the college. She's married. Promise me you won't mention it to anyone here."

"Oh, I would never." He would never do so, if anything, simply because as a rule he didn't like to gossip. He worried that his promising not to say anything to anyone about it might be misinterpreted by Klaus as a tacit moral endorsement of adultery. Of course, there was something of an irony in the situation, since he was worried that his fiancée might be cheating, and here he was listening to the secrets of a man sleeping with a married woman.

Klaus must have realized the irony too, so as if to console him, Klaus said, "It's probably nothing. I'm sure Alison isn't doing anything."

It was a strange experience receiving reassurance about his fiancée's fidelity from someone who himself was currently having an affair with a married coworker, but, then again, if there was anyone he knew who would be in a position to judge such things reliably, presumably it was Klaus.

"I assume you Skype together. The next time you talk, ignore her facial expressions, and pay attention to her voice," Klaus said.

He thought about all the tourists standing outside of Tom Gate right now, completely oblivious to what really went on within these halls. If they knew that keeping this sort of promise was the first assignment, as it were, that he received from his doctoral supervisor, what would they think? He inadvertently laughed at the thought.

"What is it?" Klaus asked.

"Oh, nothing."

"Okay. Well, we're going to be late for lunch, if we don't get going."

He went to hand Klaus the copy of *Philosophy Today in Europe.*

"No, that's yours. Keep it."

"Thanks."

Klaus stood up from the chair, went to the door, put on his coat, and waved him through. "After you."

They walked through the quad, first past the library, then the Deanery, then the Cathedral, and finally past the staircase leading up to the Hall. After rounding the corner beyond the Hall, they reached a narrow walkway to their left which he had not noticed before. "Down this way, on the right, is the SCR," Klaus said.

They took the walkway, which opened onto a closed court, with a small parking lot for the college's kitchen staff. Up ahead was the front entrance to a building whose back faced the college's meadow. When they stepped out into the court, he looked over the adjacent wall to his street down the way. His apartment was visible from where they were standing. He saw that he had left his window open; hopefully it wouldn't rain. He was about to say something about the incredible convenience of his housing accommodations, when the sound of Klaus's voice interrupted, "That's the Freind Room. There's a dining service for faculty on the ground floor. Upstairs on the first floor is a seminar room."

They climbed the entry stairs and entered the foyer, where Klaus set his coat on a rack. They took a spot in line.

"The food's not very good, but it's free," Klaus whispered. They plated their mushy salmon and sides, and sat down at a table alone.

They poured themselves glasses of sparkling water.

"Oh, sorry, I almost forgot. Phil told me to tell you he says hello," he said.

"Oh, right," Klaus said. He waited for Klaus to ask how Phil was doing, but there was an unexpected silence.

"Carrell says hello, too," he added.

"Ah, yes. I just saw Carrell not too long ago at a conference in Vermont. How is he?"

Last year, Carrell had mentioned Klaus in passing. He remembered Carrell having said something about Klaus's walking everywhere he went for the three days during the conference carrying a copy of some massive book that had been authored by another Oxford philosopher. He couldn't recall the title of the book or the author Carrell had spoken of, but he re-called vividly Carrell's tone suggesting that he'd resented what he took to be Klaus's bragging about being at Oxford. He wouldn't repeat what Carrell had said. He realized how everyday conversation was so strange, that even when three people who all knew each other talked about one another, they all had to pretend that what was being said between the two of them in the third's absence was everything that had been said. It wasn't lying exactly, but some other kind of deception. Lies were intended to deceive, but this form of falsehood was so blatant it never stood any chance of deceiving. And yet, it was such a commonplace that nobody ever thought to note it. Somehow falsehood was ingrained into the nature of everyday discussion. He assumed Carrell had things to say about him to Klaus, just as Klaus would have things to say to him about Carrell, and just as he would to Klaus about Carrell. It was a bizarre triangle of selective omissions and partial disclosures. Carrell and Klaus were sure to run into each other again at some event, if not Vermont, and they may well even be regularly in touch. For the first time since arriving, it dawned on him that Carrell might have a heavier hand in how things progressed here in Oxford than he had originally anticipated. Maybe he hadn't left Texas behind completely. It might well explain why Carrell took the news of his intention to transfer so placidly.

"Carrell's fine. I was thankful he wrote me a letter of recommendation."

"Yes, Carrell's work is some of the top stuff in the field. I've learned a lot from him. He doesn't write many books. But there's nothing wrong with being an essay man," Klaus said.

Since Klaus had brought up the topic of books, he decided to see if he could identify the book that Carrell had mentioned Klaus toting around Vermont.

"Speaking of books, anything interesting published here recently?"

Klaus's eyes lit up, and he gesticulated excitedly. "As a matter of fact, yes. My colleague, Alex Morrison, has published a fantastic work on metaphysics. The book is a colossus." This, then, must have been the book.

"Morrison?"

"Yes, Morrison. He was close with Bernard Williams, Dummett, and others from that generation. Brilliant mind. You'll meet him at some point, I'm sure."

They ate in silence for a minute. Before Klaus stood for dessert, his teacher looked across the table at him, "You know, of everyone back at the department in California, Bell was the smartest."

He could see why Klaus might judge so, though personally he thought Bell wasn't nearly as smart as Bell himself thought he was. Bell was a tactician, someone who could disect an argument, and excelled at seeing a dialectic's branches. But he lacked perspective. He lacked the deep insight of wisdom. Bell had been a braggart, always droning on to his students about how he'd studied under Brant and Hare at Michigan. The memory of Bell's mantra, delivered in that nasally voice, pierced his consciousness, "I have read all of Kant in the original German . . . " He wondered if Klaus's comment about Bell was intended to see whether it would elicit a defense of Horowitz's intellect, whom, truth be told, he did think was smarter than Bell. He thought better of it, since the line of discussion, and Klaus's purposes for raising it, was murky. He didn't really care, anyway, which of the professors back in California was smartest.

"Did I ever tell you how I got the job?"

Klaus was perceptive, so of course he knew that Horowitz thought his having landed the Oxford post was baffling.

"I put in an application without expecting to hear anything. After I'd almost forgotten about it, out of the blue I received an interview. I had to cancel all my classes and fly out. I gave a short twenty-minute lecture to some students, answered some questions from the interviewers, then went to dinner with some people. I took a walk afterwards, and when I got back to my room at the Randolph, there was an envelope at my door saying I'd been offered the post." Klaus looked at him without saying anything more.

After dessert, they readied to go their separate ways.

"I'll be in London for the next few weeks of term. But if you need anything, let me know. I host a fortnightly seminar with Daniel Fernandez, the next session of which is Thursday. There's a speaker coming to talk about Foucault."

They stepped outside together into the cold, and said goodbye. "I have an appointment, so we'll have to get coffee at the SCR another time," Klaus said.

He walked home the very short distance down the private access road, crossed the street, and then lit a cigarette at his desk after entering his room. As he looked out at the college, it suddenly occurred to him that in his three weeks here, he was yet to have a single conversation with anybody about philosophy, or any ideas for that matter, really. He sighed, and picked up a book to do some reading. With autumn here, total darkness would be falling in an hour or two. Soon, then, he would have an excuse to go to sleep, even if it was early for that.

FIVE

NOTHING had happened yesterday. After having lunch with Klaus, he had spent the following day in his room alone, leaving only once to buy some cigarettes from the corner Tesco. Today, though, he would go outside, he decided. He brushed his teeth, put on some clothes, and walked across the street to check the mail. The porters said hello, and there were ducks in the koi pond. The front entrance was closed to visitors for the day, so the long queues were forming on the meadow side of the college, which meant this part of the grounds were deserted. The sun was out, shining down on the quad's meticulous, verdant lawn. It was a shame sitting on the law was forbidden, he thought.

When he checked his pidge, he was glad he had. Klaus had completed and signed the application form for the academic scholarship. He scanned it carefully to make sure there weren't any missing details. Something caught his eye. In one of the bottom sections of the form, the supervisor was asked to rank the applicant among his other students. He looked at Klaus's entry in the box: "1st." He felt a flush of relief, then satisfaction. In a way, it was an oddly designed form, since the applicant would see the supervisor's response to the question, and the supervisor knew it. Presumably, it might put pressure on the supervisor not to answer honestly. On the other hand, the supervisor could always leave the space blank, pretending not to have noticed the question. He decided the fact that Klaus had written what he did was a genuine vote of confidence in him. He felt like whistling but restrained himself.

Elated, he crossed the street, and opened the gate to his building. He nearly bumped into a short, young Indian man. The man was wearing a blue dress suit, with impeccably styled black hair, an expensive gold watch, and shined shoes. He was the aristocratic type for which Oxford was known. "Pardon me," the man said.

39

"Sorry," he said.

"Do you live in the building?"

"Yeah. You?"

"Yes, I've just arrived from Cambridge. Theology," the man said, extending his hand.

"Philosophy."

"My name's Manan." He gave his name.

"With whom are you studying?"

"Klaus, Klaus Carman."

"On the BPhil?"

"No, DPhil." Manan's eyes widened.

"Ah, I see. Well, we'll have to get together to chat. I'm off to see my supervisor at the college."

"Who's that?"

"Prof Eliot Wood. He's the Regius Professor." He didn't know what that was, but he could tell it was prestigious. He would look it up later.

"What sort of theology are you studying?" He himself was entirely untrained in the subject, but he was interested in learning.

"The Patristics, primarily Gregory of Nyssa. But I'm interested in philosophy, too, especially Immanuel Kant. I've been reading *Opus Postumum*."

For the first time since arriving, he felt like he had met somebody else who was here for the same reasons as him, to learn and study. Perhaps he had made a friend. By the looks of it, Manan was thinking the same.

"Are you planning to attend this evening's formal dinner?"

He had almost forgotten about the American from the bank and Michaela. "Oh, yes."

"If you would like, you're welcome to sit with us. Eliot and I will be there together."

"Oh, that's very nice of you to offer. Sounds good. Are you going to the GCR event?"

Manan threw back his head and chuckled. "Sorry," he said, composing himself. "I will certainly attend the after-dinner gathering at the common room. But I won't be joining the festivities afterwards in town. I prefer to avoid the dens of iniquity." He adjusted his handkerchief. "Well, I really must be going, but it's been a pleasure to make your acquaintance." He continued, "You should come by my place later this weekend. I have some good whiskey, if you like that." He bowed solemnly, and then darted away through the gate.

At his desk, he opened his computer to check his college email. It had been assorted notes addressed to everyone with suggestions for things to do in town, notifications of looming deadlines, and tips for settling in. But today was different. At the very top of his folder was an email from Klaus. He opened it, and read with excitement. It was a note formally introducing him to Wood. Wood had already replied, welcoming him to Oxford, and offering him an invitation to a monthly discussion group he held at his residence at the college for theology students. Presumably, Manan would be there. In any case, he could ask Manan and Wood more about it tonight at dinner. He composed a short note, thanking Klaus for the introduction, and telling Wood how much he was looking forward to making his acquaintance. He sent off the email, lit a celebratory cigarette, and gazed out the window.

He was enjoying the view of the college gardens when his contemplation was interrupted by a raucous commotion below on the street. He leaned out his window and saw a group of a half dozen or so walkers approaching the gate. Judging by all the laughter and hollering, they were coming from a pub where they had been day drinking. When they stopped at the gate and began punching in the entry code, he realized they must be fellow graduate students. He looked closer, and spotted Craig among them. Someone in the group must have noticed him watching, because Craig looked up and waved, "Hey buddy!"

He waved a hand to his friend, or acquaintance, or whatever Craig was to him. Craig tapped a young blonde on the shoulder standing in front of him. She looked up to the window, her hair fluttering in her face. She laughed, brushed aside her hair, and then stared at him intensely with sparkling green eyes. He glanced away, the words of warning enveloping him, "For the lips of a strange woman drop as a honeycomb, and her mouth is smoother than oil . . . " When he thought she would finally look away, she continued staring, grinned at him, bit her lower lip, waved gently, and then walked inside with the group. His heart sank. That must be Michaela.

He remembered that he had promised to come by to meet them all before tonight's dinner. After having lunch with Klaus on Wednesday, then meeting Manan and being introduced to Wood today, he had forgotten completely. If he had been reluctant to go beforehand, seeing them now all drunk filled him with total dread. They probably would be obnoxious, and because he wasn't drunk also, they would take his composure for rudeness. He sighed. He would wait an hour, head downstairs, and introduce himself, at which point he'd only have to stay briefly before he could leave for formal.

Six

EN minutes before he would go down to Michaela's room, he was reviewing the dress code for dinner. It was full of terminology he didn't understand, so he frantically searched online for explanations of what he was being told to wear. Sometimes it was supposed to be a white bow tie and jacket with no gown, other times it was a black bow tie with gown, other times it was a black tie rather than a bow tie, or maybe that wasn't right, it had said something else. His mind struggled to recall the details of each combination. He was panicking, when a solution presented itself. He went to his window, and looked over to the college entrance, where others were gathering. Everyone had on a gown, the men with black bow ties, the women with some dangly thing he didn't know the name for. The men were in black dress pants and white collared shirts, the women in black dresses with white tops. Relieved to know what to wear, he dressed quickly, then headed down the stairs to the ground floor.

On the stairs, a young woman walking down looked back up at him. They reached the ground floor together. "Are you going to Michaela's?" she asked.

"Yes, Craig invited me."

"Oh, you know Craig. My name's Kristin." They shook hands.

They came to the door which was shut. They could hear laughter inside. Kristin knocked. "It's me. Open the door."

A few moments later, the door swung open, with Craig grinning. "Come on in, guys."

There were six others crammed into the room. Bottles of wine and liquor were strewn on a table, and everyone had a red plastic cup in hand.

"We found these in the American section at the Tesco!" Craig bellowed. "It's just like college again," he laughed.

Looking at everyone made him wonder how they would possibly make it through dinner in this state. They seemed totally oblivious to any looming social faux-pas.

Craig turned to him. "You've met Kristin." He pointed to everyone else in the room: "Emily, Erin, Allison, Frank—and that's Michaela." They all waved to him as he took a seat next to the bed, where the girls were sitting.

"Would you like a drink?" It was Emily, he thought.

"Yes, please." She poured a beer into a plastic cup and handed it to him.

"You should take a shot with us," the other girl said. It was Erin, or maybe it was Allison.

"Maybe later," he said. Emily and the other girl looked at each other and giggled.

"So serious," Emily said. "I like that," she said looking at him.

The third girl, who had been talking to Michaela, turned her head to them, and stuck out her hand. "I'm Allison," she said.

"That's so funny. That's my fiancée's name."

She laughed. "Really? One 'L' or two?"

"One," he said.

"Ah, mine's two," she slurred slightly.

"Your fiancée?" It was Michaela.

"Yes."

"That's cute. Aren't you a little young for that? Nobody's getting married yet."

He thought about saying that in the grand scheme of things he was already old not to be married, and that it was until only very recently, the last two decades really, where it was considered normal to be their age and unmarried. But he decided not to say anything, since he knew Michaela knew that too.

"Is she here?"

"No, she's in the States."

"Oh, that must be really hard," Erin said sincerely. Allison looked at Erin and nodded her head in agreement. He could tell that they had a certain respect for him now that they knew he was engaged. Michaela, however, was undeterred.

"Yes, that's quite a pity," she said smiling. She stood up from the bed, walked over to the table, poured herself a drink, and grazed her hand up against his shoulder. Her flirtatiousness evidently upset the other man who to that point had remained silent.

"I'm Frank," the man said, extending his hand.

"Nice to meet you."

"What do you study?"

"Philosophy. You?"

"International relations. You on the MPhil?"

"No, DPhil."

"Oh, a DPhil, very impressive," Allison said.

"Yes, very impressive," Frank muttered under his breath. He didn't feel like making an enemy with this man he didn't know, so he went out of his way to demonstrate he had no intention of vying for Michaela's affections.

"Well, it's a great opportunity to be here. But I miss home. I won't be settled till she's here."

Emily asked, "Do you have a date for the wedding?"

"August," he said.

"Oh, that's quite a wait," Erin said. He thought about mentioning Stuart, but once again decided not to.

"I'm sure she misses you," Michaela said bemusedly. The implication was that his fiancée probably didn't, so he shouldn't bother pretending he missed her, either. Instead, he should free himself to explore his options here.

"I'm sure she does," he countered. Being in the room with her was becoming unbearable. He desperately wanted to leave.

Craig jumped up from his chair. "Guys, can you believe it? Formal dinner at Christ Church! These gowns are so awesome. All we need are some wands, and it'd be just like Hogwarts!" The girls all laughed excitedly.

"Let's all take a picture," Frank suggested.

His heart raced. He hated taking pictures, so he was relieved when Frank moved to exclude him, by sitting down on the bed with the girls. "Set the timer, would you, Craig," Frank said.

Craig placed the phone on the table, set the timer, and jumped on the bed with the others, where they all stuck out their tongues, and held up their arms. The flash went off, and they all hollered. Just as he was about to say he had to leave, Michaela stood up from the bed.

"Well, shall we head to the Buttery? It's about time."

They all stood up, grabbed their mortar boards, and made for the door. He realized he had left his upstairs. He grabbed Craig by the arm, "We really need our caps for dinner?"

Craig failed to conceal his shock that he hadn't known. "For ordinary formal dinners only the gown is required, but tonight's welcome dinner is very special, so mortar boards are required."

"So, you're going to put yours on when you get there?"

"Well, no. It's not supposed to be worn. You're supposed to carry it under your arm."

"Ah, I see, a cap and gown affair, but not really, since technically the cap is superfluous." He laughed at his observation expecting Craig to laugh with him, but Craig didn't. "Okay, right then, I should head back to my room to get mine."

Michaela, who had been listening closely, turned to them both, "I'll go with you."

"Oh, no thanks. I'll be fine."

She smiled. "What, you don't want me to come?"

Craig cleared his throat uncomfortably. "I'll see you two at dinner."

The others left the room, and walked out the building. He stepped out into the hallway. He could hear Michaela close the door behind them. He began walking up the stairs to his room, hoping to hear her heading out the building to catch the others, but instead he heard her footsteps right behind him. He reached his door, and unlocked it. She stood at the threshold.

"I can't come in?"

"Uh, sure." He fumbled through his things, looking for his cap in his closet, as she took a seat on the bed. She stared at him without saying a word.

"Got it," he said, holding his mortar board up. "Let's go." He walked to the door and waited.

She smiled. "This is a nice room. I guess we do have to get to dinner. I suppose we should be going," she said.

When she got to the door, he stepped inside the room. "I'll see you at dinner. I have to send Alison a message," he said.

He closed the door and waited until he heard her footsteps reach the ground floor below. He took a sigh of relief. Jumbled snippets of Scripture entered his mind, "Why be ravished with a strange woman? Why embrace the bosom of a stranger? Rejoice with the wife of thy youth. Let her be as the loving hind and pleasant roe; let her breasts satisfy thee at all times; and be thou ravished always with her love." Thankfully, he would be able to avoid Michaela and the others at dinner, since he would be seated with Manan and Wood. There would be the wine reception at the GCR still to contend with, but he could skip the pub crawl.

In the Proverbs, it was said Wisdom built a house of her own. Opposed to it, there was the harlot's house. It occurred to him that the latter, perhaps, was an allegory for the ways of the world. If the house of Wisdom was ruled by the laws of righteousness leading to the kingdom of God, then the harlot's house, governed by the world and its lusts, was leading to perdition. In the Old Testament, after all, turning one's back to God was likened to whoring. He would have to ask some of the theology students or professors about all that.

SEVEN

THE clouds had departed, unveiling a host of stars and a bright full moon. Walking beside Mercury, he could hear the voices echoing from inside the Hall. He climbed the staircase, reaching the Ante-Hall, where the door on the left to the Buttery was open, with a large crowd of students bantering inside, while purchasing their bottles for dinner. In the corner of the Buttery, he spotted Craig and Michaela and the others at a table, even drunker than before. On the wall behind them was the college's collection of rowing oars, commemorating the Boating Crew's history of victories against Cambridge. The wall, he had heard, also listed the college's various Olympic rowers, which included, most recently, the Winklevoss twins, who had rowed for Harvard before rowing here. Far more interestingly, however, he thought, was the fact that these were the same twins from whom Mark Zuckerberg had allegedly stolen the software for Facebook. He knew there had been a series of lawsuits over whatever took place at Harvard, but he wasn't sure what had ever come of it. He thought of what his late friend in California had told him about corporate espionage and theft, and the Klein plane crash. Silicon Valley insiders such as these twins, he assumed, must live constantly looking over their shoulders. He was happy to be anonymous and insignificant.

He was about to enter the Hall when somebody grabbed his elbow from behind. It was Manan. Standing with the Indian aristocrat was an older man with wispy hair and glasses. The man extended his hand.

"I'm Eliot. Manan has told me that you'll be joining us tonight for dinner."

"Oh, yes. Very nice to meet you, Prof Wood," he said.

Eliot looked at him unassumingly. "Please, just call me Eliot."

The senior theologian craned his neck, scanned the Ante-Hall puzzledly, then reflected for a second before speaking. "Do either of you happen to know whether Klaus will be joining us as well? I don't see him."

"I met with him Wednesday for lunch at the Freind Room. He didn't mention dinner, so I don't think he'll be here. He's probably in London."

Manan interjected. "Yes, well, that's quite all right. Why don't we all have a seat?"

He could not yet possibly know Manan's character well enough to be certain, but he got the impression his theologian friend was quick to dismiss the question of Klaus's whereabouts in order to emphasize that Wood's presence mattered more, anyway. The fact Manan's supervisor was attending tonight's dinner, while his own was not, was something Manan probably thought would be a source of embarrassment for him, but he wasn't worried about it, since he was simply relieved to be able to avoid having to sit with Michaela and Craig's group.

This was not his first time at Hall. But till now he had not yet seen it in its full splendor. The ambient lighting was dimmed, accentuating the understated beauty of the regal lamps lining the rows of long, wooden tables. The Hall, which until the nineteenth century had been the biggest in Oxford, could seat three hundred. Tonight, it would be at capacity. Its interior dimensions were imposing, with walls that must have been fifty feet, stained glass windows, and a Renaissance hammer beam ceiling. In the middle of the far wall stood Henry VIII, his portrait looming over the High Table. Manan and Wood took seats at a table against the wall, which, as it happened, was immediately beneath the portrait of John Locke. He nearly mentioned Locke's portrait, but he didn't, for fear of sounding too much like a tourist. Then he censured himself for caring about whether he appeared too awestruck. It was undeniably remarkable to be able to sit in a place like this, so why should he be embarrassed to say so? Then again, perhaps it was worldly to feel that way, in which case it was truly best not be in a state of awe, whether concealed or not, but rather indifference. It was a privilege to be here, he knew, but for the first time since arriving, he was stirred by the thought that the only way to truly make the most of it was to bring glory to God through his work.

He was himself a bit startled by the unbidden thought, since although he had already hazily understood that his coming here was somehow providential, he had never dwelled intently on what bearing, if any, that fact should have on the philosophical work he would go on to do here. To be sure, in a place with a history like this, it was not so bizarre to put such a question to oneself. He didn't know where it was exactly, but there was a portrait on these walls nearby of John Wesley, the founder of Methodism. Wesley had been a man who seriously wrestled with the question of his work's purpose in light of God's will. Of course, he would never dare tell anyone that he had intentions of producing truly great work if he proved able. Saying so would understandably be met with thoughts that he was overly ambitious, or even deluded. But even if he were so, that didn't at all change the fact that, as far as he could tell, the age was suffering from a general malaise. Great things were a matter of historical curiosity, but the idea of anyone attempting to produce anything similar was assumed to be unthinkable. Though no one actually said so, there was always the unspoken assumption that it was immodest to think of oneself as possessing the potential to contribute something on a par with what the greats of the past had. It was a sentiment that would be understandable were it the result of a sober acknowledgment of the obvious decline in general academic standards. He recalled his father having once told him how the great grandfather knew both Latin and Greek by the time he was finished with middle school. For centuries here in Oxford, scholarship was conducted in Latin. As a relic of that bygone era, tonight's prayer before dinner would be read in Latin, although very few of those in attendance would actually understand what was being said. Many of them scorned the practice of the prayer opening formal dinners, thinking it was superstitious and silly. The fact that those who felt so were less learned than those of the past, and hence could not even understand the prayer they held in such contempt, was lost on them. He himself for his own part had taken Latin as a youth, and French too, but he'd never mastered it. In any case, modesty couldn't be the motive for such a consensus, he concluded. After all, in many ways this had to be among the most prideful, narcissistic generations in the history of the world. People took immense pride in everyday banalities, posting to social media pictures of what they ate for breakfast or the jeans they bought at a clothing store. Was it, then, truly a sense of modesty explaining everyone's forswearing high scholarly aspirations? It seemed doubtful.

The societal attitude he had in mind was one he saw unmistakably reflected in the life of the college itself. Here, for example, was a place with a legacy of having produced Locke, Wesley, and Dodgson, now operating a gift shop for tourists to profit from their memories. And for all the buzz at tonight's dinner, the demeanor of the students and dons reflected their collective awareness that the college had become more of a museum than that of a living reality. Perhaps there wasn't a single person at dinner here tonight who would do anything remotely worthy of a passing comment from a future tour guide, much less a portrait on the wall. It made him realize how little the opinion of others should control his vision. If none of the others were seriously willing to try producing something of enduring value, their opinion of him and the work he himself would go on to create was irrelevant. Taking his seat next to Manan and Wood, he resolved to produce whatever work he felt genuinely called to produce, work he hoped would be honest.

Wood poured them sparkling water, while Manan examined the menu. "Three courses, I see."

"The food isn't very good," Wood said. "But it's the experience that counts."

They chatted until the servers brought the first course. He looked at the salad, which wasn't appetizing. He almost told Wood his judgment about the food appeared to be correct, but he held his tongue. Growing up, his parents had always reminded him of all the poor people starving in the world. It was a deeply spoiled thing to complain about the food one was given, when others went with nothing. He felt ashamed for his unappreciativeness, and reminded himself that he had to work on his ungrateful attitude.

His attention redirected itself to the conversation. Manan was nodding in agreement with whatever Wood had just finished saying. The young aristocrat poured himself a glass of red wine, and said, "Yes, I think you're quite right. It's an important fact to be considered. Without Vatican II, ecumenicalism would not be the force it is today."

He had no idea what the latter term meant, but it had the sound of something that was supposed to be good but actually wasn't. Whatever it was, Wood evidently was a proponent. He considered asking a question about Vatican II, which he knew was important to Catholics. He knew many Catholics, but he had not taken the time to ask them.

"As you know, Barth was at the proceedings. He was among a select handful of Protestants who attended," Wood said.

"That does not surprise me!" Manan gushed.

"Sorry to interrupt, Manan." Manan and Wood turned to him. He could see they were intrigued to hear what contribution he might add to the conversation. Because he knew nothing of church history or dogmatics, he would ask Manan something different, though still pertinent, he thought. "Are you Catholic?"

Manan got a very solemn look on his face. "No, I'm Lutheran."

He did not know who Barth was, but he knew Luther. Well, he knew the basics, anyway. Luther the Reformer opposed the Catholic Church's abuse of indulgences. Luther who nailed the *Ninety-Five Theses* to the church door at Wittingberg.

"We'll have to work on that," Wood chided his student. "Perhaps when his time is done here, I'll have converted him to a good Anglican!"

Manan laughed, as did Wood. While he didn't know the inner workings of the church denominations and the history behind their various contentions and schisms, he did understand the ironic spirit of Wood's comment. If all the denominations were equally in the true faith, it was pointless for Wood to bother attempting to persuade Manan to abandon Lutheranism. At the same time, if the choice between Anglicanism and Lutheranism were so inessential, then it raised the question of what significance there had really been to Luther articulating the theological position he had. Presumably, then, he decided, Wood and Manan would explain that the major disagreements lie between Protestantism and Catholicism, not within the denominations internal to the former. But then, if that were the case, Vatican II, which had promoted cooperation between Catholicism and other faiths, even other world religions, ruled that out as well. And, after all, Wood and Manan had just been commenting on how they were both enthusiastic about Vatican II and ecumenicalism, so he wondered how they understood their respective personal choices to be Anglican and Lutheran. He would not dare say it to them, but the situation from the perspective of an outsider appeared to akin to diners at a buffet, all of whom were free to choose how to fix one's plate.

"If I were ever to consider Anglicanism, I should simply get on with it and become a Catholic," Manan joked.

Wood wasn't offended. In fact, the teacher found the wit of his student's comment endearing. "Yes, but as you know, Manan, any self-respecting Englishmen chooses High Anglicanism."

There were probably complicated subtexts at work here, given Manan's hailing from India, but what interested him more in the playful dynamic between Wood and Manan was not the way they were working out the legacy of British colonialism over dinner, but rather the fact that there wasn't anything particularly serious about how they were treating the question of God, as theologians. If theology was supposed to be the science of God, an intellectual venture meant to clarify man's path to salvation, the jovial banter seemed incongruous with that task.

"Was Barth Anglican?" he asked.

Manan and Wood stopped. Judging by the obvious shock on their faces, his question was a serious blunder. Manan turned to Wood, who in turn said gingerly to him, "Karl Barth was a twentieth-century Reformed theologian. He is famous for his five-volume opus *Church Dogmatics*. He was Swiss."

It was the sort of basic knowledge that even an undergraduate theological student would be expected to know before taking an introductory class in church history. He wasn't embarrassed by his ignorance, however. He had never studied church history, or dogmatics, or anything of that sort, so he had to start somewhere. Where better to have his questions answered than at dinner with a Regius Professor of Theology? He could tell Manan was surprised by his intellectual humility, as was Wood. Of course, wanting others to see one as humble could itself be a vice. He would have to guard against that.

"It's good you ask questions," Wood declared.

Manan turned to him, "What denomination are you?"

He didn't know what to say. He didn't even attend church. His mother was a lapsed Catholic, his father had been raised in an atheistic home. As a child, there had been no church attendance. His parents both said that they believed in God, and his father was fairly receptive to the idea that Jesus was the Son of God, but organized religion had simply never figured in his upbringing. In the last year or two, he had been reading the Bible more frequently on his own. He knew he believed in God, and he also believed that Jesus was the Christ. But he didn't know how those beliefs were supposed to affect his daily life. The Gospel still had the feeling of an abstract proposition one was free to entertain intellectually, and nothing more. Perhaps finding a church might help change that.

"I'm non-denominational," he said. The statement was true, although it didn't mean what Wood and Manan would likely assume it did. For them, it would suggest he possessed theological reasons for rejecting any one particular denomination, considerations that would bear directly on the issue of ecumenicalism. There was understandable puzzlement on their part, though, since somebody who claimed to be non-denominational for such reasons wouldn't be the type to have to ask who Karl Barth was. Rather than attempting to dispel the confusion, Wood redirected the conversation to a subject everyone would be able to contribute to more comfortably.

"Barth is interesting, of course. But in this context, perhaps the more important figure is Bultmann." Wood eyed him quickly, and, noticing that he was as unaware of who Bultmann was as he had been Barth, he added, "I think Rudolph Bultmann's reputation in Protestant theological circles as the driving force behind demythologization is deserved, but his relationship to Heidegger gets less attention than it should. This is probably because philosophers working in the existential tradition tend to be atheists, and don't want to acknowledge Heidegger's debt to him, while theologians are understandably wary about admitting Bultmann's debt to Heidegger, given the latter's ambiguous relationship to Christianity and theology." When Wood paused, he was about to say something about Heidegger, but decided instead to let Manan speak.

Manan finished a sip of his wine, cleared his plate, and looked at Wood. "What role do you think Kant plays in shaping their encounter?"

"Good question. In the twenties, the influence of Kant on Heidegger is very strong. This is still during his transcendental period, before *die Kehre*, so the architectonic of his fundamental ontology is in many ways reminiscent of Kant's *Critique*. In *Being and Time*, of course, the existential analytic is itself indebted to Bultmann's existential approach to the New Testament."

He decided to try another question. "Do you think Heidegger was an atheist?"

"Hah! Now that is an extremely difficult question to answer. As with so much else, Heidegger on this point is enigmatic," Wood said.

Manan said, "Oh, I think it's very clear that he was. He simply wouldn't say so overtly. Forgive the anachronism, but there's something almost Straussian about how Heidegger handles the question of God."

"Well, it would be premature to base anything decisively off an ambiguous piece of biography, but it is worth remembering Heidegger underwent a traditional Catholic burial at Messkirch." Wood waited for Manan to reply.

"Yes, of course. But that was simply Heidegger's conservative respect for tradition. He renounced Catholicism in the early twenties under the influence of Luther and others he was reading." Manan, he could tell, was pleased to be able to mention Luther's reputed hand in Heidegger's conversion to Protestantism. Of course, there was the fact that Heidegger later abandoned Protestantism, too, which Manan didn't mention.

"Well, it's true Heidegger's critique of onto-theology might indicate atheism. But in *Phenomenology and Theology*, even when Heidegger draws a firm division between the two, and claims that the former must proceed by way of an unflinching methodological atheism, he makes clear this is not to say that there is no God. He says the same thing elsewhere, even in later texts, including the *Letter on Humanism*. In fact, what Heidegger defines as methodological atheism in the context of his question of being, it seems to me, is really a formulation of Bultmann's theological anthropology. As I mentioned, there's a way of understanding the existential analytic itself as a good exercise in Bultmannian existentialism," Wood said.

"Yes, I see that. If we interpret things through Bultmann, then Heidegger's account of *Dasein's* average everydayness is simply an existential description of sinful man alienated from God. But Heidegger himself would reject that view of his description," Manan parried.

"True, but an author is not immune to misinterpreting his own work. The text must have the last word."

Manan banged the table uproariously and sipped his wine again. "How postmodern of you, Eliot!"

Wood smiled, and took a bite of his chicken which had arrived a few minutes earlier. He spent the rest of dinner listening to the two of them talk theology, making mental notes of all the figures, texts, terms, and debates with which he would have to familiarize himself. He felt like he had discovered an unknown world, and now it was time to explore.

After setting out the dessert, chocolate cake with raspberry dressing and a scoop of vanilla ice cream, the staff began taking orders for coffee and tea. There would be a port, as well.

The server turned to him. "How would you like your coffee, sir?"

"Just black, please."

He was about to ask Wood and Manan a question concerning how exactly Husserl's phenomenology figured in the relationship between Bultmann and Heidegger, when he noticed Manan's brow furrow. His friend was straining to see something. Wood and he both turned to look in the direction in which Manan was staring.

"Prof Wood, am I mistaken, or is that not Prof Carman?"

"You're not mistaken, Manan. That's indeed Klaus." Sure enough, Klaus was sitting at High Table, eating his ice cream. A brunette woman, who appeared to be in her early thirties, was giggling next to him, her hand resting on Klaus's free hand. This must be the married woman Klaus had mentioned on Wednesday, he thought. His memory turned to a comment an old friend of his had made once when they were drinking in California. "There are three types of girls: goblins, elves, and mice." His friend had laughed, enjoying the look of perplexity on his face.

"What in the world are you talking about? You mean in terms of personality?"

"No, faces. Start paying attention to it. You'll see what I mean. Sometimes it can be subtle, but every girl is either a mouse, elf, or goblin." They played a game, where he gave his friend the name of someone whom they both knew, his friend would answer which type she was, and, sure enough, he began to see his friend's point. The woman sitting with Klaus, he decided, was an elf.

"Shall we say hello?"

Wood answered Manan's question curtly, "No."

It was almost indeterminate, but Wood seemed perturbed. It occurred to him that Klaus may have told Wood he would not be at dinner tonight, and yet now here he was. Or, perhaps Klaus had promised he would be here tonight, which was why Wood had appeared to be looking for him earlier in the Ante-Hall, and Klaus had backed out of the plans to sit with them, opting instead to sit with the adulteress. He realized there were many such possibilities, there was no way of knowing which one was the case, and probably it wasn't worth knowing anyhow.

"Well, it's getting late, gentlemen. I should be going," Wood said, as they stood to leave.

They walked through the Ante-Hall, down the stairs, and emerged into the moonlight.

"Are you sure you don't want to join us at the GCR for wine?"

"Oh, very kind of you to offer, Manan. But I must be going." They watched Wood walk across the quad. The theologian opened the door to his quarters, and went inside.

Outside the Cathedral, they heard cackling coming from behind them on the Hall stairs. A group of students from dinner emerged onto the quad. It was others from the graduate apartment. He could see that Craig and Michaela and the others recognized Manan, and Manan recognized them. Their mutual dislike was impossible to conceal.

Michaela walked by, and waved at him. "See you there," she slurred.

At the fountain, one of the girls, it looked to be Erin or Emily, had to be restrained by the others from jumping into the pond. Manan shook his head incredulously. "I honestly don't know why they are even here," Manan sighed.

He didn't say anything, because he knew Manan also saw the group's behavior as indicative of the cultural decline that he himself had been noticing for years since youth, a rot from which he was realizing even a place such as Oxford was not immune. That said, he had read that in the nineteenth century, the college had been forced to ban the tradition of students dunking others in the fountain. Maybe there was nothing new under the sun.

Manan stared out across the quad to the doorway leading to the GCR. "Well, shall we? Maybe, at least, the wine will be good."

EIGHT

A
FTER reaching the first floor's landing, they made their way down a carpeted hallway, where they found the door to the GCR open. Manan went in first. Following him in, he noticed a black and white photograph of the same room hanging on the wall immediately to the left of the doorway. An accompanying plaque explained the photograph in question was taken in 1931, during the period when the room served as Einstein's guest quarters during his visit to Oxford. A letter of thanks to the college written by Einstein himself hung in the frame.

The room was crowded, with four or five dozen students mingling. Manan and he pressed through the gathering to the table where the drinks were. Manan grabbed a glass of wine; he grabbed a Jell-O shot and a beer, downed the shot, and turned to survey the scene.

"Excuse me, excuse me." A man and woman stood on two chairs, tapping their glasses. The room hushed.

"Dearest Freshers, welcome to The House!" There was clapping and cheering. "Though, of course, the others won't admit it, they know what we all know: Christ Church is the best Oxford has to offer!" There was more applause, this time louder than before. "Now, we have no desire to bore you, so we shall make this announcement as brief as possible. The itinerary is as follows: drinks at The Bear at twenty-two hundred, Turf Tavern at twenty-three hundred, and the King's Arms at midnight. In case you somehow get lost along the way, here is a flyer to remind you of where to be." There was laughter.

A stack of flyers was circulated. He took one and read. "Christ Church Freshers' Pub Crawl: the highest concentration of IQ per square foot anywhere in the world." He showed the flyer to Manan, who rolled his eyes.

57

"Yes, well, it is good they all think so. Sometimes our false beliefs are relatively harmless," Manan said as he slapped his knee laughing. Evidently, Manan was feeling the wine.

Manan collected himself, "Well, there's no reason to be rude. I suppose we should go say hello to the others in our building." Manan walked over to join Craig and the others.

"Hi," Craig said. It was clear Craig couldn't remember Manan's name, though judging by the American's garbled speech and discombobulated demeanor, he probably couldn't remember which country he was presently standing in, either.

"I'm Manan Kahn."

Craig squinted, marshalling all his strength to concentrate. "Craig," he said.

"I see you've come ready for the pub crawl," Manan said dryly.

"Indeed, he has. Remind me again, who exactly are you?" It was Michaela. She was drunk, but not nearly so sloppily as Craig.

"Ah, yes, you're Michaela, correct? What is it that you study again? Business?"

"Marketing," she said.

"Yes, same thing. I'm Manan." The Indian royal put out his hand, but she pretended not to notice.

"Very good to see you," she said, as she turned from Manan and looked at him.

"Thanks."

"Thanks? That's it," she said. The other three girls, Allison, Emily, and Erin, made their way over, along with Frank.

"It's almost time to go!" they said.

Frank turned to the girls. "Have you been to The Bear yet?"

"Emily and I have," said Erin. "We love it. It's great for supper."

"Not yet," said Allison.

"Well, then, you're in for a treat," Frank said. She giggled and rubbed his arm. Evidently, they would be pairing off tonight. Michaela looked at Frank and Allison, then at him.

"Not a bad idea," she said. "We should have a buddy system, in case any of us gets lost. Can you be my buddy?" she asked him.

"I think you and Craig would make great buddies," he said. "Excuse me."

He walked to the table, took another Jell-O shot, and decided it was time to leave. Back at the group, he put his hand on Manan's shoulder, and said loudly enough for the others to hear, "It's getting late, so I'm going to be leaving now. Thanks again for the opportunity to meet Prof Wood tonight at dinner."

"Oh, you're leaving? I was about to leave as well." Manan waved half-heartedly to the others, and walked over to another group to say farewell to some acquaintances he knew there.

"Have a good time," he said to everyone. He thought of the time when the three women at his old apartment in Texas had said the same thing to him and Timothy. He wondered whether Timothy was doing okay.

"Thanks, man," Craig said.

"Oh, you're *so* cute. The engaged man going home early," Emily squealed. She hugged him, then turned to Erin and the others. "I wish I was engaged!"

Michaela rolled her eyes. "Some people liked being imprisoned." He pretended not to hear her.

He left the room, walked down the hallway past others who were still arriving, went down the stairs, and lit a cigarette as he strode through the quad onto the street. He finished the cigarette in the building's court-yard which was empty. The night's silence had more to say to him than did any of the people back up in the GCR. His thought returned to the line from Sartre on being alone and loneliness. Tonight's events seemed to reinforce his original assessment of Sartre's claim. It was healthy to be able to be alone, when, as here, that meant not conforming to what every-one else was willing to do no matter how inane, degrading, or despairing it was. If he had gone to the pub crawl simply not to be alone, Sartre's observation would apply. Missing a beloved, and wishing she were there, however, was not at all to be equated with that.

He threw his gown and cap on the room floor, took off his shoes and jacket, and sat down at the desk. After fiddling with his bow tie, but see-ing it wouldn't budge, he decided not to bother with it for the time being.

He opened his email to find a note from Alison. "I love you."

NINE

SATURDAY, he felt, had been unproductive. Aside from taking a walk at Port Meadow that helped him escape the nagging homesickness, he had alternated between sitting in bed and smoking cigarettes at the window. The tourists were braving the cold, lining up as usual for their opportunity to enjoy a glimpse into what they thought was a Medieval fairy tale.

He had taken the walking trail along the Isis. Along the way, he had stopped to watch the ducks at the footbridge over the Castle Mill Stream. Walking, he found, helped him memorize the names of the town's streets and places. As he stared at the aquatic form of life around him, he considered why, if the ducks and fish could be happy with their existence, people weren't. What was the source of this burden he felt, that he could see everyone else laboring under as well? Heidegger had called it *Sorge*, but for Heidegger, of course, the fact that we're all burdened by our existence wasn't at all to do with our relationship, or lack thereof, with God. This, it seemed to him, was the fundamental flaw in the Heideggerian philosophy. He did not know how to show that it was, but in principle he suspected it could be shown. Perhaps it was a suitable dissertation topic. He would have to ask Klaus.

This morning had been less miserable than yesterday morning. To be sure, the ache of the loneliness wasn't as sharp. The fact he was due to meet Manan this evening probably had something to do with it. Ever since formal dinner, he had been ruminating over all the questions the discussion with Wood and Manan had generated. For years, he had grown accustomed to the experience of feeling that, at crucial junctures in the course of his thinking, he was suddenly unable to articulate his thoughts with the level of clarity and precision he desired. A brick wall would appear, the thoughts would stop, blocked by the lack of conceptual sophistication necessary to allow them to progress. But now, having talked to the theologians, he understood he was undergoing a transformation, finally acquiring a language that would enable him to express everything he'd been wanting to express. If, then, his thinking was beginning to take a theological turn, that should be all well and fine, he thought, since philosophy and theology had always stood in a fecund, if sometimes ambivalent, relationship. He understood that with the pro-fessionalization of higher education, there was an increasing tendency for everyone in academia to stay in their disciplinary lanes, no matter how arbitrary or otherwise irrational those may be, but here, at Oxford, there should be no such problem with a philosopher drawing upon the resources of theology. After all, there was robust historical precedent for thinkers having done exactly that. Turning to theology was not a swerve, but rather a natural progression, in his thinking.

Enthused by his epiphany that theology would play an important role in the work to come, it was time for a relaxing cigarette, he decided. He opened the pack to find only three left. Stepping out to buy more wouldn't be so bad. Running low on cigarettes might even be fortuitous. He did not know whom, but probably it was the scout, had reported him to the college authorities for smoking in his room. He had received a warning letter yesterday from the Junior Censor, which had come as a shock to him. It had been a reasonable assumption, he had thought, that the apartment's non-smoking policy was a mere formality, and that of course graduate students were allowed to smoke in their rooms, so long as they were discreet. Many of them were smokers, so it was strange to expect them to interrupt their reading and writing in order to continually step outside to smoke. He had never used one himself, but the image of the Oxford don, a pipe in hand, sitting by the fire in the study, entered his mind. Rather than throw on clothes and trudge down to the street in the rain and cold, he had been smoking out the window, which frankly he thought was considerate of him, since it showed a basic respect for the spirit of the rule, while ignoring its letter, which he thought was irratio-nal and served no reasonable purpose. In any event, the Censor appeared to be genuinely livid, so he would not be able to smoke as frequently in his room. Better to save this one for the street, he decided. It was a good time to take a walk, anyway.

He went through the college gardens, past the meadow, then the cricket fields, and came out in front of Magdalen. Taking the bridge to Cowley was tempting, but he decided to stroll up the High instead. He popped into a shop next to the Covered Market, buying the cigarettes, along with a six-pack of Fosters. It was drizzling, but rather than avoid the mist by cutting through the Market, he walked along the small lane toward Broad St, where a line of tourists was waiting for entry into Trinity. On the bench, he lit his cigarette, and thought about Alison. With the time difference between them, it would still be very early morning there, so she likely was still sleeping. The art show had gone well, which had relieved her, and she was undergoing a period of intense productivity. With him away, perhaps her art was becoming a way of making the most of their being apart. Her visit to Oxford was close, although it felt like an eternity still. He worried that she might not understand why he had yet to write anything. It was true to say he had been thinking, but there was no way for her to know that he was. Then again, while he knew she respected his academic work, he also knew she loved him for reasons having nothing to do with it. She hopefully would just be happy to see him. His studies would be immaterial to her, and they could simply enjoy each other's presence, and everything Oxford had to offer. And, of course, there was also the short excursion to Paris they were planning. Assuming the work went smoothly, perhaps she would never have to know anything about it. She could remain confident in the expectation that it would get done without further ado, and he could attend to her, to them. The path seemed clear. Complete the dissertation, and then take a job somewhere as a professor, like her father. He could see why, from her perspective, this was all expected, as if everything were already laid out, meaning there was every reason to enjoy the present in light of the promising future awaiting them. He agreed that things appeared relatively straightforward, but there was no denying that the academic job market was horrendous. A job, he knew, was far from guaranteed. When he mentioned this to her, she had looked at him bemusedly, as if he were worrying for no reason, as she had complete confidence in his abilities. Her assessment wasn't baseless. Klaus, after all, had already offered him an editorial position with the journal, he'd been introduced to Wood, and he seemed to be a shoe-in for the college scholarship. Maybe he was worrying for no reason. He flicked the cigarette stub into the rubbish bin, lit the last one from the old pack, which he then threw out too, ran his hand through his hair, and walked down Broad.

The exterior of the Sheldonian Theatre was awash with tourists on their way to take photographs outside the Bodleian Library. Built in the seventeenth century from a design of Wren, the neoclassical building was one of the most distinctive in Oxford. He had been inside only once, a few weeks ago, for the matriculation ceremony. The rotunda was breathtaking, its ornate wood levelled seating reminding one of all those who had come before. In addition to serving as the site of the University's ceremonies, it was also the site of orchestral concerts and academic lectures. A performance of Vivaldi's *Four Seasons* was scheduled for next month. Even though she wasn't fond of classical music, Alison might enjoy it, since it would be something for them to remember. He made a mental note to buy tickets.

He crossed the street, entering Blackwells Bookshop, which he knew would be a favorite spot of his in the years to come. Aside from Powell's in Chicago, he had never seen a brick-and-mortar bookshop with such an extensive collection of academic titles. He went to the basement for the philosophy and theology, and began browsing the shelves. It was difficult to decide precisely where to begin, but after some rumination, he would start by buying Otto, Barth, and Bultmann. An argument could be made it was unwise to start his theological studies with twentieth-century figures, but he thought doing so made good sense. By doing so, he could trace the development of the various theological doctrines to their latest state, and from there in turn attempt to reverse engineer their origins in earlier thinkers such as Luther and Calvin, Anselm and Aquinas, Origen and Augustine. A copy of Wood's own latest book was on the shelf. He would have to read it later. Orienting oneself within intellectual history, it occurred to him, was a bit like detective work. Collect all the pieces, sort them, then try to assemble something intelligible.

He took a window seat at the upstairs café, skimming through the books while sipping a coffee. When the sun began setting, he knew it was time to return to the apartment. Manan had said to come over to at six.

When he got home, if he could call it that, he took a shower and put on a white shirt and jeans. He grabbed his cigarettes and beer, left his building and walked to the building next door in the complex. Manan, who lived on the ground floor, was entering his room as he arrived. "Ah, splendid. Perfect timing. Please, do come in." He walked in, and Manan closed the door behind them.

The first thing he noticed was how small the room was. Despite just a bed and desk, there was hardly any walking space. He had thought his own room was small, but this was tiny.

"It's cramped in here, but it will just be the two of us tonight, so it should be fine," Manan said. Since his friend had brought it up himself, he decided to comment on it.

"Yeah, I thought my room was confined, but this is claustrophobic. Does it bother you?"

"Oh, actually I like it. I had my pick of rooms, and I deliberately requested the smallest one. The less space I have, the less room for clutter and distractions. So long as I have my books," he pointed to a small shelf, "I'm happy. At first, it's difficult, but in the long run I've found living ascetically to be advantageous. Athens may have given us philosophy, but perhaps I'm a Spartan at heart."

He thought about asking Manan in what ways living ascetically had proved to be intellectually beneficial, but he would hold the thought for later. "I brought some beer in case you're interested."

"Very kind of you. Let me set it down for you." Manan grabbed the beer, took a look at it, then put it on the table. It was clear he wasn't planning to touch it.

"Just got out of the shower, I see."

He didn't think his hair was wet, so he wondered how Manan knew. Then he realized. Wearing a plain white t-shirt was something Manan would consider an undergarment, so Manan must have inferred he put it on after showering. Of course, as it happened, that was correct. But he would wear such a shirt, in any case, even if he hadn't just showered. Without having intended to do so, it dawned on him that he must be developing a reputation for being the college's noble savage. Preferring cheap beer to expensive whiskey was one thing. The overly casual dress was another. But then there was the fact that his personality lent itself to social nonconformism, since he was naturally disinterested in the pomp that governed so much of the daily life of the college, especially in these first few weeks such as these, which were a period heavy on ceremonies and other formal events. He had of course skipped the GCR pub crawl. Before that, he had almost missed the University's matriculation ceremony. He had known the date, but thinking attendance was optional, he had decided to skip it. On the morning of the ceremony, two senior college officials had come knocking on his room door frantically, rousing him from bed. They assumed he had unintentionally overslept, "Overindulgence," as one of the men had explained it, but the truth wasn't that he was hung over. He simply had genuinely intended to skip the ceremony. The only thing saving him from being viewed with complete derision on the part of his peers, he figured, was the fact that people knew he was sincerely committed to a life of the mind, which meant they had to look past his social foibles somewhat, since, as they knew he knew, the entire point of being here was supposed to be scholarship. The fact that none of them cared about ideas, he knew they knew he knew, was from his perspective far more cause for embarrassment than dressing casually or wanting to sleep through a ceremony. They wanted to go through the rituals and other rites of passage that came with being here, but they didn't want to do the work. He was here to work, and couldn't care less about the rest of it. At first, he had thought Manan's indifference to the others was also due to a dedication to the life of the mind. And, to be sure, there was an ascetic streak in Manan, something he had noticed, even before his friend said anything about it explicitly tonight. And yet, he was beginning to sense that part of Manan's contempt, since it was really more than pure indifference, to the others in their cohort might actually have less to do with a disparity between their respective commitments to learning, and more so with Manan's snobbishness. His friend had not said much about his family in India, but it was apparent in his dress and how he carried himself that he was a blue blood. Of course, if it was elitism explaining Manan's derision for the others, he of all people should be the last person Manan liked at the college, since he gave others every reason to think he himself was unsophisticated. He wondered, then, why Manan was willing to make an exception of him, but not the others.

"Whiskey?" Manan raised a bottle. Manan said something about the brand and year, but as he had no appreciation for what any of it meant, he simply politely nodded his head, as he thought about other things. His friend poured two glasses.

"Cheers," Manan said.

"Yes, cheers," he said.

They clinked glasses and sipped.

"Prof Wood wanted me to tell you he was delighted to meet you Friday. I can tell he was very impressed with some of the things you had to say."

"Oh, that's very kind. The next time you see him, please tell him I say hi."

"Well, you'll have the chance to do so yourself. He has dinners at his place for some of his theology students. He says you're invited."

"Ah, yes. He had mentioned those." He could see Manan looked puzzled, but rather than explain that Klaus had already introduced him in e-mail to Wood, he kept silent. It was a minor detail not worth clarifying. He pointed to the beer on the table.

"Oh, yes, of course." Manan cracked one open, and it handed it to him.

"Thank you."

"You probably gathered from our conversation the other night, but Eliot is one of the foremost experts on Barth's theology in the world."

"I did not know that. As you could tell, I don't know anything about Barth. Or theology in general, really. I need to learn."

"Barth is probably the most important theologian of the twentieth century. Well, certainly at least the most important Reformed theologian." He wanted to ask what Manan meant by "Reformed," but he decided for now he would proceed on the assumption that it had something to do with the Reformation itself, which meant that it was perhaps a shorthand for Protestant.

"And Bultmann?"

"Bultmann is very important as well. Both are interesting in how they think theologically in the wake of Kant."

"What do you mean? I'm familiar with Kant, but not with how theologians have responded to his critical philosophy."

"Yes, precisely. It all comes down to a matter of assessing what theology can know about God after the *Critique*. I mean primarily the *First Critique*, though the others are important too. Kant's practical philosophy, I would argue, is deeply influenced by Christianity, even if Kant himself doesn't like to admit it."

"From what I remember, Kant claims that we can't know God exists."

"Yes, which means all of what the tradition has called natural theology is out the window. None of the ordinary arguments for God's existence are any longer valid."

"I guess that is similar to Heidegger, to his critique of onto-theology, I mean."

"Yes again, Heidegger certainly claims to be interested in recovering a conception of God that is different than what the onto-theological tradition had been examining, and part of that means, as with Kant, that the demonstrative arguments for God's existence of natural theology are no longer to the point. Of course, as I mentioned at dinner to Eliot, I think Heidegger was an atheist."

"And Kant?"

"Many, many people disagree. But I believe he was an atheist as well."

"So why, then, do theologians take his work so seriously?"

Manan was silent for a moment. "Kant's system leaves open the question of whether or not there is a God . . . "

"Right," he interrupted, "the famous comment 'I had to deny knowledge in order to make room for faith.'"

"Precisely! Nothing Kant says entails that there is no God. It just rules out certain conceptions of God, or at least certain ways of demonstrating his existence or knowing his nature."

He had read in passing some of the Medieval mystics. And he knew Heidegger had been influenced by some, particularly Eckhart.

"Am I wrong to think, then, that there is a way of tying together Kant's critical philosophy with negative theology, even mysticism?"

Manan almost leapt from his chair. "You have just articulated the key presupposition of what will be my thesis."

"Okay, so I get that Kant's *Critique* doesn't mean to claim there is no God. It just means that we supposedly can't know there's a God in the way theologians to that point had assumed we could. But doesn't Kant also say that we have no experiential acquaintance with God, either?"

"Yes, it is true that the Kantian system generates massive problems for religious experience."

"That seems to pose a problem for the possibility of revelation, too."

"Once again, you are correct! Eliot will have to convert you from philosophy to theology!"

"I'm sorry, I took us on a tangent. How do Barth and Bultmann fit in?"

"Barth believes that man's reason is entirely corrupt. We are in total darkness."

"Okay. How does that fit in with Kant? I always thought Kant was famous for extolling reason."

"That's true. But Kant is ambivalent. On the one hand, he says the final court of appeal is reason, but at the same time, he drastically restricts the limits of what reason can know, when compared to the traditional rationalists, such as Descartes, Leibniz, or Woolf."

"So how is Barth borrowing from Kant?"

"Because Kant has shown us that the world of experience is merely appearance, and has shown us that reason is severely restrained in what it can know on its own, this opens the way for Barth's view of revelation, that it is God who must reveal himself to us."

"Okay, but I thought Kant is thought to have shown that revelation is impossible?"

"Kant thinks so, but Barth disagrees."

"Why, then, does Barth buy into any of Kant's criticisms of traditional metaphysics then?"

"Because by humiliating reason, a little like in the way Luther did, Barth thinks that Kant inadvertently showed the depravity of man, that our noetic faculties are completely impaired after the Fall. This means, contrary to Kant, that any field of knowledge besides theology is foolishness, since the only science with any genuine basis for claiming to know anything would be the science of God, since it alone is secured by God's grace."

"And Bultmann?"

"Well, I think how the entire project of demythologization is motivated by a response to Kant is pretty clear." Manan paused, waiting for him to say something. When Manan realized he didn't know how to reply, Manan apologized.

"Oh, yes, I'm sorry. I keep forgetting that you are not a theologian. Shall I explain Bultmann's demythologization?"

"Please!"

Manan rubbed his hands together gleefully. "Okay, you'll see how it's similar in ways to what I've just said about Barth." He took another sip of his whiskey, and poured some more.

"It's good to start with Kant. One takeaway from the Kantian revolution is the critique of metaphysics. Reason is no longer said to be able to know reality independently of experience. Or rather, there are certain things we can know *a priori* about experience, but this is only because experience itself is appearance, rather than things in themselves. This has radical implications for the physical sciences, and how we understand nature."

"You mean the 'Copernican Revolution'?"

"Yes. In the wake of Newton and Copernicus and others, our view of the universe changes radically. It is the sun, not the earth, at the center of the solar system. The earth orbits the sun, rather than the sun moving above the earth. The earth is round, not flat. And then later, with Darwin, there's the theory of evolution. All of this radically undercuts what used to be the basis for certain arguments for the existence of God."

He thought about it. "For example, the argument from design?"

"Yes, that is the primary victim. Now, the beauty of what Kant does for theology is that, by drawing a distinction between appearance and things in themselves, he negates the significance of any empirical findings regarding the structure and nature of the cosmos. All of that belongs to appearance, anyway."

"So, the idea is that matters of cosmology no longer bear one way or the other on whether there is a God?"

"Precisely. Bultmann intuits this Kantian insight, which he then radicalizes with his demythologization program." It was an irrelevant thought, but he imagined how on the page, it was "programme" for the British, not "program." Some of their spellings irked him.

"How?"

"All that matters is the *kerygma*."

"*Kerygma*?"

"The Proclamation. The New Testament's doctrine that Jesus is the Son of God. Bultmann's suggestion is that everything in the New Testament, including the reported miracles and such things, can be disregarded as mythological, without that affecting the central issue, which is the person of Christ."

"This is Bultmann's way of avoiding having to defend Genesis, then, too?"

"Yes, Bultmann is happy to concede that Genesis is purely allegorical, no longer a literal account of the origin of the world. So again, all of this is very post-Kantian, and yet, at the same time, it preserves the fundamental tenets of the Christian faith." Manan dabbed his brow with that handkerchief, and swigged his whiskey.

He didn't know what to say. He had so many questions. He did know that it sounded to him, at least from what he gathered, as if both Barth and Bultmann were far too eager to settle for far too little. Having to dispense with human reason, as with Barth, and to chuck out all the miracles and other events in the New Testament, as with Bultmann, seemed extreme. Why not just take the Bible at its word, and believe what it said? Frankly, when push came to shove, why care what Kant said? Kant was just a man. It occurred to him that the stumbling block must be the cosmology. If modern astronomy, biology, and physics have revealed that the Biblical worldview was false, then the only way to purge falsehoods contained in the Bible from one's theological system was to jettison things such as angels, demons, and miracles. It felt to him like throwing the baby out with the bathwater, but he was not sure how to avoid doing so.

"I bought some books today. Barth and Bultmann. Otto, too."

"Oh, Otto is very interesting, though he receives less attention than he deserves. The *mysterium tremendum et fascinans!*"

"Yes, Kierkegaard here looms large, I take it."

"Certainly. But again, it seems to me that it's actually Kant who does more so."

"How's that?"

"In this case, I think it's the *Third Critique* that matters. The phenomenon of the sublime is very similar to what Otto means by the *mysterium tremendum*. For Kant, the sublime is awesome, overwhelming our rational faculty's ability to assign a concept to what we experience. In that sense, it's very close to mystery."

"Yes, I see that. But Otto seems to think that we know God through the *mysterium tremendum*. It's experiential knowing. Kant says that's not possible."

"Quite right. Kant does have trouble accounting for religious experience. From his perspective, much of what traditional believers take themselves to know is simply enthusiasm or madness. This is why, contrary to what many Protestants would say, it's not very crucial to read the Bible. I think it was Augustine who said somewhere that with true faith, reading the Scriptures would be unnecessary. I don't say this to my other Lutheran friends, of course, since they think *sola scriptura* means we should actually be reading it."

He could see how Barth and Bultmann could have concluded that using elements of Kant's critique of metaphysics was to their advantage, but ultimately it seemed to him better to find a way of short-circuiting the entire Kantian program, to begin with. He would have to ask Klaus about that as well, just like he would the point about phenomenology and theology.

After a couple more whiskeys it was getting late, and he was starting to get homesick. He wanted to be alone.

"I should be going."

"Ah, yes. Very good having you over. We shall have to do this again. See you around college," Manan said, as he left.

He walked outside, lit a cigarette in the courtyard, and studied the moon. He understood the fact that appearances sometimes were deceiving. Kant's entire point, of course, was that everything we experienced

was in some sense so, since it was all mere appearance. As a phenom-
enologist, though, he found himself drawn to the idea that appearance
was reality. And from what he could see tonight, not only was the moon
very bright, it also looked to be much closer than what everyone believed.
He finished the cigarette, messaged Alison, and went to bed.

TEN

W HEN the following Thursday came, it meant the time had come to attend his first session of the seminar Klaus co-convened with Fernandez. The abstract, which was posted online, outlined a paper examining Foucault's genealogical method in relation to the transcendental tradition, particularly the early Heidegger. He had once taken an undergraduate course on Foucault, and found it interesting, even if he found Foucault himself an unsavory character. Much of what Foucault said about surveillance and other systems of control seemed right to him. There was no denying, he thought, the increased regimentation of everything about our lives, and there was no sign of the bio-political, bio-digital, and bio-medical industries abating. In all likelihood, technocracy would only accelerate the dehumanization of man that everyone was already witnessing. The brave new world of a technological elite ruling over the plebes was already here, although most people were still trying to pretend it was not. Of course, the very same psychologists who charted out a plan of action to quell the masses knew this. They knew the power of denial, and they exploited it thoroughly. The average person, he knew they knew, would not admit the degree of the danger until it affected him sufficiently personally, at which point by then it would be too late to do anything to stop it. He sighed, buttoned his collared shirt, grabbed his cigarettes, and left the room.

It would be cutting things close, since the seminar started at five, but if he hurried, he could visit the Turf Tavern, which everyone had been talking about, have a pint, and get to the seminar on time. Although he was getting the hang of the town's layout, finding his way around the various colleges and faculty buildings was still challenging. Tonight's journey, he feared, might be particularly so. The Faculty of Philosophy, which now was on Woodstock, had moved to its current location a few years

72

ago. Before that, it had been in a building near the college, on 10 Merton where the History Faculty was before it moved to George. The potential hiccup was that tonight's seminar, unlike other philosophy seminars, was not held at either the Lecture Rooms or the Ryle Room. Instead, it was held in a holdover space on Merton from before the Faculty had vacated, in what was called the Strawson Room named in honor of the late P.F. Strawson. He had yet to be to the old space on Merton, so he was concerned he would get lost inside, or, even worse, he might revert to his newly formed habit, and walk off to the usual place on Woodstock, forgetting to head to Merton instead. The fact he was aiming to squeeze in a visit to the pub, he knew, only increased the danger of his wandering off in a fancy, and making an error, so he would have to be especially careful to arrive on time, and in the right place.

There were two ways into the Turf. One was to take a very narrow walkway tucked aside beyond the Bridge of Sighs. The other was to access the cobbled lane, just down the street from the King's Arms. Cutting past the Radcliffe Camera, he strode past the Bodleian, and took a right, passing beneath the bridge, darted into the narrow way, where he emerged onto the pub's front entrance. There was a picnic table outside that was full, another set of tables on a patio that looked occupied as well, and evidently more seating in the back. Before checking it out, he decided to walk inside. The interior was cramped but clean. Everything was wooden, with the feeling of being in a *Lord of the Rings* shire hut. He was sure the tourists must love that about it. He waited in line, bought a beer, and went out the way he came. He lit a cigarette, turned around, and walked down the side of the pub leading to the back patio.

The Turf had been a favorite spot of luminaries such as Thatcher and Blair. Apparently, Elizabeth Hurley, too. He sat down, and there it was. The infamous plaque.

> Bill Clinton: It is alleged that it was here at the Turf Tavern, that
> Bill Clinton, while here at Oxford University, during the sixties
> 'did not inhale' whilst smoking illegal substances . . .

As an American, he remembered having heard the infamous lie Clinton had given about his marijuana use. He had not known until now that this was the place where it had occurred. What the plaque didn't mention, of course, was that Oxford was also the place where Clinton had to leave his Rhodes Scholarship after having being accused of raping a woman. He laughed sardonically. Nobody's going to mention that one on some cute little touristy plaque here in town. Come to think of it, someone had mentioned Chelsea Clinton was currently reading for a DPhil. He wondered how the woman Clinton had assaulted felt about that, knowing her rapist had an endearing little sign at the Turf commemorating his stint in Oxford, while his daughter now attended Oxford herself. Sometimes, it seemed as if there were never consequences in this world for the wicked. He knew that there were powerful forces at play here in Oxford. He assumed he would fly under the radar, though, simply because they would have no desire to meddle in a philosophy student's dissertation. After all, it wasn't as if he were attempting to break into banking, or politics, or media. If anyone powerful ever did come to know anything about him, they would probably see him as a gnat not even worth squashing. He would focus on his work, ignore the rest, and slip right through the cracks.

Rather than dwelling on the systematic corruption of the world's institutions, he resolved to focus on what he could control here and now. He opened the copy of Otto's *The Idea of the Holy* he had brought with him. He opened to the page from which he'd left off, "The daemonic-divine object may appear to the mind an object of horror and dread, but at the same time it is no less something that allures with a potent charm, and the creature, who trembles before it, utterly cowed and cast down, has always at the same time the impulse to turn to it, nay even to make it somehow his own."

Otto's description of the numinous was as alluring as it was elusive. He could see how the German theologian was attempting to walk a very fine line, not understating the mysteriousness and incomprehensibility of God, while at the same time not denying, as Kant, the reality that the presence of God was manifest in experience. In that respect, he thought, Otto's was a thoroughly phenomenological approach, and one worth exploring, as he was. Though he had not yet read him, Jaspers was another such figure, he'd heard, someone who took seriously the Kantian claim that there were limits to what we could know, in a certain respect, while nevertheless insisting that it was possible to encounter a realm of reality beyond what Kant himself would have claimed to be accessible. Jaspers, as it happened, was for a time friends with Heidegger too. If memory served, Otto, who was based primarily in Marburg, had been also. He would have to ask Klaus, since Klaus would know. Klaus knew everything about Heidegger. Horowitz had once mentioned how when Klaus had been interviewing for the job in California, they'd driven out to the beach. The entire time all Klaus had talked about was Heidegger, Horowitz had said.

He opened his phone to check his email, hoping to find a message from Alison. There was nothing. The disappointment morphed into panic, when he realized he had indeed lost track of time, as he had feared he might. There were ten minutes till the start of seminar. He knew if he left that moment, walking very briskly, he could arrive in the nick of time. He grabbed his cigarette pack, lit a cigarette, and walked out the narrow lane, crossed under the bridge, hung a left, walked through the Radcliffe Square, passed All Souls, hung a left on the High, crossed the street, and made it to the Merton building. Three minutes to go, he told himself, as he checked the time on the wall clock. He asked a man in the lobby for directions to the seminar room, where he opened the door to find everyone about to take their seats. He plopped down in a seat against the wall, exhaled, and surveyed the room.

The room, which occupied a corner place on the building's ground floor, was adjacent to a beautiful garden outside. As for the interior, it was understated, but regal, with purple curtains and gold tassels, a thick oriental rug, and a big beautiful oak table, with about a dozen chairs. Seated at the head of the table, next to two other men, one of whom must be Fernandez and the other the speaker, was Klaus. Since coming in, Klaus had been chatting quietly with the speaker, his gaze averted from the others at the table. He stared at Klaus, hoping to nod hello, but Klaus turned from the speaker, and stared into space, his gaze trained on the back wall. Apparently, he was using the old technique of never making any direct eye-contact with those in the room, but simply scanning it, so as to make people feel like they were being seen by him, when in point of fact they weren't. It was an old Toastmasters trick his mom had described to him once.

Klaus did not ask the room to quiet. He simply began speaking in a very low, delicate voice, almost as if he were trying to wake a young child softly from a dream.

"Thank you all very much for finding the time out of your busy schedule to be with us tonight. Our speaker tonight, for our first session this Michaelmas, has come from Sussex. Prof Gardner, as many of you in the phenomenology world will know, is very-well known for his work on Heidegger. In particular, he has been focusing on the nature of conceptual change, and how that bears on various issues in political philosophy, but also aesthetics. Tonight's paper, 'Foucauldian Genealogy:

A Heideggerian Critique,' will explore some of Foucault's thought's transcendental elements, and argue that those aspects, which largely remain undeveloped by Foucault himself, might be best understood from within the perspective of Heidegger's existential analytic." Klaus waved to the speaker, indicating the floor was his.

"Well, first of all, before turning to the paper itself in earnest, let me offer some prefatory remarks. First, of course," he motioned to Fernandez on his right, then Klaus on his left, "my sincerest thanks for the opportunity to present my work here tonight. This seminar is a unique space, in that it affords the sort of long and serious discussion of philosophical ideas that I think all of us here tonight value so greatly. So, thank you." Klaus nodded and Fernandez smiled.

"Second, let me caution you all not to get your hopes up. This paper is not nearly as ambitious as it may sound. It is part of a much larger book-length project that I am currently in the earliest stages of conceiving. The idea, to put it as briefly as possible, is to trace the history of how transcendental philosophy, beginning with Kant and ending with Heidegger, has handled the question of the relationship between conceptual content and aesthetic and political experience. As you might expect, a key text will be Kant's *Third Critique*, but tonight I focus instead on Foucault. Finally, a disclaimer. I am not a Foucault expert, so although I hope to avoid any obvious howlers when it comes to my interpretation of his views, I am in reality more interested in a particular philosophical thesis, which I believe can be justifiably attributed to Foucault, and found throughout his works, but which frankly stands on its own terms, and warrants our consideration, even if it ultimately doesn't capture Foucault's own view perfectly. It is, as I shall explain in due course, a claim that we also find in the Heidegger of *Being and Time*. To that claim I now turn."

The speaker read the paper which was riveting. When the questions and answers period came, he desired to ask a question, but he was too nervous to do so. It was the first time he could recall ever being too afraid to speak in public. Just as he was about to get down on himself, a man sitting at the opposite end of the table from the speaker and co-convenors began to speak. Neither Klaus nor Fernandez had yet asked for hands, much less called on anyone, but apparently the man felt entitled to take the floor. When nobody else in the room seemed surprised, he realized that this must be some sort of custom. Evidently, judging by his smug face, the man in question, who was somewhere in his fifties with fair hair and glasses, relished the attention, though he strained hard not to appear he did, a theatrical display of false modesty that only accentuated the very narcissism he wanted to conceal. He rarely disliked anyone this much upon meeting him, but something about the man rubbed him the wrong way. The man had the attitude of a fox, or maybe a snake. The garish red sweater he was wearing, which was highly obnoxious, didn't help things, either.

"Many thanks for a stimulating and thoughtful presentation that has given me a lot to digest. While I don't pretend to be able to do it full justice, given the immense robustness of the various and layered issues it touches upon, I do hope to ask a question that might help me clarify some confusions I had in my mind, as I listened to your paper. In particular, I have in mind a concern regarding your use of Heidegger, which, if I understand you correctly, is meant to enlist him as an ally of Kant's, but which, I do wonder, does so at the express cost of running afoul of what Heidegger himself considers to be the fundamental distinction at the heart of any proper philosophical inquiry, as he understands it. I mean, of course, the ontological difference. I worry, in other words, that the elements in Foucault's thinking, which you wish to appropriate to the transcendental tradition, and which you think can be satisfactorily explicated by appeal to Heidegger's existential analytic, in fact on the contrary distorts the very picture of good philosophy, as Heidegger understands it, by turning philosophical genealogy into a form of merely ontic inquiry, whereas Heidegger would insist that it must remain strictly ontological . . . "

The question went on for another minute or two. He followed everything the man was saying, but was frustrated by it, because it could have been stated more briefly. His initial impression seemed to be confirmed. Here was a man who loved the sound of his own voice.

"Wow, thank you so much for that absolutely fantastic question, Thomas. I'm afraid I won't be able to do it nearly the justice it deserves." The room laughed heartily, evidently awed by the man's display of erudition. Thomas—this, he realized, must be Prof Thomas Quiller, the seminar legend of Oxford.

The speaker and Quiller went back and forth for a long while. By the time they were finished, the room was exhausted. Quiller stood up from the table and addressed the speaker. "My apologies for having to leave now, but family obligations require my attention." He waved to Klaus, and slipped out of the room, closing the door behind himself.

Fernandez surveyed the room. "Any other questions?" The implication was that there shouldn't be, because it was time to go.

He worked up his courage, and raised his hand. Fernandez raised an eye-brow. "Yes?"

"Thanks, I know we're about at time, so perhaps the speaker would prefer to answer the question after we conclude here, but just quickly: what, if anything, can be said about how the later Heidegger, rather than the early one, might shed light on what you're seeing in Foucault?"

The speaker's eyes light up. His question was intended to let the speaker exercise some creativity, since, from what he could tell, the paper had been working itself up to claim something that it never actually got around to suggesting explicitly. "Well, I hadn't mentioned it yet tonight, either in the paper or during discussion, but the next logical step, which frankly is the one that interests me most, is precisely that. A lot of ink has been spilt on the early Heidegger's relation to genealogy, but not nearly as much when it comes to the later Heidegger, which, if you think about it, is very strange, since Heidegger's rhetoric about poetic thinking and so forth, it stands to reason there might be resources there for thinking through certain issues raised by Foucault's analysis of conceptual scheme in the realm of aesthetics. That isn't a detailed answer, I know, other than to say you've encouraged me to think I'm indeed on the right track by thinking there is something important there to mine. Thank you."

There was a long silence. Fernandez smiled, "Well, please thank our speaker for a wonderful talk. As usual, everyone is welcome to join us for further discussion and drinks at Quod."

The room clapped. He stood up from his chair, waiting for the speaker and convenors to walk by. The speaker smiled and nodded hello as they passed, but Klaus said nothing. Everyone walked out of the room. He stood in the emptiness, debating whether to go to Quod or whether instead to go back to Turf, or whether instead simply to go back to the room. Because he knew not going to Quod would leave him with an incomplete sense of the seminar's full arc, he decided to catch up with the group, which by now had reached the exit, and was about to head onto the High.

He caught up to the back of the group, where two other new philosophy graduate students whom he had met previously at orientation events said hello. Klaus opened the glass door to the restaurant, holding it open for the speaker and the others. Inside, the waitress put them at a large table. The restaurant was one of the more elegant in town, with glass and crystal and white linen everywhere. Under the glow of the bright interior lights, everything was shining.

There were eight of them. Some ordered meals, others did not. He ordered a gin and tonic. He could stop at the kebab van on the way home, and anyway he for whatever reason had always been uncomfortable eating with strangers. He would nurse his appetite. He sat in silence, listening to the conversation. Everyone had his piece to offer, and the litany of items, all the figures and texts and debates, piled up one after another on top of each other, the procession of new things he knew he'd have to learn about only pausing when the meals were served. Klaus had ordered a hamburger and fries. His supervisor took a fork and knife in hand, sliced a fry in half, and put it in his mouth. He wondered whether it was typical for the British to eat their fries, or chips, he reminded himself, with a fork. He looked around, and noticed the others were all using their hands.

"I have a question for the table," Klaus said.

Everyone got quiet. "What are your feelings about the etiquette of phones?"

Gardner turned his head to Klaus, "What do you mean?"

"The other week, I was out to dinner with a group, and one of my students had his phone out, texting during dinner. I'm wondering whether that's considered normal now, or is that still considered rude, as I remembered it being the case not too long ago?"

A few people at the table laughed. One of them said, "Oh, Klaus, that ship sailed long ago. Phones are everywhere, and they're a part of life. I think it's obnoxious when somebody texts during a conversation, but apparently it's considered harmless."

Klaus nodded, "I see."

The conversation continued on about phone usage, which led to more general questions about the nature of technology and its impact on society. Inevitably, that led back to Heidegger, at which point the group had been gathered for over an hour. The plates were cleared, it was getting late, and it was time to go. They all stood, paid their tabs, and walked out the glass door. On the sidewalk, he was about to leave for his room when Gardner approached him. "Magnificent question tonight. Thank you."

"Oh, you're welcome. It just seemed to me that what you were saying led in that direction naturally, and I wanted to see if that was the case, so I'm happy to have seen it is."

"Yes, it was very helpful. Sometimes you can get so close to a topic that you begin worrying whether what your thinking is reflective of what's in these texts. So your insight was a welcome confirmation that I'm not down in the weeds."

They paused. The visitor from Sussex asked, "Whom are you studying with here?"

"Oh, Klaus. Prof Carman, I mean." He could tell Klaus had not told Gardner about him.

"I see. Well, it's a shame we didn't have a chance to talk earlier today when I was here in town. I met some other students at a lunch this afternoon; it's a shame you weren't able to attend."

He could tell Gardner was hoping to determine whether he had been invited and chosen not to bother attending, or whether he had not received an invitation. Assuming it must have been Klaus or Fernandez responsible for organizing the lunch, he did his best not to say anything that would suggest they hadn't invited him. Gardner might infer, then, that it had been rude of him not to come, since he would understandably surmise that he'd been invited, but he hoped the fact that he had asked the question at tonight's seminar would compensate. Maybe Gardner would think he simply had another engagement this afternoon, and had been unable to make it.

The speaker pulled out his wallet and gave him a card. "Those are my contact details." Gardner glanced at Klaus, who was standing silently, then back at him. "Let's stay in touch."

"Oh, thank you. I'd love that," he said.

Klaus and Gardner began walking up the High. It occurred to him that Gardner would probably be staying in the spare room at the college Klaus had mentioned, so to avoid the appearance of following them when making his own way home, he decided to cut through another side street off the High, where he then passed through the gardens, avoiding both of the college entrances completely.

He set Gardner's card on the desk, lit a cigarette, and thought things over. He wheezed slightly from the smoke. When Alison later asked him how it had gone, he knew he would not be sure what to tell her.

Eleven

THE next morning, he awoke, and lit a cigarette at the desk. If the Censor didn't like it, so be it. It was overcast, but on the horizon blue sky was visible, so perhaps there would be sunshine later in the afternoon. To his surprise, he found an e-mail from Klaus, asking whether he would be available to chat at the office today at "1530 hours." British clock time annoyed him, but he was doing his best to grow accustomed to it. His supervisor's note did not disclose the precise reason for the chat, but he assumed it might have something to do with Gardner's seminar talk. He reached to light another cigarette to think it over, when he saw he was low. It would be necessary to run to the shop, so he put on some clothes, checked to make sure he had his keys, and was about to head out the door when he opened his wallet, only to find his bank card was missing. He patted down his pockets, then went through the bed linen, and even looked through the desk drawers. It wasn't there. He walked to the sink and checked there, but it was just the toothpaste and hand soap. It didn't make sense to do so, but in the interest of thoroughness, he checked his closet, rummaging through all the pockets of his clothes. The search turned up nothing. Then it occurred to him he must have left the card at Quod. He wasn't sure whether they were open for lunch, but it was worth a shot.

The sidewalks were crowded, with busses and taxis whizzing by on the High. It felt good to be outside, to melt into the city bustle. As he was nearing the restaurant, a small blue plaque on one of the buildings caught his eye. He had time, so he stopped to read.

> In a house on this site
> between 1655 and 1668 lived
> ROBERT BOYLE
> Here he discovered BOYLE'S LAW

and made experiments with an
AIR PUMP designed by his assistant
ROBERT HOOKE Inventor Scientist and Architect
who made a MICROSCOPE
and thereby first identified
the LIVING CELL.

His memory turned to all of the philosophy of science debates those he'd known in Texas had at the bars and cafés. The Aristotelians, he remembered, would cling ferociously to the role of teleology in scientific explanation, though of course the others held such a view in derision, given the fact that, as far as they were concerned, modern natural science had eliminated the need, indeed the very viability, of any *telos* in nature. After Newton, in physics, there were simply efficient causes, conforming to the laws of mechanistic nature. And after Darwin, in biology, once again ends had been eliminated. Just months after the publication of *On the Origin of Species*, there was a famous debate here in Oxford between Thomas Huxley and Bishop Wilberforce. Everyone was familiar with the Royal Society's roots in Baconianism and London, seeing as it was founded in 1660 at Gresham College. But it had roots among the physicians and natural scientists in Oxford also. Looking at the plaque, he realized it was very strange how the theory of evolution was silent on the origin of life itself. It only purported to explain the mechanism by which new lifeforms evolved, yet not the origin of life as such.

His thought drifted to what Manan had said the other evening about Bultmann's demythologization. He could appreciate why the theologians would feel pressure to disown Genesis, as a literal account of creation. In Genesis, after all, the earth was said to have been formed before the stars, the birds and whales before the reptiles and insects, and the plants before the animals. According to Darwinian evolution, however, the order of events was said to be precisely the opposite. He wondered what the chances were of that. And, of course, evolution's account of the order of formation of life was in a way the least of the problems for theology. If the evolution of species on earth occurred over billions of years, this was because the cosmos as we know it is completely different than what the Bible claimed. To begin with, the earth is not at the center, the sun is. He had meant some fervent Thomists who still clung to the theoretical plausibility of geo-centrism, given certain considerations of relativity theory. But that didn't alter the fact that there was much more that couldn't be reconciled with what science had shown us. The earth, for example, is not a unique land mass, but just another planet among the others. The stars above are not within the firmament, but reside lightyears away in distant galaxies. Furthermore, the sun does not circle over the earth, but instead it is the earth, which is round, not flat, that orbits the sun. The moon is not another light, but merely reflects the light from the sun. This is why many atheists he knew loved to mock the story of Joshua. How could God have stopped the sun, as it was written, when in reality it was the earth moving? The entire biblical cosmology, so it seemed, had been exposed by Newton, Copernicus, Darwin and others, as the ignorant opinions of ancient man. Bultmann and the theologians, who were desperate to preserve the Gospel of Jesus Christ, had been forced to strip the Scriptures down to the bone.

There was an irony here. It seemed to him that looking at the situation from a Heideggerian perspective was illuminating. According to Heidegger, everyday language is fraught with empty claims that are constantly circulated by those who really have no genuine evidence for them. They merely repeat what "one" says or thinks—"idle talk," Heidegger called it. He found it amusing how many of the same atheists and materialists who bandied about scientific claims they did not truly understand, much less ever verified for themselves, were thereby without realizing it basing their beliefs on hearsay. They believed what they were told. We all did, he thought. He remembered the first time he saw a globe as a young child. At first, he didn't know what it was.

"That's the Earth, son," his dad had told him.

His dad pointed out the continents and oceans. While watching his dad spin it, he became confused. The ground beneath his feet wasn't spinning. And the ground was flat; he had never seen a curve. Then he was given all the explanations. We don't feel the planet's spin because we ourselves are small in comparison. It's a matter of relativity. We don't see the curve with the unaided eye, but we can see traces of it on the sea shore, when we look out to the horizon and see the boats disappear. And then there was outer space, if anyone should ever doubt what we're told. Yes, there were all those photographs of the earth from space. His dad had once shown him photographs taken by the astronauts in space on one of the Shuttle missions his dad had worked on. Of course, neither his dad nor anyone else he knew personally had ever orbited the earth or seen it from space for themselves. They believed what the astronauts told them was there to be seen. He laughed. The same atheists who would dismiss the testimony of the Apostles were those who immediately believed what some employee working for a government agency said.

His thought continued, as he studied the plaque. If nobody could feel the earth's axial spin, nobody could feel its circuit around the sun, nobody could see its curve with his own eye, while everybody dismissed the fact that the sun and moon both appeared to be near, and that the moon appeared to have her own light, in what sense was what they believed truly empirical? To the contrary, it seemed like everyone was believing things contradicted by their senses. Why, then, were they so readily dismissing what their own senses appeared to deliver to them, only in the name of testimony based on authority? As he thought more about it, the entire situation to him seemed eerily reminiscent of the very mentality that the skeptics and atheists accused religion of inculcating in its believers. Ignore the self-evident, don't think for oneself, only believe what the authorities say. He thought about it counterfactually. If, for instance, the Bible had claimed that the earth was round, that it was spinning on its axis and orbiting the sun, that the moon did not possess its own light, and so forth, he was sure all the atheists would point out everything he had just thought: nobody has ever seen the curve with his own eyes, nobody can feel the spin, the sun appears to circle over us, and the moon clearly gives off its own light. The fact they didn't point to such things, he decided, was simply because they wanted to believe the Bible was false, so if they were told that science had shown so, they were willing to deny their own senses and experience, if that was what believing in what science told them it took. The absurdity of it all, he thought, came into clearest focus when it came to life itself. The plaque here says Boyle discovered the living cell, yet the same Oxford and London Royal Society scientists had ended up claiming life originated in a primordial soup struck by lightning, a completely speculative, and preposterous, view that frankly belonged in a bad science fiction novel, rather than a science textbook, he thought. It was fine for a fairy tale to be absurd, but this was supposed to be true. He shook his head incredulously and walked on.

Quod was open for lunch.

Through the doors, he saw a maître de waiting for him to enter.

"Good afternoon, sir. Table or bar?"

"Oh, neither, actually, sorry." He was developing the habit of saying sorry for everything, as the British do. "I'm here because I believe I may have left my bank card last night."

"I see. What bank?"

"Barclays."

"Let me take a look. One moment." The man disappeared. A few minutes later, he returned, a big smile on his face.

"You're in luck. One of our staff must have found it. Here you are."

"Oh, great. Thank you!"

He had an hour before the meeting at Kilcannon. He took Merton down to the back entrance of the college, walking through Peck and the library, and then took a seat on the quad. He smoked some cigarettes, and tried not to worry about the meeting. It occurred to him that he might knock on Wood's door, but he decided against it. There would be a chance to talk again soon, as one of those dinners he'd been hearing about was coming. Five minutes before the meeting, he buzzed himself into Kilcannon, walked up the big stairs, and came to the double doors. He listened for a moment, but didn't hear anything inside. He knocked gently. There were a few seconds of silence.

"Come in."

He walked in and took a seat on the big couch. "I'm sorry I'm a little early." Klaus waved his hand, to say it was no problem.

"Thanks again for having mentioned your seminar to me. I'm glad I was able to attend. I thought Prof Gardner's paper was very interesting."

"Yes, Sacha does excellent work. I saw he gave you his card."

"Yeah, that was nice of him. I told him I was sorry I missed the lunch."

"Yes, well, that was my mistake. I forgot to mention it." Klaus seemed distracted. He decided he would pause, and see whether Klaus would say whatever was really on his mind.

Klaus shifted in his chair, "How are things with Alison?"

"Oh, they're great. Feeling better."

"Good. Glad to hear it. I thought it was nothing." Another silence.

"Listen," Klaus said, "I have to tell you something." Klaus sighed, then stammered, "I, we, well, Zoe's husband found out."

"About the affair?"

"Yes."

"How? Did she tell him?"

"No, we got caught texting." He didn't ask what was in the texts, but they must have been incriminating.

"Wow, so what's going to happen?"

"That's the worst part. I'm completely helpless. I don't know. She told me she needs time to think things over. I'm not sure what she's going to do."

"I'm sure it'll be fine." He didn't know what to say, since he felt that in a way Klaus had gotten what he deserved. The husband probably felt terrible. Klaus must have read his face.

"Maybe it was foolish. I don't know. The husband came here to confront me."

"What?"

He couldn't be sure, but he thought Klaus almost smiled. "Yes, I was having lunch at the Freind Room yesterday. He came right in. He's a boxer. When I stepped outside, I brought my wineglass."

"How did he know where to find you?"

"Zoe must have told him."

"What did he say?"

Klaus stared out the window. "He said I'm morally depraved." He could tell Klaus was deeply bothered by the comment, though it was ambiguous. It was hard to tell whether he felt badly because he realized he were depraved, or simply because somebody thought he was and had said so.

Klaus turned to him, then stared out the window again. "Everything is dark."

It was unclear what more should be said, so he waited in silence for Klaus to steer the conversation.

"I'm sorry for bringing you in for this. But again, I would greatly appreciate your discretion, while Zoe and I try to work this out."

"Of course."

They stood from their seats, fist-bumped each other, and Klaus showed him out.

TWELVE

THE next week passed with nothing of any note happening, other than the fact that its coming to an end meant he was now one week closer to seeing Alison. Last week's talk at the Strawson Room felt like it belonged to a different age, each subsequent day ever since having been an endurance test in boredom and restlessness. He was growing stir crazy in his room, but when he would resolve to go out, he would look outside and see the gray and the rain, and decide he would wait for it to clear. It never did, and before he had known it, a week had gone by. The others in the building had stopped bothering to invite him out, since they knew he would politely but inevitably decline, Klaus was in London, and while there was always Manan, he didn't want to wear out his welcome. In any case, tomorrow night would be the theology dinner at Eliot's, so the present stretch of nothingness, he hoped, would soon be over. As he was gazing out the window, he startled, for a moment thinking he was simply hearing things, but on the third ring, he realized the phone was indeed ringing. He walked to the wall, fumbled with it, answered right before the call would go to the voicemail system he had yet to set up, and nearly dropped the receiver as he brought it to his ear.

"Hello?"

"Hi!" It was an unfamiliar female voice.

"Hi. Who's this?"

"It's Anna." He almost asked who it was again, since he couldn't recall anyone that he knew by that name. Then the memory came to him. He did know her. She was an anthropology student from the college, a Fresher too. They had spoken once at dinner a couple weeks ago, since some of her friends lived in the building.

"Oh, hi. How's it going? How did you get my number?" He was certain they hadn't exchanged numbers.

She laughed. "I asked the porters, silly!"

"Oh, right, of course. Stupid question, sorry."

"Don't be sorry. I'm glad you answered. You're very mysterious. It's been hard to find you." She laughed again.

"Yeah, I've been staying in. The weather . . . "

"Oh, tell me about it! I can't stand the gray. It makes me miss home terribly. It can be so lonely here." He waited for the point.

"Anyway, I thought I'd just call to see if you possibly wanted to go see a movie tonight with me at the Phoenix." The independent film house was in Jericho, a little neighborhood near the Faculty that he liked. And he enjoyed films. It would be good, also, to get out of the house, or rather, the room. He found himself tempted to say yes, but something felt off. He wasn't sure what it was, but he knew it was something. He knew she had a boyfriend living in Germany, but he wouldn't mention that.

"Who else is going?"

"Oh, nobody. I haven't asked anyone but you. Just you and me, I figured." She didn't use the word, but it was clear what this was.

"Well, it's very nice of you to get a hold of me. Tonight's not going to work for me. Maybe later this weekend, or sometime next week. I could call Ben to see whether he'd be interested in joining us." Mentioning a mutual acquaintance from college, he hoped, would make things clear enough without having to say it directly.

"Okay. If you ever change your mind, let me know. I'll be there at nine-thirty." She gave her phone number and hung up.

He put the phone down, and walked to the desk and sat down. He'd like to go to a movie tonight with Alison, but she was thousands of miles away. He went to bed early, so that tomorrow's dinner at Eliot's would come sooner.

The next evening, the sky had cleared and the moon was out. Perhaps it was a good omen, though, of course, he didn't really think it mattered either way. That was all superstitious. And in any case, it would be terribly self-involved to think the moon was shining tonight just for him and for tonight's occasion. He smiled, as he recollected Jackson Nowak back in Texas. The moon might not be for him, it was for everyone, which was just to say that it wasn't simply a pure being indifferent to what was happening below. Her light told us something, even if he couldn't put it into words.

The quad was still, but when he reached Eliot's door, he could hear voices coming from the back garden. There would be more people here

tonight than he had expected. He knocked on the door, and two students
he'd never seen before opened it. He was about to say hello, but they immediately turned away, evidently confused as to where to go themselves,
since from the looks of it, this was their first time here as well.

Another guest came into the foyer from the study. "You'll want to go
that way," he pointed down a hall, "everyone is in the garden for drinks
before dinner. Eliot's in the kitchen cooking."

He followed the instructions the man had given the two guests in
front of him, and walked out to the garden. It was like walking into the
thing of storybooks. The outdoor heaters were on, and the starlight was
shining down on a Medieval courtyard, the vines on the stone walls as
thick and lush as the tangled web of ambitions he knew had driven the
others to come tonight. A garden party at the grandest college at the most
prestigious university in the world was something that could easily go
to anyone's head. If one already had a predilection for power, breathing
in the night air here in the garden would be an aphrodisiac. He could
tell a number of others must have felt that way, and they were giving in,
because they were all evidently much tipsier than one would expect to
find at an early evening gathering of theologians. Nobody, it seemed, was
immune to the charms of Dionysius. There were about two dozen guests,
all young and dressed smartly, laughing and talking, with wine glasses in
hand. He spotted Manan, who waved when he saw him.

"Well, good evening! I see you've made it to Prof Wood's jolly party!"
Manan was already at least on his second glass.

He smiled. "It's good to be here. I'd been languishing away in my
room."

"Yes, well, with the company one would have to keep back at our
building, I don't blame you. Pure philistines, frankly. But not tonight, my
dear friend! Tonight, you will get to see Oxford."

He wondered how Manan thought he was in a position to know so,
but then he remembered his friend from India had said he'd been studying at Cambridge before coming here. This would not have been his first
wine party in the garden.

"I must introduce you to someone," Manan said. His friend scanned
the garden. "Hm, I don't see him . . . Ah! There he is," Manan said, pointing to the man who'd given the directions to the garden, who was now
himself coming out of the house.

"Joseph, I'd like to introduce you to my philosophy friend."

"Pleasure to meet you," he said. He gave his name.

"I'm Joseph, Joseph Bingley. American, I see. Where from?"

"Texas. That's where I was living before moving here. Originally, I'm from California."

"Ah, California. I miss it."

"What part?"

"Los Angeles. You?"

"Bay Area."

"Well, nobody's perfect." The three of them laughed.

"Manan tells me you're a philosophy DPhil?"

"Correct. I'm studying with Carman."

"Yes, Klaus Carman. He runs the seminar at the Strawson Room. I missed last week, but usually I'm there."

"And you study?"

"Theology. I'm a JRF." By now, he knew the term, which was short for Junior Research Fellow, the equivalent of a postdoc.

"You certainly picked quite the college," Joseph continued. He outstretched his arms.

"Yes, you know, it's funny, because when I was asked to select a college to which to apply, I knew nothing about all of them. I just picked this one, because I figured it would be convenient to be at the same college as my supervisor."

He could see Joseph could tell he was being honest. It wasn't the answer Manan's friend was expecting, since he understandably would have expected him to brag about the college's history, or finances, or some of the faculty. Although it had momentarily thrown him for a loop, it looked like Joseph found it refreshing.

He asked Joseph the same question. "Where are you?"

"Wolfson."

Founded in the 1960s, Wolfson was far from being one of Oxford's prestigious colleges. Joseph must have been relieved, then, to see he hadn't thought to brag about being at Christ Church, since it made it easier for him to say where he was, a place with little comparative history, best known, if memory served, for being where LinkedIn's Reid Hoffman had studied while at Oxford. He almost made a comment about how silly the whole pecking order among the colleges was, but he decided not to, since he could tell Joseph agreed anyway.

Manan interjected, "We've recently been discussing Kant."

Joseph lit up. "Kant! Very good. What about exactly?"

Manan waved a hand to him, encouraging him to be the one to answer Joseph.

"Well, I guess we were discussing a number of things. But mainly we were discussing Kant's relationship to theology, or rather, the impact he's had on modern theology."

Manan looked at Joseph with a smile. "I've been teaching him Barth and Bultmann!"

Joseph said, "Yes, well, if you're going to be spending any time around these parts, Barth is a name you'll have to get to know. Manan probably has mentioned it, but Prof Wood is one of the world's foremost experts on Barth. If I'm not mistaken, he's working on a multivolume systematic theology, which will be drawing heavily on Barth."

Manan turned to Joseph, "Oh, I would do anything to be able to see that manuscript." Joseph didn't say anything, but the appearance of delight on his face suggested he had seen it.

"You've seen it!" Manan almost started jumping in place. Joseph smiled, and lifted his wine glass in the air. "To the wine gods!" They clinked their glasses, and took a sip.

"Excuse me," Manan said. He walked over to another group in the garden.

Joseph turned to him. "So, I see you've made friends with the college's Indian royalty."

"I guess so!"

"You know, he's not the sort to mention it, but Manan's from a very wealthy, very prominent family. From what I hear, he has serious political ambitions." Joseph was about to elaborate, but he clammed up, when he saw Manan walking over.

Someone came out to the garden. "Prof Wood kindly invites you all inside now. It's time for dinner."

In the dining room, which was capacious enough to have accommodated a crowd of fifty, stood a large table, the placements set out. He looked at Manan and Joseph.

"Where do we sit?"

"Anywhere, I suppose," Joseph said. They all took a seat next to one another. People made small talk for a few minutes, at which point Eliot entered.

"Thank you all for coming. I see you're all settled." Servers came in with plates. When everyone had a dish, the guests looked to Eliot.

"Let's say grace."

Eliot closed his eyes and bowed his head. He felt uncomfortable praying before a meal in the presence of so many strangers, but because he didn't want to be rude, he closed his eyes and bowed his head. When the grace was given, they opened their eyes, and began eating. For about thirty minutes, there were many conversations going on at once, but each one progressively waned, subsumed by another, until the only one remaining happened to be Eliot's. The entire table listened in hushed silence, as Eliot made a personal comment about another famous British theologian.

"Not many people know this about John, but he believes in literal fairies. He's told me so. I guess he runs around the forest looking!" The table erupted in laughter. The young theologians apparently liked the idea of mocking something they felt they could view as silly, since they would not themselves be on the receiving end for a change. Here in Oxford, as elsewhere, belief in God was often not taken seriously at all.

"But enough stories about John. The real question that's been on my mind, given what's been in the news, is Vatican II." He still didn't know what Vatican II was, and he didn't know what had been in the news. Perhaps something regarding the Pope.

"I should put the question to the table. Is last week's news a good or bad development for the church?" Given the way he put it, evidently Eliot didn't mean just the Catholic Church, but the Anglican Church too, or apparently the entire body of believers, regardless of their denomination. A barrage of voices began speaking over one another.

"It's preposterous! The conservatives were right all along . . . "

"So very glad to see it. It's about time that the ordination question is taken seriously with no evasions."

"Nonsense! It's fashionable to mock the traditionalists, but they're on to something. The ordination issue is just an appetizer before the Mass debate, which is the real elephant in the room."

"A mixed bag. It's hard to say. Time will tell."

Eliot quietly raised a finger, and the room fell silent. Everyone was on the edge of his seat, waiting to hear his opinion, and to watch how he would begin sorting through the competing positions. As he waited too, he was hoping simply to figure out what was even up for discussion.

"I think it's time for dessert." Everyone broke into laughter.

An older man who was sitting next to Wood looked at the table, "That's Prof Wood! Ever the politician. But we all know what you really think!" Eliot shrugged his shoulders playfully, and whistled out the room.

He turned to Manan. "I'm sorry, but I have no idea what everyone is talking about. What's the issue?"

Manan was in a heated discussion with Joseph and another man. "I'm sorry, I'll have to explain later."

He listened for another few minutes, but when it became apparent that he was never going to figure out what was being discussed, he decided it was time to leave. He stood up, and went to the kitchen with his plate. He set it down on the counter.

"Thanks very much for dinner tonight, Prof Wood."

"What, you're leaving? We haven't yet had dessert!"

"Oh, I know. But I should be going."

Eliot smiled. "Well, you're invited next time as well. I'm sure we'll be seeing one another around college. Do tell Klaus I say hi."

When he stepped out into the quad, he couldn't help compare tonight with what he had seen last week among the philosophers in the Strawson Room. The theologians were just interested in theoretical puzzles and political infighting. The philosophers, it seemed, were right to ignore the question of God, if the way the theologians treated it were any indication of its actual worth. At the same time, there was something no less off-putting about the philosophers, since their own way of thinking proceeded as if God could be safely ignored entirely. The theologians were correct that there was something myopic, even monstrous, about that. One discourse claimed to get to the essential but was really frivolous, the other didn't even pay lip-service to the issue. What was needed, he was seeing, was a discourse that did not wholly ignore God, like the philosophers, but did not trivialize him, either, like the theologians. He got back to his room and lit a cigarette gloomily. He didn't want to be a defeatist, but it seemed to him the writing was on the wall. He would be working alone.

THIRTEEN

THE next morning, the wheeze was back, and this time he coughed a couple times. The thought he should quit entered his mind briefly, but he knew he wasn't ready, so to suppress the thought, he lit another cigarette, and ignored the cough. Smoking was not the only familiar comfort whose powers of satisfaction was in marked decline. He had found reading Otto intriguing, though somehow nevertheless unfulfilling. Barth was simply tedious. He assumed Bultmann would be too. He had been reading for so many years, so many books of the wise, all in their own ways attempting to shed light on existence. But none of them ever really did so. They were all somehow alienated from what they discussed, their words a reflective mirage of the source they could not penetrate.

The Scriptures, he was finding, were not so. They were alive, illuminating everything around him. They spoke of the matters of the heart, and with authority, knowing things about him nobody but God could know. They were not mere words, for in them was life. Reading the books of men only left him frustrated. Their complexities provided intellectual stimulation, but the process of moving from one text to another was unending, each work another exercise in cataloguing the errors of the others, itself sure only to suffer the same fate. The Scriptures were simple—and yet, inexhaustible. The depth of their truth was unfathomable. He knew he had only begun scratching their surface, and yet he had already learned more from them than he had in years of reading everything else. Perhaps it was called the Book for good reason, after all.

He lit a cigarette and sighed. The trouble with the Bible, of course, and the reason he suspected others hated it even if they had never seriously read it, is that it was a source of moral correction, sometimes brutally painful correction. The idea of eternal judgment was bound to

94

enrage anyone who knew that he was not yet prepared for it. Naturally, the idea would be rejected, even hated, since nobody wanted to believe he would be damned for doing what he currently desired to do. He knew, for instance, that he personally should quit smoking, and knew he should quit getting drunk. He should also stop watching pornography completely, though he took some solace in the fact that he no longer watched it as regularly as he once had, or as much as other men his age did. Alison had raised a very good point once: if looking at another woman naked in the flesh was cheating, why then was it okay to do so online? When he thought about it that way, he had begun seeing why pornography had once been considered a societal evil, and was criminalized. The mental, physical, and spiritual harm it did to the men who watched it, and to their relationships as well, was no secret. Of course, if Alison was right that he should stop consuming pornography, the Scriptures were clear that fornication was a sin too. As it happened, the Greek word in the New Testament for fornication was *porneia*. When he would come across a verse in Paul forbidding fornication, his heart would sink. Over time, he had begun reading much more selectively, deliberately skipping over the chapters where he knew the vexing verses were waiting to accuse him, but that didn't do anything, other than intensify the conviction, since he knew he was avoiding the words he couldn't bear to read. He had thought about the issue many times. If there truly was nothing wrong with pre-marital sex, as everybody he had known growing up had told him, and as the prevailing societal consensus maintained, why then did he feel so guilty about it? Freud had said that conscience was simply the internationalization of societal norms, but the norms regarding sexual morality were not at all Biblical anymore, and yet he found himself naturally, as it were, censuring himself for behavior the Scriptures condemned. It was hard to believe it was a coincidence, and not that the Scriptures spoke with some sort of insight into human nature. He had confessed his feelings of guilt about the issue to Alison, and she had been incredibly supportive over his decision to wait till they were married, but his resolve had been half-hearted. It wasn't long before he caved to temptation, not without regret and self-loathing, but at this point, with the wedding drawing nearer, he had decided to carry on, rationalizing his unchastity by telling himself that at least it would be short-lived.

He took a final drag of the cigarette, and blew the smoke out the window. Barth, he recently learned, had kept a mistress for years. He wondered how a theologian of Barth's stature could have lived in adultery for so long. He also wondered why none of the scholars thought this fact about Barth's life, or character, was relevant to assessing his work. He understood the notion of separating a work from its author, but in matters of theology, the cleavage didn't seem so clean. It was very hard to take seriously a man purporting to investigate divine things who fell so far short of basic decency in his own personal affairs. Barth, it seemed to him, had probably written everything he had with a bad conscience. The theologian's tortured, convoluted prose suggested a man who was self-servingly overcomplicating what was actually simple, in order to avoid having to confront whatever it was about himself he didn't want to confront. Socrates had written nothing. Neither had Christ written anything. That wasn't to say writing itself was a sin. But it could be an indication that one was coping with something that remained to be settled "off the page." Maybe Barth never would have written all those huge volumes on dogmatics, if he simply had done what the Scriptures commanded, and been faithful to his wife.

He wondered whether Barth had ever had children. Probably he had. If he did, he imagined Barth's children would have had good reason to disregard the works of their father. What a terrible form of judgment, he thought. To dedicate so much intellectual labor into writing volume after volume, only to realize that one's own children would have no reason to take them seriously, because of how he had mistreated their mother. No argument, no matter how clever or learned, could overcome hypocrisy of that magnitude. If he himself ever had children, he resolved that whatever he wrote, they would be able to read it, and be able to take it seriously. He would not let whatever was "off the page" negate the words on the page. It was something to think about, not simply a flight of fancy, since, in all likelihood, he would be a father soon. In fact, there was a good chance he and Alison might start a family after they were married and still here in Oxford. If their children were born here, he wondered whether that meant the children would have dual citizenship. His mind drifted to the matter of passports and other bureaucratic details, and as he pictured the American Embassy in London, he decided that a trip to the Old Smoke was past due. He didn't particularly like the city, but taking the train there would give him something to do. At least it would get him out of this room.

At the station, he got a ticket. He would have to remain mindful of the time once he got there, since the last returning train from London left Paddington before midnight. Spending the night stranded in London was not something he wanted to end up having to do. He took a seat on the platform bench, watching the others. When the train arrived, he grabbed a window seat, where he stared at the countryside. He thought about trying to count the sheep and cows, but when they pulled into Paddington a little over an hour later, he realized he must have drifted off to sleep somewhere before Reading. He walked off the train, hopped on the Circle Line, and got off at the stop for the Tate Modern. He didn't care for modern art, but he thought it was good sometimes to interrupt old habits, so rather than looking at more Impressionist art, which was what he would have preferred to view, he would spend the afternoon looking at what he didn't esteem.

As expected, the museum felt clinical and cold, the art itself was uninspiring, and aside from the nice view of the Thames from the café terrace, the excursion was forgettable.

Outside the museum, the sun was setting. He lit a cigarette, and ignored something in his gut that told him it was time to get back to Oxford. Probably nothing, he thought, as he dismissed the unease. He walked through the streets, the grim surroundings reminding him why he never bothered to come to London. He was about to turn back to find a tube station, when he heard voices coming from down the side street to his left. He peered down the way, where he saw a large group of shoppers exiting an outdoor market. As he approached it, he read the sign, Borough Market. The shopkeepers were closing up for the day, but across the street, The Market Porter was open. The brick corner building was handsome, with charming green shutters on the first floor, and inviting signage on the ground floor. The bright interior was crowded, but there was space on the unlit sidewalk, where evidently drinking was allowed. He discounted the feeling of nagging foreboding, and stepped inside.

In the past, he had realized how the depth of his melancholy was able to conceal itself until he drank. Then he would feel it. Of course, he realized that it may be the drinking itself that exacerbated the sadness, but in any case, all he knew was that after having two pints here tonight, he was sad. It didn't help that everyone around him was in groups, laughing and talking excitedly. It was an odd mix of tourists and locals from the neighborhood. Surveying the scene, he decided he would smoke a last cigarette, and leave. He fumbled for his pack in his pocket, opening it to find it empty. A middle-aged man dressed in construction gear was standing a few feet away smoking.

"Excuse me, I'm out of cigarettes. Could you spare one?"

"Aye, of course, mate." The man handed him a cigarette. He lit it and was about to turn away.

"American, eh?"

"Yes."

"Visiting on a trip?"

"Oh, no. I live here. Well, not here. Oxford."

"Oi, Oxford. A clever chap, I see." The man started wheezing from his laugh, his nicotine-stained teeth unsheathed from his chapped lips.

He knew that by clever the British simply meant smart, but he still hadn't broken the habit of hearing the word with the American subtext, which often carried the connotation of being shrewdly pernicious or conniving.

"I guess so."

"What you doing here tonight?"

"I was at a museum. Ended up walking around and found this spot."

"Ah, I love this spot, mate. I come here every day after work."

"Where's that?"

The man smiled, tapped his hard hat, and then pointed, "I work over there." There was a massive skyscraper nearby under construction.

"Wow, you work on the triangle building?"

"Aye, mate. The Shard. I'm the chief engineer." The man didn't look it, but then he realized that he wasn't in the construction business himself, so he wasn't in any place to judge. All things considered, the man probably was what he claimed.

As they were talking, a young blonde woman, who looked Dutch, came riding down the lane on an orange bicycle. The woman rode by them, glanced over, and kept riding.

"Aye, now there's a little lass," the man said, raising his eyebrows. The engineer watched the woman, who, reaching the corner, stopped the bike, and turned it around, riding back toward the pub.

"She coming back? God, I hope so," the engineer said.

The woman pulled up to the two of them. She looked right at him, then at the engineer.

"I'm lost, can you help me?"

The engineer smiled. "Where you trying to get yourself to little lady?" His attention shifted to other things, as the engineer gave the woman directions. When the engineer finished his explanation, he was expecting the woman to ride away, but instead she set the bike against the pub wall.

"Mind if I join you?"

The engineer was exuberant. "Of course, not! We'd love to have you stop for a chat."

"Great. Let me pop in for a pint. I'll be right back."

The young woman walked inside.

The engineer leaned in to him, and with those teeth out, said, "So, mate, you want to go twosies on her?" It took him a second to realize what the engineer was proposing.

"Uh, no, no thanks," he said. Before he had to struggle to decide what to say next, the woman had returned, her pint in hand. The engineer began saying something, but she faced him instead. She looked right at him, like she knew what he was thinking.

She grinned. "If you leave now, you might catch the train in time." He didn't know what to say.

"Don't worry," she continued, "You're right. The orange bicycle does look just like Johno's." He felt his spleen move. A shudder went through him.

She laughed. "Don't be so scared, darling. I did read your mind. You've never met a clairvoyant?"

The engineer lit a cigarette, and cackled through the smoke, "Aye, mate, this one is a little bonkers. You know what that means!"

Without saying a word, he chugged his pint, downed the whiskey shot he'd been nursing, strode down the sidewalk, and turned the corner. A few paces up the sidewalk, he looked through the pub's exit door facing the Borough Market, in order to see whether the woman had entered the pub from the other side where they'd been standing. He didn't see her. A few storefronts later, he paused. A dread he'd never felt before overtook him. Nearly frozen in fear, he could feel himself being watched. He turned slowly around to see the woman, her head poking around the corner, waving to him with a knowing grin. "You know who I am. Come back," she said.

Though he went by the name Prince of Darkness, in principle, the evil one presumably was capable of taking any form he wished, including a woman. He went straight to Paddington, boarded the night train, leaving whoever, or whatever, that was in London behind.

Fourteen

The next morning, he woke up at what was an early hour for him, having never fallen asleep soundly. He lit a cigarette, hoping it might settle his nerves, but he knew there would be no forgetting what he had experienced. He coughed harder than usual, but he didn't care. His thoughts turned relentlessly to the pub. The Dutch woman's diabolical grin was etched in his memory. The most unsettling thing about it was just that, the fact there was no denying what it had given him to understand.

As bizarre as he knew everyone would believe it was, the woman had truly read his mind, even flaunting the fact she had done so, and then taunting him as he fled because of it. Perhaps fled was not the right word, he thought. To be sure, he had been afraid, but he hadn't left in cowardice. It had been sound judgment. There was wisdom in not meddling with evil, especially evil of that degree. The fascination of the encounter had nearly gripped him to the point of staying. The thought of what may have happened if he hadn't left made him shudder. Of course, there was nobody to tell what had happened. He knew it would sound insane, and it wouldn't be reasonable to expect anyone, even Alison, to comprehend what had happened. In any case, even if he could tell somebody who would believe him and understand, it would still fall to him to decide what to make of it, and how to live in light of it. He would have to come to terms with it remaining an entirely solitary event. The isolation of the encounter had heightened his anxiety on the night train back, and he had assumed at the time that the fact he wouldn't ever be able to communicate it to others would be an unavoidable burden. But now sitting here on the desk, he was finding the event transformative precisely for that reason, as it was already beginning to open a depth of interiority in him previously unknown. A fragment from Colossians entered his consciousness, "And whatsoever you do, do it heartily, as to the Lord, and not unto men."

He got dressed. A walk, either through Port Meadow or the University Parks, would do him some good, he decided. He brushed his teeth, splashed some warm water on his face, sent Alison a love note, and left the room. Down the street, he popped into a shop selling sausage rolls and other breakfast items.

The older woman who ran the place, and who had a knack for remembering faces, lit up when she saw him. "Ah, it's our new American friend again."

"Yes, good to see you. How are you?"

"Oh, I'm doing okay. We've been busy, which is good."

"Large coffee and two sausage rolls, please."

She poured the coffee, placed the rolls in a bag, took his bill, made the change, and handed him the food and coffee. "Here you go." He had been noticing it was more common here than back home to use cash rather than card, especially for small purchases. He liked that.

He smiled, "Thanks."

Another customer behind him in line, a mother with two young children, looked at him when he turned from the register, and said kindly, "Wow, you have very beautiful blue eyes."

He blushed, "Thank you."

The mother turned to the woman working behind the counter.

"I didn't mean to embarrass him! But doesn't he have such beautiful blue eyes? And his lashes! Look at them! They're so long."

The woman at the counter said, "Well, I wasn't going to say anything, but yes, he does have very handsome eyes."

He walked out as the two women continued talking.

There was the question of where to head now. He mulled it over walking up the street. Given that he was still jittery from last night, he decided in favor of the Parks, since it would be more crowded there. If he wanted to assess what had happened calmly, something scenic would potentially be unnerving and hence counterproductive, so Port Meadow was out of the question. As he was thinking things over, someone called to him from the quad inside the college's gates. He stopped to see Manan.

His friend came onto the street.

"Hey, how are you? You disappeared at dinner on Friday." It was hard to believe it had only been two nights ago. So much had happened, yet it was all impossible to tell.

"I'm sorry about that. I didn't mean to be rude. I made sure to thank Prof Wood for dinner before I left."

"Well, you must have done something right. After the other guests left, Eliot had Joseph and I and a few others stay for a late discussion. I won't repeat precisely what he said, but suffice it to say he was impressed with you."

Were he not so distracted by what had happened in London, he might have felt exhilarated, or at least relieved, to hear what Manan was telling him. His friend must have been able to see something else was preoccupying him.

"Perhaps I've caught you at an inconvenient time. I apologize; I didn't mean to intrude, if you're busy. Why don't you come by my room tonight for some whiskey and theology talk?"

It occurred to him that it didn't make sense why Wood should have been impressed with anything he had said at dinner. He'd hardly spoken a word. Maybe Wood appreciated his taciturn demeanor, since others invited to such a party might well have gone out of their way to try to impress others, only to have said too much.

"I don't mean to be rude. I just woke up, and I'm out for a walk to think through some things. I'll probably be more functional after I've had some of this coffee."

"How about nine then?"

"Sounds good. I'll see you then."

Manan bowed, and walked off to the building. He stood outside Tom Gate, lit a cigarette, considered going in to see the koi, but then changed his mind, and headed up Cornmarket past the old graveyard, then down Broad. When he reached the Parks, he took a seat on a bench, devoured the rolls, and threw out what was left of his coffee, which by then was lukewarm, along with the wrappers. He went to light a cigarette reflexively—better to wait a few more minutes, he thought, as he shoved the pack in his jacket pocket. It was partly sunny, but hardly bright, so he took off his sunglasses, wiping the lenses as he replayed the encounter at the pub.

Memory could be distorting, he conceded, but if one plumbed an event's details while it was still recent, it wasn't an entirely fruitless endeavor to attempt to recover what might be a crucial detail, or to notice something that had yet to be appreciated properly. He felt like he should scrutinize the encounter from as many competing perspectives and interpretations as possible, to ensure he was entitled to hold the judgment he had formed of it, given how extraordinary he knew that it was. Even if others weren't in a position to challenge his understanding, since they had not been there and he would not tell them, he could do so himself, to some extent, at least.

No matter how many skeptical questions he put to himself, no matter how strenuously he tried to doubt what he thought he had seen and heard, there was no evading the reality of what had happened. The given was manifest. The occult, or the demonic, was real. It didn't offend his sense of reality, as it might others, since he had always been open to the possibility that genuinely sinister powers were behind the events unfolding before everyone in the everyday world. The world was full of so much evil that it was hard, he thought, to understand how anyone couldn't take seriously the idea that there were powerful forces at work in things. Frankly, he had long been of the mind that only the gullible or willfully ignorant could come to any other conclusion than that the world was run by psychotic criminals. As even a cursory look at the course of human history revealed, the world's institutions were fraught with corruption. He wondered, then, whether it was apathy, selfishness, or cowardice, or some combination thereof, that led those who denied it to do so. Maybe they knew it was as bad as it is, but they were pretending not to know simply because it was too overwhelming, and they figured they were powerless to do anything about it anyway. Better merely to pretend it wasn't the case, and go on with things, hoping that one's own life was minimally affected. Of course, this was precisely the attitude evil relished, since it amounted to a form of compliance, something that in turn only hastened evil's grip on things. The famous metaphor of the frog in the boiling water pot was apt. But instead, he pictured a mouse, still in denial, chewing its cheese obliviously, as an anaconda slowly wrapped itself around its victim and squeezed it to death. Most people, he sighed, were like that mouse. Although nobody was ever blunt about it, the fact was that so long as most people were still given a hamburger and access to pornography, they would do whatever the state and the corporations told them to do. Evil knew this, and so evil exploited it accordingly— bread and circus, just as the Roman Emperors had known. History was simply the sum of everything that had happened as a consequence. To be fair, he realized that anyone walking by him on the street might well form such an opinion of him, that he was just another peasant willfully blind to the truth about the powers that ruled the world. When he thought about it, after all, he had never done anything to demonstrate he had the knowledge he did about how the world really worked. Maybe, then, others around him were the same, aware of how evil and corrupt everything around them was, but unable to find a way to oppose it. He wasn't sure how, but one day, he felt, he would find a way to expose and oppose evil in his work. It was a long-term goal, something he would keep to himself, but not an idle daydream. He was sure of it.

For the first time since coming to Oxford, he felt like putting some of his thoughts to paper. Not these thoughts he was having about the role of the demonic in the world, or thoughts about the systemic corruption and evil of the world's institutions. He might never find the right opportunity to write about those things, or at least not for a while. For now, he was merely content to jot down some notes that might later be usable when it came time to begin writing his dissertation. When he returned to his apartment, he would list the works he knew he still had to read, ordering them in order of most pressing to least so. Then he would list some key concepts he was interested in exploring further. And, depending on his mood, he might then also list some tentative thesis ideas, the sort of substantive claims that were potentially befitting of the kind of sustained textual, argumentative treatment a dissertation would merit. In the wake of his recent conversations here in Oxford, and his reading of the Bible, it was appearing that it would be necessary to say something about the relationship between philosophy and theology. That itself was a massive topic, probably something too vague for a thesis, but if he could decide how to approach it within the scope of more limited terms, the idea of contributing something constructive to the question was not a total pipe dream. Perhaps the road to do so was through an analysis of Heidegger's existential analytic in *Being and Time*. Evidently, Bultmann had things to say about it. Klaus, he worried, might not particularly welcome the theological implications motivating his reasons for doing so, but such a dissertation, even if it clearly laid the groundwork for wider ambitions to be explicated in future work, would at least stick to a text with which he knew his supervisor and examiners would be comfortable. It might ruffle some feathers, but nothing too dire would come of it. In any case, at least he would not be met here with the same resistance such ideas had been in Texas with Carrell. He threw his cigarette butt in the bin, left the park, and on the way home bought two tickets for the upcoming Vivaldi performance. He wouldn't tell Alison, since he thought it might be a nice surprise.

He wondered what the engineer and the Dutch woman from last night were doing now. God only knows, he thought.

That night, he found Manan dressed casually, as the last time. Only to be wearing Khakis and a button-down was, he assumed, his friend's way of showing they were on more intimate terms, and his friend was getting comfortable enough not always to have to maintain the appearance of Indian aristocracy.

"Ah yes, come in," Manan said, opening the door. The tininess of the room again startled him.

"I didn't bring any beer this time, sorry."

"That's fine. As you know, I prefer the whiskey. Please have a seat." He sat down on Manan's bed, as Manan poured two glasses of whiskey.

"I forgot to mention that next week I have some old friends from Cambridge coming to visit. Henry is a very good friend of mine, and a very sharp theologian. I will be sure to have you over when they're here, because it would be good for you to meet them."

"Sounds good."

"Henry's an Anglican, so I'm sure he and Prof Wood will be sure to make a couple jokes about Luther. They like to tease me when they can."

He didn't tell Manan that he was beginning not to understand the denominational battle lines. All of the denominations had their doctrines that it seemed to him clearly contradicted the Bible. Picking a denomination, it almost seemed, was like selecting which man-made system one preferred most in lieu of the simplicity of the Scripture itself. He knew if he ever said such a thing, Manan would dismiss it as the judgment of a theological neophyte, who didn't have a proper grasp of church history or whatever else. But that reaction in a way underscored his entire suspicion. The more learned one became in such matters, the more confused one became, and the farther one moved from the truth. He thought about the words of Paul to Timothy, about those "Ever learning, but never being able to come to a knowledge of the truth."

Perhaps he was the victim of some misunderstanding, but if not, he felt he was uncovering a serious dilemma for the theologians. Either the Scriptures were plain, and they could be sufficiently understood by anyone sincerely desiring to do so, which, as it happened, seemed to him to be Paul's own counsel to Timothy. The words came to his mind, "All scripture is given by inspiration of God, and is profitable for doctrine, for reproof, for correction, for instruction in righteousness. That the man of God may be perfect, equipped for all good works." The passage, as he was understanding it, was of course presupposing precisely what was at issue, but it did seem to him that the Scripture itself was teaching what he thought was the case. After all, if it was not capable of rendering itself comprehensible to those who desired to understand it, how then could it reveal the nature of God and his commandments? It would be a very odd form of revelation, one that frustrated itself. On this view of Scripture, then, theology was unnecessary. This led to the other horn of the dilemma. Or, the Scripture was not accessible to anyone seeking to understand, in which case here one might say the need for theology became apparent. Theological thinking somehow supplemented, or indeed completed, what was said in the Scripture. But where did that leave those who were unlearned? Were we to conclude that God had relegated them to an incomplete, even flawed, understanding of his ways, such that the fuller picture reserved itself only for scholars? In that case, why have bothered to bestow the Scriptures to man at all, since in effect they would be little more than an item of intellectual and scholarly amusement for a handful of exegetes and theologians? He thought it over. Either the Holy Scripture were sufficient until itself, in which case the purpose of theology was unclear, to such an extent, in fact, that it might even be otiose, or else theology was essential, in which case the need for the Scripture was unclear, since it would be unable to do anything more than serve as a source of inspiration for intellectual contention.

He recognized it was an odd opinion coming from someone who had traveled all this way to Oxford in order to study, but it was becoming more evident every day that the truth resided in the word of God, not the theological tomes and systems of men. If what he was intending to write in his own dissertation was not to be pointless, he would have to think about why he was even here.

What he knew, he was fairly certain, was that there was precious little fear of God in anything he was seeing around him, especially among the theologians, who one would think would constitute the remnant in today's secular society, if there were one. Then again, he was unsure whether he himself truly feared God. The fact he was unsure, he decided, was probably compelling evidence that he didn't, since, after all, actually fearing God didn't seem to be the sort of thing that would be shrouded in mystery.

"What are Henry's reasons for being Anglican?"

Manan mulled it over. "Well, Henry comes from a very traditional, upper-class family. He has the refined sensibilities of somebody who enjoys the High Anglican mass." He thought about secularists, who, in criticizing faith, claimed that religion was mostly an aesthetic phenomenon anyway, something people enjoyed because of how the ritual and music and comradery made them feel. Manan knew this too.

"Of course, he wouldn't put it that way. He claims to have his strictly theological reasons. But I find those unconvincing. That's why I'm a Lutheran. But I do understand the appeal of the High Church, since the ceremony is very beautiful." They both took sips of their whiskey.

"You know, that is why many Protestant traditions have been so concerned about the form of worship itself. Having a sparse ceremony can be good. The Quakers feel this way, although there's problems with their doctrine in other matters."

He thought about asking Manan a question of the role of icons in Orthodox liturgy, and how those aren't simply idols, but he knew the theological explanation Orthodox theologians had would be too sophisticated for him to understand. So, he said nothing.

"The fact that there is a danger of temptation even in religious service is interesting, I think. It raises a more general point," Manan continued.

He felt Manan was working up to something his friend had been meaning to say from the beginning of his visit, maybe what even was the entire purpose for inviting him over tonight.

"What's that?"

"Every man has to deal with three great temptations in life: sex, money, and power."

"I think I see your point."

"One of them is a priority and so something he has to struggle with, one is something to which he's largely indifferent but not completely, something he would prefer to have all things considered, while the other is something that has no appeal to him whatsoever." He could tell Manan wanted him to disclose his ranking, but instead he waited, forcing Manan to go first.

"Sex to me seems like a waste of time. I see the majority of other men around me ogling anything with a pair of breasts, and I just don't understand. Money, I suppose, is nice, and I would prefer not to be without it, but it does not drive me to do anything I desire. My great temptation is power."

Manan took a sip of his whiskey and chuckled softly to himself. "As Augustine would put it, *libido dominandi*," Manan sighed.

He did not say so to Manan, but he found the lust for power shallow, vulgar. He had never understood its appeal. The idea of being a politician, or corporate hotshot, or whatever, repulsed him. Those types of men were buffoons. Frankly, he'd rather live under a bridge.

Manan waved his whiskey glass toward him. It was his turn.

"Thinking about it, I guess I'm the opposite. I guess my temptation is women. Money is something that is good, but I don't need it. Power is something for which I really have no desire at all. I mean, I think that's why I'm so happy that I'm engaged. Being with Alison is more satisfying to me than money or power."

"Yes, I see." Manan, he could tell, was ruminating over something.

"I can't explain it, but I have this unquenchable urge for power."

"What kind of power?"

"Political. I haven't told you, but I come from a prominent family in India. There is no history of political service in our family, but we are wealthy. My father is a famous Bollywood director."

He thought about mentioning how Joseph had said something about Manan's background at Wood's dinner, but because he didn't know whether Joseph would want Manan to know he'd mentioned it, he didn't say anything. Again, here was the same dynamic he had reflected on before in the earlier context of he and Klaus and Carrell, or he and Klaus and Horowitz, everyone never saying everything that had been said.

"One day, my hope is to be Prime Minister of India," Manan said flatly.

In any other circumstances, it would only be fitting to laugh at such a comment. But not here, he realized. If the college had produced more British prime ministers than any other Oxford or Cambridge college, then surely it could produce an Indian one too. As interested in theology as Manan was, he realized Manan's real reason for being here was to build the *résumé* he would need, in order to launch a serious political career at home in India.

They finished their whiskeys, while Manan discussed Gregory of Nyssa and apophatic theology's relationship to Kant's critique of metaphysics. When it was getting late, he stood to leave.

His closest thing to a friend in Oxford, the man aiming to be Prime Minister of India one day, opened the door. "Don't forget about Henry and my visitors! I'll let you know when they're here."

When he got to his room, he opened the Proverbs, since he felt he might come across a nugget of instruction pertinent to whatever exactly it was that he was facing presently. Something was awry, and not solely because of what had happened in London, though he couldn't put his finger on it.

FIFTEEN

H E stirred from sleep, gathering his bearings in the midst of the fogginess from last night's whiskey. It being Monday, he realized, meant exactly two weeks to go, two weeks till she would be here for the visit. It was strange how time protracted when waiting on something desirable, even stranger, he mused, how it was possible already to feel the sadness for its passing before it had yet to occur. He had spent so much time pining over Alison, wishing she were here, only now to find that, with the visit nearly upon him, he was beginning to feel despondent over the very fact. Because the visit would only be for a week, it wouldn't be too long before she had come and gone, and then the real waiting would begin. After that, it would be many months till he might see her again.

He shuffled over to the desk, lit a cigarette, and opened his email. There was nothing from Alison, but there was a note from Joseph Bingley. He scanned the note. Evidently there was another dinner at Eliot's this Friday, a smaller, more intimate gathering than the other typical dinners. Manan and his friends from Cambridge would be there, along with a few others from before. If he was interested in attending, he should let Joseph know by Wednesday so that Eliot knew how much food to prepare. He replied to say that he would be there.

To assuage the pit in his stomach, he decided it might be nice to walk down to the shop for a coffee. He brushed his teeth, put on some clothes, grabbed his keys, and stepped onto the street. The overcast sky sometimes would allow the sun to penetrate. Today, however, was not so. The black clouds were thick and menacing, boiling as if in a cauldron, because a storm was brewing. If he hurried, he might be able to make it back without getting drenched in the rain. Taking an umbrella was always an option, and almost everybody had one, but he didn't like using his, so he'd simply use the hood on his jacket, if need be.

He came into the shop, and took a place in the queue.

"The lightning will be here soon," a workman in front of him said to his friend.

"We'll have to move the equipment."

"Ah, it's always something, ain't it?" The two men laughed, then went back to staring into their phones.

When his time came to order, he knew he should order some food, but even though he was hungry, he only ordered coffee. The woman with a talent for remembering faces, Cecilia was her name, smiled softly at him. She could tell he was distressed.

"You have a good day, sweetie," she said.

"Thanks, you too." He looked out the storefront glass. "Looks like I'll be able to make it home just in time."

"Good luck," she said.

When he got onto the street, the rain began pelting, and he noticed that the tourists had all left Tom Gate. He heard claps of thunder in the distance. With a storm like this, there might be flooding. He got upstairs to his room, unlocked the door, and shut the window before the rain could puddle on the desk.

By the time he finished his coffee and smoked a number of cigarettes, he was genuinely worried. It would be three or four in the morning by now in Texas, and still he hadn't heard anything from Alison. That afternoon, she had said she was planning to stay home and work on her art, and usually she would say goodnight. He decided to call her.

The line rang five times without an answer. He called again, but again nothing.

He set his phone down, lit a cigarette, and about halfway through, his phone rang. He knew it was going to be dreadful.

"Hello?"

It was Alison. "Hi, what's up?"

"Um, I'm just wondering whether everything's okay."

"Yeah. Why?"

"I didn't hear from you." He could hear loud music and voices in the background. So, she was out.

Alison was defensive. "Well, I'm sorry, I didn't think it would bother you."

He thought about asking her how the art was coming along, but since he didn't want to waste his time working his way to the truth, he decided to ask her directly. Klaus's tip about paying attention to the sound of the voice entered his mind. "It's past three in the morning. Where are you?"

"I'm just out with Sandra and Stephanie at Barbarella." He knew that as hard as he might try, he was about to lose his temper, and they would argue. He tried to stay calm and to compose himself, but it only angered him, since the idea he was supposed to be okay with the situation was itself a manipulative power-play, he felt.

"You're at a nightclub at three in the morning?"

"I don't want to argue about this. There's nothing wrong with it."

He had never mentioned it to Alison yet, but he suspected that Sandra and Stephanie weren't happy with the engagement, and would like to see her go back to Justice. If they knew that Alison and he had made an agreement to cut back on their drinking and avoid certain places, it stood to reason, then, that they would be encouraging her to frequent them. It might get the two of them arguing, and over time, it might be enough to dissolve the engagement. He was afraid to ask, but because he assumed that the night's itinerary had been lined out by Sandra, there was a high probability they'd also been to the bar where Rusty had been killed. They had promised one another never to return. Alison knew the question was coming.

"Did you go there?" He didn't say where, but she knew where he meant.

She was quiet for a moment, "Yes," she said. There was resentment in her voice.

"Why are you acting like I'm getting upset for no reason? We agreed it was a terrible place, and you promised you'd never go again. Now I call you, and you're out at three in the morning, after having been there."

He could hear Sandra's voice. "Is everything okay, Alison?"

He lost his temper, and began yelling into the phone.

"I'm going to go," Alison said. She hung up. He tried calling a number of times, but she didn't answer.

An hour later, he got a call on his computer from her. She was drunk, with a vacant look on her face, lying on her bed.

"Sandra and Stephanie drove me home. Happy?"

"Yes, I'm so happy that you decided it was fair of me to interrupt your fun at three in the morning."

"Stop yelling at me," she said.

"I'm not yelling." He sighed.

He knew she was blacked out, which meant that she wouldn't re-member any of this. When he drank, he never blacked out, which meant, for better or for worse, he remembered everything. He sometimes wondered whether everyone else truly blacked out, as they claimed, or whether they just pretended, in order not to have to talk about what they had done while drunk. Probably, he decided, people did black out, but maybe not as frequently as they said they did.

"I can't believe you're trying to justify this. You broke a promise. Of course, I'm going to be upset to find out my fiancée is out at a nightclub at three in the morning. I don't think that's controlling at all. Maybe our braindead, degenerate society thinks it is, but frankly that doesn't bother me. It just proves my point about why I have no intention of caring what everyone else thinks is normal." He continued ranting for a few more minutes, until he realized from her snoring that she must have fallen asleep.

He hung up, and stared out the window, listening to the rain drum against the roof. Here he'd been suffering through terrible homesickness, pining over her daily, counting down the days until her visit, only to find out that she'd lied to him, saying she'd be home working on her art, instead of going *there* with her friends. That little miserable Sandra, he thought. What a manipulative little wretch. He put on an old song he used to like, Alkaline Trio's "My Friend Peter." It would only worsen his mood, he knew, but he wanted to plunge deeper into the despair.

He knew it was petty, but he wanted revenge. When the song had finished, he walked to the corner Tesco, bought a bunch of beer, walked back to the room, cracked one open, and started drinking. By early eve-ning, he had finished all the beer, and because he still hadn't heard from Alison, he decided there was no point in stopping now. He flung open his door, stomped down the stairs, opened the gate, and walked down the street. When he got to Turf, he bought two gin and tonics, sat down in the corner, and guzzled the first one. He nursed the second one for a half hour or so, then went to the counter for more. By closing time, he was numb, and he wandered through the empty streets, slowly meandering to the apartment. When he reached his room, he checked his email, hop-ing to see an apology from Alison, but when it wasn't there, he was glad, since he told himself it justified his decision to go on the night's bender.

Despite being soaked to the bone, he realized that till then he'd been completely oblivious to the rain. He tossed the empty pack of cigarettes out his window, shut it, fell into bed, and stared at the ceiling until the dark enveloped him completely, and he was plunged into an angry sleep.

Sixteen

E heard nothing from Alison on Tuesday either, but on Wednesday he did.

"I'm sorry," she wrote. "I understand why you're angry. I shouldn't have gone. I was just getting stir crazy, and I figured it would be just one time."

He wrote her back. "I'm sorry too. I shouldn't have gotten so angry." He considered saying something about Sandra, but he assumed Alison already knew how he felt. He didn't want to start another argument, especially so close to her visit, so he said nothing of it.

"My mom's driving me crazy with the wedding planning," she said.

"How?"

"She keeps going over and over the invitation list."

Alison and he had known her parents wanted the wedding in Texas, but they had always preferred California. Stuart and Linda hadn't said anything about it to Alison, but she was discerning enough to know her parents were resentful over the decision not to hold the wedding in Texas. They had picked a small adobe garden on the central coast of his home state, in the same town, in fact, where his parents currently lived. He thought it was charming, and Alison seemed to like it as well, which was all that mattered, as far as he was concerned. He deliberately had been trying to stay removed from the wedding planning, because he didn't want to have to mediate between Alison and Linda. He wasn't intending to leave Alison to do all the work herself out of selfishness. It was prudence. He suspected that Linda wanted to irritate Alison, in order to draw him into the drama. He had not been participating in the planning, thus avoiding whatever trap Linda was setting. He didn't want to explain this to Alison, since he knew she might not believe her mother was conscientiously trying to provoke them into an argument, but the problem was that, as a result of not explaining his rationale, Alison, he could tell, was assuming he was simply ignoring the planning process out of disinterest. It was a reasonable explanation for her to form, and he wished he knew a workable way of disabusing her of it.

"I told her that we want a small ceremony. But she's inviting all of her friends. She has more guests than I do."

"I'm sorry."

"We should just elope." She said it half-jokingly, but seriously enough for him to know she was testing to see how he might react to the proposition.

He smiled. "That would be nice. You know I hate weddings, anyway. I could talk to the people here at the Cathedral." The college, he thought, would be an ideal place to be wed. He pictured the two of them standing alone together in the Cathedral, exchanging their vows. Maybe they could tie the knot next week, when she was here. He floated the possibility.

"Really? Please, please do. I don't know how much longer I can deal with my mom."

In addition to the location of the venue, there had been questions about the size of the wedding party. Eventually, they settled on five groomsmen and five bridesmaids. On her side, there were the twins, Sandra and Stephanie, another longtime friend from Texas, May, and two friends from the university, Kelsie and Enrique. He knew Alison knew he thought it was bizarre for a man to serve as a bride's attendant, but because Enrique was a homosexual, Enrique knew everyone would brush it off and pretend it was normal. It wasn't the sort of thing worth arguing about. He liked Enrique, anyway, more so certainly than he did Sandra, and if it was what Alison wanted, he wasn't going to object. He would show her the same courtesy that he knew she was showing him. After all, there was no way she could be pleased with his choice of groomsmen.

His recollection turned to that summer earlier in the year, when she had met two of them for the first time in Palm Springs. He had been in California for a visit to his parents, and her family was on the way to her cousin's wedding. They made plans to rendezvous in the desert resort, near the wedding venue. His childhood best friend, Andy, the one who now went by Moto in New York City, was himself home on vacation in California. So, their mutual childhood friend, Bert, who had lived in Los Angeles for a decade, invited Andy and him over, with an eye toward them being introduced to Alison and her family. Andy, the former aspiring screenwriter and actor turned office employee, had always had an ambivalent relationship with Bert. Up through middle school, he and Andy had been inseparable, while Bert, though close to Andy, was not nearly as good of friends with Andy as he was. By their sophomore years in high school, however, Andy had begun using drugs and drinking, and so for a time, he and Bert became best friends. But then Bert began getting up to the same trouble as Andy had, so Bert and Andy ditched him. He had become a social liability to them both, given their new friends from high school. But as much as Andy and Bert partied together in high school, he knew Bert never truly respected Andy. Bert and he attended the same public high school, and on the rare occasions when they would talk at lunch, Bert would tell him about how Andy had no self, and how Andy tried too hard to fit in, and so on. As for Andy, whom he saw even less frequently than he did Bert, the feeling was mutual. Andy told him about how one time Bert had pretended to get sloppy drunk at a house party, only to discover that he'd really just been drinking fruit punch the entire time. Everyone at the party had let Bert play act for hours before finally telling him that they had all let him embarrass himself. The successful party prank, according to Andy, was all the proof anyone needed to know that Bert, not he, was the phony.

Now recollecting the shifting dynamics among the three of them in high school, he recognized the same pattern of selective omissions and partial disclosures was at work then as was now with Klaus and Carrell, or with Joseph and Manan. Probably, he assumed, all of them had done the same thing with their own friends as adolescents, behavior they now carried over into adulthood. He had always felt that, because Andy wanted to fit in socially, his friend had been willing to tolerate terrible abuse from Bert that Andy never would have accepted had it been coming from others. His thought turned to the time when Bert and he and some others from the neighborhood were in Bert's yard shooting a potato cannon they had made. With his parents away on vacation, Andy had come over after drinking his very first beer at home alone. For some reason, the beer didn't sit well with him, and he nearly passed out in the yard, falling to the ground where he began convulsing. Everyone was terrified, except for Bert, who laughed sadistically, and started kicking Andy in the head, as he thrashed violently on the ground. Thinking about it now, he wondered whether Bert and Andy had always resented each other, simply because they recognized in the other what they despised about themselves.

The same pattern had continued into their college years. They all had reconnected after he himself had begun drinking, and now, a few years on after college, things seemed to be congenial among them all. Andy had accepted his invitation to be the best man, and Bert would be one of the groomsmen. Although the three of them had not been keeping in as regular touch as before, he had known them for over twenty years. It seemed only natural that they should be his groomsmen. He knew that he would probably not be either of their own best men, but he wasn't offended by it. He had no expectation that they should have to reciprocate.

When he got to Bert's house in Los Angeles, the first day things had gone fine enough. Bert seemed genuinely happy to see him, and Bert's girlfriend, Maggie, who lived with him, was very welcoming. The next day, when Andy arrived, things became strained. It was not hard to understand why. Bert was working on a PhD in psychology, which was something they had in common, given the fact that he was about to go off to do his own PhD work in philosophy. Of course, Oxford was more impressive than Claremont, but he knew Bert could tolerate the disparity in prestigiousness, because in comparison to Andy, Bert was doing well indeed. Andy, after all, had no higher degree of any type, and he was stuck working an office job that Bert knew was one Andy only a few years beforehand would have considered a failure—an "office drone," had been Andy's own derogatory phrase to describe what he had since become. Bert, in fact, he saw, was taking a sick satisfaction in watching Andy's film aspirations fail to materialize, since that meant he had everything he knew Andy wanted but didn't, a career path that would be personally fulfilling, a stable girlfriend, and plenty of leisure time to indulge in hobbies and use recreational drugs. Andy, who was resentful of how his life was turning out, felt exposed, since unlike those he knew in New York, there was no way of pretending with Bert and him that he was sincerely happy. Andy knew they knew he was miserable. He could understand how, from Andy's perspective, having to be here in Palm Springs to see Bert and him in order to meet Alison might feel like being back on that ground again, getting kicked in the head when he was down. To make matters worse, Andy had recently broken up with his latest girlfriend, which, thinking about it now, had likely precipitated what happened next in Palm Springs with Alison.

Bert, Maggie, Andy, and he had driven out to the hotel where Alison was staying with her family. When they parked the car in the lot, Alison ran over to hug him. They kissed, and he turned to introduce her. To his horror, nobody had yet come out of the car. The two of them stood there awkwardly for a few moments, until Maggie finally got out of the front passenger seat.

"Hi, I'm Maggie. Very nice to meet you."

"Hi, I'm Alison." They both hugged.

"Congratulations! I'm so happy for you two," Maggie said.

Bert reluctantly got out of the driver seat.

"Alison, meet Bert. Bert, meet Alison."

Bert put out his hand, which Alison shook.

"I don't know whether you guys are interested, but my mom wanted to let you know that our family is going out for dinner tonight. It's for part of my cousin's wedding. She wanted me to let you know that you're all invited. She thinks it would be nice to meet you, since you're going to be groomsmen at our wedding." Alison looked so sweet, so joyous, so loving. He could tell she was genuinely expecting them to accept the offer.

"Oh, we're not going to be able to make it," Bert said without explanation. Maggie looked surprised, and almost said something, but then didn't. They all chatted superficially for a few more minutes. Nobody asked how he and Alison had met. Nobody asked anything about Alison. It was like she and the wedding didn't exist.

"Okay, well, we should be going," Bert said.

They all said goodbye, Bert and Maggie got in the car, and drove off. Andy, his childhood best friend and best man, had never gotten out of the car.

He didn't know what to say, as he turned to Alison, who was visibly upset.

She appeared to be on the brink of tears. "Did I do something wrong?"

"No, no, not at all. I have no idea why they didn't want to come to dinner."

"I mean, we came all this way, we're right here, and they don't even want to spend any time with us? Andy didn't even get out of the car." He could tell she wanted to say Andy was supposed to be his best friend, but to spare his feelings, she held her tongue.

There was no point trying to excuse any of it. It was inexcusable. He was genuinely disappointed. He never imagined that Andy might do something so rude to Alison, whom he knew Andy knew he loved.

"I'm so sorry. I don't know what's going on."

Sitting at his desk here in Oxford, he remembered hugging her in the parking lot, wishing there was a way to assure her that what his old friends had done was not at all her fault. They had always been mean-spirited, he wanted to say. Of course, since that were true, there was the question about why he had wanted them involved in the wedding. He didn't have a good answer to that. It was the inertia of time, maybe, or maybe the hope that something he thought he remembered from their childhood together could somehow be restored. Looking out the window onto the college gardens, he knew he was lying to himself. If he were going to be honest, he should just ask someone at the Cathedral about eloping.

SEVENTEEN

THERE was a knock at the door. That would be Manan. The week had gone by relatively fast, and now in a few minutes, it would be time for dinner at Eliot's.

"Come in."

Manan raised a bottle. "I got it," Manan said.

"Oh, great. One second." He fumbled in his drawers for change. It was silly in a way to pay Manan for a bottle of wine, when obviously Manan could himself more than afford it, but it was the thought that counted. He offered him a bill.

"That won't be necessary."

"Please, I insist."

"Thank you." Manan took out his wallet, put the bill away, and placed the wallet back in his pocket.

"I guess in a way that entire exchange was pointless, since neither of us is really a money guy." He waited for a laugh, but Manan looked on expressionlessly. He knew Manan must remember their earlier conversation about the three sources of great temptation, so it was strange that Manan would pretend not to understand the reference.

Manan looked at his watch. "Oh! If we hurry, we shall be right on time." They walked out of the room, and he locked the door. At the bottom of the stairs, they saw Craig and Michaela with Emily and Erin. He was about to wave when he realized they were too drunk to notice. In any case, before he could, the group disappeared down the hall and into Michaela's room. As they opened the building door, Frank came in.

"Hello," Manan said.

"Yeah, hi," Frank slurred as he nodded to Manan. Frank walked by without looking at him, his concentration focused on trying to find Michaela's room.

"Pity," Manan said.

At the college gate, they saw Joseph approaching Eliot's door.

Manan called across the quad, "Joseph!"

Joseph waved, and waited at the doorway stairs.

"I see Melissa won't be joining us tonight," Manan said, as they all shook hands.

"No, I'm afraid not. She's away on a trip to Berlin."

"The next time you talk to her, please give her my best regards." Melissa must be Joseph's wife.

"What does your wife do?"

"She's an anthropologist."

"Ah, interesting."

"Manan tells me you're engaged. Congratulations. Melissa and I will have to have you and Alison over for dinner."

"Oh, that sounds good. I'm sure Alison would love that."

He noticed that Joseph entered without knocking. Inside, there was a fire in the study, and a smaller table than last time was set in the dining room. The residence, which was quiet, felt somber tonight.

"Everyone must be having drinks in the garden," said Manan. They made their way outside.

"Henry!"

"Hello, old chap!" A young man in his earlier twenties, with ruddy cheeks and curly brown hair, waved to Manan. They embraced warmly.

"It's so good to see you."

Henry turned his head over his shoulder. "Guys, over here!" Two others, both in their early twenties, walked over with big grins on their faces.

"William, George, so good to see you both," Manan said.

Then Manan cleared his throat. "Allow me to make the introductions."

"Henry, George, William, these are my friends, Joseph and—"

"Excuse me, everyone!" A loud voice called out from the door. The garden fell silent. "Dinner shall be served."

When they sat down, things came into focus. There were Manan's three Cambridge friends, Eliot, and two others whom he recognized from the last dinner. Counting Manan, Joseph, and himself, that made nine tonight, fewer than half as many guests as last time. The others who had come before with their wives were alone. None of the female students present last time were here either. Tonight was men only.

The food was served, and the table wasted no time in beginning to talk shop.

"If Rahner is wrong, I don't see how to explain the possibility of salvation prior to the Incarnation," said one of the older guests, an albino man in his early thirties.

"Oh, James, you would think that," the other guest from last time said.

James laughed. "Christopher, don't you start with me!"

"Enough banter. It is a serious issue. I know you both feel that way. It's a good question, what are we to think concerning those who lived before Christ?" The table fell quiet in light of what apparently was a strong rebuke from Eliot.

James, who felt he was on familiar enough terms to use his given name, responded to the Regius Professor, "But, Eliot, you're a universalist!"

He was still a theological neophyte. But he had been reading as much as possible to attempt to bring himself up to speed. Born in Freiburg, the home of Husserl's and Heidegger's phenomenology, as it happened, Karl Rahner was a Jesuit priest and theologian famous for his notion of "anonymous Christians." According to Rahner, people who had never heard the Gospel could nonetheless be saved through Christ. A Buddhist monk, for instance, who followed his conscience, might attain salvation through Christ, even if he had never received the Christian revelation. The idea, so far as he understood it, amounted to the view that the nature of consciousness was, as a matter of its transcendental structure, always already oriented toward God. This in turn made it possible for those who had not yet heard the name of Jesus to live a life that was consistent with his teachings. Depending on how one took it, Rahner's transcendental openness to God might seem to be a precursor to a view on which everyone was saved, even if they did not know it. In short, Rahner's theological anthropology appeared to open the door to universalism. Given James's comment addressed to Eliot, this, he assumed, must be Eliot's own view.

Eliot looked bemusedly on the young theologian. "Do you think so little of God's love, James?"

"Oh, Eliot, we've all had this conversation a thousand times!" The table laughed.

James's face grew more serious, "To uphold the doctrine of eternal hell is not to falsely circumscribe God's love. I don't deny that it can appear difficult to reconcile God's love with eternal judgment, but it does us no good to shy away from the hard truth, that this is what both Scripture and tradition teach."

One of Manan's Cambridge friends piped up, "Ah, said like a good Catholic!"

"There is worse company to keep, I suppose. Augustine and others agree," the albino said.

"That's just an appeal to authority," the young Cambridge man fired back.

He was still intimidated by these discussions, since he recognized the limits of his own understanding. But he felt strongly compelled to speak. He wanted to say that, if universalism is true, then there would be no reason for the Incarnation. The idea behind universalism, of course, was that God's love was boundless, and so grace in no way depended on man's deeds or response to the Cross. The Cross was absolute. But if that were the case, this implied that God could reconcile everyone to himself by any means, in which case it rendered Christ's own life otiose. Why should Christ have been made man, suffered, and died, if nothing about it made any material difference? On the universalist assumption, God could just as well have forgiven everyone without any Incarnation or Resurrection at all. Then of course, there was the point that, according to Paul in Acts, the reason for the Resurrection was to warn everyone of the judgment, that each of us would one day be resurrected from the grave, and stand before God. If universalism were true, the doctrine of eternal judgment was negated, and then the entire purpose of the Resurrection too, at least according to Paul. As for the *kerygma*, Bultmann, it seemed to him, completely misunderstood it. That was another point that was beginning to bother him. All the theologians around him at the table appeared to equate the Gospel itself with the "life, death, and resurrection of Jesus Christ," but whatever that was supposed to mean exactly, it couldn't be correct, since according to the Gospel accounts themselves, Christ was commanding his own disciples to preach the Gospel before he had died, before he had been resurrected, and indeed before everyone who knew him even had a clear picture that he was going to be crucified. If, then, the Gospel were what the theologians said it was, how was it being preached before Christ's death? Obviously, what Christ said the Gospel was differed from what the theologians were saying. He laughed to himself. Maybe the philosophers were those who ignored Christ, the theologians those who argued with Christ.

Poised to speak, his lips opened, but on the cusp of uttering the first word, Henry spoke. "I like to believe Eliot is right about the liberality of God's judgment!" The table laughed, as evidently everyone there knew why Henry would say so.

"Well, Henry, don't be too hard on yourself. Nobody's perfect," Eliot laughed. He could tell that Eliot was alluding to whatever Henry had been alluding to as well. When he thought whatever that was would remain a mystery, James said, "Yes, well, even we conservatives learn to experiment from time to time back at the college."

Henry turned to James, "Indeed! They don't call it Peter House for nothing." The entire table erupted in uproarious laughter.

"Kissing in the dorms has been going on there for many years, gentlemen," Eliot said. "You all know that."

Extremely uncomfortable with the turn the dinner had taken, he turned to Manan. Instead of finding Manan horrified or even remotely disoriented, as he'd expected, Manan was grinning widely and nudging Joseph. Evidently all of the young, promising conservative Oxford and Cambridge theologians at tonight's dinner had been engaging in homosexual activity, and they were all openly joking about it, with Eliot's full approval.

"Dessert will be served shortly, and then we can all retire to the study. But, before that, I must show you all something," said Eliot.

They all looked at each other excitedly, and stood up from their plates. Eliot walked down the hall, and waved to them, "C'mon, this way."

They followed behind Eliot in a single file to a room with a staircase leading downstairs. That was odd, because this was the ground floor. It must be a basement, he deduced.

"You know, very few people know this, but the college spends millions of pounds a year maintaining the grounds, partly because of a very extensive tunnel system beneath the buildings. There are run-off issues."

Eliot flipped on a switch and led them down a flight of wooden stairs to a concrete chamber. The ceiling was extremely low, and it was cramped. "There's a system of chambers just like this, connected by tunnels. I could show you more, but you get the idea."

One of Henry's friends looked confused. "What's it all for?"

"Storage, I suppose. At least in the old days," said Eliot. "Well, it's damp down here. Why don't we go back upstairs?"

They walked up the stairs, shut the door, and walked to the study where dessert was to be served. Joseph and Manan took a seat together on a loveseat, and the others took seats as well. Whiskey was being poured, and although the study looked exactly how anyone who had never been there would imagine an Oxford fireside chat to look, he wanted desperately to leave.

He turned to Manan and Joseph, "Excuse me." He found Eliot, clearing plates from the dining room table.

"Hi, Prof Wood."

"Hello, so glad you could make it tonight. I hope I didn't scare you with the tunnels."

"Oh, no, not at all. I don't spook easily." Eliot's eyes narrowed, and his lips pursed.

"No, I don't think you would," he said.

"Anyway, I must apologize, but I must be going. I'm afraid that once again that means no dessert for me."

"Yes, that's a shame. Well, thank you for coming."

"Thank you."

He opened the door and stepped onto the quad without looking into the study. When he got to his room, he lit a cigarette, and thought about Alison. Making sense of what he had seen tonight at Eliot's could wait. For now, he would first simply clear his mind.

Eighteen

I T was noon, and he had been up since nine, so lunch seemed appropriate. Last night's dinner was still a shock and he thought mulling it over a meal might bring clarity to the situation. It was one thing to have already seen that the theologians treated the question of God frivolously, as mere sport for intellectual amusement and sparring. More disconcerting was the apparent fact that many of them, some of whom were very powerful and famous, presented a veneer of traditional respectability to the public and others, while carrying on quite differently behind the scenes. He wondered how many of their wives and family knew they were secretly homosexuals and engaging in extra-marital affairs. Having grown up in California, naturally he had heard talk about the existence of a Lavender Mafia, but it was still certainly something to see such a network alive and well in one of the most exclusive dining parties in Oxford. He himself was not a homosexual. In fact, he had never had a homosexual encounter of any kind, though of course he had seen so many others he knew experiment in their youth. There had been the time he and his friends found the photographs of Andy making out with Tad, and there was the other time that Bert had ejaculated on Eric's face during a sleepover at Andy's house. At the time when everyone told him about what Bert had done, he had thought it was sick but funny. But in retrospect, now that he was older, he realized how incredibly dark and depraved it was. What had seemed like a risqué prank now looked more like straightforward sexual abuse or assault. The wider childhood context only made it worse. Years later, for instance, an older boy from the same neighborhood had been arrested and convicted of possessing and distributing child abuse images, and was serving a prison sentence in Nevada. The same boy's father had been a Little League umpire when they were growing up, and his mother an elementary school drama teacher. It was suspicious, he now thought, that the sex offender's own parents would have been around children, only to have their own son turn out to be so sexually damaged. He wondered whether there was any connection between that and Bert. Perhaps Bert himself had been groomed or molested by someone in the neighborhood. It was impossible to say. In any event, that sort of sadistic sexual behavior, he assumed, had only continued when Bert had joined a fraternity at college. As for Bert and Eric, they had remained friends over the years despite the incident, and thus Eric, along with his twin brother Craig, were both going to be groomsmen at the wedding. If Eric and Bert were comfortable around one another, he saw no reason to bring up what they all knew had happened between them. Alison thought it was cute that both she and him would have a set of twins in the wedding party, so there was no reason to spoil that. He would keep quiet about what had happened during the sleepover in Andy's basement. Then again, there was always the possibility of eloping, which would render it all moot. He would have to stop by the Cathedral soon.

It was hard to know definitively, but he was beginning to suspect that most of the men he knew, particularly those in academia, had some sort of homosexual history. When Alison had first met him, she was absolutely shocked to discover that, unlike Justice and his friends, he had never had any such encounters. He knew it was common to claim that those who opposed homosexual activity on moral grounds were themselves merely repressed homosexuals. And maybe in some cases that was the case. But armchair psychology such as that cut both ways. One could just as easily argue that those who alleged others were secretly latent homosexuals were simply doing so because they themselves couldn't accept that there were others who were genuinely heterosexual and comfortable with it. If that were the case, then it was bad faith to contend that everyone was doing it, and to believe that anyone who said he hadn't was a liar or repressed. But popular psychology wasn't what mattered. What mattered for his purposes was finding a way to deal with the institutional reality he was currently faced with. Suffice it to say, he was going to be very adamant about not entangling himself in whatever world it was he had been shown a glimpse of last night at Eliot's dinner. If that ultimately posed problems for his career advancement, so be it.

He took a seat at a booth in the restaurant. Typically, he avoided the Covered Market, but he felt like a change of pace. The food here, in all likelihood, would not be anything to write home about, but as notorious as the English were for their bad cuisine, he had been finding it reasonably tolerable thus far.

The waitress came to the table. "May I get you something to drink?"

"Yes, a lemonade, please. I think I'm ready to order."

"Sure. What will it be?"

"I'll have the Armenian Lamb, please."

"How would you like your meat done?"

"Medium, please."

"Anything else?"

"No, thank you."

A few minutes later, the waitress returned with his drink. "Here you are."

"Oh, thank you. I'm going to step out for a cigarette," he said.

"Not a problem," the waitress said.

Rather than step onto the High, he went out the back instead. Workers in their yellow hard hats were busy renovating a building exterior, and a number of tourists were walking by with their selfie sticks. He lit a cigarette, and looked down the way to Cornmarket. As he was finishing his cigarette, he turned, and, to his surprise, there was Klaus, walking with a woman down Turl. Judging by the look of pure elation on his supervisor's face, it must be Zoe. It was, from what he could tell, the same woman from the formal dinner at High Table. They disappeared from view behind the corner, and there was no point in trying to catch them to say hello, so he walked back to his booth. It would be interesting to hear what Klaus would have to say about the situation the next time they met up. There was no telling when that would be, but hopefully sooner rather than later. If Klaus were in town from London, it stood to reason he should have time for a meeting. But he hadn't received any word from Klaus. He sighed. To guard against any resentment setting in over Klaus's blowing him off, he decided to think about Alison's coming visit.

The lamb was tasty, even if the side vegetables were too soggy. Alison didn't much care for lunch, he knew, but he would keep the place in mind as an option, since it might be worth coming back here together. He paid the bill, finished his lemonade, thanked the waitress, and stepped onto the High. Next door was a café. He was feeling a little groggy, so he bought a coffee, and walked back to the building.

At the gate, Manan, Henry, and the two others from Cambridge, were coming out.

"Hi, guys. Good to see you," he said.

Henry smiled, "Likewise!"

Manan said, "We'll be back at my place after dinner tonight. You should join us. Nine?"

"Sounds good. See you then," he said. No doubt they all would be keen to feel out his reaction to last night's dinner, just as he was to gauge theirs. He was beginning to sense that he was being tested, played with even, and that was fine. This was Oxford, after all, it would be strange if there weren't going to be mind games. He was ready.

Although usually he showed up precisely on time, tonight he made sure to show up forty-five minutes late. Doing so, he figured, might throw an initial wrench in whatever plans Manan and the others had. It would be good to put them off balance. When Manan opened the door, he could see the Indian prince was agitated by his late arrival.

"Yes, come in," he said.

The whiskey was out on the desk, but Manan did not offer him any.

"I see I'm the first to arrive," he said to Manan.

"Yes, I'm not sure where Henry and the others are. They were supposed to have come over straightaway after dinner, before you were due here at nine."

He could see Manan was lying. Manan was saying what he had been planning to tell him if he had arrived, as expected, promptly at nine. So, the plan had been to have it be just Manan and him here alone, while the others pretended to be running late. Manan would get a preliminary read on him, and the others would then take their cue from Manan once they arrived. It would be interesting, then, to see how they reacted when they came to the room, only to realize that Manan had nothing to provide them, since he hadn't shown up when they had been expecting.

Just then, there was a knock on the door. "It's us!"

"That must be them," Manan said distractedly.

He opened the door and Henry, George, and William came striding in. He quickly hopped off the bed, and took the one seat. The others all plopped down together on the bed.

"Sorry we're late," William said to Manan.

"We ended up stopping for drinks on the way back," George explained.

He could tell they were waiting for Manan to join in the banter, but when he didn't, sitting there stoically instead, they got uncomfortable. They could see that things had not gone according to plan.

"Perhaps you should all run to the store and pick up some wine. I'm not in the mood for whiskey this evening." Taking the hint, the three of them got up, and went to run the errand. As he was ruminating over why Manan would send them away, there was another knock on the door.

"It's me," the voice said. It was a familiar one.

"Yes, do come in." Manan's voice was more chipper this time, but it was strained.

In walked Joseph with a young man he had never met before. The man was in his late twenties, with a crew cut, and olive skin. They set wine down on Manan's desk, shook hands, and then turned to him.

"Hello! So good to see you," Joseph said to him. He stood up, shook Joseph's hand, and turned to the new man.

He stretched out his hand, a warm smile on his face. "I'm Ben." He gave Ben his name.

"Well, do have a seat. I'm afraid we might not have room when the others return."

Manan never would have invited more guests than he could accommodate at once, so the fact that Joseph and Ben had shown up now, around ten, suggested that Manan must have been intending to stagger his visitors. By this point in the night, Manan had expected him to have already left after having shown up at nine. He wondered what Manan and the others had thought would have led him to leave in between when he was supposed to have arrived at nine and now.

"I hear you're in philosophy," Ben said.

"Yep! You?"

"Me too, actually." Ben paused. "BPhil or DPhil?"

"DPhil. You?"

"Same."

"Is this your first year?"

"Yes, just arrived."

By his accent, he could tell Ben was from Canada. "Which province?"

"Alberta." He considered mentioning how his old friend from Texas, David, was from Alberta too.

"I've only been to Canada once, to Ontario. I'd like to visit again. It seemed nice."

"Yes, that's a very Canadian way to put it! 'Nice,'" Ben laughed. "You're from the States?"

"Yeah, California. Bay Area."

"Who's your supervisor?"

"Carman."

"Never heard of him."

"Yeah, he's fairly new to Oxford. Yours?"

"Walker."

"Ah, so you work on Kant, like Manan?"

"Yes, I'm focusing on Kant's practical philosophy, specifically his account of the connection between duty and character formation."

"I see."

"As a Christian, I'm interested in trying to make my philosophical research as applied as possible." There were many things he could say in reply to keep the conversation going, but he wasn't in the mood to talk philosophy, so he held a silence.

Joseph interjected, "Well, Ben, you'll have to meet Prof Wood at some point. We've recently introduced him," Joseph pointed, "to Wood. There are regular dinners. If you're potentially interested, do let us know."

"Oh, that sounds great. I'd be very interested. Doesn't Prof Wood work on Barth?"

Manan, who by now looked completely deflated, mumbled, "That's correct." Ben was confused why Manan was so inexplicably dour, so he turned to Joseph instead.

"I joined a squash club recently. I don't know if you like to play, but let me know."

Joseph said, "I'm not the athletic type, I'm afraid."

Although it had just appeared Manan had decided to check out of the conversation, he unexpectedly said, "Ben, forgive me for having been rude, I should have asked. How's Winnie?"

Wincing, Ben lowered his eyes, then quickly composed himself. "Oh, she's fine."

"It's a shame she didn't come tonight," Manan continued.

"Yes, well, she's back in Canada right now at her mother's."

"Well, when she gets back, she'll have to come over."

Joseph added, "Yes, Manan's right, Melissa and I will have you two over for dinner." By the looks of it, though, Winnie, who evidently was Ben's wife, wouldn't be coming back to Oxford anytime soon. It had the smell of a separation, with divorce on the horizon.

Just then, the door opened, and the three Cambridge men came bumbling in from the store. His plan of showing up late had now paid dividends, because there was no way to accommodate everyone, and everyone was forced to recognize it was bizarre of Manan to have overbooked his small room. He looked right at Manan, and held his gaze, to let Manan know that it hadn't been by chance that he'd decided to come to the room late tonight. Manan smiled faintly, as if to concede defeat, and then turned to the others standing at the door.

"Well, this is awkward. I don't know what I was thinking. My apologies to everyone."

"Don't worry. I'll be going," he said. He stood up, waved to Joseph, and shook Ben's hand.

"We'll have to get coffee soon," Ben said.

"That sounds great. Send me an email." He wanted to tell Ben, who was clearly naive, that he was swimming with sharks. But he would have to learn for himself.

George and William looked confused to find Joseph and Ben in the room. Manan, who recognized their confusion, did his best to iron things out on the fly.

He turned to Ben, "Ben, please meet, Henry, George, and William. They're theologians from Cambridge, and old friends of mine. George and William are staying at the Randolph, because the room is small. I'm only able to accommodate one, and the lucky winner is Henry." Holding his gaze on Ben, Manan pointed casually to Henry, "He'll be sleeping on the floor, of course. It's uncomfortable, but the floor in college is better than the street, isn't it Henry?" Ben looked even more confused, but didn't say anything.

He had reached the door, and, without looking, he shut it behind him, glad to have extricated himself from whatever plot Manan, and potentially Joseph with him, had been hatching for tonight. He could not prove it, but whatever it was, it probably originated in the mind of Eliot. These, he now realized, were simply the minions the professor was using to groom, and blackmail, newly arrived students. He didn't really want to know the details, but it was not the sort of activity Eliot would be engaging in alone. There must be a network.

NINETEEN

W HEN he checked his email the next day, he shook his head. To be sure, it was a relatively harmless lie, but still a lie. According to the note Klaus had sent him last night when he was over at Manan's, his supervisor had been busy all day in London, and he would be returning to Oxford for the first time in weeks next week. Well, he thought, if Klaus did actually make an appearance, it would mean Alison would be able to meet him. Looking at the screen, he told himself that would be good, but when he acknowledged the terrible trepidation that he couldn't help but feel, he knew that it would probably not be.

A coughing fit came over him, and after it passed, he lit a cigarette, which he held out the window. It was sprinkling outside, but this was not a good time to get another note from the Censor. Despite the frequent gray, it had been relatively mild since arriving, but with winter fast approaching, it was now cold. Even with his sweater on, he would have to close the window and turn up the heater. He had not yet bothered to use it, so it would take a minute of fiddling to figure out.

He walked to the heater, which was on the wall, next to the bed. He put his hand over it, and confirmed that the air coming out was too cool. He turned a knob on the top clockwise, and moved his hand over the heater again, to see whether he could feel any change. When the air became cooler than before, he tried turning the knob counter-clockwise, which seemed to work. It might take a while before he felt any appreciable difference, but it was better than nothing. He was poised to crack open the Bultmann book finally, when something caught his eye. He pressed his head against the wall, to get a better look. He couldn't be sure, but he reached his hand down behind the heater, grabbed hold of something, and pulled it out from against the wall. Well, this is very odd, he thought. A pair of skimpy, lace red women's underwear. They certainly weren't his.

If Alison had been the one to find them, she understandably wouldn't have believed him if he'd denied knowing how they got there. It appeared to him that someone had put them there. He felt a huge relief having found the underwear before she had. But there was also the question of what now to do about it.

He walked over to his desk, and opened a tab in his Internet browser. If memory served, there was a Facebook group for the graduate students in the building. Thank you, Mark Zuckerberg, he said to himself, while chuckling. He had never posted anything to the group, but now he would.

> Hi, everyone. I'm in Building 2, Room 9. My apologies for what might seem to be a bizarre note, but I feel I must send it. A few moments ago, I went to adjust my space heater, when I discovered, to my surprise, a pair of women's underwear nudged against the wall by the bed. I say surprising, because I'm currently engaged, and my fiancée is living overseas in the States, and the pair of underwear is not hers. I frankly have no idea how they got there, but I just wanted to make a note of it to the building that if anyone happened to sneak into my room to play a prank, please understand that it wasn't funny. My fiancée is coming for her first visit to Oxford next week, and if she had gone to use the heater and found what I did today, she understandably would have assumed the worst. I have no desire to find out who was responsible, but I do hope that if it was someone from the housing on St Aldates, it won't happen again. Thanks.

Five minutes later he heard footsteps from somebody running up the stairs. There was a knock at the door.

"Come in."

Frank and Craig came rushing into the room.

"Dude! We read the note to the group," Craig exclaimed. "You're kidding, right?" They were scanning the room.

"No, I'm not." He grabbed the panties from his bed and held them up.

"What? That is so weird," Frank said. He walked over and grabbed them.

Craig looked completely discombobulated. "Who would do that? How would somebody get into your room?"

"The better question is why," Frank said.

"I really have no idea who it was," he said. "I'm just glad I was the one to find them."

"Oh, yeah, man. That would have been game-over if your fiancée had found them."

"Exactly," he said.

He could tell that Frank and Craig were clueless, just as Ben had been last night. He tried to imagine what their reaction would be if he tried to tell them what he had seen last night at Manan's, or over at Eliot's, or back in London.

"Wow, man, that's super creepy," Frank said. Frank went to set the underwear down on the bed.

"You keep them," he said to Frank. Craig and Frank laughed.

"See you guys later," he said, as he walked them out.

He listened to their excited voices travel down the stairs. "Michaela and the others aren't going to believe it. So weird—he wasn't kidding. I wonder who did it."

Space, he thought, was odd. It wasn't objective. Descartes, for instance, had mathematized space, claiming that it was simply pure extension. But that clearly was false. Space, in a human sense, was situational. Or better, human space was a place. Multiple individuals could occupy the same geometrical space, this room for instance, and yet inhabit completely different places. Frank and Craig, for instance, were in Oxford, lived in the same building as him, attended the same Hall for dinner, frequented the same pubs, shopped at the same stores, viewed the same sites, rode the same buses, and walked the same streets. Yet their situation here was entirely different from his. In that existential respect, they were so far apart, that they may as well have been on another continent. It was all abduction, a bit like detective work, which meant nothing was determinate, it was all hunches, inferences, surmises, and judgments. But his gut told him that somebody, probably the scout, had been told by someone to place the underwear there. It was unclear when it happened, since today was the first time using the heater, but if he had to guess, he surmised they were put there after Anna had called and he'd refused the date, certainly after he had rejected Michaela's advances here in the room before formal.

Someone might come to the conclusion that the likely culprit was Michaela herself, but that was too superficial. Most likely, whomever had been instructing Michaela to throw herself at him was also the one behind the planted underwear. Michaela had just been a pawn.

It was Eliot, probably, he believed. One of course could reasonably make the case for believing Klaus also may have had a hand in it. But that would be to fail to see the situation fully. Klaus, after all, from what he was gathering, was not anywhere near the top of the totem pole. His supervisor only did what his handler, Quiller, permitted. And above that, there were those who told Quiller what to do. Probably, then, it would have either been Eliot or Quiller, or perhaps both, he decided.

What a stroke of luck, he thought, that he had gone to use the heater when he had. Then he corrected himself. Not luck, Providence.

TWENTY

I T was hard to fathom, but it was here. He pinched himself, really, the day was here.

He had arisen earlier than usual because of the anticipation, taken a vigorous walk around the college meadow, leisurely smoked some cigarettes in the quad, checked in on the koi, then strolled back to the room where he changed his shirt. Everyone on the streets and at the college were in exceptionally fine spirits, absolutely delighted with what back in the States would be termed an unforgettable Indian summer day. Evidently, it was by far the hottest day on this date in Oxford recorded history, a beautiful, balmy twenty-one degrees, or seventy Fahrenheit, as they would say back home, shattering the previous record of fifteen degrees. In fifteen minutes, the bus from Heathrow would arrive at its stop, which, as it happened, was located right in front of the college. And with that, for the first time since arriving, home would be here.

He got to the stop, leaned up against a streetlamp, finished his orange soda, lit a cigarette, and watched the people streaming up and down the street. It was difficult to decide what he should show her first. It made best sense, he figured, to start with the college itself, since they were right here already, and it was one of the most impressive destinations in the entire city, anyway. After that, maybe an art museum. There was the Ashmolean, which he liked, but, even more charming, he thought, was the college's art collection housed in the Picture Gallery. Knowing her, she would love that. And, since he had already resolved not to fret anymore about the fornication issue for the rest of the engagement, there of course would be the sex, which was unbelievable. Love, he was seeing, was about allowing oneself to be transformed from within by another, power, by contrast, was about exteriorizing oneself into what only proved to be an abyss. The line from the Proverbs came to mind, the one about the woman more priceless than rubies. He just simply couldn't wrap his mind around power guys, such as Manan. It made no sense, he thought, shaking his head incredulously, before turning his face upwards to meet the sun.

He took a deep breath. He would be sure not to delve into any of the issues that he was dealing with regarding Klaus and Eliot, or Michaela and Manan, and all the others. She did not have to know about the silly intrigues, he knew that she didn't want to know, and he knew she didn't want to know because she fundamentally trusted him to handle whatever proved necessary to handle. And he would. Over the past few days, he had considered everything carefully, and when he was honest about it, he accepted his time here was shaping up to be quite the battle. There would be no avoiding it, unless he were to compromise himself, and he was never going to do that. He knew he was a marked man as it was already, and the longer he attempted to remain a lone wolf, in order to focus strictly on his work and take his degree with his integrity and autonomy fully intact, the more he would incense whatever powerful enemies there were here in Oxford to make. Invariably, he knew, they would put up a colossal struggle to stop him once they had realized the threat he posed to their system. That was fine, he would overcome it, because evil was weak. In a way, it was irritating to him, knowing not just what was going to have to happen, but knowing that those who would decide to oppose him would find it necessary to play it all out. Evil men were predictable like that, because they lived in denial. He would be forced to defeat them before they would accept that it had been obvious from the beginning that he always was going to do so, but again, that was fine. He was ready. In any case, since he knew he would end up taking care of whatever he was forced to take care of later, he would bracket all that for the week, and put all of himself into the present, being thankful for every second he had with her. There was absolutely no reason to let the machinations and petty mind games of the network do a thing to sap the joy out of their time together, by preoccupying, much less disconcerting, him. The words enfolded him, "Consider the lilies of the field . . . "

He looked back up at the blue sky, and smiled. He would build for them a private world where evil could not intrude. That is what a man does.

Twenty-One

I F time had previously been coagulated, choking him into a knot of malaise, with the longing for her presence finally fulfilled, the future now no longer rose up against him as a demoralizing penal sentence consisting of a series of plodding days all laced with nothingness, but instead reconstituted itself into something entirely different than before, the old empty horizon that had been responsible for his unending restlessness obliterated, consumed by the flames of an exuberance capable of at last rendering the present sufficient to itself. In short, seeing her step off the bus was a mini-eschaton. It could not be otherwise in an event like this, he thought, since in the face of the beloved was the trace of God. Before he could fully ruminate over the mystery of existence, over the facts that they were in love, and that she had come all this way to see him, she was in his arms, and it was as if the night at the magnolia tree had never ended.

They kissed, and he reached for her hand, "I love you."

She looked directly into his eyes, and smiled, "I love you too," she said.

She reached for her luggage, a rolling suitcase, but before she could grab it, and begin walking to his address, he took it and walked to Tom Gate.

"We can leave it at the Porters' Lodge for now, when I show you around."

"Ah, very fancy, my Oxford man!" she laughed sweetly.

The Head Porter, a Frenchman who had never seen him in such spirits, smiled widely at him, and tipped his cap to Alison.

"Hello," she said.

"Hello, miss," he said.

They walked up the stairs and into the Lodge.

Alison looked back outside. "Is he French?"

"Yeah, François. He's really nice. He moved here a few years ago. Pretty cool job, if you ask me, though I guess it probably gets annoying herding all the tourists in the summer."

"There's so many of them, even now! And they all have those stupid selfie sticks. I had been seeing people online with those in pictures, but I didn't know they'd be that popular." They both started laughing.

He walked to the counter where two other Porters were sitting. "Mind if I leave the suitcase here for just a bit?"

"Not a problem, mate. We'll keep an eye on it for you." They smiled at Alison, who smiled back.

He looked at her. "Okay, well, where to go?"

He could see an idea come over her, "Let's see the koi!" She trotted out the door, and he followed behind. As she hurried over to the fountain, she would turn her head back to smile, and their hands met just as they reached the pond.

"Oh, it's so beautiful." The lilies were not in bloom, but the koi were active, gliding across the surface, sticking their mouths above the water, exploring the boundary between their respective worlds.

She smiled. "I wish we could feed them."

"You know, I've never seen anyone feed them before. They must do it at night. And look at this lawn. It's perfect."

"It's ridiculous! So green. You can't walk on it?"

"Almost never, no. I think when there's a college ball, they allow it."

"Stupid Brits," she said playfully, "with all their rules!"

"Oh, yeah. You're going to crack up. They are very serious about their queues. The people here are so docile, it's any totalitarian's fantasy. I swear you could order them to walk off a cliff." She laughed.

She stuck out a finger for a koi. It nibbled on her finger, as she gently patted its head. He almost made a comment about the Empress of Japan, but didn't.

"That's Mercury, I guess," he said, pointing to the statue. She stood up, and they hugged, her head resting on his chest. He could feel her soft breathing, and he wondered whether she could feel his heart beat.

She looked up at him. "Where to next?"

"Well, I could show you the Cathedral. And there's also the Hall. I booked us for a formal dinner later on the trip. You'll love it, I think. There are also all the private gardens in the back. I just remembered I should check my mail. One second," he said, as he began walking to the Lodge.

"Is there a bathroom, or loo, or whatever?"

"Yeah." He pointed to the doorway down the way from the Lodge in the corner, the one that led to the GCR. "Upstairs above the bathroom is the room Einstein stayed in."

She started laughing. He laughed with her. She knew he knew she didn't care, and he liked that about her. It wasn't about the history surrounding all the famous and powerful people who had come before, it was simply about enjoying the place in its purity together. He reached the door to the Lodge, and waved to her as she stepped inside the staircase.

There was no mail, so he came out to the quad for a cigarette while he waited.

"Hey!"

He turned to see Ben. "Oh, hi, how are you?" He thought it was so insincere how some people would say someone's name they had just met, in order to prove they remembered it, so to avoid any appearance of disingenuousness, he didn't say Ben's name.

"I'm doing great. How about this weather?" Ben took off his sunglasses and looked up at the sky. "Just unbelievable!"

"Yeah, given how hot it is, unsurprisingly this is the hottest day on record."

Ben stuck out his chin and mused. "Really? Very cool. A little bit of Oxford history made here today, and we didn't have to do a thing." They laughed.

Ben looked at him. "Do you mind if I have one? I usually don't smoke."

"Oh, sure. No problem," he said, handing him one and the lighter.

"Thanks," he said, lighting up.

They stared across the quad. At first, they both weren't sure that they were seeing what they were seeing, but when there was no denying it, he could feel Ben fidget.

"What is that? Is she—" his voice trailed off.

A young blonde woman dressed in a heavy black trench coat came walking past the Deanery. She was barefoot, and evidently naked beneath the coat. It would be bizarre enough in cold weather, but on a sweltering day such as this, it was surreal. Judging by the smug smile on her face, she was enjoying all the stares.

"What in the world?"

"That's Lavinia," he said.

"Lavinia?"

"Yeah, I've never met her myself. But I've heard about her. She's an undergraduate here, the one dating the flamethrower guy." At an undergraduate party a few weeks before, the Porters had been called, because one of the college's philosophy students, one of Klaus's, had been shooting a homemade flamethrower in the quad. The incident had made the BBC, causing the college authorities considerable consternation. In an email to the entire college, the Senior Censor had euphemistically referred to a "safeguarding" incident.

"Oh, right, I heard about that."

The college's nudist paused in front of the Censors' office, greeting a group of other students.

Ben stared even more incredulously. "Who are they?" One of them, an extremely tall man, was dressed in drag, while the rest were in body paint. The tourists were staring.

"That, Ben, is our college's alphabet brigade."

Ben laughed. "Ah, yes, I see. You would think at a place like Christ Church this sort of spectacle wouldn't—"

He almost interrupted with a comment about how, given the existence of debauched societies like Piers Gaveston involving infamous stories like the one about David Cameron and the pig's head, it really wasn't too surprising at all, but he decided not to say anything. It would be a topic Ben wouldn't understand, and it would bring out a dark side of Oxford that he knew Ben would prefer to ignore. Better not to spoil the carefree mood.

As they continued watching, a group of the college's officials and some photographers with their gear descended the Hall staircase, joining the students on the quad. The students posed for a group picture, and there was hooting and hollering. Some of the tourists, mouths agape, covered their young children's eyes.

He felt a tap on his shoulder. It was Alison.

"Ben, meet my fiancée, Alison."

"Oh, very nice to meet you." He stuck out his hand, which she shook happily.

"He was just talking about you the other night at Manan's."

"I hope it was good!" she joked.

Ben smiled broadly, his hope in humanity momentarily restored at the sight of their love. He could see there was an understandable element of wistfulness, too, since seeing Alison and him had clearly reminded Ben of when he himself had first fallen in love with his wife. He made sure not to bring up anything about Winnie. Alison was observant, so she was sure to notice his ring, but she would be too shy to propose making any couple's plans.

Alison took a cigarette from him, and lit it, as Ben and he were finishing theirs. As he was about to offer his new friend another one, Ben's face momentarily crinkled.

"Well, I should be going," he said. "It was nice to meet you," he said, looking at Alison.

"You too!"

"See you around," he said to Ben.

He turned to Alison, who was looking out across the quad to the Censors' Office.

"Who are those weirdos?"

He laughed. "Those are the college cool kids. Don't worry about it."

She took a drag of her cigarette.

"I never should have gotten you smoking," he said.

"It's fine. I'm not addicted. I can quit anytime I want."

"That's what you think! That's how it starts," he laughed.

"We'll quit together," she said.

"I really should," he said. "Hard to believe I've been smoking now for over five years."

"We need a healthy Koala," she said in a quirky voice, squeezing his hand. That was her nickname for him.

"Heal me, Barnancle," he said. She smiled at the use of his for her.

They walked through the cloisters.

"Is that the gift shop?"

"Yeah. Want to take a look?"

"No." They laughed.

He tried guessing which of the gardens would be her favorite.

"I bet I know which one you'll like the most," he said.

"Oh, yeah?"

"Ask me when you've seen them all."

They passed from the cloisters and stepped into the shade from the Meadows Building.

"The garden's that way," he said.

They were about to step through the gate to the Masters Garden, when something caught her eye.

She exhaled.

"Oh, what's that?" He hurried to catch up, as she entered the first of the gardens behind the Cathedral. It was a small space, with an immaculate lawn, and ancient stone walls. But what set it apart, he thought, was the tree for which the garden was named.

"What's it called?"

He looked at the tree, with its mossy trunk and thick, twisting, low-hanging branches.

"It's a Pococke, I think. It's rumored to have been the inspiration for Carroll's *Jabberwocky*. Did you have to ever memorize it at school?"

"No."

"Our English teacher in fourth grade, Ms Kearley, had us all memorize the poem and then recite it to her and the class. I still remember that," he said. He thought about the mystery of time, how as a school child memorizing Carroll's poem, he never dreamed he'd be a young man about to be married, looking with her at the tree that had inspired the topic of his homework assignment. He pictured the sun room in the old house where he had memorized the poem, and the French doors that had opened to the used brick steps leading down to the yard. He wondered whether the house was still there, or whether someone by now had bulldozed it and built something else.

"I would have been so nervous! I hate speaking in front of others."

"Yeah, in retrospect, I see the rationale for the assignment. Familiarize us with an important writer, show us poetry can be fun, and help us learn to speak under pressure."

She sat on a branch, her feet barely dangling off the ground, and patted the space next to her. He climbed on, and she rested her hand on his lap. They stared at the Meadows Building for a while, listening to the sound of voices coming from the Broad Walk on the other side.

"It doesn't sound like anyone is in the other garden. Let's go see," he said.

They hopped off the tree, and walked through the gate into the Masters Garden.

There was some croquet equipment somebody had left on the lawn, and another young couple sitting on a bench.

"Wow, this is beautiful." She took a seat on the grass, then lied down, with her face up to the sun.

After lying in silence for a while, she spoke. "I'm so happy to be here. I missed you."

"I missed you too." They kissed.

"How's your work coming along?" She had a senior exhibit looming.

"Better than I expected. You know me, usually I wait right till the end, but this time I've been trying to get a little bit done at a time." He could detect the uncertainty in her voice.

"You're a great artist."

"No, but that's okay," she said. Arrogance was irritating, and he was very glad she wasn't, but it was frustrating in a different way to see how hard she was on herself. He wondered why she couldn't see her talent, why she felt so fundamentally bad about her work. Maybe it was just perfectionism. Then again, the fact that Linda and Stuart didn't support her art didn't help.

"Are you inviting people to the show?"

"Yeah, Enrique and Kelsie. My parents, too."

"How are they?"

"My parents? They're fine. My mom's obsessing over the wedding details. My dad's in the lab, as usual."

"I'm sorry that the wedding is becoming an ordeal. Originally, I was looking forward to it, but now I just want it to be over."

"I agree. It's turning into this big spectacle, which I never wanted." There was a pause. "Did you talk to the Cathedral?"

"Not yet, I thought you might want to be there with me when I asked," he said.

"Ah! Good idea."

"Want to go tomorrow?"

"Yeah," she said. "We had a meeting with the wedding planner before I left, and it went on forever. My mom kept talking, and it's like she doesn't listen. Angela kept trying to answer her questions, but it never ended. I barely got to say anything."

"I'm sorry. I'm deliberately staying out of it. I think if I got involved, that would only complicate things worse," he said.

He could tell she was wondering whether what he said was the whole truth, or whether part of him was simply uninterested, and using Linda's annoying personality as an excuse.

"Well, the main thing is that you're here, and you can see what we'll have together next year."

"I know! It's so exciting! I can't believe we're here."

She looked at him. "How's Klaus?"

"Fine, I guess." He thought about his promise not to tell anyone about Zoe. His supervisor had said not to mention it to anyone at the college. Mentioning it to his fiancée was different, perhaps. "Is he here?"

"No, London I think."

"Why would he want to live in London when he could live here?"

"I don't know. I agree. I think it's much nicer here." His mind turned to the night at the Borough Market.

"Speak of the devil," he said. She turned to look at the gate. Klaus and Zoe had just entered the garden, and were standing under a tree by the gate facing the Broad Walk.

"That's him?"

"Yep."

"Who's she?"

"Long story. I'll tell you later."

He thought it would be nice to have them join them on the lawn, but after a few minutes of talking to one another quietly, Klaus and Zoe left the garden without looking over, or saying a word.

He turned his forehead to touch hers. "I'm sure you'll meet him later."

After cuddling for a while, they left the garden, and stepped onto the Broad Walk.

"This is the Meadow," he said.

"Oh, wow, it's gorgeous."

He pointed over to his building. "That's the apartment."

"Unbelievable!"

"Want to go for a loop? This is where I go for walks when I'm thinking."

She took his hand, and they walked to the Cherwell, where the ducks were out.

"I hear there are supposed to be swans, too, but I've never seen any. One day," he said.

"I love swans," she said.

"Aren't the duckies so cute?"

"Yes, I love them," she said. She laughed to herself. "Want to know something?"

"Yeah."

"I still cry whenever I read or watch the *Ugly Duckling*." He started laughing. He knew she was embarrassed, but he found her sensitivity noble.

They followed the trail along the Meadow till they reached the Isis.

He pointed. "That's Folly Bridge. I've never crossed it to see what's on the other side of town. This is where the swans apparently come out." They kissed again, and looked out across the Meadow back to the college.

"It's beautiful," she said.

"You should see it at night, when the college is lit up under the moon."

"I can't wait."

They walked back to the Meadows Building.

"There's another garden this way," he said. They turned left, toward the street, where the War Memorial Garden was.

"It commemorates all the guys who died in World War I. They have their names all listed on the Cathedral."

"Oh, wow. That's so sad," she said.

"Yeah, I was surprised to see how many guys from the college fought and died." He wondered whether the young men who had died in battle would think it had been worth it, if they could see him and the others standing here now. There are some things for which it is impossible to adequately respond. This seemed to be one of them. Thinking about all the young men who never had wives and children of their own, who never got to grow old and experience life—it was only natural to feel fundamentally unworthy of such a sacrifice, he thought. He thought back to the thoughts he'd had about Tarawa, and the Indianapolis, and Manzanar, the day at the Prison Museum in Texas. He felt that same feeling of fundamental guilt, or debt, mixed with that peculiar gratitude, welling up from within. Maybe that's how Alison felt in general, that her very existence was a gift for which she was unworthy. He wished he could make her see that she was worthy.

Before he knew it, they had crossed the street to his apartment, and come up to his room.

"It's so cute!" she said.

"It's okay. Great location, certainly."

"Look at the bed! It's so tiny!"

"Yes, the English are notorious for bad beds."

She looked confused. "There's a French philosopher I know who told me that once. He's a life member at one of the Cambridge colleges. Anytime he visits, apparently he can't stand the beds. He says the English have uncomfortable beds." They both laughed, picturing a grumpy Frenchmen muttering to himself, thrashing on his bed.

Later, they were entangled on the small single bed, her head on his chest, as she slept. After the long flight, the bus from Heathrow, and walking around college, she was exhausted. He gently slipped out of bed.

She smiled with her eyes closed. "Where are you going?"

"We forgot your bag at the Porters' Lodge. I'm going to go get it."

"I'll come with you," she said.

"No, no. That's fine. You're tired. Get some sleep. I'll be back soon. Do you need anything when I'm out?"

"I have a blister on my foot. Could you get me band aids? I know we'll be doing a lot of walking, so I don't want it to get worse."

"Sure, no problem."

"Thanks, I love you so much."

"I love you."

He got dressed, grabbed his wallet and keys, stepped out of the room, locked the door, and lit a cigarette on the street. He realized he should have told her to smoke out the window because of the Censor, but he had forgotten to mention it. In any case, she would probably be sleeping the whole time he was gone.

Tom Gate had been closed for the night, so he buzzed himself in.

"Hi, guys," he said inside the Lodge.

"Hello," one of the Porters said. "Your bag's where you left it."

"Great, thanks." To avoid the stairs, he decided to exit the Lodge on the side with the ramp. He stepped onto the quad, when something struck him. Joseph, Manan, the albino, and some others, were milling about in front of Eliot's. They all knocked on the door, and another face he recognized from one of the dinners answered. They all went inside. Evidently, he was no longer being invited to the theology dinners. Well, no matter, he thought. What really mattered was sleeping back in his room.

He picked up the band aids and got two coffees, and went home. The college bell would be tolling soon.

She smiled when he opened the door, "You're back."

"I'm back."

"I thought you might want a coffee," he said.

"Thanks." He laid out the band aids and put her suitcase by the bed.

"You forgot to ask," she said.

"Oh, that's right. Well guess which one?"

"I think you think my favorite is the Masters Garden."

"Nope! I think it was the Pococke Garden," he said.

"How'd you know!"

"I know you," he said. He grabbed his coffee, lit a cigarette, opened the window, and sat down on the desk.

"We can smoke in here?"

"Technically, no. It's against the rules. I've already gotten a warning notice about it. But if we keep the cigarettes out the window, we should be fine."

"Koala! Already getting into trouble. I don't want them to evict you," she said.

"They won't evict me for smoking. They have a kid operating a flamethrower in the quad, for heaven's sake," he laughed.

The next day, he felt her slip out of bed and walk to the desk. There was the sound of the lighter and then the window opening. He opened his eyes to find her smiling at him.

"Making sure to follow Koala procedure," she said, saluting.

"Thanks," he said.

He sat up in bed. "What's that?"

She held up the piece of paper. "Making a list of all the different things we have to do before I leave." She had a habit of making to-do lists, especially when traveling. He found it cute.

"What do you have down so far?"

"A few restaurants, pubs, some of the museums."

"Which restaurants?"

"There's supposed to be a really good place down the street called Chang-Mai. Heard of it?"

"I went once for lunch. It's awesome," he said.

"Great, maybe we could do that for dinner, tonight."

He suddenly remembered. "Oh! I forgot to tell you. That might not work. There's a concert at the Sheldonian tonight. I got us tickets. It was supposed to be a surprise."

"A concert?"

"Yeah, Vivaldi."

She smiled widely. "That's so sweet." He knew she knew he rarely planned ahead for anything, much less organized events, so she knew he was doing his best to let her see how happy he was that she was here.

"Well, I'm sorry, I know you're not a great admirer of classical, but the venue is beautiful, and it will be quite the experience, I think."

"Sounds good," she said.

"What other restaurants?"

"There's one in Jericho called Mama Mia's. The pizza is supposed to be excellent."

"Oh, you'll love that neighborhood. It's right by the Faculty. There's a cool movie theater there, too, the Phoenix. Maybe we could see something when we go for pizza." He told her about Anna.

"Nobody gets to have my Koala! I can't believe she called you like that out of the blue. That's weird. I bet her boyfriend would be furious." He thought about telling her about the Borough Market pub, and Michaela, and the underwear, and Eliot's dinners, but he bit his tongue.

"Pubs?"

"I have down Turf. You've been there, right?"

"Yeah, it's great. You'll like it. I was thinking we could pop in after the Sheldonian."

"But it'll be cold," she said. They looked out the window. Yesterday had been a complete one-off. It was now gray and windy.

"That's the best part, actually. They have these really amazing outdoor fire space heaters."

"Oh, that sounds nice," she said scribbling. "Okay, so there's that. What about the King's Arms? It's supposed to be close to Turf."

"It is. Right down the street. That was one of the stops on the GCR pub crawl I told you about."

"The last one I have down is the Bear."

"Yep, that one was on the crawl as well. It's just on the other side of college. It had great food. It feels like stepping into Bilbo's shire.

"Is the Ashmolean worth it?"

"I think so."

"Okay," she said, jotting it down.

"What about the other ones? The Pitt?"

"I don't know. They're popular, but to me they look boring."

"Good. Me too. So, we'll scratch those off."

He started laughing. "How much research did you do? You seem to know the city better than I do!"

"We're going to be living here! I have to know what's going on," she said.

She stood up from the desk and kissed him.

He leaned out the window, looked at the street approvingly, then looked back at her. "What about London?"

"Eh, I don't know. I'm not too interested. I mean, since we're here, we should go, I guess. Maybe we could show up a little early on Saturday before the train."

"Yeah. I went to the Tate Modern. Didn't like it. But I'm thinking the National Gallery might be nice. They have a huge Impressionism collection."

"Okay, I'll put it down. Saturday morning: National Gallery, London."

"Very official."

"Thank you," she said laughing.

"We should get snacks for the place. I eat out most of the time, so I don't have anything," he said.

"Sounds good," she said.

He got dressed, and then sat on the bed, waiting for her to get ready. She smiled at him in the mirror, as she was doing her hair.

"You're beautiful," he said.

"No," she said.

"Well, whatever, you don't know what you're talking about," he said.

She laughed. "Sorry I'm taking so long."

"It's fine. I guess that's going to be part of being married. Waiting for my wife constantly!"

She put a down jacket over her dress, put on her boots, and threw a scarf around her neck. "Ready?"

"Ready," he said.

They walked up Cornmarket.

"I should stop at the bank." He walked over to the machine, pulled out some money, handed her the bills, and pointed in the direction of the Tesco, which was up the street, past the graveyard.

"They have so many coins here, I noticed," she said.

"Yeah, cash is way more common here."

"I'll sound like a change monster, with all the coins jangling, as I walk," she said.

They stepped onto the sidewalk.

"Brr, it's cold," she said.

"Oh, this is nothing. Wait till the sun is down."

"I'm sorry," she said.

"For what?"

"Now that I'm here, I understand how it could be really lonely here."

"It's okay. I wish you were here, but it is what it is."

"Thanks for what you're doing."

"For what?"

"For building us a future. I'm sure everyone's going to be going crazy to hire you when you're done with the degree here. Maybe they'll want to keep you."

In principle, it was possible. Nothing with God was impossible. But realistically, it would be unlikely. He thought about explaining how his work was equally alienating to the theologians and philosophers, but he decided not to worry her. Either he would find a way to succeed, or he wouldn't. Worrying her over it wouldn't change that.

"Imagine our kids with funny little accents," she said.

He smiled. "We'll have to make sure they're instilled with a healthy dose of American questioning of authority."

"Oh, with how stubborn we both are, I'm sure that won't be a problem. They're probably going to be nightmares to control," she laughed. They reached the supermarket and went inside.

"Oh, look at that," she said, pointing to the signage. "Foreign foods. Sounds interesting." They took the escalator down to the basement level.

They reached the floor.

"Hah! There's an American section? Let's see what they think we like," she said. On the shelves were all the familiar artificially-flavored candies and other junk food items from home. When they were finished stocking up and had checked out, they decided to drop everything off at the apartment before heading to the Cathedral.

They put the groceries away in the shared kitchen.

"Where are the other floormates?"

"I never see them."

"Weird. Who are they?"

"It's a guy and a girl. I can't remember their names."

Alison raised an eyebrow playfully. "A girl, eh?"

He laughed. "Don't be stupid," he said. Though it had not occurred to him till now, he quickly dismissed the possibility that the floor mate was the one to have left the underwear in his room. She didn't seem to be the type.

On the way down the stairs, they bumped into Craig and Frank.

"Ah, so this must be the one," Craig said smiling.

"Guys, meet my fiancée, Alison."

"Alison, this is Craig and Frank. They're Americans, too."

"Coming from Texas I hear," Frank said.

"Yeah," she said.

"Well, he's smitten with you," Craig said, turning to him, "all he does is talk about you."

She looked at him and smiled.

"Glad you sorted out the whole underwear thing," Craig continued. Alison looked confused. "Underwear?"

Frank and Craig started laughing. "You didn't tell her?"

He told her about the underwear.

"That is so weird," she said.

"Well, guys, we have to be going. There's a concert at the Sheldonian soon."

"Good to meet you," Craig said to Alison.

"You too," she said.

When they got onto the sidewalk she looked at him. "Do you think it was Anna?"

"No. I think it was somebody else."

"Who?"

"I'm not sure, but I think it was a girl named Michaela."

"Michaela?"

"Yeah, she's another international student who lives in the building."

"You never mentioned her."

"Yeah, I saw no reason. She's an idiot," he said.

"She likes you?"

"I guess so," he said. He didn't know how to explain what he thought had really been going on with Michaela.

She laughed. "Well, I guess I'll have to keep my eye on her, too! All these sluts. They're everywhere!" He thought about telling her the bit about Klaus and Zoe, but that could wait.

At the entrance to the Cathedral, there was a group of tourists blocking the door.

He pointed to the names on the wall. "Those are the names of the war dead," he said.

Inside, there were candles burning. Evensong would be starting soon.

"Wow, it's beautiful," she said, admiring the stained glass.

"Yeah, the choir is very nice too."

He scanned the interior. "Let me see if I can talk to somebody," he said. He walked to the office, and tapped on the door which was ajar.

"Yes? Come in."

They walked inside to find the College Chaplain sipping tea.

"Hello, how may I help you?"

He gave his name. "I'm a member of college, and this is my fiancée, Alison."

"Very good to meet you," the Chaplain said.

"We're set to be married next summer back in the States. But recently we've been toying with the idea of being married here. Would it be possible for somebody at the college to hold a quick ceremony here at the Cathedral?"

"Well! How romantic," the Chaplain smiled. "But I'm afraid the Cathedral is booked for at least a year."

"I see. I'm sorry for the confusion, but we're not interested in having a ceremony with guests and so forth. We simply are looking for somebody to perform the vows for us."

The Chaplain shifted. "I see. Well, in principle that makes things far less complicated, as you note. Are you members of the church?"

"I'm a Christian, but neither of us is Anglican, no. But as a member of the college, my understanding is that the Cathedral is available for a ceremony."

"Yes, that's true. Do you have a date in mind?"

Alison and he laughed. "This week," he said.

The Chaplain laughed. "This week! Well, you two are really very serious about this, aren't you?"

"Yes," Alison said.

"Well, I feel terrible doing this, but I'm going to have to disappoint you. There's no way to perform a ceremony here at the Cathedral on such short notice. I hope you understand."

"Of course," he said. "Thanks for taking the time to discuss the matter with us," he said.

"My pleasure. Please accept my blessings for your future," the Chaplain said.

They walked outside onto the quad.

"Cigarette?"

"Yeah," she said. "I really thought for a second she was going to say okay. I could see she was seriously thinking about it," Alison said.

"I know. Obviously, it was an unusual request. They do weddings here, but they're huge productions with tons of guests planned out way in advance."

"I mean, all we need is somebody to administer the vows. I don't get it. Oh, well," she said.

They were quiet for a second. "I thought the Chaplain was supposed to be a man," she said.

"Long story. It's the Anglicans," he said.

"We better hurry if we're not going to miss the performance," she said.

They left Tom Quad, passing through Peck Quad on their way to the back exit.

"What's that?"

"That's the Library. Beautiful, right?"

"It's exquisite."

The French Head Porter, who usually would be working the front gate, smiled as they approached.

"*Monsieur* and *mademoiselle*," he said, tipping his cap.

"Hello, François," she said. When they left the college, she grabbed his hand, and whispered, "I have to start practicing my French. It's only a week until Paris!"

"I know, me too. I hardly know a word. I'm going to be a savage over there. You know how much the French hate tourists," he said.

"I like the French version of your name," she said.

"Yeah, it's not bad."

They walked past Oriel onto the High, and cut through Radcliffe Square, where they found a long line waiting for them at the theater. He realized he was underdressed, but he didn't care, since nobody would know who he was. It occurred to him that Alison sometimes probably wished he would dress up, but she never said anything about it. He would make sure not to let her down at the upcoming formal.

About ten minutes before the orchestra was to begin, they took their seats on the upper gallery. The venue was small enough that where one sat didn't affect the acoustic quality much. At least, not for their own purposes. He was far from an aficionado of classical. His ear was untrained, he knew frankly nothing about music theory, and he was here to enjoy the music naively. There was a great deal about tonight's performance that would be lost on him, that would be appreciated by a sophisticate. Then again, maybe there was an integrity to a primitive experience of the music with which a trained ear over time only lost touch.

"Somebody's waving to us," Alison said.

He looked down to see Manan seated a few rows in front of them.

"Manan, I didn't know you would be here tonight," he said.

"Nor did I expect to see you," Manan said.

"Manan, please meet my fiancée Alison," he said.

"Nice to meet you," she said. Manan nodded.

"Is anyone else joining you tonight?"

"I'm afraid not," Manan said. "Henry is still in town, and we've made dinner plans, so I'll be meeting him afterwards." Manan didn't pause to tell Alison who Henry was. Come to think of it, Manan hadn't made an effort to say anything about himself. He realized Alison must be lost.

"I'm sorry. Manan lives in the building. He's a new graduate student as well. He studies theology with Prof Wood," he said, turning to Alison.

"Ah, I see," she said smiling.

"Yes, that's correct," Manan said. He glanced down at his watch. "Ah, it seems the performance is about to begin. Good talking to you," Manan said, looking at him. The Indian prince turned around to face the orchestra.

The performance was nice. A little more boring than he'd expected. Really, what he enjoyed most was her company. Probably the highlight of the night was when she put her head on his shoulder. After everyone was finished clapping for the symphony, Manan turned around quickly, looked at him and said, "Well, goodnight, I'll be seeing you at college."

When they got outside, the stars were out.

"It's beautiful," she said.

"Yeah, there's no place like this at night. Look at the bridge," he said.

"What's it called again?"

"The Bridge of Sighs."

She was quiet for a minute.

"Do you think he liked me?"

"Who? Manan?"

"Yeah."

"Why?"

"He seemed not to. He hardly said a word to me, and he only looked at you the whole time."

"I noticed that too," he said. He didn't know how to explain the background about what had been unfolding at the college in Eliot's dinners. "You know, he's the son of a famous Bollywood director, he's an aristocrat, someone who wants to be a politician. I think sometimes that means he can be aloof."

"He's conceited," she said.

"Yes." There was no point in denying it.

"I think he doesn't like women," she continued. Coming from Alison, that was something. She had never made an observation like that about anyone before.

"Yes, Indian men can be very misogynistic."

"It's not that. It was something else." She paused. "I don't know, I don't want to be paranoid, but I'd be careful about him," she said to him.

They walked under the bridge. "It's through that little alley."

"Oh, wow, this is so cool," she said.

They emerged onto the front patio.

"It's a little shire! Just like you said," she laughed.

Inside was crowded, but eventually they were able to press up to the counter. The bartender came over to them. "What'll it be?"

He looked at Alison who looked back at the bartender. "You go first. I'm still deciding."

"I'll take a cider, please," he said.

"Hot or cold?"

"Cold, please," he said.

"Okay. And for you, miss?"

"Hot cider? Sounds good."

"It is," the bartender said.

"Okay, I'll have one of those, please," she said. She gave him the bill, and took the change.

She turned to him and laughed when the bartender left to make the drinks. "More change for my collection!"

The bartender set the ciders on the counter.

"Thanks," he said.

"Cheers," the bartender said.

They squeezed through the crowd, and stepped onto the side of the pub, where they took the walkway to the back patio.

"It must be our lucky day," she said, pointing to a small table right next to the fire.

"Perfect, let's snag it," he said.

She sat down, put her purse on the table, and took out her phone and set it down. She looked over at the sign. "Ha, Clinton was here?"

"Yep," he said.

"I'm sorry, but I'm going to have to take a picture of us," she said.

"But you know I take terrible pictures," he said.

"C'mon, just do it for me," she said.

"Fine," he said.

They took a picture together, at their table next to the fire burning, with the stars shining down. It was a little slice of something from a dream.

"A cider in the shire," she laughed.

They talked about everyone in Texas, and the future. Before they knew it, they had already had three ciders each. They were tipsy, it was getting late, the pub was emptying, and it was time to go home.

"Well, let's go," he said.

They walked through the little alley, back under the Bridge of Sighs, down the High, where they made a left on St Aldates, which took them past Tom Gate right before reaching the apartment.

"Do you want to see the koi again?"

"We're allowed in at night?"

"Yeah, I'm a member. I can go whenever I want."

The quad was still, the only sound the crunching of their feet against the frost quickly forming on the night ground. She wrapped her arm through his, kissing him on the cheek. "I love you," she said.

"I love you too," he said.

The moon was not bright, so it was dark, which meant they couldn't see the pond clearly, but they could hear the koi rustling in the lilies.

"I love it here," she said.

"Me too, but it's not the same without you."

He decided he didn't care what Sartre thought about it. He turned to her. "I'm nothing without you."

"I'm nothing without you. We're two peas in a pod," she said.

The next morning, the rain was pelting against the window, but rather than making him sad, as inclement weather usually did, today it made the room feel quaint.

When she could feel him stirring, she said, "I checked the forecast last night. It's supposed to clear up early this afternoon." She nuzzled her head under his chin. "I'm not really in a rush to leave anyway."

"Oh, wow, look." He pointed.

"A rainbow!" She leapt out of bed to get a better look. "Come here! It's a double rainbow!" The sun was breaking through the clouds, and the rain had stopped.

"It's magical here," she said.

"Yes, it's hard to believe sometimes."

"Is something wrong?"

He looked at her. "No, I'm fine. I just sometimes need to remind myself to make the most of this. I hope my work will turn out okay."

"Your work will be amazing. I miss you back in Texas, but now that I'm here, I see why you decided to take the opportunity to transfer. They brought you over here for a reason," she said.

She took her list off the desk and studied it.

She smiled, "Well, how about the King's Arms today?"

"Sounds good," he said. "Try not to take so long today to get ready!"

"I'm trying, I'm trying," she laughed. "Could you maybe run down and get me a coffee?"

"I was thinking we could stop at a place when we're out. There's one on Cornmarket I think you'll like."

"Okay, sounds good," she said.

When she was ready, they stepped onto the street. The rainbow had faded, but it had left its mark, imprinting the surroundings with an auburn afterglow. His thoughts turned to the passage from Genesis about the rainbow, about the covenant God made with man after the flood. He thought, too, about God's instructions to "be fruitful, and multiply." There was something noble about a man and a woman in love, two complementary pieces, fitting together to form a whole. It wasn't the fulfilment of Plato's *mythos*, the idea of completing oneself in another after one's own self having been split in two. It was, rather, about forming a higher whole altogether. His mind turned to the words of Christ, "Have ye not read, that he which made them at the beginning made them male and female, And said, For this cause shall a man leave father and mother, and shall cleave to his wife: and they twain shall be one flesh?" The words in the next verse followed, "So they are no longer two, but one flesh. What therefore God hath joined together, let not man put asunder." He wondered what was tearing Ben and Winnie's marriage apart. Of course, his bond with Alison was not immune to such danger. He understood that. That is why he would have to be vigilant to protect it. Stuart, after all, had been scheming from the outset to prevent them from marrying. And as much as he didn't want to admit it, Stuart probably wouldn't stop after the wedding. If anything, it might only incite him to struggle harder than he already was. No matter, he thought, Stuart was a weakling. It would be fine.

"This is it," he said, approaching the outdoor coffee stall.

"Oh, it's cute," she said.

"Hi," the man working said.

"Hi," he said.

The man looked to Alison.

"Uh, I'll have a nonfat latte, please," she said. The man started to make the drink. A half minute later, he placed the drink on the counter, waiting for the bill.

"Oh, I think he wanted something too," Alison said pointing to him.

He waited for the man to turn his attention to him, but the man didn't.

Alison asked him, "What do you want, sweetie?"

"Just a black coffee," he said.

"A black coffee, please," she told the man.

"Sure thing," the man said to her.

They took their drinks and walked into the street.

"That was weird. He didn't even look at you," she said.

"Yeah, whatever, it's fine. Muppet man liked you, so I guess he decided to be a tough guy with me," he said.

"Muppet man?"

"Yeah, he looked like a Muppet." She laughed, and hugged him.

They passed the graveyard, turning onto Broad. Standing on the wide promenade, with the Sheldonian in the distance, it was one of the most impressive views in all of Oxford.

"The King's Arms is on that corner across the street from the Sheldonian," he said.

When they got to the pub, it was crowded, so she took a seat at one of the last open spots on the benches. "I'll get you something," he said.

"Thanks."

"Same thing as last night?"

"Yeah, thanks, it's freezing," she said shivering.

When he came outside with the hot ciders, seeing the theater reminded him of the Vivaldi performance, which in turn led him to almost begin thinking about Manan and the theologians. He shook his head, and sat down.

"What is it?"

"Oh, nothing," he said.

They sipped their ciders, huddled together on the bench, listening to the conversations of everyone else.

"Excuse me." He came out of his daydreaming, and realized the man sitting across the bench was addressing them.

"Sorry, I was distracted. Yes?"

"When did you two get married?" The man wore a wrinkled dark blue collared shirt. He looked like he hadn't slept the night before, and although he looked to be in his early forties, he was probably considerably younger, given the obvious toll a long history of partying had clearly taken on him. He wasn't a vagrant. Instead, he had the demeanor of a hedge funder who had just learned he'd lost his fortune in a bad trade, or a film producer whose once famous company had just gone under, or a tycoon who'd just had his yacht repossessed. Whatever had been brewing for years, the crisis had arrived, and the man was in the midst of coping over it with a pint at the King's Arms. The man, desperate to talk, needed someone to listen. He decided to let the man get to his story.

"No, not yet. But close! We're engaged," Alison said.

"Oh, well then, congratulations," the man said.

He looked at the man kindly and gave his name. The man shook his hand.

"I'm Richard, Richard Squires." He looked at them. "I know, it sounds so, but it's not a fake name." The man stared into his pint. "Are you two just visiting?"

"I moved here recently. She's here for the week," he said.

"Ah, I see. You going to uni here?"

"Yeah." He could tell the man didn't want to know the details, so he didn't elaborate.

"Well, I'm from around here." There was a pause, as the man waited to see whether they were willing to listen.

"Yeah?"

"Yeah. Well, I have some family in London. But the main house is out here in the country," he pointed off in the direction of Headington. "Big, big mansion. The kind you would see in the movies," he said.

"I see." Alison was interested, but also a little uncomfortable, so she was letting him do the talking.

"I, uh, came out here last night with some friends. Stayed later than I had intended, ended up getting ditched, no way back to the house, lost my wallet, so I figured I'd just sit out here for a while before I decided what to do." The man didn't say so, but by friends, he got the impression the man meant prostitutes. It appeared the man had been robbed and was too embarrassed to call home for help. He could see why the man would feel so. He was way too old to be calling his parents, or whoever was back at the mansion, to drive into town and take him home after some party had gone off the rails.

"I'm sorry," he said.

The man sighed. "Yeah, well, when you been at it as long as I have, it's bound to happen. I think this may be rock bottom," the man laughed, as he sipped his pint.

"Want a cigarette?"

"Oh, yes, please. That would be great," the man said.

They all lit their cigarettes.

He looked at the man. "So what do you do, Richard?" He made an exception to his rule, because the man seemed so low, he thought it would buoy his spirits to know somebody was listening, that somebody did remember his name.

The man laughed. "I don't really know, to be honest. I don't really do anything. My family is fantastically rich, so I've never worked. I just live in the mansion and have people over. Big, big parties. That's it." The man pulled out a card. It had his name with the family crest.

"It's not really a business card. I don't work. But I'm supposed to have one, since it would be improper not to."

He took Richard's card and put it into his wallet, "Thanks."

"Oh, you're welcome. Well, really, I should be going. If you ever want to come over, let me know. I'll be around," the man said. He stood up, shook their hands, gazed off vacantly into the distance, and lumbered away.

Alison took out her phone. "I looked up the name. There's a Squires family in the area, and they're rich. Seems legitimate."

"You want to go party with that guy?"

"No! No way. I'm just saying it wasn't some scam. I thought maybe it was. It looks like he really was telling the truth. He seems sad. I wonder what happened," she said. They looked down the street, but he had disappeared.

They finished their ciders. She put her hand in his.

"What time is dinner?"

"It starts at seven-twenty."

"Want to get another coffee on the way home?"

"Sure, but not at the Muppet Stand. I'm boycotting him for now."

She laughed. "I was actually thinking of trying a place called the Grand Cafe. It's on High. Have you been there?"

"I've walked by it a bunch of times. But I never went in. I thought it would be fun to try it for the first time together. It's the oldest coffee house in England."

"Yeah, it says 1650 here."

"Sure, let's check it out."

They sat in the café for a while, sipping their coffees, and watching the buses and taxis drive by. In the time there, they counted no fewer than five different languages being spoken by customers.

"Tonight, after dinner, I'll have to try memorizing more of the basic French words we'll need," she said.

"Good idea. I should do that too."

When they got outside, it was starting to rain again, but only lightly. She opened an umbrella, and they strolled up the High.

When he had dressed into his suit back at the room, she adjusted his tie.

"Very handsome," she said.

"Don't laugh. Unfortunately, I have to wear the gown."

"It looks like a cape," she said.

He laughed, "That's one way to look at it."

They left the building, where he took her up the private access road, the one leading to the courtyard outside the Freind Room. When they got to the courtyard, they kissed. They took a photograph together that they both knew was one they would show their children one day. Here was mom and dad in Oxford when they were young, he thought.

He pointed to the building. "That's the Faculty dining hall."

"Ah, I see."

"I mention it because I should tell you something."

"What's that?"

"Klaus is having an affair with a married woman here. Her husband came here and confronted him about it. He told me not to mention it to anyone at the college, but I figured I'd tell you just so you would be aware when you met him, and so that you don't think I was being weird, if you felt like something was going on."

"That's crazy. The woman from the garden earlier?"

"Yeah, her name's Zoe."

"Her poor husband. What a piece of garbage she is," she said.

"What's going to happen?"

"I don't know. When I first got here, they were seeing each other. Then they got caught, and Klaus told me she had decided she needed some space. Now evidently they're back together."

She checked the time. "Oh! We have to go. It starts in five minutes." They put out their cigarettes, and walked up the stairs to the Ante-Hall.

He took her to the Buttery, where he told her the story about the Winkle-voss twins and Facebook. They got a bottle of wine simply for the sake of the ritual, and sat down to dinner. The food wasn't particularly good, and they had nobody else to talk to. But they liked it that way.

That night, back at the room, he watched her dream after she had dosed off in bed with her French dictionary out.

He woke up the next day with a pit in his stomach. The first three days of Alison's visit had flown by. Tomorrow would be the last day in Oxford, then it would be off to the station in London to catch the train to Paris. The stay in Paris would be short, three days, and then she would be back off to the States, and his exile in Oxford would resume.

He realized she must have felt his sadness, because she stroked his arm gently when she woke up. "It's not over yet," she said.

"I know," he said. Time was strange like that, he thought. It was all a matter of scale. In principle, everything was finite. Their entire life together was ultimately fleeting, he knew. If he was so sad about the brevity of their next few days together here in Oxford and Paris, in a way the fact that one day they would both die should make him even sadder. But it was too remote, too distant, or at least he hoped so, for it to register. Of course, there was the afterlife anyway, though he knew that Alison still wasn't sure about that. He knew all the arguments for discarding the hope for a heaven, arguments that alleged it was simply the desire for a "revenge against time."

People who made that argument misunderstood. They thought only people who couldn't accept suffering for what it was had the hope of something beyond this world. What a confusion, he thought. He was entirely reconciled to suffering. Though he knew he had still not yet done so, he understood that he had to care first for God and the kingdom, and not Alison. He knew she probably secretly resented this about him, since from her perspective it meant he didn't love her fully, but that was untrue. He loved her more than she knew, even if there was no way of proving it. The trouble was that she didn't yet understand the love of God, so she misunderstood his love for her. She saw his love of God and his love of her as being in competition. But they weren't. He knew there was a way to reconcile them harmoniously, not only leaving both intact, but actually magnifying each in turn. He would find a way, and he trusted God to show him that way. To her, what seemed to be selfishness or indifference, was really selflessness. He knew that would sound self-serving if he said it, but it was true. Maybe this was his sacrifice: that in loving his wife more than the husbands who were without God loved theirs, he would be misunderstood, taken by her, and others, to somehow love her less than they loved their wives, when in fact he loved her more. "Love suffers all things . . . "

Of course, that was simply the way of the world. There were men who would drink, and gamble, and cheat, but they were admired as big men of the community, respected by their friends and family, envied by their coworkers. Men whose view of love was dictated by whatever conformed to their golfing schedule or whatever other vain amusements they spent their time on. He had seen it before growing up with his friends' parents. They pretended to have a shared life together, when really they didn't. The emotional estrangement was defended by everyone in the name of supposedly avoiding falling prey to co-dependency. But he had always felt, even as a child, that was a lie. The husband and wife simply didn't like each other, so they veiled the fact through the pretense of having their own friends, and hobbies, and interests. In a way, there was a shrewdness about it. After all, these men knew their wives secretly liked it that way, since there was the appearance of devotion, as if these serious men of the world had put their wives and family first, the proof being that by their own admission they cared more about their wives than even God, since, after all, many of them were proud atheists, so their wives and family and friends would tolerate their marital indiscretions and other failures. They had mortgaged themselves to the world, so that meant everything they did was forgivable. The one thing that was unforgivable would be to die to the world and live to God. That was treason. Secular women could usually accept a man who had another woman. But they could not accept a man who had God.

For everyone who went that way, mortgaging themselves to the world, they would pursue whatever idea they had of happiness, invariably hurting themselves and others along the way as they failed to find it. He thought it was telling that those who did not know God would dedicate their lives to seeking something illusory that the Scriptures didn't even once bother to mention. Existence was not about attaining happiness in this world, but most people chose to pretend that it was. To be sure, they had reason to think that what he wanted to seek, the kingdom of God, was merely a mirage. But what they were seeking was a known impossibility, a true phantom, and yet they persisted in chasing after it nonetheless. Seeking after happiness was a dishonest optimism, a disfigured idealism. People acted as if pursuing happiness were nobly braving fate, but really, if it were so noble and exceptional, it wouldn't be the case, as it was the case, that nearly everyone he knew was living that way. There wasn't anything extraordinary about it at all, since it was so typical, so average. If they were being honest, what they really wanted, or should want, was joy. Happiness was said to come about in that elusive equilibrium between oneself and the world, between one's desire and reality. Joy, however, came entirely from within, and had nothing to do with the world, because it came from gratitude. It was eternal.

To find joy, peace with God was necessary. But because the pursuit of worldly happiness was precisely the willful rejection of God, it only led to what he saw everywhere around him, namely misery. What a paradox. People who in the name of happiness chose misery, all simply because they were willing to forgo joy, so long as that meant being able to ignore God. He realized he could not control the future, or defy time. All he could do is make the most of what he was given.

"I love you," he said.

"I love you," she said. They kissed, because there was no point in talking.

Today was Thanksgiving in the States, and here today at the college, there was a special dinner being held for the American graduate students at the Deanery. But after last night's formal dinner, he was getting cold feet. He put on his usual white t-shirt.

She looked up at him, "Do you want to go to the dinner tonight?"

"Honestly, not really. I hope that doesn't disappoint you."

"No, it's fine. I was hoping you didn't want to go, either. There's always next year," she said.

"What else is on your list?"

"There's the arboretum.

"Oh, that's very nice. I've walked through a couple times. You'll love it. Let's do that."

She got dressed faster than usual, and smiled. "There! How was that?" She walked up and kissed him.

"Want to walk through the college on the way?"

"Yeah, I want to check in on our little fishy friends."

At the fountain, he stared at Mercury, as Alison played with the fish. The more he thought about it, the less sense the statue made to him. He was going to have to figure out what it symbolized.

She hopped to her feet. "Ready?"

"Yeah," he said.

They walked up the stairs when they heard a voice calling him.

"Hey, it's me," said Klaus. Klaus was evidently heading back to the office at Kilcannon after getting out of a Governing Body meeting.

He walked up to them.

"Klaus, this is Alison, Alison this is Klaus."

Klaus smiled, "Hello."

"Good to meet you," she said. There was a pause. "He's so happy to be here," she added, pointing to him.

"Yes, well, Oxford is a great place, isn't it? How long are you here?"

"We leave for Paris tomorrow," she said.

Klaus turned to him. "You didn't say you were going to Paris. You should have said something. I have friends there with whom I could have put you in touch." He could tell Alison wanted to say there was still time for Klaus to do so. He was relieved when she didn't.

"Well, I must be going. I have a student to meet with. See you tonight at seminar?" He had completely forgotten. Tonight there was a speaker giving a talk on Hegel at the Strawson Room. He could see Klaus resented the fact it appeared he was not coming to the talk. If that were so unacceptable in Klaus's view, how, he wondered, did Klaus justify lying so egregiously all the time. Klaus, after all, was not really off to a tutorial, as he said. Klaus, who had already said the college had relieved him of teaching duties, must have forgotten what he'd said. The trouble with lying was trying to remember them, in order to fit them together.

"Oh, right. Yes, see you there," he said.

"Good to meet you," Alison said. "Excuse me, I have to use the restroom." She smiled, and started across the quad. She had left unexpectedly, before Klaus had managed to leave, so it was just the two of them. There was a silence for a few seconds, and then Klaus looked right into his eyes.

"What's your favorite film?"

It was an odd question, obviously, but he knew that Klaus knew he would understand that it was Klaus's intention, to ask a supposedly innocuous question, but in a somewhat awkward context, just to see how he would react. Well, it wasn't simply to see how he would react, since the answer itself, presumably, would give Klaus valuable insight into his mindset too.

"*Drive*," he said without blinking.

Klaus was genuinely incredulous. He had answered so fast, so nonchalantly, yet assuredly. Klaus clearly had seen it too, and his supervisor was at a complete loss as to how he could have thought so highly of a film that Klaus hadn't liked at all.

"*Drive?*"

There would be no retraction, not even an intimation of one. In a flash of insight, he knew his reason for loving the movie corresponded directly with the very same reason Klaus had so disliked it. There were natural men, and there were spiritual men. In the flesh, it wasn't what one knew, but only what one could prove. And proof was always a matter of what others would find satisfying. If others couldn't be convinced, then it wasn't proof, and because knowing was taken to presuppose proof, one accordingly was said not to know. In the Spirit, it was different. Something could be known, even if it couldn't be demonstrated to others, even, in fact, if they thought it was bizarre or baseless. Something could be given to understand to one alone, in a clearly compelling way only one was positioned to see for oneself, and it was up to one to act on it. That was what discernment was. Being misunderstood by others who did not see what one saw simply came with the territory.

"Yeah," he said, with just enough trace of surprise to suggest he was shocked that Klaus hadn't liked it.

He waited for Klaus to respond, holding the silence. Klaus looked over his shoulder back to the restroom where Alison was.

"Well, anyway, I have to go. See you tonight," he said.

"Sounds good," he said.

A few minutes later, Alison returned.

"So, that was Klaus," she said.

"That was Klaus. I'm sorry, I completely forgot about tonight's seminar."

"Don't worry about it. You take care of what you need to take care of. Don't worry about me," she said.

"I can go to the talk. If you want, you could meet us all at the restaurant after? We're usually there around six-thirty."

"Okay. Which restaurant?"

"Quod," he said.

"Oh, the fancy one on High?"

"Yeah."

They were quiet for a little while.

"I don't trust him," she said finally. He could tell she thought he wouldn't want to hear it. In a way, he didn't want to. He had come all the way to Oxford, and his career was in this man's hands. It was distressing to know that something clearly was off about it.

"I know," he said.

"He's mean to you," she said. "He ignores you."

"He's busy," he said.

"No, he's not. He just pretends to be. He could make time. That's his job," she said.

They were quiet again.

"He actually reminds me of someone."

"Who?"

"I'm trying to figure it out," she said. She stuck out her finger. "Oh, I know. He reminds me of Bert," she said. Given the fact that Bert had been so rude to her in Palm Springs, it stood to reason that the individual in question would be someone with whom she had formed a negative association. But he could see there was more to it.

"How's that?"

She looked into space and crinkled her brow trying to think of how to explain it. "I don't know. Big face, smug, always has something to say . . . "

He started laughing. "Yeah, I know what you mean," he said.

At fifteen till five, he left for the Strawson Room. She would stay behind at the room, and then meet him at Quod. After having spent so much time in the world of the theologians at the college, it felt odd reentering the world of the philosophers. Quiller was in his usual seat, wearing his same red sweater. He took a seat and did his best to concentrate on what the speaker had to say. When the speaker concluded, Quiller asked his customary first question, he listened quietly to the exchange that followed, and then listened to the other questions too. Ordinarily, he might want to interject, and he had a number of things that he thought he could say which were relevant, but he no longer saw the point. He was still trying to find the words for what he really wanted to say, what he would try to say in his dissertation, and the discussion tonight really had nothing to do with any of that.

When they came to the restaurant, Alison was waiting outside. Klaus walked by without saying anything, and the group went in, leaving the two of them alone on the street for a moment.

"How'd it go?"

He wanted to be positive. "It was good. The speaker seems nice," he said. He opened the door, "We don't have to stay long. Thanks for coming," he said.

They took a seat at the table with the others and listened to the conversation continue. The speaker was busy explaining the finer points of some disagreement between Hegel and Habermas. He listened attentively, but did not say anything.

The meals came. Klaus had a burger, like before. He took a knife and stabbed a fry. He glanced over at Alison, whom was watching Klaus eat. The meal ended, and they said their goodbyes.

"We'll have to talk more about your dissertation next month," Klaus said.

"Sounds good. Send me an email whenever you want to set a meeting," he said.

They got outside and started up the High Street. He waited for it.

"Did you see Klaus using a fork?"

"Yeah, I wasn't going to say anything. I wanted to see if you would. I saw that last time, too."

"That's so weird. Does everyone here do that?"

"I'm not sure," he said.

"Do you think he does just to look fancy?"

"Maybe," he said.

They both laughed. If his supervision was going to be a challenge, that was fine. He would keep a good attitude about it, which meant laughing.

Their last two days in England were a blur. First, there were all the other college gardens they saw. Maybe their favorite was the sunken quad at Worcester, although the finest garden in all of Oxford was maybe at St John's, a place Alison particularly loved. The movie at the Phoenix wasn't any good, but the pizza at Mama Mia's was excellent, and he knew walking home that night in Jericho would be something he'd never forget. Then there was the bookstore. At Blackwell's, he had been standing in the philosophy section, staring at all the volumes, ruminating over how in the world he would find something worthwhile to contribute to all that had already been written. She had walked up behind him, after finishing her own shopping there, and, intuiting his concern, said, "Don't worry. One day you'll have a book here too." She smiled at him, and he knew she was right. It would simply take time. In London, they were drowsy from waking up early, and the traveling made them anxious, since they had to keep an eye on their luggage and the time. When they reached Paddington, they went straight to the museum. They ended up splitting apart as they made their way through the exhibits. He found himself alone, and felt a way he'd never felt before, as he looked at the painting before him, Bellini's *The Agony in the Garden*. He stared intensely at it for a long time, pondering whether he himself was forsaking Christ. Getting married was not the issue. Far from it. It was being here in Oxford. That was the issue. How to create work that wasn't a betrayal, that was the question haunting him.

They took the Chunnel to Paris, with Alison's head on his shoulder as she slept, their hands entwined. They were there for three days. They saw the birds at the market on the Seine together, and he was so content he felt like he could die.

Twenty-two

FTER the visit, the months passed, if albeit slowly. He came to know the city well, even settling into a routine, reading voraciously and writing frequently, while attending as many seminars and talks as possible. He was soaking up as much knowledge as he could. At the same time, there were the ordinary affairs of life, finding his favorite restaurants and cafés, making a habit of exploring the city's extensive walking trails. By the end of spring, Oxford had become as close to home as it ever could be without her. Still, he knew challenges lay ahead.

Indeed, they were fast approaching. For although nobody he knew there said so to him, everyone recognized that both intellectually and institutionally he was an orphan. Klaus was barely going through the motions, Quiller had remained aloof, and Eliot had withdrawn after his advances designed to recruit him to the network met with failure. The other students were all invested in the system, obsequiously doing whatever they were told to do by their supervisors, hoping that if they complied, they might be one of the lucky few rewarded with an academic job somewhere. The world of academia, he realized, was a cult, and most of his fellow students had Stockholm Syndrome.

The fact he didn't want to participate in what was supposed to come with the professionalization process of graduate school meant that he had focused solely on the work itself. As a result of his efforts, he had a serviceable thesis already taking shape. Once they had moved into a place here in Oxford after the wedding, he would set a viva date to defend the thesis next year, and when he had the degree, they would see what came next.

Perhaps they might move to Europe, since although he still hadn't told her so, it was appearing increasingly less likely that Oxford would ever want to keep him as a fellow. And presumably, there was always California waiting. His old teachers at the philosophy department, including Horowitz, had mentioned the availability of a lectureship there. In some ways, that might be the best option, since the idea of moving home to California was appealing to him. But Europe was Alison's strong preference. When he had floated the idea of California to her, she was adamantly against it. According to her, it would be selling his work's promise far too short to return to his undergraduate department. He should instead keep his options open, she thought. Of course, her judgment that he would have employment options from which to choose presupposed that his work would actually be allowed to speak for itself, an assumption he knew wasn't likely to hold. The trouble, of course, was that there was no way of explaining to her the existence of a powerful international cabal of people, including some of those here at Oxford whom he knew personally, who didn't like the direction his research was taking, and who would gladly stop at nothing to destroy it, if the opportunity presented itself. Then again, if California were off the table, living with his wife in Paris as a writer would not be so bad at all, he thought to himself, as his focus drifted back to the page he was reading here at the desk. He realized that his mind could easily descend into an endless maze, ruminating over what the future might hold, but it was fruitless to do so. The words entered his consciousness as a welcome admonishment, "Lean not on your own understanding, in all your ways submit to him . . . "

Tomorrow was his transfer of status meeting with Quiller and Hodges, so he was preparing by reviewing his notes. He wasn't nervous, as it was merely a formality, something virtually everyone passed, and even if he was already potentially subject to heightened scrutiny from the powers that be, the objective standards for passing were sufficiently low for it to be impossible for anyone at this early juncture to plausibly contend his work was below grade. If anything, then, he was looking forward to it, since tomorrow's discussion would force Quiller to engage with the work seriously, to some extent, at least. He would be able to gauge what sort of criticisms Quiller and others might be planning to use against the work later at the viva. It was a bit like cards, and tomorrow the other side would have to show its hand. He wasn't anticipating any substantial philosophical criticism of the work. He knew that both Quiller and Hodges weren't sufficiently versed with the texts and figures he was drawing upon to do so. It would be interesting, then, to see how they tried to attack the work. Probably, they would use the fact that this was only a transfer of status meeting, the work's first official review, as an excuse to avoid discussing the content carefully, pretending that it was still too inchoate for any sustained discussion. Eventually, though, they would have to face it, since there would be the confirmation of status meeting later too, which served as the dress rehearsal for the viva itself. And, in any case, it was tradition for students working in his area to give a talk at the Strawson Room. The point, he knew, was that there was only so long before Klaus and Quiller would have to publicly address the work, and he knew that everyone knew they weren't yet prepared to do so. It was exactly what had happened with Carrell in Texas, so he wasn't surprised, though it was disappointing. He had hoped things might be different here. He looked out the window and sighed. Human nature is human nature, he thought.

He set his pen down. It would be golden hour soon, which meant walking over to the quad. It was a habit he had developed as the spring progressed, and the daylight hours increased. On his way out, he reached the ground floor where he could hear laughter coming from Michaela's room. Many of them had only come on a one-year master's program, so they would be growing ever wilder as their time in Oxford drew to a close, and they attempted to make the most of it. Soon, after all, it would be back home to the States for them, where they would be lucky to find a job commensurate with their education, or where, even if they did, it would end up being something soul-draining, certainly nothing to compare with the elation of the year they'd been able to spend partying in a private fantasy world reminiscent of *Harry Potter* or *Alice in Wonderland*. Some of them probably hadn't cracked open a single book the entire time they were here, he realized. As far as they were concerned, all that mattered was that the degree would be on the résumé, and they would have stories with which they could regale everyone they knew at home. In a technological world wherein even an educational institution as Oxford had been so commercialized and corporatized, the others in Michaela's room had paid for an experience, and gotten one. It was an investment, nothing more, nothing less.

He sat on the steps of the quad and lit a cigarette. Some students were walking with dinner from the Hall. A few dons were leaving their offices to go home. In a few minutes, the quad had emptied entirely except for a couple of porters patrolling the grounds. Though the sun was still out, the moon was also visible, and a golden aura enshrouded everything in majesty, the twilight's transitory manifestation between day and night reminding him of the fleetingness of existence itself, hovering as it did so fragilely between birth and death. His mind turned to Tertullian, whom he knew had said something about how nature itself, including the celestial bodies, was a reflection of spiritual matters, including the Resurrection.

When night fell, overtaking day completely, he stood to leave, when suddenly he was pierced by an urge to walk through the college's cloisters, something he rarely did. Deciding his transfer notes could wait a while longer, he walked across the quad, past the Hall, and through the cloisters, which took him to the Meadows Building. What he found surprised him.

At the gateway to the Masters Garden were two imposing security guards from outside the college. Standing in front of them were a man and women with a list, evidently a guest list. The man was somebody from the Censors' office he had seen before and recognized. The woman, who was dressed very smartly, looked to be some sort of event coordinator, but not with the college. He could see the tops of white guest tents that were set up on the lawn, there was the sound of jazz coming from a live band, the voices and laughter from dozens of partygoers carrying over the garden's stone walls. He couldn't recall receiving any email from the college about an upcoming soirée, though it wasn't too uncommon for the college to host private events. Curious to see more, he walked to the gateway.

"Sorry, sir, this is a private event," the woman said politely but firmly.

"Oh, yes, of course, but I am a Member. I'm simply out for a walk here at the college," he said.

Recognizing that he knew she herself was not a Member, she softened her tone slightly, but iterated her point. "Are you on the invitation list?"

"No, I certainly would never intrude." He looked at the private security. "Nonetheless, presumably it's not Top Secret. What's the occasion?"

The man standing next to her grinned, evidently admiring his wit, and the woman with the guest list, who was obviously flummoxed, was saved from having to respond by the sudden arrival of a boorish group of partygoers attempting to enter. There were three of them, a snobbish woman in her early fifties with black hair, a man, who appeared to be her date, also in his fifties, with silver hair and tan skin. She was dressed expensively, with lots of diamond and gold jewelry, her breasts drooping out of her low-cut top, while the man was wearing jeans and a crimson Harvard sweatshirt. The third, a younger brunette woman apparently in her thirties, perhaps an assistant, since it was clear she wasn't their daughter or friend, trailed behind the couple.

"Excuse me, excuse me, sir," the woman with the guest list said.

"Is there a problem here?" the woman on the Harvard man's arm snapped.

"Are you on the list, madam?"

"Am I on the list? Who do you think you are? My assistants drafted up the list, you little twat. Tonight's dinner is only happening because my friends at the college here provided the space at the last second when I asked for it after Balliol bungled everything." One of the security guards at the gate whispered into the ear of the woman working the door.

"I'm, I'm, I'm very sorry, Ms Max—" the woman's voice trailed off.

The man was interjecting, "Don't worry about it! She's like that with everyone," he laughed goofily. Evidently, the man was enjoying immensely the fact that they had been stopped at the door, largely because of the way he was so badly underdressed.

The snobbish woman turned to the woman behind her. "Sarah, where's Andy? Have you seen Andy, Jeffrey?"

"I think he's already inside, G-Max," the female assistant said.

"Well, I want you to tell him that—". She paused, and looked at the woman holding the list. "Tell me, what is your name?"

"Eleanor."

"Right, yes, whatever. Tell Andy that someone has to fire Eleanor. It's unseemly to have someone so thick as this bothering guests."

The man with her in the sweatshirt laughed, "Sorry, she's incorrigible," he said, and the three of them all walked inside, leaving Eleanor and the man from the college both shaken and speechless.

He looked at them both. "Who are they?"

Nobody heard his question, because there was already a flurry of activity on the radios, with various assistants now buzzing around, all thrown into a tizzy by the snobbish woman's dust up with the people working the door. He stepped onto the Broad Walk, took the access road back to the street, entered the building, and took a seat at his desk. Three cars were arriving across the street at the college. They were very fancy, two Edinburgh green Jaguars and a black Bentley. They idled at the gate to the access road for a few minutes, then drove up the road, where they parked in the courtyard to the Freind Room, where, he remembered, Klaus had been forced to confront Zoe's husband with the wineglass. The drivers stayed in the cars, while some security exited the vehicles and formed a perimeter. He was bored, and this was all very intriguing, so he looked up the license plate of the Bentley: "AY03 DOY." At first, he was shocked by what he read, but then he realized he shouldn't be. If the Queen herself was the college's Visitor, it wasn't so inconceivable that her son might pop in for a visit too from time to time. He wondered who else was in attendance tonight at the garden party. For one thing, the couple he had just encountered at the gate had certainly acted like they were very important.

TWENTY-THREE

IT was ten minutes till the meeting would begin, which was to be held at an office on Mansfield. He stood down the street smoking a cigarette, composing himself. He had all his major claims worked out, and he had prepared a number of responses to various objections he might receive. He was confident. More important than the actual philosophical material itself was his demeanor, he knew. Quiller, who was shrewd, would be probing him, testing his character, studying his personality, and trying to size up how exactly to move forward. It was important to give Quiller as little to go on as possible. Presumably Quiller, or at least whoever handled him, had access to his electronic communications, which would mean Quiller would know a lot more about him than either of them could acknowledge openly in any professional setting. Both each would know the other knew this, and the question then was how to exploit it to his own respective purposes. He was of course familiar with the longstanding relationship between British Intelligence and Oxford academics. A.J. Ayer, for example, himself a philosopher at the college last century, had worked for MI6. Surely many others had as well, though of course clandestinely, including probably Quiller. Quiller's aura of invincibility gave it away, since it was so obviously the attitude of a man who was thoroughly relishing the fact that he thought he knew something nobody else around him did. Hodges, who would be there as the second examiner, wasn't worth worrying about. He was there simply because Faculty procedure dictated there be two examiners for the meeting, and he would be deferring to Quiller in everything.

At the hour, he knocked on the door.

"It's open, please come in," Quiller said.

He stepped into a large office, though still less spacious than Klaus's. There were the trademark white bookcases with the volumes, a rare but understated rug, an antique desk, a couch, and two chairs.

Quiller walked to the rug, and gestured to the couch. "Have a seat." He sat and nodded to Hodges. Hodges nodded.

"Can I offer you anything? Tea? Coffee?"

"Tea sounds good, please," he said.

Quiller smiled. "Yes, of course," he said, adjusting the collar over his red sweater. He always took coffee, never tea, and Quiller knew this. The fact that he took tea here instead, Quiller recognized, was his way of telling Quiller to junk the scouting report. He wanted Quiller to know he was entirely on his own now, that everything Quiller might have thought he knew about him or this situation didn't matter, and that Quiller would have to improvise accordingly. Some silly psychological profile Quiller had read about him wasn't going to cut it.

"Black or green?"

"Black," he said. He could see Quiller had expected him to say green.

"One minute." While Quiller brewed the tea, he and Hodges chatted about nothing.

"Here you are," Quiller said, setting down the tea.

"Looks great. Thank you," he said.

"You're most welcome. Well, with that out of the way, why don't we turn to business?"

Hodges spoke, "Yes. I'm here in capacity as a second assessor, so I won't be saying much, though if I have any pressing questions, I will be sure to ask."

Quiller leaned back in his chair, put his hands on his lap, and crossed his legs.

"I will have a number of questions in due course, but before we get to those, why don't you lay out what you take the central claim, or claims, to be of your current project as you currently envision it developing."

He laid out the central philosophical claims he wished to defend, a little bit about their historical origin, as he understood it, mentioned a few objections he thought it would be necessary to address, and then said a bit about how all of this related to certain key texts which were at the moment being widely read in Paris. There was, he thought, the perfect balance between originality and inheritance, philosophical argument and exegesis.

Quiller framed his response in terms of Heidegger, which was what he had expected Quiller would do.

"If I'm not mistaken, it sounds as if you have in mind doing something Kierkegaardian. Would you consider the overall thrust of your argument to be an internal, or an external, critique of Heidegger?"

There followed a fairly long back and forth about the existential analytic, the relation between philosophical anthropology and fundamental ontology, the role of methodological atheism in Heidegger, and then, toward the very end, the relation between philosophy and theology. When it became clear that his command of the ideas was beyond question, and there would be no way to plausibly suggest he was undeserving of passing, he could see Quiller begin laying the groundwork for how to regroup for the confirmation meeting, and, eventually, the viva itself.

"I think you have a number of very interesting and very promising ideas here," Quiller said looking at him. Quiller looked to Hodges.

"Yes, yes, I agree fully," Hodges said.

"The issue, if there is one at this stage, to my mind concerns the matter of the literature. What sort of contribution are you intending to make with the thesis? It will be important that is made clear to your examiners at the viva. In order to focus the contribution, you intend to make, I think it is imperative that you draw more extensively than you have thus far on the secondary literature."

It was now clear. Quiller, who could not object substantively to any of the work on philosophical grounds, would deploy a forking move he'd seen used against the work of other students. If one focused on the primary texts themselves, one was accused of ignoring the relevant secondary literature. If one instead focused on the debates in the secondary literature, one was accused of not engaging sufficiently with the primary texts. Either way, there was no winning, and regardless of which path one took, one would be criticized for not having taken the other one instead. He had known about this trick coming into the meeting, so he had frontloaded things with the primary texts only, knowing that the criticism doing so would elicit, that he had not sufficiently consulted the secondary literature. At the next meeting, then, Quiller would praise the way in which he had addressed the original lack of treatment of secondary sources, but then allege that there was insufficient attention paid to the primary sources. It was all very predictable. It would be tedious having to jump through the hoops, but he knew, given how the meeting here was going, that he could navigate it. Quiller was pinned with the work, and there was nothing Quiller could do about it.

Quiller and Hodges stood.

"Thank you for coming today," Hodges said.

"Thank you for taking the time to discuss my work with me," he said.

"Thank you," Quiller said.

"Thank you," he said.

He was about to leave when Quiller spoke. "Oh, I presume you'll be at the Strawson Room tonight?" There was a talk.

"Oh, yes. As it happens, Prof O'Malley is a former student of Prof Carrell's," he said.

"Ah, yes, that's right," Quiller said. Quiller let him out, "Well, I shall see you there."

The speaker, Maureen O'Malley, was an established, fairly senior professor from Sussex. She had studied in Texas under Carrell, though he himself hadn't ever met her, since by the time he entered the program, she had already finished her work and moved on to Sussex. If he went to the talk, it was certain that O'Malley would mention Carrell at the dinner, since Carrell was still a mentor to her, and somebody with whom she regularly collaborated. Klaus, of course, would be there too, so it would be an opportunity also to see how Klaus chose to speak of Carrell. He thought about it. O'Malley would know that he had once studied with Carrell, she would know that he had transferred here to work with Klaus, and she would be duly intrigued. In all likelihood, she and Klaus would speak about it all sometime today before this evening's talk, though there was no way to know what Klaus would say about the situation, or what Carrell might have O'Malley say about it to Klaus on his behalf. Many people in such a situation would allow curiosity to get the better of them, asking questions they shouldn't ask, or saying things they shouldn't say. He would exercise extreme discretion, and say as little to anyone as possible. He thought about it, how what he had recently read in the Proverbs somewhere counseled something to that effect, "Whoso keeps his mouth and his tongue keeps his soul from troubles." For the first time in months, the prospect of attending a talk at the seminar filled him with genuine enthusiasm. If he were wise, it could really provide insight into the state of affairs, and where he stood, as he prepared for the homestretch toward the viva.

At the talk, things went as one would expect. Quiller was in his red sweater in his usual seat. Fernandez wasn't there, but Klaus was. Manan and Joseph were, too. Seeing Joseph there was not too surprising, but seeing Manan there was. Usually, the theologians never attended the seminar. Seated next to Manan was Ben, who looked uncharacteristically disheveled and glum. He would have to ask what was wrong after the talk.

"Hi guys," he said, as he took his seat at the table.

"Hello," Manan said.

"How've you been?" Joseph asked.

"Really good. I had my transfer meeting this morning, which I think went well. I've been getting a lot of writing done, and I feel like my ideas are coming together." Manan and Joseph, who both knew Quiller had been one of the assessors, glanced over at Quiller. Quiller looked and smiled.

"Fabulous to hear you seem to be making such fine progress," Joseph said.

"Thanks. I guess the talk's about to begin, but if you're going to dinner afterwards, it would be great to catch up."

"Yes, that sounds great. I won't be able to stay long because Melissa and I have plans, but I'll certainly be able to stay for a drink."

"I'm afraid I won't be able to make it for dinner after the talk. Eliot is having over some people," Manan said. Ben, who was still staring blankly at the wall, said nothing.

"Oh, that sounds nice. If you would, please tell Prof Wood I say hi." He knew Manan knew he knew he was no longer being invited to the dinners. Being cordial about it, and going out of his way to tell Manan to tell Eliot hello, was his way of letting Eliot know that it didn't matter to him.

"I'll be sure to do so," Manan said, slightly flustered.

"All right everyone," Klaus said, raising his voice. "We should get started. Thank you all for attending our fortnightly seminar here at the Strawson Room. Our speaker tonight is Prof Maureen O'Malley from the University of Sussex. I could go on and on about all the things she's published, but I'll simply draw your attention to her forthcoming book, due out with OUP later this year, about the role of the emotions in practical reason. Tonight, Maureen will be speaking about Levinas."

"Thank you, Klaus. It's a delight to be here." She made some other preliminary remarks, and read the paper. Quiller asked his first question, and after he received a response from Maureen, he stood to leave. "I'm very sorry, but I have family obligations to which I must attend." He nodded goodbye to Klaus, and left. The other questions were unremarkable, and when the discussion had lost its steam, Klaus spoke.

"Okay, please thank our speaker." There was clapping.

"Those of you who are regular attendees of the seminar know that we have dinner at Quod. It's an opportunity to continue the conversation. Everyone is welcome to join us," he said. The table stood up, and everyone began meandering out the building to the restaurant. Something Maureen had said about the Face in Levinas had triggered a thought in Joseph about Herder's treatment of language. As they walked up the High St, he listened to Joseph work out the idea.

"The more I think it through, it seems to me Levinas would want to dismiss Herder's account of the origin of language out of hand, simply on the grounds that because it's naturalistic, it fails to capture precisely what makes human language human. Perhaps there's something to that sentiment, though I think most people sympathetic to Levinas's view grossly oversimply Herder's position." As they reached the door, he considered noting how the disagreement between Levinas and Herder seemed to be a matter pertinent to a thinker such as Buber, but he was so tired of talking about Buber after years of having listened to David back in Texas, that he decided not to bring up Buber. His memory turned to the day out at the lake, and how he had felt then that all the talking his friends did never went anywhere. It wasn't any different here, however, he realized. Whether it was on a Texas lake or in an Oxford pub, the debates were endless, with no satisfactory resolution ever drawing any closer. A metaphor came to mind to explain it. It was like a game from childhood. But instead of playing with action figures, like Teenage Turtles or GI Joe, as adult academics, everyone selected a favorite thinker. One then dressed up one's favorite thinker, retrofitting him with armor and weapons, those were the interpretation one gave him that made him special and superior compared to the others, then put him in the ring and watched him fight the other figurines. People who enjoyed spending their time this way claimed that's precisely what made it so invigorating, but he found the open-endedness frivolous, even monstrous. Discussing ideas was not in itself wrong, of course. He did so too, which was why he was at tonight's seminar. But to stake one's entire existence on that level, as if that were how a life should get on, to him seemed so superficial, inhuman actually. He thought part of the reason Joseph enjoyed talking to him was because part of Joseph felt that way too, though Joseph never said it.

There were eight of them at dinner. He took a seat next to Joseph, across from Klaus and Maureen. Klaus got the burger and fries, Maureen a salad, and he decided only to get a drink. As he was about to get comfortable, he realized Ben wasn't there. He turned his head to the street, and saw Ben walking by the front window dejectedly. "Excuse me," he said to Joseph.

He opened the door and stepped onto the street. "Ben!"

Ben spun around. "Oh, hey."

"You're not coming to dinner?"

"No, not tonight," he said. There was a silence.

"Okay, well maybe next time, right?"

"Yeah. I'm sorry. I don't want to get into it now, because I know you're busy, but I'm getting a divorce. Winnie's not coming back from Canada," he said.

"I'm sorry," he said.

"Oh, it's okay. I think it's for the best. She was always very abusive." They were quiet again.

"I'll see you later," Ben said, and then he walked away.

Back inside, when he sat down at the table, Klaus turned to him. "No food?"

"Yeah, no food. Not hungry," he said.

"I'm sorry, we haven't met," Maureen said, holding out her hand. That was technically true, though of course she knew by now who he was.

He gave her his name and shook her hand. "Klaus is my supervisor."

"I see." She turned to Klaus.

Klaus looked at him, then at her. "He's a fellow Carrell disciple," Klaus said.

She turned to him with a big smile on her face and raised an eyebrow. "Really? Is that so? What are you doing out here then?" So, she was going to take the blunt approach by playing dumb, he saw.

"Well, I don't know about a disciple. I think Carrell tries to instill independence in his students. At least that's what he told me when I was there working with him."

"Yes, of course, I didn't mean to suggest otherwise," said Klaus.

Maureen's face turned a bit more serious. "You worked with Carrell?"

Of course, she knew that, and she knew everyone knew she knew it, but they all had to pretend that she didn't. "Yes. You did as well too, right?"

"Yes, I loved working with Saul. I learned so much under him. After finishing my dissertation there, I moved to England." The implication was that she had profited just fine by staying put in Texas, so it was arrogant of him to have thought to transfer elsewhere. He was getting the impression that her hostility was coming from whatever Klaus must have said earlier today about him before the talk.

"I learned a lot too. Seeing the continuity between Kant and Heidegger was very transformative for me." Her face softened a bit, since that was one of the ideas central to her own work. The rest of the dinner passed rather uneventfully. Mostly he talked to Joseph, and listened to what others had to say. The check came, Klaus paid the bill with a Faculty credit card, and everyone stood up.

"Well, I need to be getting back to London, but the rest of you are of course more than welcome to carry on." Klaus paused and pointed to him. "He's at college too, so maybe he can show you to the college. There's a pub nearby that you might want to check out called The Bear." Klaus looked at him. "Sound good?"

"Oh, yes. I live right across the street from college, so I'm walking that way. The Bear is very nice. If you're not too tired, we could pop in for a pint," he said looking at her.

"That sounds great," she said.

Klaus looked at him. "By the way, I spoke to Quiller. He and Hodges will have the paperwork to the GSC soon, hopefully by the end of this term, if not, then first thing next term after summer. You passed," he said.

"Oh, that's great," he said smiling.

"I have no idea what you two are talking about, but congratulations," Maureen said.

"He had his transfer of status examination earlier today. He's passed, which means he's now a full DPhil student after a year as a Probationary Research Student."

"Ah, I see. Well, very impressive. Congratulations," she said, smiling at him.

"Thanks," he said.

"Goodnight, you two," Klaus said.

He looked at Klaus. "Say hi to Zoe," he said.

Klaus froze. "Oh, yes, thanks. Yes, I'll tell her you say hi."

The Bear was very crowded. There wasn't a single seat left on the benches, so they squeezed inside, where it took a while to get a round.

When they found a spot to stand, Maureen looked at him. "So, any plans for the summer?"

"Yeah, actually I'm getting married in August," he said.

"Wow, that's great," she said. "What's her name?"

"Alison," he said.

"Is she here?"

"No, she's back in Texas finishing her degree." He thought for a second about mentioning how Stuart might actually know Carrell, since they both were on the faculty. There was a chance that Maureen might have even known Stuart, or at least heard of him. But he didn't bother.

"Oh, that must be hard. My husband and I had to spend some time apart due to distance," she said.

"He teaches at Sussex too, correct?"

"Yeah, he's in the art program," she said.

"Very cool. Alison's an artist," he said.

"What kind of art?"

"She's really into large-scale drawings. Charcoal."

"Very interesting," she said.

There was a pause.

"So, what are your plans when you're done here?"

"I'm not sure. I guess we'll go wherever I get a job, assuming I get one," he said.

"Yes, the job market is absolutely terrible," she said, her hand brushing up against his arm. She had drunk a lot of wine at dinner, and now nearing the end of her Guinness, she was standing very close to him. The fact of the pub's being crowded was obviously just a weak pretext that only made the unnecessary contact more awkward.

"Want another round?" she asked.

"Sure, one more," he said. "I'll be right back."

He got two beers. "Here you go," he said, handing her one.

"Cheers," she said.

"Cheers," he said.

They finished the beers, and then it was time to walk back. They stepped out of the pub, took the narrow lane out to the main street, where they went left which led them to Tom Gate.

She stood at the gate which was closed.

"Can you get in?" he asked.

"Oh, yes, Klaus gave me a fob," she said, pulling one out of her purse. "I have a room at college." Evidently, she was staying in Klaus's spare room.

"Yeah, I live right over there," he said, pointing to his building. He was about to say goodbye, when she spoke.

"You know, I'm organizing a volume on Carrell's work. I'm going to get former students of his and others influenced by his work to contribute. Would you be interested in editing it with me?"

"Oh, sure. That sounds very interesting. I've never edited something like that, but I'd be happy to help."

"Fantastic. I'll be in touch when I have more details," she said. He could feel that she was assuming he wanted to come into the college to continue the night, and was about to say so.

"Well, I hope you enjoy the rest of your visit to Oxford. Goodnight," he said.

"Oh. Yes, goodnight," she said.

He turned around and walked to the apartment. When he got to his room, he lit a cigarette and stared at the ceiling on his bed. It had been a bizarre first year here. Of course, it could have been far more bizarre, if he had not been so extremely careful to stay as far away as possible from all that he had. There was more to come, he knew, but he could worry about it later. He'd passed the transfer exercise which was the main objective. Later this week, he would be on a plane back home, and shortly thereafter would be the wedding. It felt good to know he could forget about everything here for a while.

Twenty-four

I T was late afternoon when he landed. After collecting his luggage from the carousel, he waited on the curb, and before long he was drenched in sweat. He had forgotten how humid it could be here, but after months of the gray and cold, the heat was invigorating. Because of the car accident that had killed her siblings, Alison had a fear of freeway driving. The fact she was coming to get him was a testament to how much she must have missed him. He had offered to take a cab to her apartment, but she insisted on picking him up. As he lit a cigarette, the car came up the ramp and pulled up to the curb.

"I can't believe it! Mr Koala is finally home! You're here," she said.

She had done her makeup and was in the green dress with white polka dots, the one she had bought on the High St on her visit. He knew she knew how much he loved that dress on her, and he knew she was wearing it to remind him that they had almost made it. In just a few days they would be married, and then they could truly start their life together.

They hugged, he put his luggage in the trunk, and they faced each other.

"I love you," he said.

"I love you too," she said.

"I'm so glad to be back."

"I missed you," she said.

"Me too. Well, let's go," he said.

They got in the car, and drove off from the airport. When they merged onto the highway, Alison spoke.

"Are you too tired for dinner tonight? If you are, that's totally fine. We can reschedule."

"Oh, no, don't worry about it. I'll be fine," he said.

They would be going to dinner tonight at Linda and Stuart's house. That he was tired from the flight wasn't the issue. He wouldn't want to go anytime, frankly. He laughed to himself over how much had changed in a little over a year. When they first began dating, the closest they had come to a real argument was over her parents. Only, at the time, he had been the one defending them from her objections. She was always reluctant to go see them, and when Linda would invite them over, he couldn't understand why she didn't want to go. Linda would make comments about how she didn't see Alison enough, and Stuart would have a look of sadness when Linda spoke about it. He had begun feeling sorry for them, actually, wondering why Alison was so distant and aloof from her parents who seemed so nice.

"You don't understand," she said once when they had been driving over for a dinner she was dreading.

"They seem fine to me," he said. "They just want to spend time with you," he had said.

"No, it's not like that. This is what they do. They manipulate others into thinking they're the victim. But when you know who they really are, you see it's all an act," she said.

Here now in the car, he could see what Alison had been trying to tell him. They had manipulated him too, of course, pretending not to understand why Alison didn't want to spend time with them, pretending to be doting parents who were having their love rebuffed by a selfish, inconsiderate daughter whom they loved anyway unconditionally. Then the veil had been lifted, and he had seen how it really was. There had been the power-play Stuart had made in the office at the engagement, and then the ensuing manipulation over the wedding itself. Stuart and Linda were paying for the wedding, which ordinarily would have been a nice gesture. But it was actually the opposite. It was about control. Not merely control over the wedding itself, but personal control over Alison, her emotions, and, above all, their future marriage. Linda was using the fact they were paying for everything as a way to guilt Alison. Anytime there was a disagreement about the wedding, Linda could claim she was simply interested in making it as wonderful as possible, thereby insinuating that Alison was being unnecessarily difficult, maybe even ungrateful. There were two obvious flaws in Linda's plan. To begin with, Linda and Stuart were racking up a massive bill to cover expenses that had nothing to do with what Alison herself desired. In fact, Alison had explained on a number of occasions how she felt the wedding had expanded way beyond anything she had wanted. It made no sense, then, for Linda to act as if Alison should be grateful when Linda was the one insisting on all the extravagances. Furthermore, there was the fact that his own parents could easily have paid. Linda and Stuart were acting as if they were doing what they were out of love for Alison, as if the wedding she desired would be impossible otherwise, but it wasn't the wedding she desired, and it would have been possible anyway, assuming she had desired it, because his parents would have been happy to pay for it themselves.

"Angela has been a saint," Alison said. "I don't know how she's put up with my mom."

He laughed. "Well, it's her job. I bet she's really looking forward to the wedding being over, though," he said.

Alison glanced over at him. "So am I. I just want to be in England with you," she said.

"I know. Me too," he said.

His perception of Alison's parents was not the only thing that had changed. So much else had as well, at least with regard to the situation in Texas. He thought about everyone. Mick had ended up in Australia with an academic job. David was in Alberta. Karl had left the city, probably for Austin, as he had thought Karl would. Tony was now gone to Miami. Cody was home in West Virginia after being rejected by all the graduate programs to which he'd applied. Apparently, he was now married with a newborn child, the result of an unplanned pregnancy. He was surprised to hear they hadn't aborted the child, since that would have seemed to be more in keeping with Cody's attitude about everything being atoms and the void. Maybe Cody was changing, after all, he thought. Clara had not yet left the city after breaking up with Paul. He could find out more about everyone if were to ask Jack, who was still here, but Jack had no interest in seeing him anymore now that the group had dissolved. Then there was Timothy, who had vanished completely. He thought about going to the old apartment to see whether he could find any information about his whereabouts, but he knew it would be futile.

They pulled up to the apartment and parked in one of the spaces. They lit cigarettes in the car, rolled the windows down, and enjoyed the gentle breeze. It made sense to sort out the state of his situation in Oxford.

"So, how did the meeting go?"

"I passed."

"You passed! You didn't even tell me," she said.

He smiled. "I wanted to make it a surprise. It's nothing official yet. I still am waiting on the paperwork."

"So, it went fine with Quiller?"

"Well, it went fine enough. I know he doesn't like me or my work, but there's nothing he can do about it at this point."

"Klaus?"

"Same," he said.

"You know I don't trust him."

"I know," he said.

"I'm so excited. This is wonderful news. Now we can relax," she said.

"Yeah, it's great timing. I wouldn't have wanted to be worrying about it over the summer," he said.

"So when will you defend the thesis?"

"There's still the confirmation of status meeting. But that will be easy, too. That'll be sometime next year. Then I'll set a date for the viva."

"So exciting! I wonder where we'll end up. Do you think we'll stay in Oxford?"

"I don't know," he said.

"Well, we better hurry, or we'll be late. I don't want my mom to call asking where we are," she said.

He set his luggage on the studio apartment's floor, changed into a white collared shirt, and brushed his teeth.

"Ready when you are," he said.

"Ready!"

She came up and kissed him. "Thanks for doing this," she said.

"Duty is the essence of manhood," he said laughing. It was a famous quotation from Patton that he'd mentioned to her before. She laughed.

"You're my little koala soldier," she said.

As they walked down to the car, he thought about how stupid war was. The military industrial complex Eisenhower had warned about was only worse now. He knew so from personal experience. His father, who had worked at Lockheed Martin during the height of the Cold War, had told him everything.

He called to mind the conversation he'd had recently with his dad about the world.

"It's all a fraud, Son. Think about it. How did Schwarzkopf do what he did? They claim that he took all the Army Divisions and pulled this massive flanking maneuver on the Iraqis by suckering them into thinking he'd be attacking from the other direction with the Marines. It's absurd.

That sort of logistical maneuver may have been possible during World War II. That's what they say the Germans did to the French, by coming through the Ardennes rather than across the Maginot Line. Okay, what's the problem with that story though?"

He knew what his dad was driving at. With today's satellite and airplane technology, it would have been impossible to conceal a massive troop movement the size of the one Schwarzkopf was said to have orchestrated in Kuwait.

"We're supposedly fighting the Soviets. Okay, so you're telling me that the Soviets wouldn't simply tell the Iraqis what we were doing?" The implication was that, because they hadn't told the Iraqis, the Cold War itself had been a charade.

"It's all theater," his father continued. "We drive Saddam out of Kuwait, and then on the way to Baghdad, we just stop?" At the time in the nineties, his father had been confused as to why Bush hadn't finished the job. In retrospect, as his father now saw, it had all become obvious.

"So, we leave this terrible tyrant in office, mess around for years with the no-fly zone, then finally invade again. But there's no WMD. It was all a lie. Powell made the whole thing up at the UN. Then we're in Afghanistan, just like the Soviets themselves were beforehand, fighting against the same forces that we had previously been funding to fight the Soviets. Osama Bin Laden was a CIA asset back in the eighties. Now he's the big boogeyman? Try to figure that one out. It's not about freedom for the Afghanis or stopping terrorism. You know what's it all about."

"Opium," he said.

"Yeah, just like Vietnam. They have the Special Forces over there guarding the drugs. That's why they popped Tillman." His dad was referencing the late Pat Tillman, the former NFL football player who'd joined the Army Rangers after 9/11, and who had been murdered by friendly fire in Afghanistan.

"Tillman figured out the whole thing is a circle jerk. I mean, look at 9/11."

"I know, Dad, I don't understand how people can't see it," he said.

"The week of the attack, I went over to Grandpa and Grandma's house. I was talking about how it didn't make sense how the Towers could implode like that. I'll never forget what he said. My dad shifts in his seat, looks at me, and said, 'Well, you know Scott, the thing that really gets me is the Pentagon.' Even Grandpa knew," he said.

His grandfather, who at the time of the conversation about 9/11 had been retired from Lockheed for twenty years, had worked at Skunk Works. Before that, in his youth, he'd flown in the Army Air Corps. He remembered the story his dad had once told him about how the grandad had known of the SR-71 and Stealth Fighter years before they were ever declassified. On his grandpa's home office wall were memorabilia from the first ever American satellite missions that he'd worked on.

His dad continued recounting a related story.

"I went over to the house, because I was all worried the Soviets were going to invade West Germany. This was in the seventies. We were getting all these intelligence updates from the field that an attack was imminent, and everyone at Lockheed was freaking out. The Soviets had more tanks, more men, more planes. We seemed to be outmatched. I drove over to the house and sat down on the patio. I was telling my dad about how we were hosed, and he just looked at me. Then he pretended to be some radar operator in a Soviet command center: 'General! General! We can't track it! What is it?' My dad waved his hand to make a plane motion. I realize now that he was trying to tell me about the Stealth Fighter. He told me even Carter didn't know about it at the time. 'We can tell everybody anything we want,' he had said. I didn't understand at the time. My dad was trying to say that the President and others are all figureheads. They don't do anything. But he also meant the public. You can tell the public anything, and they'll believe it. That's what he meant about the Pentagon. My dad knew it wasn't really a passenger airliner. 'Nothing can hit the Pentagon,' he had told me. It was probably really a cruise missile, but that's not the point. The point is that the air defense system had to be disabled in order for anything to hit the building, which means it was an inside job. My dad knew all those guys. He knew Rumsfeld and Wolfowitz. He said they were all idiots. I was in a meeting with the former Director of the CIA at Lockheed once. Had to give the dork a briefing. These guys are all blowhard morons. It's a scam."

His dad continued, "I've been watching it my whole life. Look at the Bushes and the Clintons. The Bushes were running drugs with the CIA way back in the eighties. Clinton gave the Chinese all of our ballistic missile technology in the nineties. Clinton was part of a student organization that visited the Soviet Union. How did he even get a clearance?"

"I know, Dad, it's all a scam. You know, Chelsea Clinton is working on her little DPhil over here right now, too." They both laughed.

"It's so stupid," his dad said. Then he paused. "You know, Son, I didn't want to say anything at the time, but there's a big problem back in Houston with Stuart's lab." His dad laughed.

"I know, it's obvious, but everyone's too dumb to see it," he said.

He recollected the occasion his dad was mentioning. It had been shortly after news of the engagement, on a trip his parents had taken to meet Alison's parents. They'd gone to the university, where Stuart had offered to take his dad and him on a tour. Of course, in a way the tour was pointless, since he was already a student there, and his dad wouldn't be impressed. His dad had seen top secret military labs for years, so Stuart's lab was nothing. But they had to humor Stuart, in order to keep the peace. They had walked through the lab, and he knew his dad would notice that most of the postdocs were Chinese nationals. When they got outside the lab and Stuart had left for his office, his dad turned to him.

"Are you kidding me? How is Stuart doing that? You can't have foreign nationals from a Communist country in a government-funded lab like that. It's a national security violation. How does the guy know the students in there aren't working for the PLA?"

"I know, Dad," he said, shaking his head at the absurdity. "The Chinese Consulate is just down the street too. Most of the guys in the lab probably are told what to do by the Consulate."

"Unbelievable, Son," his dad said. "So, Stuart's taking US taxpayer dollars to develop technology for the US military, and yet the Chinese can walk right into his stupid lab and syphon it off right in everyone's face? Why did we even fight the Cold War? I told you about the clearances. The FBI, CIA, NSA, it's all a fraud. They ask you whether you've ever cheated on your wife, whether you're a closet homosexual, whether you've ever used drugs, they even ask whether you've ever been molested. I remember Mark Griffith at Lockheed. When he'd get his clearance renewed, he'd also come up to me and complain about how he had to tell them about how he'd been molested as a child by a priest. It didn't make any sense why they'd want to know that. You won't believe it, Son, they had us all so brainwashed. They told us that we had to give them any sensitive information that the Soviets could potentially use to compromise us. Well, now the entire government is taken over by the Communists, anyway. Bush and Clinton are criminals, Stuart has the CCP in his lab, and we're all supposed to pretend we have a country still. I figured it out. They take all the information to blackmail people. It's why Hillary had the FBI files in her closet in the White House. Look what they did to Foster.

Murdered him right in front of everyone. Then you go watch a movie like *Enemy of the State*, and all the people in the theater are too dumb to know the NSA is really spying on them. They put it right in the movie," he said.

"Truth in the movies, lies on the news, Dad," he said.

"Exactly."

When he had told his dad about Eliot's dinners, his dad immediately understood. Then he told his dad about Piers Gaveston, Lavinia and her friends at the college, Jacob Rothschild, the British Royal at the college soirée, Klaus's affair, and all of the women they had been throwing at him.

"That's what I'm telling you, Son. That's how it works. We used to be told by the counterintelligence guys: 'If you're on a business trip and some chick at a bar approaches you, don't do anything.' All these guys in academia and defense and the rest of it, they're all on videotape humping a mistress or whatever. That's the dirty secret. The reason Stuart has the PLA spies in his lab is probably because he got blackmailed, too. Don't worry about Stuart. Whenever he tries to provoke you, don't respond. Just let him twist in the wind. Eventually Alison will see it, and then he'll have to disappear. Howdy Doody's not worth it, anyway. Don't waste your time getting into a pissing contest with the guy. Focus on Alison, and protecting her," he had said.

His dad had fallen silent for a moment. "You know, Son, think about all the guys my dad knew who died in the war. Do you think they would have died at Tarawa, if they knew that we'd have a country where Stuart can sell us out to the Chicoms? Do you think all the guys at your college who died in the wars would do it again? I mean, why do they even bother having clearances? Everything that we supposedly could be blackmailed for in the seventies and eighties is now public policy. Adultery, pornography, homosexuality, drugs, gambling—all of it. They took what the vice squad used to arrest people for doing, and transformed it all into a national pastime. As the degradation grows worse, so does the obviousness of the fraud. I don't know how anyone takes the world seriously anymore. It's like watching a bunch of junior elves walking around inside Santa's Village still trying to pretend it's all real."

Driving over now to the house with Alison, he saw that his dad had been right about everything. His job was to support Alison by not escalating anything with her parents. They had been probing for months, and he hadn't taken the bait. There were only a few more days to go, and then after the wedding he would be in a position of strength. Stuart would know this, so he would have to be prepared for some silly mind games tonight at dinner. He knew how this would all unfold if he remained patient. After the wedding, Linda and Stuart would try to undermine the marriage while simultaneously pretending to be supportive. They would wait for a moment of weakness, probably when he finally faced an inevitable challenge at Oxford over his work, throw gasoline on the fire, and try to persuade Alison he was a failure whom she should leave. Stuart would leverage his contacts in the academic and defense worlds to undermine him further, to make it as difficult as possible for him to build the life with Alison Stuart knew his daughter was expecting she would have. If he tried to explain this to Alison when it began happening, she understandably wouldn't want to believe it, Linda and Stuart would play dumb, in order to guilt her into thinking he was being unfair to Stuart, and eventually Alison would leave him, convinced he was a delusional loser and failure. To avoid all this from happening, he would have to allow Stuart to bury himself under a mountain of lies. When Stuart's behavior finally became too bizarre for everyone to explain, Linda and Stuart would disappear from their lives without a trace. They might still continue spreading lies about him to people they knew in Texas, but eventually everyone would see what had really happened. This would all take much longer than it should, due to people's denial, cowardice, and selfishness, but eventually it would. The hard part would be waiting for everyone to accept the reality he already saw. He sighed.

"Is something wrong?"

"No, sweetie, I love you," he said as they pulled up to the house.

Twenty-five

T HEY rang twice, and the door opened.

"Sweetie! You're here, it's so good to see you guys," Linda squealed.

Linda and Alison hugged. Then Linda hugged him too. "Come on in, dinner's almost ready. Daddy will be down soon, he's finishing some work," Linda said as they walked into the kitchen.

"Do you guys want something to drink?"

"Sure, how about a beer?" Alison asked.

"They're in the fridge. Help yourself," Linda said.

"What's Dad working on?"

Linda was quiet for a second. "Oh, well, I don't know if I should get into it," she said, with a look of worry on her face.

Alison took the bait. "No, tell us. What is it?"

Linda pretended she was torn, that she was about to say what she was with great reluctance. She lowered her voice.

"Daddy's having an issue with one of his students in the lab," she said.

Alison was concerned. "Oh, no, what is it?"

"It's one of his new postdocs. She's been having issues."

"Well, I know Dad has such high expectations, maybe she's just getting used to the pressure," Alison offered.

Linda was quiet for a moment. "Yes, I know Daddy can be difficult. He's such a perfectionist. But that's not it. Her work is fine. It's something else," she said.

"What?"

"She's having to take a leave of absence. Daddy's concerned because they're in the middle of a major experiment, so now he's having to scramble to re-allocate the work."

"A leave of absence? Why?"

Linda looked uncomfortable. "It's a medical issue, I guess," she said.

"Oh, no. I hope she's okay. What is it?"

Linda looked at Alison. "She has an eating disorder. Apparently, she wants Daddy to do something about it, but he's not going to. He's had to have a conversation with her about it."

"What do you mean?"

"Daddy's not going to be approving the absence. If she leaves, that will be it."

"What?" Alison was mortified.

"What? It's Daddy's lab. There's work to do. She knew that coming in," Linda said.

"She has an eating disorder! It's not fair for Dad to hold that against her. Why can't she come back?"

"Because she made a promise to Daddy that she would be able to do the work. She isn't following through, so he has to move on," Linda said.

Alison was angry. "Why doesn't he want to help her? Doesn't he care?"

"She's being unfair to Daddy. It's not his job to worry about it. She's making demands of him that are unreasonable."

"It's unreasonable to expect your supervisor to help you when you're facing a serious medical condition?"

"That's not it. It's a personal issue of hers. Daddy has no obligation to deal with that," Linda said.

He had watched enough. Linda had gone fishing, and he wasn't going to bite.

"Want to sit outside, sweetie?" he asked Alison, changing the subject.

She looked over at him, then back to her mother. "Dad should help her. I want to talk to him about it," she said.

"Oh, no, not tonight, please. Maybe some other time. It's already stressful enough for him. I know he just wants to be able to enjoy dinner," Linda said.

"Fine," Alison said. "Let's go outside."

They sat down at the patio table.

"I can't believe it," she said.

He was silent. He could tell she was starting to get angry with him too, mistaking his silence for tacit agreement with her parents. This was the spiritual trial. This was the test. This was the collision between the world and God. The temptation was to speak, to tell her everything he already knew. The temptation was to make himself understood, to reassure her in a way that she would understand. But that would be to lie.

The truth was that he couldn't speak, since the truth demanded that he for now keep silent, even if that meant her resenting him. It pained him to know she might question his love, but love demanded it. He thought about the story of Abraham and Isaac, about Kierkegaard's analysis of it. The words of Silentio entered his mind, "I *think* myself into the hero; I cannot think myself into Abraham." The tragic hero, Agamemnon or Brutus, is still within the ethical, still within the external and the visible, still mediated by the universal and hence by language, and so can still make himself understood to others by rendering his reasons in terms they will accept and comprehend. But Abraham is not the tragic hero, for what he does, though done in love, cannot be understood—Abraham cannot speak. "The paradox is that he cannot explain himself to anyone else, for the paradox is that he as the single individual places himself in an absolute relation to the absolute." Such is the suffering of the Knight of Faith. He looked across the table, and could see the pain and frustration on Alison's face. He wanted to tell her that he understood, that she didn't have to worry, because he understood more than she did about who her dad really was, and that he was going to be sure her dad paid for everything he had done to hurt so many people over the years, this postdoc in his lab included.

He smiled softly, "I love you."

She looked at him and sighed. "I love you too," she said.

"Just a few more days."

"I know," she said.

Stuart came down the stairs and popped his head onto the patio through the door.

"Hi, Alison," he said grinning.

"Hi, Dad," she said.

A few minutes later, Linda and Stuart came out with dinner. Linda asked a few questions about Oxford, but when it became clear that nobody was going to ask about the transfer of status meeting, Alison tried changing the subject to the wedding.

"Oh, you know, it'll be so good to be settled in California in a few days," Linda said. She turned to Stuart. "I know it'll be hard for Daddy, though, with all the traveling he's already been doing. He just got back from a two-week trip to China."

Alison looked surprised. "China?"

"Yeah, Beijing and Wuhan. Tell them about it, Stuart," Linda said.

"I have a colleague at a university over there. He invited me to share some work," Stuart said.

"Daddy's so happy to be home. The food was terrible. They took him to a special dinner where they served delicacies like snake," Linda chuckled.

There was so much he would like to say. To begin with, there was the fact that the university in Beijing was a known hub for CCP military and intelligence efforts. More importantly, there was the fact that the CCP was persecuting the Uyghurs. Christians too. Then, of course, there was the fact that the CCP operated a massive surveillance and censorship grid that stripped the people of China of all the civil liberties people here in the West still thought they had, even though they really didn't. And finally, there was the fact that the research Stuart was developing in his lab would be used by the CCP, in order to exploit its own population, and eventually it would be used against the American people themselves. In short, the CCP was a godless, totalitarian regime abusing the people of China's human rights. Stuart traveling to work with them was the equivalent of an American scientist traveling in the thirties to collaborate with Hitler's or Stalin's military scientists. But in the morally decayed, ignorant society in which they all lived, none of these facts mattered, and if he tried to point them out, Linda would simply pretend that he was ruining what was an innocuous story, and Stuart would sit there and play dumb. It was frustrating to watch Stuart and his criminal friends openly sell out their very own country they pretended to be working for, but in a world this corrupt, with institutions this debased, there was nothing to be done about it. Stuart and his science colleagues had sold their souls for sex, money, and power. And everyone they knew, even their own families, were simply collateral damage. He sighed.

Linda turned to him. "Is something wrong?"

"No, Linda. Everything's fine. I was just thinking about something," he said.

They finished dinner, said their goodbyes, and got in the car. He felt exhausted.

"I can't believe my mom is defending my dad over not helping the girl in his lab."

"I'm sorry," he said.

"Let's go home. I love you," she said.

TWENTY-SIX

"HEY, Dad, there's a problem," he said.

"What is it?"

"Alison's gone," he said.

"What do you mean? Where?"

"I'm not sure. I think she went back to the hotel."

"Why?"

He looked around the crowded house, and decided it would be better to have the conversation outside on the sidewalk. It was the night before the wedding, and there were dozens of guests mingling at his parents' house for the rehearsal dinner. The night had started fine enough, with the wedding party taking photos on the back patio. Then the other family and friends arrived, there was dinner, and now everyone was enjoying themselves over drinks. He hadn't had a real opportunity to talk privately with Andy or Bert or the other groomsmen, but they seemed happy, and they were all settling into that old familiarity they had known growing up together. Everyone was stunned by the exquisite state of the house, a classic Spanish adobe, which had been recently beautifully renovated, and it was clear that Alison deeply appreciated the extent to which her future mother-in-law had gone to organize a wonderful evening.

They got out to the curb and stood by the purple Bougainvillea.

His dad looked at him. "Okay, tell me what's going on," he said.

"I went into the bedroom, because I'd noticed Alison was missing. She was changing out of her dress with Sandra and Stephanie. Alison looked a little discombobulated, and I could tell the twins were trying to hide something. I think they convinced her to leave."

"Why would they do that?"

"Long story. Then I came down to the street looking for her, after she wasn't in the house, and I found Stuart and Linda coming up the stairs. I asked them if they'd seen her, and they said they hadn't."

"Bullshit. They saw her leave."

"Yeah, exactly."

"Okay, so let's go find her. Should I tell Mom?"

"No, don't mention it. Linda and Stuart want us to panic and make a big deal about it. Let's just slip out and take care of it."

"Okay, I'll drive you down to the hotel."

He returned inside to grab his phone. On the way to the front door, some of Alison's other bridal party, who were sitting in the living room, turned to him.

"Where's Alison?" Kelsie asked. Enrique looked concerned. May was silent.

"I'm not sure. I'll be back."

He got in the car with his dad. When they reached the hotel, he told his dad more.

"Listen, I think part of the problem is that Linda and Stuart had always promised Alison money if she didn't go off to Wheaton. That was her dream school. We've been counting on the money, and knowing them, they've probably told her they're not giving her the money anymore."

"Stuart's such a little demon," his dad said. "He's going to try to tighten the screws on you financially. Don't worry about it. You keep focusing on your work at Oxford, and you know I have you financially."

"I know. I'll be right back."

When he got inside, he saw Sandra and Stephanie sitting at the hotel bar with their dates. The four of them looked at him surprised, and didn't say anything.

"Hi, guys, great to see you here. By any chance do you know where my fiancée is? She disappeared from the house and the rest of the bridal party is concerned, as you might imagine."

Sandra glared at him. "I think she's upstairs with Linda," she said.

"Oh, thanks so much," he said.

At the top of the stairs, he could hear crying. On the other side of the lounge, at the top of the staircase, was Alison, sobbing into her mother's shoulder, who was patting her on the back. As he walked over, Linda almost jumped out of her skin.

"Oh, hi," Linda said nervously.

"Hi, Linda," he said. "Is everything okay?"

Linda was quiet.

Alison, who apparently was so grief stricken she hadn't noticed his presence, was mumbling, "He doesn't love me. Why doesn't he love me?"

Linda turned awkwardly toward Alison and whispered, "That's not true, honey. That's not true." So, somebody at the rehearsal dinner, probably Sandra, must have lied to Alison. He heard footsteps and turned around.

"I think you should sit down," Stuart said, gesturing to the couch.

"Oh, I'd be pleased to," he said.

He sat down across from Stuart.

Stuart looked at him sternly. "What exactly is going on here?"

"I thought you might tell me that. Alison left the house without saying goodbye to anyone, and everyone is worried. I asked you outside whether you knew where Alison was. Evidently," he gestured to the room around them, "you did."

"I'm more worried about focusing on the problem," Stuart said. The implication was that he himself had done something to cause it.

"So am I. Maybe you can tell me why you're here and not at the rehearsal, Stuart?"

Stuart was snared in his own scheme. Unless he had actually seen Alison leave and knew where she was going, there would be no reason for him to be here. What had really happened was clear. Someone at the rehearsal, Sandra probably, had told Alison that he didn't love her, maybe made up some false story about what she supposedly knew about him, then whisked her off to the hotel, where Linda was manipulating her into calling off the wedding. Now that he had shown up unexpectedly, Stuart was doing damage control.

Then he saw Stuart startle, like he had seen a ghost. Stuart hopped to his feet. "Oh, uh, hi . . . "

His dad strode up the stairs, looked at Linda, and walked right up to Stuart.

"Hi, Stuart."

"Well, I should be getting back to the room. I'm glad to see Alison is doing okay," Stuart said. "C'mon Linda. Let's go," Stuart said.

Linda stood up and slinked away from Alison, stood next to Stuart, and was silent.

"You two have a good night," his dad said. Stuart and Linda disappeared down the hall to their room.

"You talk to Alison. I'll be outside waiting for you in the car. I love you, Son."

"Thanks," he said.

"No problem. He's just a little Howdy Doody," he said. They hugged.

Inside, he sat down next to Alison, who was still disconsolate.

"Honey, it's me. What's wrong?"

She was sniffling, her chest heaving. "You don't love me," she said.

"I don't love you? That's absurd. Why would you think that? Of course, I love you."

He could tell she was surprised he had come to find her. She was beginning to see that his coming here to find her didn't fit with whatever she'd been told. She started composing herself, as the truth dawned on her.

"I'm sorry."

"I'm sorry, too. I know how stressful this has been. I should have been more active in the planning. I'm sorry I didn't find a way for us just to elope in Oxford."

"That would have been nice. It's okay, though. I love you," she said.

"I love you too," he said.

"Tomorrow's the big day, and then we can put all this behind us, and just have each other," he said.

"I know," she said. He wiped the tears from her cheeks, and let her blow her nose on his shirt. She smiled.

"Listen, my dad's outside waiting. He needs to take me to the rehearsal. You stay here and relax and get some rest."

"You sure you don't need me to come back?"

"No, it's fine. Just get some rest, and I'll see you tomorrow," he said.

They kissed, and he left.

Down in the hotel bar, the others were sitting there. He walked up to the table.

"Everything's squared away. I hope you enjoyed the rehearsal at the house tonight. I know my parents appreciated the opportunity to welcome you all into their home. See you tomorrow," he said. They sat in silence, embarrassed.

When he came into the living room, Kelsie ran up to him.

"Is everything okay?"

"Yeah, it's fine. She's tired and went back to the hotel," he said.

"Oh, okay, good. I'll tell the others."

"Thanks." They hugged.

When the guests had left, and his parents had gone to sleep, he went out alone to the front patio overlooking the downtown. He lit a cigarette, stared at the mountains, and then watched the stars. He walked down the stairs, and lit another cigarette at the bougainvillea. He could feel his own nothingness before God. He felt relieved, even calm. The words from the Psalm came to him as he reflected upon that evening's events at the hotel, "For they intended evil against thee: they imagined a mischievous device, which they are not able to perform." He put out the cigarette and decided to go to bed. Tomorrow would be a blessed day, and nobody would ruin it.

TWENTY-SEVEN

THE serene melody, which floated gently through the sunny afternoon breeze, as if animating the rustling oak leaves it was fanning with a whisper, reached his ears, dilating his heart, taking him to a place where he was no longer present there with everyone, but was now alone only with her. Love had bracketed the world, reducing those sitting before him in their chairs to a matter of indifference, as she walked slowly down the aisle. Watching her approach, there was no doubting Debussy's *Claire de Lune* had been the perfect choice. Yes, to be sure, the moon was not for him. It was for everyone, a reminder of God's ever watchfulness over his creatures, including the affairs of men. He could feel that frankly everything was a gift from above—the sun, the trees, the grass, the clouds, and the birds. "Marry and you will regret it; do not marry and you will regret it; either way, you will regret it." Drifting out of his reverie, he returned to the altar, where he stifled a laugh at the words which had just crossed his mind, since he knew the others at the ceremony would understandably find it an odd moment in which to laugh, if he had. He was simply struck by how the words in question revealed the false presupposition behind them. Love, he realized, was not a feeling, nor a fleeting emotion. Or, at least, it was not meant to be. When it flowered properly, it was eternal, a promise, which of course was precisely why it should take the form it was currently taking here, the vows that their union was about to bring about generated by a love that could not be extinguished. The aesthete's error of thinking that regret was inevitable no matter what he chose to do, he now understood, was the consequence of holding an entirely impoverished conception of love. With love, there could be no regret.

Then, her hands were in his. His hands were sweaty, of course, but he didn't care. It was good that she would know he was nervous.

The officiant administered the vows, Sandra and Andy handed over the rings, and before he knew what had happened, they were one flesh. They kissed and walked down the aisle to cheers and applause. Part of him knew very well that he could count on just one hand the number of people there who would really be there for them if Alison and him ever needed it, but that didn't matter. Nothing could detract from the elation, because it came from within, from God, and so it had nothing to do with the others, anyway.

The reception was held in the adobe garden under the trees. Before dinner would be served were the toasts. Or, rather, there was the one toast. His groomsmen had all demurred, and neither he nor his dad had any intention of giving a toast, either. Better to let the situation be what it is by simply speaking for itself, they had all thought. The guests all gathered around the edges of the dance floor and hushed as Stuart grabbed the microphone.

"You know, I always tell the story of the time he came to my office to ask whether he could marry Alison." There was strained laughter. "I almost reached across the desk and killed him—"

His mind drifted from the speech, other words now commanding his attention instead: "Whatsoever things are true, whatsoever things are honest, whatsoever things are just, whatsoever things are pure, whatsoever things are lovely, whatsoever things are of good report: if there be any virtue, and if there be any praise, think on these things." His bride was certainly lovely, so he would think about her. He looked at her and smiled, she smiled at him, they kissed, and squeezed one another's hands.

"Your hands are so sweaty," she giggled.

"I know," he said. He paused, then whispered, "I'm sorry."

"For what?"

"I'm having a bad day."

"It's okay," she laughed. Angela was coming over to have them take pictures with the photographer, and he was self-conscious. He knew he photographed poorly as it is, and today he was not looking very handsome. Of all the days, of course he would be having a bad day on their wedding day. Alison had noticed it the moment she'd seen him before the ceremony, but to be kind, she had done her best to pretend she didn't notice. They stole away from the toast, took the photos, then returned to the reception by which point everyone was eating. In the whirlwind of activity that followed, it was a couple hours later when, as the reception was beginning to wind down, that they finally realized they'd forgotten to cut the cake.

Alison put her head on his shoulder as they sat together at the table. "We should head to the hotel for the drinks reception," she said.

"Sounds good," he said.

They stood and waved to some nearby guests and stepped onto the street, leaving the garden behind them.

"I can't believe it's over," she said.

"Me too," he said.

"We're married!"

He stopped in the street, turned to her, and kissed her.

As they turned to continue walking to the hotel, suddenly there were footsteps behind them, and then a voice.

"Alison!"

They turned around. Stuart was running up to them.

"Alison, wait!"

"What?" There was irritation in her voice.

"You need to take off your dress," Stuart said.

"What? Why?"

"You'll get it dirty on the walk over," his father-in-law said.

Alison, he saw, understood the preposterousness of it.

"It's not going to get dirty. Who cares anyway? I'm not going to wear it again. We want to walk over," she said. Stuart winced at the word "we."

"Alison, just change before you go. It's not a big deal," Stuart said.

He almost asked Stuart why, if it was not a big deal, Stuart was making it into one. But he bit his tongue. He would let Alison handle this herself, since he knew Stuart wanted him to get involved, so that Stuart could accuse him of interfering in a situation that wasn't his concern. If he replied to Stuart by insisting that it was in fact his concern, Stuart would then accuse him of being controlling and unnecessarily aggressive. If he told Stuart to take a hike, which frankly would be perfectly understandable, Stuart would accuse him of ingratitude and rudeness, and make more of a scene than he already was. He didn't want to fall into the trap of being the stereotypical "controlling husband," so he would make Stuart work for the false narrative, by keeping quiet no matter how absurd or pathetic the provocations became both here, and in the future.

"Dad, this is outrageous. We just got married, we want to walk over, and I'm not changing," she said.

Alison looked at him. "Come on, let's go," she said. She turned away from Stuart who was speechless.

When they were out of earshot, he said, "I'm sorry for not saying anything. I didn't want him to have the excuse."

"I know. Thank you. It's so stupid," she said

The encounter with Stuart in the street be it as it may, the honeymoon had begun. There was that evening's reception at the hotel, then a brunch the next morning, after which the guests all said their goodbyes. Stuart and Linda were leaving for a vacation up the coast, his friends all had to get back to work, and her friends had places to be as well. He actually felt relieved when it was over. That night, they moved their things into an apartment they would have for the week. Alison was on the couch playing on her phone with all the photographs, the windows were open, and there was the sound of crickets coming from outside.

"My feet have blisters again! Could you maybe get me band aids from the store?"

"Of course."

When he got out of the store, he stood in the empty parking lot, listening to the silent night. He felt like he was floating, like he was ten feet tall. This wasn't simply a transitory euphoria to nowhere, but the beginning of something he knew that God would ensure would never end. He was a husband now, and it was good. He would make sure to kiss her when she opened the door, so she knew he had no regret.

He knocked, but there was no answer. He remembered the spare key under the mat, unlocked the door, and stepped inside. Nobody was in the living room, but he could hear Alison's voice coming from the bedroom. He walked down the hall, and opened the door. His wife turned to face him, with a haunted look of frustration and desperation on her face.

She put the hand to the receiver. "It's my dad."

"Your dad?"

"Yeah. He wants me to come see him."

"About what?"

"He says he has to see me."

He sighed. "When?"

"Now," she said.

"Now? It's nine at night."

"He wants me to come to a coffee shop and talk to him. He says if I don't, he'll never see me again."

"This is absurd. I told you there's something really weird about this guy. Unbelievable. It's the first night of our honeymoon and your dad is calling you to come down to see him, or else he'll never talk to you again? That's normal." He put his hands in his palms and laughed incredulously. "I thought they were supposed to be taking a trip?"

"I know, I know. They're leaving tomorrow," she said. He stood in the doorway watching her talk.

"Dad, I'm sorry, but I'm not coming. First the dress a couple days ago and now this, it's too much. You need to respect our space," she said. She hung up the phone.

He knew she would internalize Stuart's call by blaming herself. And even though it made no sense to do so, since she was utterly blameless, she would convince herself that he now regretted marrying her—no doubt Stuart had placed the call to her tonight knowing that it would make her feel precisely that. Any daughter who treats her own father this cruelly, so the perverse logic went, is not the kind of woman truly worthy of love or worthy of a husband. That was the implication of the call. If Stuart could not have her, and she would not do as Stuart said, then she must be made to feel anyone else claiming to love her, even her new husband, only must be lying. She would be made to feel that she was unlovable. As patently absurd as what Stuart was suggesting may be, he could see it was taking her in. After so many years of so many nights just like these, of all the ultimatums, the manipulations, the coercions, and the false promises, she had become so used to it, she even believed she deserved it. Stuart and Linda had made her feel unworthy of anything else. He wished he could find a way to make her see it was a lie. He had no regret, and she should feel no guilt. He was about to speak when he was overwhelmed with that old familiar feeling. Sometimes, he thought, there is no point in saying anything, since words do nothing. He left the room, and they were silent the rest of the night.

Twenty-eight

"Righty-o, if you just sign and initial here, I'll grab your keys, and you'll be all set," she said.

"Many thanks, Sally," he said. He signed his name on the agreement, then handed it to Alison, who did the same.

The Treasurer looked over the document, nodded approvingly, stood up from her desk, and retrieved two sets of keys from a metal wall cabinet.

"This one," she said holding up the larger of two keys, "is for the main door. The other one is for the side gate that leads to the yard. Rubbish is collected on Tuesdays. If you have any maintenance requests or need anything else, we have a team that'll service any issues for free, simply get in touch with us."

"Beautiful, thank you," he said.

"You're welcome," she said smiling.

They grabbed their keys, stepped into the upstairs hallway, walked down the stairs, and walked out onto Tom Quad.

Alison did a twirl and smiled. "Let's go see the fish," she said.

"Okay."

She opened an umbrella, and they walked to the fountain.

"Hello my little fish men," she said, extending a finger.

He looked at Mercury. Alison looked up from the pond smiling, expecting him to be watching her at play with the koi. When she saw that he wasn't, her brow wrinkled in worry.

"Is something wrong?"

"No," he said. "I just—"

The summer had ended, it was autumn, and they had moved everything across the Atlantic. It was their first day back in Oxford, and by nightfall they would be in their first place together as a married couple.

He knew he should be grateful, but something was weighing on him, even if he couldn't identify what the source of the concern was precisely.

"Don't be worried about the meeting. It'll be fine," she said.

In a way, she was right, although for reasons she did not yet fully understand. The meeting was indeed nothing to worry about. Tomorrow, he would see Klaus for coffee at the SCR. The situation in which he found himself was by now clear, he thought. The meeting itself was merely a surface phenomenon, something that would further reveal a much deeper undercurrent. As far as he was concerned, the issue facing him, then, was not the meeting itself, or the larger set of circumstances of which it formed only a small crumb, but rather the fact that there was no way of explaining any of this to Alison, since the nature of the situation, he knew, was unapparent to anyone but him. He would have to let it play itself out until she saw it for herself, as he did the best that he could to navigate his way through it in the meantime.

He tried to imagine how, if he were to accept that nobody would believe him and simply try nevertheless to tell somebody what he knew, he would characterize the situation in Oxford. Something roughly as follows, he thought. Threatened by the direction his work was taking, and the fact that he could not be compromised, Quiller and Eliot had instructed Klaus to redirect the supervision along a path the network could tolerate. If he did not acquiesce, Klaus would be told to terminate the supervision. His career at Oxford would come to an abrupt end, there would be no doctorate, and his future as an academic would be over. Naturally, if it did come to this, everything would be done in such a way to ensure that it appeared that he had brought the ruin upon himself unnecessarily, something which in turn would cause Alison understandably to resent him. She would be led to believe that he had betrayed their future, by throwing away the life they should have been theirs. There were others close to the situation who stood to profit. Carrell was one beneficiary. After having failed to scuttle the work in Texas, Klaus was now being instructed to do so here in Oxford, and Carrell, who would know this, would consequently turn a blind eye, allowing things to run their course. For all he knew, Carrell very well may already be in touch with Quiller about everything. But whether or not Carrell was actively coordinating with those in Oxford, both Quiller and Klaus were right to rely on Carrell not presenting an obstacle to their plans, since all three of them had an equal interest in destroying his work. Then there was Stuart. It would also be in Stuart's own personal interests to permit Carrell, Quiller, and Klaus to go ahead with the plan to professionally destroy him. With his son-in-law's academic career and reputation ruined, Stuart's goal of imploding the marriage would be made easier. It was impossible to know, but his intuition was that Carrell and Stuart would already have discussed all this in Texas, or at least would discuss it eventually. At any rate, Carrell and Stuart would have a mutual tacit understanding with one another, that it was in both their interests to let the hurricane currently brewing offshore to reach land. He sighed as he looked at the koi. If he was about to reap a whirlwind here in Oxford, nobody in Texas was going to do a thing to help him. He was on his own.

"Depending on how the coffee goes, I may have to stay late tomorrow for dinner and then drinks," he said.

"Is Zoe going to be there too?"

"Probably."

He wanted to tell her the fact that Klaus was bringing Zoe was designed to have the effect it was, to make Alison nervous and uncomfortable. It was all mind games.

"Okay," Alison sighed.

"I'm not like him," he said.

"I know you're not," she said.

"Let's pick up some things for the house before we go in," he said.

She stood and smiled, "Sounds good."

It was only drizzling, so when Alison was in the shops, he went outside, lit a cigarette, and leaned over the graveyard's wrought iron fence. Most of the headstones were so old that time had eroded the names. If they were able to communicate, how many of those buried here would say they had regretted the way they'd lived? He had heard the list of things people were reported to have said they regretted on their deathbeds. Not spending more time with friends and family, worrying too much about their jobs, and so on. He could see the rationale for regretting all that. But such lists rarely mentioned the regret of never having become the individual God had wanted someone to become. That, he thought, must be the worst thing to have to regret about one's life—that it really had never been a life, just a performance for others, one elaborate attempt to stifle the claim God had exerted on one. He took a long breath, leaned up against the fence, and watched the people passing by. Nobody so much as glanced at the gravestones. How telling, he thought, to have an ancient graveyard located in the midst of the bustling city center, only for everyone to be completely oblivious. The walkers, and cyclists, and motorists, were all as immersed in their present cares as the dead had once been by theirs. Probably, those buried in the graveyard behind him had themselves been as indifferent to the dead as the now living were. Whether the words that entered his mind were a cause for sadness, or for joy, he didn't know: "For all flesh is as grass, and all the glory of man as the flower of grass. The grass withereth, and the flower thereof falleth away."

Watching everyone around him resolutely ignore death made him melancholy. There could be no genuine community, or sincere solidarity, among men when the world, and those who loved it, pretended that they would all be here forever. Living as if the fact that they would not be here forever mattered so little to them that it was entirely beneath contemplation, as if it deserved to be banished completely from their consciousness. That, it seemed to him, could lead only to the societal dysfunction everyone saw. People complained about the injustice and inequality in the world, yet they inhabited the very shallow, narcissistic attitude responsible for allowing such evil to reign unchecked. The memory of death was nothing to them, when in truth it should matter more than anything. Since time was finite, but everyone pretended that it was not, all that resulted from that attitude would be a pretense, too. There was a clear motivation for the mindset. To countenance the transience of all things was a very short step from raising the question of God seriously, and those who clung to time, blunting the claim of eternity, had no intention of letting God intrude into their lives. Hence, the graveyard was ignored, along with all the dead that had come before, since their nameless headstones were a reminder of something beyond the time leading to death, something those living wholly dispersed into the world did not want to acknowledge. In a way, things really hadn't changed essentially any since Eden, when Adam and Eve hid themselves from God. Society, he saw, was just a big joint enterprise, in which everyone was hiding from God while pretending not to be. There was something deeply unsettling about how things carried on so absurdly, without anyone ever seriously questioning how he was even here, or why. Evidently people liked it that way.

"Ready!" It was Alison.

"Okay, great, let's go see the place," he said smiling. He could tell she wanted to tell him to stop worrying about whatever was worrying him, but she said nothing.

They walked down George, then across the roundabout, and then past the train station. Just up the street, near the corner, was the place: 1A Cripley Road.

"It's so cute," Alison said, sitting down on the stone wall in front of the flat. The limestone building was handsome, with the blue and white trimming for which Oxford flats were famous. The building itself was two stories, their flat on the ground. The front door facing the street led to the upstairs unit. "This way," Alison said, grabbing his hand, as they followed the walkway against the fence leading to the side door.

"This is it," he said. "You do it."

She turned the key and the door opened. There was a small kitchen and bathroom, a bedroom with a view looking onto the yard, a living room with a view to the street, and a laundry room in the back. It was a small space, but he liked it immediately.

"It's quaint," he said. Alison, who he could tell was a bit let down but afraid to say so, opened the door in the kitchen leading to the back yard. Thankfully, the yard was nice, which made up slightly for the plainness of the interior.

"We'll have to get furniture for outside," she said. "It's so nice out here. Our very own English garden!" She kissed him. After she finished taking pictures and they had unpacked their things, it was time for bed. He stared at the ceiling, as she rested her head on his chest.

"Everything will be fine," she said drifting off to sleep.

"I know," he whispered. He wasn't lying. It would be fine, he knew, even if he currently couldn't see how that it would be. There was no other choice. He would walk by faith.

Twenty-nine

A FTER checking his email, he opened the bedroom window, lit a cigarette, and watched the sparrows on the patio, finding what would be his new morning routine. He had been anticipating what he had just read, so it did not put him off balance. The only thing to do would be to pay attention to detail, which above all would mean guarding what he said to others. He would be sufficiently engaged to be polite, but not loquaciously so. Klaus would be looking for clues. The less he could give Klaus and Quiller to go on, the better.

Alison woke from sleep and sat up rubbing her eyes. "What's wrong?"

"Nothing. Klaus cancelled the coffee. He wants to meet for dinner instead at the Hall."

"Informal or formal?"

"Formal. They'll probably want drinks at the SCR after that."

When evening came, he put his gown under his arm, said goodbye to Alison, and walked to the college. François was at the gate.

"Hello, it's been a while," the Porter said.

"Yes, hello. My wife and I just arrived yesterday. We were in the States for the summer."

"Ah, well welcome back. Where is she?"

"She's at home tonight. I'm here to have dinner with my supervisor."

François looked at him intently.

"Klaus Carman."

"Oh, yes, I know Klaus," the Porter said.

"Have a good night," he said.

"You too," François said.

When he got to the Ante-Hall, Klaus was not there. He ordered a shot of whiskey at the Buttery, drank it down, then looked over to the Ante-Hall. Still no Klaus. The doors to Hall would be closing in just a minute. He ordered another shot, gulped it down, then walked back into the Ante-Hall. Just as the dining staff was closing the doors, Klaus came running up the stairs.

"Sorry I'm late," he said, as he walked into the Hall.

They took a seat together, then a few seconds later stood for the grace.

Everyone bowed his head, and the words began echoing through the Hall, "*Nos, miseri homines et egeni, pro cibis—*"

His thought drifted to when he was young and had been studying Latin. He tried to recall all the conjugation tables and declensions, but it was all gone. What a shame, he thought. All that knowledge wasted. There had been a time where he could read the *Aeneid*. Now he couldn't even understand the grace at dinner. It was a decline, and a humbling one. The prayer ended, and they all took their seats.

Klaus turned to him. "Wine?" Some others sitting near them had extra bottles and had offered one of theirs.

"Sure, thanks," he said. He watched the glass fill, and he recalled all the cheap boxed red wine he used to buy when he had lived in Texas. After all the drinking, he'd never felt any happier. From what he'd seen, all it did was make everyone sadder. He sighed.

"Something wrong?"

He turned to Klaus, "No," he said.

"How's April?"

"She's good. Tired from the travel."

"So, you're married now?"

"Yes."

"Congratulations."

"Thanks."

"I'm sorry I wasn't able to attend." Before Alison and he had suspected that something might be off with Klaus, they had invited him.

"Oh, it's fine."

"I'm sorry we haven't discussed your work as much as we should have. Last year was very hectic for me, as you know," Klaus said.

"How's the situation?"

"It's great. We're now a couple."

"And the husband?"

"She's getting a divorce. I've made plans for her to meet you tonight after dinner at the SCR."

"That's good."

"Heard from Carrell? You were back in Texas for the summer, right?"

"For much of it, yes. No, didn't hear from Carrell. I assumed he was busy." He could see Klaus wanted him to ask whether Klaus had been in touch with Carrell, but he didn't ask. Klaus would say he and Carrell hadn't spoken, but it was now clear that they had.

"Remind me, what is April's, I mean Alison's, family situation? She's originally from Texas, correct?" Klaus was very sharp, but when the situation was this obvious, there was no natural way to conceal the truth. Klaus had been asked to see what sort of information he was likely to give those he trusted. The first question about Carrell, and now the follow-up question about Alison's family, was meant to give Klaus and others insight into his present state of thinking. They would want to see whether he would open up about Stuart and Carrell, and what he would say, if he did.

"Her mother is retired. Used to be a lawyer. Her dad's a physicist."

"A physicist? Interesting," Klaus said

"Yeah, he does research funded by the Defense Department. You know, designing weapon systems to kill people in illegal wars," he laughed. That would be enough to change the subject. Klaus poured them both another glass of wine, and took a bite of his chicken.

"I've spoken to Quiller." He waited for Klaus to continue.

"He's very impressed with you. But there are concerns that the project, as currently envisioned, is overly ambitious for a graduate thesis." He had been expecting the negotiations to start after dinner at the SCR. The fact Klaus would bring up Quiller and the thesis now meant they were even more eager to resolve the problem than he had thought they were.

"I'm happy to hear he's impressed with the work. I think the main takeaway from the transfer meeting, at least in my opinion, is that both he and Hodges wanted me to delve further into the secondary literature."

"Yes, that will certainly be important," Klaus said.

"Were I to do so, would that resolve the concern that the thesis is too ambitious? Or is that a separate concern?"

"It's related, to be sure. But, yes, addressing the dearth of secondary literature won't by itself resolve the concerns regarding the ambitiousness of the thesis. A DPhil must be tight and polished. It is better to focus on something limited, and do a job with it that will persuade one's examiners, than to bite off more than one can chew. There will be time for that later," Klaus said. Of course, there would only be time for it, assuming he passed, and he would pass only if he pleased his examiners, and he would please his examiners only if Klaus and Quiller were first pleased. They held the keys to the kingdom, and if he wanted to step into the world of academia as a professor, he would have to learn to do what he was told. Klaus liked the fact that he was smart enough to understand all this, but Klaus also resented him for being reluctant to do what one was supposed to do. He didn't think Klaus resented him for simply wanting to be a non-conformist; Klaus resented him because part of Klaus himself wanted to be one too, but had chosen not to be. He knew that for Klaus, seeing him was for Klaus probably like encountering a younger version of himself, when Klaus had been faced with the same choice. If Klaus and the others had done what they were led to believe was necessary to get to where they were, nobody else would be allowed to run an end-around the way things were done. One does what one's supervisor says, or else. Quiller had made clear to Klaus what Klaus was to tell him, and if he didn't do what Klaus asked, Quiller would tell Klaus to dump him.

"I thought Maureen's talk last term was very interesting," he said.

"Yes, me too. She does good work," Klaus said.

It would only be natural for Klaus to broach the topic of the Carrell volume that Maureen was intending to edit, but Klaus didn't touch it. He wondered why not. Maureen would almost certainly have mentioned the volume to Klaus. Still, it was possible that Klaus didn't yet know about it. Then again, even if Maureen had in fact mentioned the volume to Klaus while she had been here in Oxford, if she had told Klaus the fact that he would be editing it along with her, Klaus might be avoiding the topic for that very reason, since Klaus's student having the opportunity to edit such a volume would only make it harder for Quiller and Klaus to claim he truly wasn't able to make a contribution to the scholarly literature. They were trying to lay the foundation for a narrative that his work wasn't up to par, so the invitation to edit this volume would only undermine that. At any rate, if Maureen had told Klaus about the volume but not also invited Klaus to contribute, that also would explain the silence. Perhaps Klaus was simply jealous at being excluded. Or, perhaps Maureen had invited him to edit the volume merely as a test to see how he would react, to see whether he would mention it to Klaus or Carrell. In fact, despite being invited to edit it, it wasn't inconceivable that he'd never hear from Maureen about it again. There were just too many possibilities to narrow it to one. All he knew is that psychological intrigues over who was, or wasn't, invited to contribute to some academic volume wasn't the kind of life he wanted for himself. He just wanted to be able to write philosophy, not play professional mind games with others for the chance to write something.

The college, and the worldly lifestyle it epitomized, was the pinnacle of everything modernism stood for. To be sure, there was the lip service to ideas and knowledge. But it was really all about a social existence, a community in which everyone achieved his freedom by way of institutional recognition of others. The truly astounding thing, he thought, was that otherwise intelligent adults took it seriously. It was like little girls and boys playing house or army, only now the adults believed the game was real. How strange that Klaus and the others would choose to lead a life whose very accomplishments were inevitably brushed aside so cavalierly by others anyway. The problem with seeking the esteem of others was that it was pointless. He had seen it so many times before during all the drunken academic conversations over the years. A truly great thinker, a Plato or a Kant, for instance, became a little name tossed around as if it were nothing, a mere prop for whomever was speaking to be able to hog the spotlight at some party, or dinner, or bonfire, or barbeque. It was like watching hyenas tear at a carcass. Only stranger, because the hyenas themselves all desired to become the meat one day. Seeking recognition from others was foolishness, he thought. That, probably, was why he had never understood the appeal of Hegelianism. Take, for example, the Carrell volume at stake. It would go virtually unread when it was published, just as Carrell's own body of work had. And when such academic work was read, it was usually read only by a handful of others looking for the slightest reason to dismiss it as wrong-headed or otherwise inadequate, to attack it, either out of professional jealousy or personal animosity, or a combination of both. Even when what was said in the work was true, it would provoke scorn or resentment in those who read it. When the end goal was winning the esteem of others, the truth itself was no asset. If what one wrote were true, then others would simply deny its originality, claiming everyone already knew what it said. If it happened to be both true and original, there was always the further option of questioning the sincerity or purity of the motives for one's having said it. What one said, then, regardless of whether it was true or not, original or not, honest or not, would be seen by others as little else than a trampoline for themselves and their own careers. The world of academic scholarship, and the life it demanded, was more Hobbesian than anything else: "Solitary, poor, nasty, brutish, and short." Carrell's own life exemplified it. If one were truly lucky, perhaps one might earn a building on campus named in one's honor or maybe an endowed chair. In Carrell's case, success meant a *festschrift* before retirement, a professional swan song before death in obscurity. It was pathetic and vulgar. Even when it was deserved, such social recognition, or esteem, was elusive, since the pride and jealousy of others would prevent one from garnering it. And when it was received, it was hollow and unsatisfying, precisely because one knew how everyone really felt, even though they would never say it. He took a sip of his wine, and sighed. If he were ever to write something, it would not be for professional recognition, or for social approval, or for the praise of men.

"There's an upcoming conference in Canada. They've accepted the paper. It's the reduction chapter, which is central to the thesis, as it stands. If I present it there, maybe I'll receive some good feedback," he said to Klaus.

A look of panic flooded Klaus's face. Klaus composed himself. "That might be good. Who else will be there?"

He listed a number of very prominent scholars, some of whom were from Paris, and who were more senior and powerful than Klaus. He would share the work publicly with them, receive positive encouragement, then let Klaus know he had received the positive feedback he had. This would put Klaus in the difficult position of having to pretend the work was not strong when clearly it was. The aim was to force Klaus into a situation, where he would be forced to disagree with others, rather than solely with him. Klaus knew this is what he was doing, but Klaus couldn't say not to do it, since Klaus wasn't able to come out and explicitly say that the quality of the work itself was irrelevant to whether or not the examiners would pass the DPhil. Things were shaping up to be a game of chicken, and it would be a question of who would swerve first.

"I watched *Drive*," Klaus said. He waited for Klaus to say more. "Didn't get it," Klaus said shaking his head.

He held his tongue. Deception, lies, and ulterior motives thrived in the darkness of ambiguity. If he were to give himself any chance of getting through the program with a degree and his integrity still intact, he would have to dispel the ambiguity, by shining a light on things, and forcing people to reveal themselves by their deeds. Judgments and inferences and surmises would only get him so far.

As Klaus was about to say something more, the dining staff began serving desert. One server would set down a piece of cake, while the other server would pour the chocolate sauce. The server reached them, setting down the cake. The second server poured sauce on his plate, and then moved past Klaus. Klaus looked at him baffled, then turned to the server, raising his voice and his arms.

"Hey!"

The server turned to face Klaus.

Klaus pointed incredulously to his plate. "Where's my sauce?" Judging by Klaus's angry face, Klaus thought the server had skipped him intentionally.

"Oh, I'm so sorry, sir," the server said apologetically.

"No need to apologize. Thank you," Klaus said.

They ate their cake in silence, and when they were finished, they stood to head to the SCR.

At the door, Klaus punched in the code. "Welcome to the Senior Common Room," he said. Inside was a large fireplace, a big espresso machine, and a number of leather couches. Zoe, who was with a young man from the college whom he recognized, stood to greet them.

She stuck out her hand. "It's so good finally to meet you," she said.

"It's nice to meet you," he said, shaking her hand.

"This is Thomas," she said

"Hi," he said, giving his name.

Thomas looked at him. "So, you're reading for the DPhil in philosophy?"

"Yes. You?"

"I'm a JRF. History," he said.

"I see. Well, congratulations. I know how competitive those posts are."

Thomas looked slightly surprised he didn't seem envious. "Oh, thank you. Zoe and I were about to have another glass. Shall I pour you one?"

The question was directed to him, but Klaus answered. "Yes, please. Actually, it appears we'll be needing more wine shortly. Zoe, do you want to come with me to get some?"

He sat down next to Thomas on the couch as Zoe and Klaus left the SCR. Thomas took a sip of his wine, crossed his leg, and turned to him.

"So, you work with Klaus?"

"Yes. You know him?"

"Fairly well, yes. I know Zoe as well." So, Thomas knew about the affair, and was fine with it. It was now his turn to say whether he was fine with it.

"I've known Klaus for a number of years. This is my first time meeting Zoe."

"I see. I didn't know you knew Klaus prior to coming here to Oxford," Thomas said.

The conversation continued like this, weaving around the essential, everything that was worth being said remaining unsaid, but implied nonetheless. It was not that he was unable to play the game, it was that he found it boring. Others were titillated by it but not him. Just as he was growing exhausted, Klaus and Zoe came in giggling.

"More wine," Zoe said plopping down on the couch. Klaus took a seat next to her. Judging by their flush faces and the amount of time they were gone, they clearly had just had sex.

Zoe looked at Klaus. "What if the Censors find out?"

"It will be fine," Klaus said

"Eventually they'll notice," she said.

"You worry too much," Klaus said, pouring everyone more wine.

Klaus turned to him. "We just came from the college's wine cellar. I'll show it to you sometime. It's quite the collection."

He realized they must have stolen the wine from the cellar, and now Zoe was worried that if the college authorities ever found out it was them, they might also start asking questions about the affair. The college Blue Book forbade sexual relationships among colleagues, unless they were disclosed. Because Zoe had been cheating on her husband, which was scandalous, Klaus and Zoe had not reported the relationship to the college. That must have been why Klaus had told him not to mention it to anyone when he had arrived last year.

Klaus and Thomas began talking, while he sat silently and listened. He could feel Zoe staring at him. When the next bottle was opened, she stood from the couch, and took a seat next to him. He looked at Klaus, who kept talking to Thomas.

"So, I hear you're married?"

"Yes, this summer," he said.

"Fantastic. Congratulations. You must be over the moon," she said, grabbing his wrist.

"Yes, we're very happy. I'm sure you'll have a chance to meet her soon," he said.

"Oh, I would love that. Klaus and I should have you over in London. We have a place right near Paddington."

"Excuse me, I'm going to step out for a smoke," he said. He walked out to the quad, lit a cigarette, and sat down. He wasn't in the mood to get back inside, so he smoked two. When he knew that everyone in the SCR might start thinking he had left, he decided to return.

"Oh, there you are! I was starting to worry you'd run off," Zoe said. His mind pictured the Dutch woman from the Borough Market in London.

He sat down where he'd been before. He looked at Thomas, who continued talking to Klaus.

"More wine?" Zoe giggled.

"Oh, no thank you. I'll probably be going soon," he said.

"But it's still so early!" Zoe rubbed her foot against his leg, then down to his foot. He waited for Klaus to look over, or to say something, but he didn't. He sighed softly.

"You seem stressed," she said

"I don't think so. I've always sighed my whole life."

She ran a finger down his forearm and smiled at him. "It's so good to meet you finally," she said. She was badly inebriated. In all likelihood, she wouldn't remember anything from tonight. He turned to Klaus.

"Klaus, I should be going. Thanks so much for dinner tonight. And thanks for the feedback on the dissertation. I'll have to think more about what Quiller said."

He stood, and so did Klaus. They shook hands and said goodbye. Thomas leaned over and was immersed in conversation with Zoe. There was no point in saying anything to either of them, since they were both gone.

It was only when he got home and removed his jacket that he realized how flustered he was. Alison looked at him worriedly.

"Where's your gown?"

"Ugh, I can't believe it. I left it at the SCR."

"How'd it go?"

He looked at her and laughed grimly, "You have no idea."

"That bad?"

"Worse," he said. Explaining that his supervisor was currently attempting to groom him into having sex with his mistress, in order to be able to blackmail him, was not a conversation worth having.

"You'll figure it out. You always do."

THIRTY

"KOALA, hurry! Look!"

He jumped from his desk in the bedroom, and ran into the living room. Alison was cozied up underneath a blanket reading on the couch, the soft lights from the Christmas tree filling the room. She pointed out the window. "It's snowing!"

He ran back to the bedroom and looked out the window onto the patio. The ground was already covered in snow.

"You're right! It's really coming down," he said.

In the living room, they walked to the window together, and pulled open the blinds fully. The falling snowflakes trembled underneath the street lamps, wafting down like feathers.

"Come on, we have to go outside," she said excitedly.

"But you hate the cold!"

"I know, but it's so beautiful. It's our first Oxford snow." She put on her big down jacket and boots, and went outside, where she twirled in the street. A few of their neighbors had come outside as well.

"Merry Christmas," they said.

"Merry Christmas," she said.

They took photographs, and she made a snow angel. When there was no sign of the snow letting up, they decided to take a walk through the town center.

"Think about how pretty Tom Quad must look right now," she said. "Let's go!" She stuck her arms through his, her teeth chattering from the cold, as they walked to the college.

"Oh, no!"

"What?"

He caught up to her at the fountain pond.

"The fish! It's frozen," she said. "What do you think happens to them?"

"They're probably alive. I think it's just the surface that's frozen."

"I don't know, it's so shallow. Do you think it froze all the way through?"

"I don't know, maybe they're dead then."

Alison thought for a moment then smiled. "I'm sure the college removed them from the pond in preparation for the snow. They're probably fine," she said.

He looked at her, "Want me to take a picture of you?"

"Sure," she said.

The entire quad was sunken in snow, the green grass buried beneath the white powder. The storm was swelling, the snowflakes now coming down in violent flurries. The wind was stinging their faces, and their hands were numb.

"This is what I imagined when you first told me you'd been accepted," Alison said, with happy tears in her eyes.

"I know, me too." They hugged.

She smiled, "What do you think everything else looks like?"

"Let's go see," he said.

They walked through Peck Quad and onto the street. They crossed the High, and took a seat on a bench on Broad. He looked at the gargoyle faces lining the walls at the Sheldonian. The men here in Oxford might be ugly, he thought, but the heavens and the earth were not. A night like this was a reminder that there was a God in heaven, and that all would be well. He would have to remember that whenever he might later feel like giving up. He smiled at Alison, and kissed her.

THIRTY-ONE

"Everyone please thank tonight's speaker," Fernandez said. There was applause. "Next time, we'll be hearing a talk from one of our very own Oxford graduate students." Fernandez paused and turned to him. "What is the topic?"

"The phenomenological reduction in Husserl and Heidegger," he said.

"Well, there you have it, folks. Very interesting, so you will want to be sure to attend. As usual tonight, feel free to join us for food and drink at Quod." Everyone stood to leave.

Joseph Bingley approached him. "Nervous?"

"A little bit, but not really. Once you realize that the worst that could happen is being wrong, it's not such a big deal. If I'm wrong, I want to know, so there's really nothing to worry about," he said.

Joseph smiled. "I like that. Good point. Are you coming to Quod?"

"Yes. You?"

"I'll pop in for a bit. Melissa's away, so I don't have to hurry home," Joseph explained.

"Any new developments with the Herder?"

"Actually, as it happens, yes. I think the last time we spoke, I had said I'd hit a wall. But I had a breakthrough recently."

"Great! Tell me," he said. They strolled out the building and down the street to the restaurant. Inside, they put their coats on the rack, and took a seat at the table.

Tonight's seminar speaker, William Maddow, was from Sussex like Maureen. He didn't know whether Maddow and Maureen were close, but they certainly knew one another. Maddow had given a paper on Fichte's transcendental account of the origins of property rights. It was a testament to the speaker's remarkable charisma to have been able to make such a dry topic interesting. He would never say that to the speaker, of course, but, in any case, there was no need to say so anyway, since he could tell that the speaker obviously derived satisfaction in knowing he had been able to do so. The man was in his fifties, with glasses and a mousey appearance, thick brown curly hair, and in a gray suit like a businessman. He could tell Maddow had been waiting for an opportunity to introduce himself, which Maddow now took.

Maddow turned to Joseph casually, and looked at them across the table. "Herder?"

"Yes, Herder."

"Now that's a name one doesn't hear enough," Maddow said.

Joseph smiled, "Agreed!"

Maddow turned to Klaus who was seated next to him. "Is this the new student of yours?" Klaus was silent.

"No, I think you must mean him," Joseph said, pointing to him.

"Ah, I see. Well, I'm William. Very good to meet you," he said, extending his hand.

"Likewise," he said, giving his name.

"So, Daniel mentioned that you're the seminar's next speaker. Husserl and Heidegger?"

"Yeah, we'll see how it goes."

"You're addressing the reduction. Very important topic. It seems you didn't fall too far from the tree, after having studied with Carrell. Maureen told me about you." He could see William was waiting to see whether he'd mention the volume. Best to be quiet, he thought.

"I hear there's a volume in the works," William said, turning to Klaus. "Volume?"

"Yes," William said, turning from Klaus to him. "Maureen said you might be doing some editorial work on it with her." William and he looked at Klaus, whose eyes flashed with anger. It was unclear whether William was taunting Klaus, or whether he was simply fishing for gossip about Carrell. Perhaps both, he decided.

Klaus turned to him. "You never mentioned any volume to me," Klaus said.

"Yes, there's a volume on Carrell's work in the works. Maureen asked if I was interested in helping her co-edit it."

William interjected, "Oh, Klaus, don't be angry. I'm sure he didn't mean anything by it. When you're young like that, you're still learning the ropes." William turned to him. "Did Maureen tell you that you could mention it to anyone?"

He looked at William. "No, she never said anything about that either way."

"See, there you go, Klaus. He was simply being prudent. It's reasonable to assume in a situation like this that Maureen was expecting confidentiality," William said to Klaus.

Joseph cleared his throat, and asked, "So what's the central claim of the paper?"

"I'm going to summarize the reduction in Husserl and Heidegger, then turn to how developments in France suggest a different way of looking at the reduction."

William appeared interested. "Which texts from France will you be examining?"

"Primarily *Reduction and Givenness*," he said.

"Ah, yes, something of a classic," William said. "Would you mind sending me the paper when it's ready? I'd be interested in reading it."

"Oh, sure. I'd be happy to." He looked at Klaus. "Actually, I'm going to be presenting it at a conference in Canada next month. I'll want to polish it in light of the feedback I receive there. But after that, I'll send it on," he said.

"That would be fabulous," William said smiling. William turned to Klaus. "What do you think of the issue?"

"It's a big topic. We'll see what Quiller and Dowell have to say," Klaus said.

The waitress brought menus.

"I should be going. An emergency back in London," Klaus said. William was confused.

"Should I come with you? I haven't had a chance to get into my place yet," William said.

"I need to head to the train station now," Klaus said. Klaus stood up, put his jacket on, and said goodbye to the group. When he got outside, William stood up as well.

William glanced at Joseph and him. "Please excuse me. I'll walk with Klaus down to the station, and then come back. Hold that thought on Herder."

An hour later, William returned, though by then Joseph and everyone else had left.

"I'm so sorry about the delay," William said. "Where were we?"

"Joseph was going to lay out some insights into Herder. It's too bad he had to leave."

"Yes, it's a shame. I'm interested in hearing more about the reduction paper, though," William said. They talked for another hour, having the kind of intellectual exchange he had always imagined he would have at Oxford. It was something of an irony that the conversation should take place with a professor from elsewhere.

William looked at his wedding ring. "Married, I see," he said.

"Yes."

"How long?"

"Not even a year yet," he said.

"Ah! Newlyweds. Fantastic. Is she here in Oxford?"

"Yeah. Which is great. My first year here she was still home in the States."

"What does she do?"

"She's an artist."

William smiled. "Is that so?"

"Yeah."

"Well, it's a shame I wasn't able to meet her tonight. Let me give you something," he said, as he fished into his shirt pocket. "Here," he said.

It was a business card. "Tell her to feel free to get in touch with me. If she's ever interested in applying to the Ruskin, I could help her get in," William said.

"Wow, thank you. I know Alison will be thrilled. She's been thinking about going to graduate school for the arts," he said.

William looked around the room. "It's getting late. I should be going."

"Yes, me too," he said. They stood and shook hands, and walked outside.

"Good luck with your work," William said.

"Thank you."

They went their separate ways into the night. He couldn't be sure, but when he got home, he felt like he could tell Alison he had made a friend.

Thirty-two

WHEN he arrived to the Strawson Room, nobody else was yet there. He took a seat down at the head of the table, and waited. The talk would begin at the bottom of the hour, which was twenty minutes from now, and the early birds would begin arriving within the next ten minutes or so. He laid out his paper on the table, and reviewed the notes he'd written down on a pad.

The oak doors opened, and two regulars, Phil and David, came in.

"Hello, hello," David said waving.

"Hi, guys," he said. They sat down and unpacked their things.

Phil looked at him excitedly. "Ready?"

"I think so."

"I'm very interested to see how it goes this evening. I read the abstract online. Sure to stir up some controversy, I think, given all the Heideggerians here," Phil said. David chuckled.

A few minutes later, others he did not recognize entered. Then some theology students followed. He was surprised when Manan entered the room. His old friend bowed politely and took a seat. A minute later, there were voices outside the door, and then Quiller came in chatting with Joseph. Joseph waved, as Quiller took his usual seat at the far side of table. He was beginning to get nervous. He stood up when Klaus came in and walked over.

"We'll start at five-thirty on the dot," Klaus said. He had just worn a white t-shirt. He could see Klaus wanted to say something about it, but Klaus didn't.

"I'm going to run down to the store to get a soda. I'll be right back," he told Klaus. He walked out to the street, grabbed a bill from his pocket, got an orange soda, and came back to the Strawson Room. By now the table was full, and all the chairs lining the walls were taken too. It was the most crowded he'd seen it. Quiller and Klaus were talking to one another quietly at the other end of the table. The doors opened again, and this time it was Mike Dowell, a prominent American Heidegger scholar on a fellowship here in Oxford for the year. Dowell took a seat next to Quiller and Klaus. Phil looked over at him, nodded toward the three of them, and then winked at him.

The room fell silent when Fernandez entered and took a seat next to him. "I'll introduce you, and then we'll begin," Fernandez said.

"Okay, sounds good."

After Fernandez's introduction, he provided some opening remarks about the paper, by sketching the origin of the ideas, and how the material in the paper fit within the dissertation as a whole. He was nervous, and he felt like his voice sounded shaky, but he knew that once he began reading, the nerves would settle quickly. He took a breath, and began reading. Most of what followed afterwards was a blur. He could sense it was going well, because when he would look up from the page to view the room, everyone was smiling and nodding, and many were scribbling notes excitedly. Even Quiller chuckled when he quoted approvingly a humorous passage from the young Heidegger's recollections of his early disillusioning days in Göttingen: "For a whole semester Husserl's students argued about how a mailbox looks." Heidegger's point, which was one of his own paper's too, was that philosophical reflection on the meaning of existence must itself be serious, yet there was a persistent tendency among academic philosophers to fall well short of that mark. When he finished reading, the room erupted in enthusiastic applause and a number of hands shot up immediately, since many people were eager to ask questions. Quiller, who would be the first to ask one, was instead silent, since commenting on the work here tonight would disqualify him from later serving as an examiner for the viva. But if Quiller had to keep his powder dry, Mike Dowell did not.

Fernandez called on Dowell, and everyone turned to watch him ask the question.

"Thanks for the talk. Very interesting. I have a number of questions I could ask, but I guess I'll stick to just one. It has to do with your handling of Kierkegaard. I worry that you're enlisting him in support of a view that's not really his own, although you suggest that it is. You seem to suggest that Kierkegaard's conception of being an authentic self entails some sort of decision to die to the world, but that's not how I understand his view of the God-relationship. Could you explain where exactly you're getting this view of his work?"

"Sure, thanks for the question. Well, having read a lot of Kierkegaard, I'm not sure what else to say. It seems to me obvious that one of the recurring themes of his life's work is the idea the world in some sense is false, or a lie, as he would say, and that the entire point of life is to focus on eternity and God in such a way that one's relationship to time exhibits the understanding that the most important thing about existence is our relationship to God."

"Yes, I think you're right that Kierkegaard stresses the importance of the God-relationship in orienting us to our temporality, but I still disagree that Kierkegaard thinks that means necessarily first recognizing the phenomenon of what you're calling vanity." By vanity, he had meant a relation to the world that might alternatively be called melancholia, or what a longstanding spiritual tradition called *acedia*. It was the disgust with finite things, the sense that they were empty or somehow meaningless because they were ultimately unsatisfying. Until one had such an experience and responded honestly to it, the possibility of entering into a proper God-relationship was foreclosed. One would remain lost in the world.

He looked at Dowell. "But I think that's precisely what Kierkegaard means," he said.

Dowell was now visibly agitated. Dowell had assumed he would take the comment at face value, as if it were a clear correction. That he would publicly challenge Dowell had evidently not crossed Dowell's mind. "But again, I just don't see where you're getting that in Kierkegaard. Where does Kierkegaard suggest that the ultimate goal of existence is simply readying for eternity?" he said.

The room turned to him. "That's what was written on his tombstone," he said.

Klaus flinched, Dowell looked shocked, and the entire room was tense. In the name of challenging the interpretation of Kierkegaard offered in the paper, Dowell had shown everyone his ignorance of what Kierkegaard had really said on the matter. He knew that Dowell and the others at the seminar would later look up the hymn on the gravestone, which undoubtedly showed that Kierkegaard had himself viewed temporal life as a mere prelude to eternal life. He thought about reciting the hymn to the room now anyway, but there was no need. Better to let Dowell go home and read it for himself.

In a little while,
I shall have won,
The entire battle
Will at once be done.
Then I may rest
In halls of roses
And unceasingly,
And unceasingly
Speak with my Jesus.

After that, the remaining questions were much more collegial. When it was all over, everyone clapped. Quiller, Dowell, and Klaus stood from their seats, and were the first to leave. None of them said a word to him, or even looked his way. It was just like being back on the baseball field with Rick and Johno, he thought. The others at the seminar milled around for a while, chatting enthusiastically while readying to leave for Quod. Phil and David came up to him.

Phil was ecstatic, "What a talk!"

"That was even more intense than a viva," David said.

"Yes, yes it was. I've never seen anything like that before," Phil exclaimed. They both patted him on the back, and shook his hand.

He walked with Manan and Joseph to Quod, where Alison was waiting at the door. She kissed him. "How'd it go?"

"It was a great talk," Joseph said before he could reply.

They all took a seat at the table. Klaus wasn't there, a sign that Klaus would make him pay for what he had done tonight. He didn't care. It was worth it.

THIRTY-THREE

THE next morning, the email he expected was waiting for him. He read it carefully, leaned back in his chair, threw his hands up, and lit a cigarette at the window.

"What is it?"

He turned to Alison and smiled ruefully. "Klaus."

"What did he say? Is he angry?"

"You can read it."

"No, just tell me," she said.

"He wants to meet this afternoon at his office."

"Maybe that's good. Usually, he ignores you."

"Exactly."

"What? I don't get it."

"Usually, he ignores me, because he feels like he has everything under control. After yesterday's talk where everyone saw my work, he and Quiller have to do damage-control, so he wants to see me. They're pissed."

"Oh," she said.

He thought about telling her about Maureen and the Carrell volume, William Maddow, and the upcoming Canada conference. He took another drag.

"Don't be angry at me," she said.

"I'm not. I'm just thinking."

He wanted to tell her the stress they were putting him under was meant to affect his mood so as to interfere with their marriage, by making her think he was angry with her. If he said that, however, she would understandably think he was simply making excuses, which would only make it worse. No doubt Quiller and Klaus knew all this, which is why they were applying the pressure that they were. The more turmoil they could create at home, the more prone he was to make a mistake professionally. He might simply even quit and go home. Everything they would do would be all about trying to induce a mistake on his part.

"Things are going to get very bad very soon, I think," he said. "I'm sorry. I'm going to need you to trust me. Sometimes you're just going to have to take my word on things, even if I can't explain it to you."

"That's not fair! This is my life, too. I married you. We have a future. What happens to you professionally impacts me," she said.

"Exactly."

"What does that mean?"

"They know that. So, the more they interfere with my work, the more stress at home. They're messing with you."

"You can't just run off and do whatever you want and expect me to deal with the fall-out. That's not fair. I should have a say also."

"I'm not saying you shouldn't have a say. I'm saying that there are some things I'll have to do that I might not be able to explain. That's not disregarding your opinion or your feelings. It's just saying that there are limits to what you'll understand."

"So, you're saying I'm stupid?"

"No, I'm saying that you haven't spent years in higher education, you're not in the meetings, you don't understand these institutions and their norms, so you're not in a position to pick up on all the details. I have to do that, because it's my job."

She looked at him frustratedly.

"Who was the second assessor for my transfer meeting?"

She looked surprised. "I don't know. Why are you asking me that?"

"Hodges. It was Hodges. I'm making a point. How are you going to expect me to explain the intricacies of what's going on when you don't even know who one of my examiners was? You were expecting me to take care of things, you assumed you didn't have to know anything, and now that I'm telling you it's going to be complicated, you're acting like you have a right to know everything. Well, there's no way for me to explain the situation, if you don't know something as basic as who Hodges is."

She stared at him.

"Who's the DGS?"

"What's the DGS?"

"The Director of Graduate Studies. It's the person at the Faculty who's going to have to mediate between Klaus and me, if there's any complaint about the supervision filed. Who's the DGS?"

"I don't know."

"What college is the DGS at? Which other people at the Faculty are at that same college?"

"I don't know."

"Which Faculty does the Senior Proctor work at?"

"Senior Proctor?"

"Look up the Proctors' Office. They're the body that handles academic appeals."

"Academic appeals? You passed your transfer of status meeting!"

"I'm going to have to file an academic appeal, if anything happens with my viva."

"What would happen with your viva?"

"They'll fail it. Hence the eventual need for an appeal. Who's the Proctor?"

"I don't know," she said, throwing her hands up.

"I'm not attacking you. I'm just making a point." He looked at the time and sighed. "I have to go. I'm supposed to be meeting numb nuts at one. I want to get lunch first." He went to leave.

He heard Alison's voice from the room. "You're not going to kiss me?"

He went back in. "Sorry." They kissed. "I love you."

"I love you too," she said, squeezing his hand. "I'm just scared."

"It'll be fine," he said.

When he got to the blue doors, he knocked twice.

"Come in."

Klaus was sitting at his desk. He took a seat on the couch. Klaus was scribbling something down on a piece of paper. When he was done writing, he stood up and took a seat at the chair.

"I want to talk to you about last night," Klaus said. He waited for Klaus to continue.

"Why don't you tell me how you think it went," Klaus said.

"I think it went very well. The talk was well-attended, which suggests to me that everyone finds the material interesting. Some of the questions were pointed and challenging, but I think that's a testament to the originality of the work. It's good, I think, that it provoked a strong response. A number of people afterwards came up to say they thought the talk was great, and they hadn't seen an exchange like that before, even in a viva. So, I think it was all positive."

Klaus put on a look of bewilderment. "You think it went well? Really?"

"Yeah," he said.

"What's your interpretation, then, of Dowell's line of questioning?"

"I gather he thought I had fundamentally misread Kierkegaard. I didn't think my handling of Kierkegaard was central to the paper, so I'm not sure why he made a point of focusing on it, but because I've always been an admirer of Kierkegaard, I was happy to talk about it."

"Your comment to him about the gravestone! That's not how it works. That's not how you do it." Klaus had read the hymn evidently. Dowell must have too.

"Do what?"

"Mike is an eminent, senior scholar. He was asking you a question. That's not how you answer his question."

"He brought up the subject. I simply addressed it in turn."

Klaus sighed exasperatedly, "What about the rest of it?"

"What do you mean?"

"For starters, your handling of the secondary literature."

"You mean the parts on Heideggerian authenticity?"

"Yes," Klaus said. In the course of the paper, he had quoted from a recent volume of essays to which Dowell and Carrell had both contributed. Klaus had written an endorsement for the book jacket. The fact that he had drawn on the material only to criticize it had obviously upset Klaus.

"Did I misread the essays?"

"Dowell was right there in the room," Klaus said. The implication was that it had been rude to quote Dowell's work critically when Dowell was in attendance.

"I wrote the paper long before I knew Dowell would be there. Was I supposed to take out the quotation simply because he'd be there? During my transfer meeting, Quiller told me I had to focus more on the secondary literature. That's what I did," he said.

"Not like that," Klaus said.

"So, Dowell can ask me a question implying I'm completely wrong about Kierkegaard, and I'm obliged to answer, but I can't quote his own work when it's directly relevant to a point I'm making in the paper?"

"There are rules about this," Klaus said.

He laughed. "Rules? I didn't come all this way to Oxford to write book reports, Klaus," he said.

Klaus's face turned beet red. His eyes began watering, and for a moment, it appeared he would burst into tears. He was livid.

"*Book reports?*"

"Yes, book reports. I didn't come here to sit around regurgitating what everyone else has already said. If somebody wants to know about that, they can read what others have said. That's not philosophy, though. Quiller told me to add secondary literature to the thesis, so out of respect for the process, I did so. Now you're upset that I did."

Klaus stared at him for a half a minute.

"This is not how it works," Klaus said. "I need to talk to Quiller, and then I'll be in touch." Klaus stood to show him the door.

When he got outside to Peck Quad, he lit a cigarette, and watched all the students head into the Library. What an absurd situation, he thought. To come all this way to Oxford with the aim of writing something that might be worth adding to a library, only instead to have everyone here do all they could to actively thwart him from doing so. He sighed. When he got home, Alison would see the meeting had gone badly, and it would be impossible to explain why.

He opened the door gently. She was napping. When she heard him come in, she stirred from sleep.

He stood in the doorway. "Do you want to talk now?"

She smiled in her half-sleep. "Sure," she said, nodding her head.

"It went terribly."

"What happened?"

"Quiller and Klaus are angry that everyone liked the paper. Dowell's angry too. They're telling me to stop, and if I don't, they'll probably sink me completely."

"How? They can't do that," she said.

"Who will stop them?"

"What about the DGS and the Proctor? You just mentioned them."

"It's not that simple," he said. "There aren't any rules. It's all fake. The people I'm dealing with can do whatever they want."

She sat up in bed and lit a cigarette. "When you left, I read a terrible story in the local paper," she said.

"What?"

"It's about three guys sentenced today for sex-trafficking young girls here in town. Dozens of victims," she said.

"Yeah, they use the harems as a cover for trafficking," he said.

"The police got them, at least."

"Some of the low-level guys, yes. The police don't ever touch the VIP pedophile rings, though. We never got around to watching the Johnny Gosch documentary," he said.

She looked at him, "Want to watch it tonight?"

"Sure," he said. They were both quiet. "Look, honey, I know most people we know would never believe me. I know it sounds crazy. But tonight, when you're watching the documentary, understand that there are very powerful people and institutions running these things. It's everywhere, including academia. Some of those people are here in Oxford and London."

"What's your point?"

"My point is that if law enforcement will look the other way when top government officials, corporate heads, celebrities, and others are being blackmailed by the intelligence services for abusing children, then certainly Quiller and Klaus are able to bend the rules over a philosophy viva. Oxford is a corrupt institution. Look at Clinton. He should be in jail for money-laundering and drug-running and God knows what else, and instead his daughter's right here reading for the DPhil, as if there's nothing wrong with it." He paused. "And you know I'm not picking on the Clintons. All that right-left stuff is nonsense. The Bushes are just as bad. They were running drugs too with the CIA back in the eighties."

"I know," Alison said.

Thirty-four

A LISON was out shopping at Sainsbury's. When he looked at his phone, which was ringing, he was surprised to see it wasn't her calling. It was a number he didn't recognize.

"Hello?"

"It's Klaus." He composed himself. Klaus had never called him before. Whatever Klaus was calling to say was something Klaus didn't want to leave in writing over email.

"How are you doing?"

"I've talked to Quiller."

"And Dowell too?"

"That's not the point." So, he'd spoken to Dowell too. They were all working together.

"Okay, so what is?"

"The Canada conference: you're not going. If you want to continue working with me, you need to spend the next few months intensely re-working the dissertation, nothing else. I don't care about conferences, or other papers, or anything like that. All you need to care about is pleasing your examiners, and that means pleasing me."

"What about the Carrell volume?"

"That can wait."

"Isn't that Maureen's decision, not yours?"

"I just told you. Your priority is reworking the thesis in the way that will please your examiners."

"And Quiller still wants to be the internal examiner?"

"That is the expectation. He serves as the internal examiner in this area."

"If I receive feedback on the paper in Canada, won't that make the paper stronger? The paper is in the dissertation. So how is going to Canada not working on the thesis?"

"I don't care what anyone else thinks about the work. And it doesn't matter if your work is published. All that matters is what I'm telling you. The term is over, take the summer to make your decision." Klaus hung up the phone.

He sighed, adjusted his scarf to blunt the cold, and looked up at the moon. According to all the university statutes and regulations, as well as Faculty and college procedure, a doctoral supervisor was supposed to be actively helping the student share his work at conferences and publish. And here was Klaus doing the exact opposite, even going so far as threatening to terminate the supervision if he continued doing what he was supposed to be doing as a student. He hadn't been asking Klaus to help him with any of the things Klaus was supposed to help with anyway. And now Klaus wanted more, telling him to shut everything down. It was all standard psychological warfare, laid out precisely according to Biderman's Chart of Coercion. First was isolation and monopolization of perception. The goal was to shape his view of his own work solely in light of what Klaus and Quiller said. That wouldn't be possible if outside experts were still seeing the work and thinking well of it. Hence, Klaus's command not to go to Canada. If he continued not complying with Klaus, next would be humiliation and degradation. Then, of course, there were always the threats. At this stage, the main threat was to fail his viva, which is why Klaus kept speaking about the examiners. If Klaus and Quiller thought the situation warranted it, owing to the situation having intensified, so the severity of the threats might too.

Alison came smiling down the street with groceries.

"It's so cold," she said.

"Here, let me take that," he said, grabbing some of the bags.

"Thanks," she said.

They set the groceries down on the kitchen table.

"Is something wrong?"

"Klaus just called."

"He called you? That's weird. You just saw him for a meeting. What did he want?"

"He says I can't go to Canada."

"What? Why?"

"Do you want what he said, or what's really going on?"

"What's really going on," she said.

"Okay. Quiller's been trying to shut down the work. Klaus is under instructions to do so, and so far, I haven't listened. I made it to the talk at the Strawson Room, and now that everyone's seen the work, Quiller and Klaus are panicking. It's getting too embarrassing to pretend the work is fundamentally flawed when it clearly isn't, so in order to block it at the viva, they're trying first to hide it from others. If I share the work in Canada, they know that's just more exposure, which will make their goal more embarrassing."

"What are you going to do?"

"I'm going to go to Canada. Klaus is bluffing. No matter what I do, they're going to flunk me out."

"What did he say he wanted?"

"He said no Canada. No other conferences, either. No publishing. No circulating the work with others. He said to focus entirely on the dissertation only."

"What about the Carrell volume?"

"That's off the table, too," he said

"What? He can't do that. What about Carrell?"

"He'll get a hold of me, if he wants to," he said. He didn't want to tell her yet that Carrell was probably already working with Quiller and Klaus. He hadn't heard from Maureen. It was looking increasingly likely that she had been asked to invite him to edit the volume simply to see how he'd react. Now that Quiller and Carrell or whomever else had the information they wanted, Maureen had been told to disappear.

"What about Dowell?"

"Dowell wants a job at Oxford. He'll do whatever Quiller says. That's why Klaus brought him over for the year. It's a trial run. If Dowell gets in the way of what Quiller and Klaus are planning to do to my work at the viva, they won't bring him over permanently. Dowell's going to play dumb and pretend to stay out of it. He's not going to help."

"Okay, maybe don't go to Canada," she said.

"And then what? Don't you understand? The entire thing is a farce. They pretend it's about the quality of the work, but it's really just a compliance test. People whose work is terrible pass easily. Others who have great work languish for years, and eventually quit. Even if I don't go to Canada and do everything they say, they'll just stick me in a loop where I'm constantly receiving new objections to the work, and being told to revise it. It'll never end. Look at Alex and Joe. They've been working forever on their theses, even though their theses are obviously already good enough. But somehow Beth flies right through? It has nothing to do with the quality of the work."

Alison had met Quiller and Klaus's other doctoral students at a Faculty cocktail party. She knew that Beth was a bit of a ditz, while the other two were very sharp. It made no sense how she could supposedly be poised to pass her viva, while Alex and Joe were being told their own work still required fundamental changes before it would be ready.

"Do you want me to end up like them? The chains are never broken. Once you submit, they own you the rest of your life. They write the letters, sit on the hiring committees, and control the publishers. Do you want me to be forty years old worrying about whether I'll get tenure all based on whether Quiller and Klaus are happy with me?"

He could see Alison shudder. "No," she said.

"Okay, so it's now or never."

"So, what does that mean?"

"It means I'm going to Canada, and I'm going to push through this by the work. That's what it's all supposed to be about, anyway. It's not my fault the system is phony," he said.

"Okay," she said. "We forgot to watch the Gosch documentary. Let's watch it tonight."

When the film was over, he thought about saying something. But he didn't. She gave him a kiss, turned over, and went to sleep.

Thirty-five

He woke up with a pit in his stomach. He went to the window, lit a cigarette, and stared at the birds. It was summer, but it was still cloudy. He coughed heavily. His lips hurt and he could feel his body rejecting the smoke, but as unpleasant as smoking was, he couldn't quit. He was addicted. He would like a cigarette to think, to relived the stress, but it didn't work, he knew. When he did smoke, the stress never abated, and the fact that it didn't only intensified the desire for another one, which only in turn led to further dread when it didn't do any better to alleviate the stress any better than the first one had. . Sometimes now when he smoked, he felt like he might be dying, which he knew was preposterous, but it didn't matter if he knew it was irrational. That's simply how he felt.

"I'm so tired of the clouds," Alison said from bed.

"Me too."

"We should take a trip," she said.

"We should."

"Where do you want to go?"

"Florida? I've always wanted to see St. Augustine."

"St. Augustine? Let me look it up. Oh, it's pretty. We could go there."

"Where did you have in mind?"

"I don't know, maybe the Riviera."

"That would be nice. You know, I never mentioned it, but Horowitz has a place in Montenegro."

"Montenegro?"

"Yeah, look it up. The coast there is beautiful. It's affordable, too."

He put out his cigarette. He was about to light another one, when he decided not to put it off. He would check his email. He sat down at his desk and opened up his laptop.

He laughed incredulously.

"What? What's wrong?"

"Well, it's really kicking off now," he sighed.

"What? Tell me."

"Klaus just reported me to the DGS. You'll be happy to know that he's currently enjoying himself in Barcelona on vacation. I guess I'm supposed to sit here and wait for him to return."

"Reported you? For what?"

"Just read the email yourself. I can answer your questions after that," he said, handing her the laptop. He watched as she read carefully.

She looked up at him with a panicked expression.

"So, he's claiming that you're ruining the supervision? I don't understand. Are you in trouble?"

"He's setting up a narrative with Quiller. They have to be able to pull the plug on the supervision, which means they have to start building a paper trail showing that there supposedly was a problem. They know I might file a complaint against Klaus, so they decided to get out in front of that by having Klaus be the one to go to the DGS first." He told her how it was a breach of University regulations for Klaus to have forbade him from attending the conference.

"Okay, so he says here to the DGS that there's a problem with the supervision. But he doesn't say specifically what it is. So, what is it? What's he going to say?"

"He's deliberately left it indeterminate for now. He wants to see how I react, so that he and Quiller can decide how to respond."

"So, what are you going to do?"

"I'm going to talk to the DGS."

"What are you going to say?"

"I won't know until I see her in person. Then I'll know," he said.

Alison fell into the pillows, and put her hands over her face. "This is a nightmare," she whispered.

"I know. They're making it that way. That's the point," he said.

He wrote the DGS, introducing himself, and asking whether she might have a time available at which they could meet. She responded that same day, saying she would be in touch with a meeting time once she had heard more from Klaus about the precise nature of Klaus's concern.

The weeks dragged on, and he heard nothing.

One night, Alison came into the living room where he was staring at the wall. "Where is the DGS? It's August already."

"I don't know," he said.

"What are you going to do?"

"Wait. I'm going to wait." He turned to her and smiled, "Do you know Psalm 37? 'Rest in the Lord, and wait patiently for him: fret not thyself because of him who prospereth in his way, because of the man who bringeth wicked devices to pass.' That's what I'm going to do. Wait."

She sat down next to him and clasped his hand. "I'm sorry," she said.

"For what?"

"It wasn't supposed to be like this," she said.

"It was inevitable. I should have been more honest with myself. I thought I could come here and slip through. I was lying to myself," he said. She began sniffling.

"I just want everything to be okay," she said.

"I know. I'm sorry. I should have told you what was going to happen," he said.

"I didn't sign up for this," she said. He could see she saw the words stung. "I'm sorry," she said, "I didn't mean that."

"You know, the next thing they're going to do is say I'm crazy. That's what conspirators do. They attack the credibility of the one being targeted by accusing him of being crazy. It's funny, because that's what they did to David," he said.

"David?"

"Yeah, King David. He knew his enemies were plotting against him, but those who knew him dismissed it." He sighed.

"I don't dismiss it," she said.

"I know, I'm sorry. I didn't mean to suggest you do. I just meant the others. Our friends and family at home. Everyone here in Oxford. My dad knows what's going on, but other than that, nobody else will ever listen," he said. He thought about mentioning Stuart, but he knew it was too soon for that. It would only lead to an argument.

"I'm going to bed," she said quietly.

He stayed up, and before he knew it, sun rays were coming through the blinds. Morning had come. He left without saying anything, since Alison was still sleeping. The sun was out for the first time in weeks. He went to the college and checked his mail. There was nothing there, but it felt good to be out. He crossed the street, and bought a coffee and sausage rolls from his old spot. When he got home, Alison was in the kitchen.

"I was wondering where you were," she said. "You didn't get me any coffee?"

"No, I'm sorry. I thought you would still be sleeping," he said.

"That's okay."

"I'll be right back. I can get you one," he said.

"No, no, you don't have to do that.

"I want to," he said. "Muppet Man will be so disappointed it's just me," he said. She laughed.

The rest of the week passed by as the previous weeks had. When it appeared nothing would happen, finally there was a note from the DGS. She would see him tomorrow afternoon at three-thirty at All Souls.

He told Alison the news when she came home.

"Okay, this is good. I can't believe it took so long. Is Klaus back?"

"I assume so. I haven't heard from him, though."

"What's the DGS going to say?"

"I don't know."

She looked at him. "Do you want to get dinner?"

"I would, but I have to do something. I need to go to the college," he said.

"Now?"

"Yes, now."

"What for?"

"I need to talk to Wood," he said.

"Wood? Why? You haven't seen him since last year."

"I know."

"Okay, fine, whatever," she said, throwing up her arms. "Do you want me to wait for you to get home?"

"You don't have to do that. But if you do wait, I can pick something up on the way home. Pizza?"

She smiled. "Mama Mia's?"

"Sure," he said smiling. He kissed her. "I'll see you soon."

"Be careful," she said.

At the college, a number of parishioners were leaving the Cathedral. Wood, who would have attended Evensong, would be due back to his place soon. He waited at the door.

A few minutes later, Wood came down the quad to the door.

"You'll have to attend an Evensong one of these days," Wood said.

"Yes, it's been a while, I'm afraid," he said.

Wood fumbled for the key. "Well, for you to turn up at my door like this, I assume it's important. Why don't you come in?"

"Thank you."

They took a seat in the study.

Wood looked at him. "How was your summer? It's been a while."

"It was good. Alison and I got married. We're doing our best to settle in now over on Cripley."

"And the work?"

He laughed. "Good question. I'm pleased with it, but not everybody else is."

"I see," Wood said. "What's the issue?"

"Have Joseph or Manan mentioned the talk I gave at the Strawson Room?"

"Joseph said something about it. Apparently, it was a talk on the reduction. He said he thought it went quite well."

"So did I, but evidently Klaus doesn't."

"Well, that's between you and him, I'm afraid. Is it the theological turn in your thinking?"

"That's partly it, I think." They were both quiet.

"I tried reading Barth."

"You did?"

"Yes."

"What did you think?"

"He's brilliant."

"I can tell there's a 'but.'"

"There is."

"What?"

"I feel he overcomplicates things. He doesn't let the Scriptures speak for themselves."

"In what way?"

"Are you a universalist?"

"I am. But I thought we were discussing Barth."

"We are. I'm just giving an example. The Scriptures repeatedly talk about judgment and damnation. Yet you're a universalist. You have a systematic theology wherein that makes sense. But that's the problem. The system has nothing to do with what the Scriptures actually say. I feel that's what Barth does. He twists the Scriptures to say what he wants them to say, rather than conforming his thinking to what they do say."

Wood laughed. "Well, if you've already alienated the philosophers, you may as well do so with the theologians, too, I see," he said.

"I guess so," he said quietly.

"What else is on your mind other than the mysteries of salvation?"

"I simply have a clerical sort of question. Tomorrow, I'm meeting with the Faculty of Philosophy DGS. Klaus has written her to complain about the supervision. I wanted to ask: in your experience, are footnotes counted toward the word-count for a DPhil thesis?"

"Footnotes?"

"Yes, footnotes," he said.

"No, not at all. I mean, I've never seen anyone make an issue of it," Wood said.

"Okay, thanks."

"I didn't know Klaus had gone to the DGS. I suppose this is serious. What's going on?"

"I don't know, which is part of the problem. He wrote the DGS weeks ago, and I hadn't heard anything about it until today. Have you seen him? At the time, he said he was in Spain."

"We had a Governing Body meeting last week, so he's back."

"Well, that's good to know. The next time you see him, give him my regards."

"I'll be sure to do so," Wood said.

Out on the quad, he lit a cigarette, and mulled it over. Wood was intending to sit this one out until there was a clear winner. Wood would not intercede on his behalf, but neither would he actively support Klaus. Everything must be coming at this point solely from Quiller, then. He coughed for a few seconds, until he regained his breath. He would have to make sure not to smoke before the meeting with the DGS.

The next day, he arrived at All Souls. Inside the gate, the porter stopped him.

"Sorry, sir, the college is closed to the public."

"I'm a Member of the House. I have an appointment here," he said, pointing to the DGS's office, which was on the main quad.

"Oh, I'm very sorry."

"It's fine," he said.

He knocked on the door. The DGS opened, and smiled warmly. "Come in," she said. It was their first time meeting one another in person. She was short, with wavy brown hair, and glasses. She was probably older than she looked, but because she was tan and thin, she looked vital for her age.

"Please sit down," she said gesturing to the couch.

"Thanks."

She took a seat at her computer. "I wanted to check again just to make sure," she said. She was quiet for a minute. "Yes, that's so," she said to herself, as she turned to him.

"I have still not yet heard anything definitive from Klaus. When he originally emailed us, I asked whether he would like to Skype. He said that he would, but he missed our appointment. He should be back from Barcelona, but he has not responded to my subsequent messages," she said.

"I see," he said.

"At this point, I'm not sure what I can do for you until I've spoken to him. Why don't you come over here, and we'll draft a message together." He walked over to the computer.

She started typing. The message was short and to the point. Klaus was asked to reply, so that he could explain to her his original reasons for having written her.

"Do you want me to tell him that we've spoken?"

"No, I think not," he said.

"Yes, I think that's prudent. Okay, here it goes," she said clicking the send button.

"When I hear from him, I shall let you know," she said. "Do you have examiners lined up for your viva?"

"Quiller will be the internal, I think. He was my transfer assessor, and he'll be acting again as an assessor for the confirmation."

"And the external?"

"I really have no idea. I was assuming Klaus would arrange that, but now I'm not so sure."

"Have you talked to the Placement Director about all this?"

"Not yet," he said.

"You should. Are you participating in this year's Placement Scheme?"

"I was intending to."

"Okay, good. Next term, when letters of recommendation are due, have a chat with the Placement Director about your viva."

"Okay, thanks." She let him out.

He took a seat on a bench on the High, and lit a cigarette. The tourists surrounding him were lost in their own world, worried about where to go to dinner, or what to see next. They hadn't the faintest idea about what Oxford was really like, he thought.

The Almond tree had already bloomed, and now it was fading. Another year gone by, he thought. There was no telling whether they'd even be here next year to see it bloom again.

Thirty-six

SEPTEMBER was fading, which meant he had returned from the conference in Canada. It had gone even better than he could have hoped. The feedback on the paper had been incredibly positive, which only confirmed his judgment that those in Oxford attacking it were doing so in bad faith.

The email he'd been waiting for arrived that night. He turned from his desk.

"What is it?"

"Klaus," he said.

"What does he want now? I thought he disappeared."

"Well, I'm back from Canada now, so he and Quiller have had time to talk it over. He wants to see me tomorrow."

"What's he going to say?"

"He'll ask me if I went to the conference, since he knows I did. That'll be his pretext to reignite whatever he was trying to hatch earlier in the summer."

"Okay, so you went to the conference. So, you're trapped."

He lifted a finger and smiled. "*Au contraire, mademoiselle.* Klaus has snared himself, although he doesn't yet know it."

"How?"

"Want to see?"

"Sure."

"Come here," he said. She walked over and sat on his lap. "Look," he said, pointing to the screen.

He opened the exchange with the DGS, and sent her a note, asking whether she'd yet heard from Klaus. "Watch."

A few hours later, the DGS replied.

"She says Klaus hasn't talked to her yet," she said.

"Exactly."

"So, what? Klaus isn't going to try pretending that he has. Why would he do that? It would be stupid to lie about something like that, when you could find out so easily," she said.

He shrugged his shoulders. "When you lie for so long, you get lazy. Klaus has been lying for years. He probably doesn't see the risk. God has blinded him," he said.

He responded to the DGS thanking her for the update, and told her that he would be meeting with Klaus the next day. She replied again, telling him to let her know how the meeting went.

The next afternoon, when he got to the blue doors, he smiled. He thought about the story Andy had told him about Bert, about the time Bert had gone to the party and pretended to be drunk, when really it had only been fruit punch he'd drunk. This was a bit like that, he thought. He would enjoy watching Klaus carry on while Klaus was thinking he was in the catbird seat. Frankly, it would be interesting to see how Klaus would behave when he thought he was in the clear, when he thought his lies were winning the day. He knocked.

"Come in."

Inside, Klaus was already in a seat near the couch. He had a smile, and waved. So, Klaus would pretend everything was resolved. It made sense. From Klaus's perspective, things were resolved. Quiller was backing him, and with Quiller due to act as the internal examiner for the viva, there was no way for him to get the DPhil without their approval, assuming they ever even let him sit for the defense.

"How was your summer?"

"Pretty good. Yours? I see you spent some time in Barcelona."

"It was nice. Zoe had never been before. We had the chance to meet family, too," Klaus said. Klaus looked out the window, then back to him. "I want to apologize," Klaus said.

"For what?"

"The footsie at the SCR. Zoe gets like that when she's been drinking," Klaus said.

There was silence. "Well, before we talk about the work you've done on the thesis over summer, I should tell you I've heard from the DGS," Klaus said. He waited for Klaus to continue. Klaus was trying to be nonchalant, but the glee was palpable. Klaus felt himself to be like a judge at a sentencing hearing, thoroughly enjoying the power.

"She agrees with me that you were out of line. It's not my job to read the books you think I should for the dissertation. The direction the dissertation takes is up to me," he said.

"I see. Well, the fact you're telling me that the DGS has said you don't have to read *Reduction and Givenness*, in order to supervise the thesis would have presented a problem, I think."

"Would have?" Klaus's eyes narrowed.

"Yes. It's all moot now." He could see the worry flood Klaus's face. His supervisor knew he had somehow fallen on his own sword, though he didn't yet know how exactly, and in any case, it was too late to do anything about it.

"What are you talking about?"

"I also spoke to the DGS last night. Well, I suppose I shouldn't say 'also.' We've been in touch since you wrote her from Barcelona. We had a meeting at All Souls last month. She says she's been trying to reach you, but you never replied. Apparently, you blew off a meeting you'd scheduled with her. She says you've never talked to her about the supervision since. You're lying."

"When did you last talk to her?"

"I told you. Last night. She told me to tell her how today's meeting with you went. I'm going to have to write to her to tell her I'll need to arrange a change of supervision. I can't work with someone I can't trust, and I can't trust you after you'd lie to me like this. By the way, I just got back from Canada. It went great. I'm glad I went. It'll open up a lot of avenues for discussion during the confirmation meeting with Quiller, I think," he said.

"With whom are you going to work?"

"I don't know yet. Perhaps Quiller will have a suggestion," he said.

"Perhaps," Klaus said.

"I'll organize the paperwork, and leave it in your pidge for your signature. The DGS will have to sign as well," he said. He stood up and left.

When he got home, Alison was at the door.

"How'd it go?"

"It was fine. I told him I knew he was lying, and I want a change of supervisor."

"Did he deny it?"

"No, he couldn't."

"So, what did he do?"

"He basically just sat there. He'll try to scheme up something again, but it won't matter. This was the first big move. From here on out, they're on defense."

"Who are you going to work with?"

"I'm not sure, but I have some ideas. I have to take care of Quiller first," he said.

He sat down at his laptop, and sent a note to the DGS, saying that Klaus had lied by claiming he'd talked to her about the supervision. He told her, too, that Klaus and he agreed a change of supervision was necessary. Then, he wrote a note to Quiller, telling him about his decision to change supervisors. He mentioned the Canada conference, and asked whether Quiller had any suitable recommendations for a new supervisor. He thought about emailing Carrell also about the change of supervision, but he would deal with Carrell later.

As for the other thing, it was purely a judgment call, as to whether he would do so now or later. May as well keep the pressure up, he thought. He drafted an email to Maureen.

"I want to read you the email to Maureen. Tell me if it sounds okay," he said. He read the note.

"Yeah, sounds good," she said. "Do you think she'll reply?"

"Probably not." He printed out the change of supervision paperwork, and filled out what he could. He lit a cigarette, and looked at the birds.

"What about the supervisor?"

"Morrison," he said.

"Morrison? Who's that?"

He turned around. "Alexander Morrison. He's at St Anne's. He's bigtime. In some ways, it's probably better to work with him than Klaus, anyway."

"Is he theology?"

"No, philosophy."

"What kind?"

"Remember that big book I told you Carrell had said Klaus was walking around with everywhere in Virginia," he said.

"Yeah," she said.

"That's Morrison's book. He focuses on Kant, but he knows a lot of other things. At this stage, the thesis is mostly done. I just need someone to write me a letter of recommendation for the job market, and to help me find an external examiner for the viva," he said.

"Is he friends with Quiller?"

"I don't know. They must know each other."

"What about Klaus?"

"Even if Klaus and Morrison are close, which I'm not sure whether they are, Morrison won't be able to defend Klaus lying the way he did. Klaus really blew it."

She sighed with relief. "Oh, if this works, it would be so good. I hope he'll work with you."

"Me too," he said. "Let's see." He sent an email to Morrison, introducing himself, and asking for a meeting about a potential supervision. He was not by any means yet out of the woods, but at least there was a path forward.

Seeing his good spirits, Alison broached the topic he'd known she had been thinking about for a while.

"My mom's waiting on an answer," she said.

"Yeah, that's fine. I told you it's fine with me if we go back to Texas for Christmas."

"We can go to California, too."

"We don't have to do both. That's a lot of traveling. After the Atlantic flight, it might be better to stay in one place," he said.

"But I like your parents. I want to see them," she said.

"Okay, well then we'll see them too. It's up to you whether you want to go to Texas first and then fly home from California, or whether you want to visit California first, and then fly home from Texas."

"Let's do Texas first, then leave from California," she said.

"Okay, sounds good."

"I'll let you know when I've booked the tickets."

They were quiet.

"You know, maybe we'll be able to celebrate," she said.

"I don't know, don't get your hopes up."

"Isn't December when news of interviews comes in?"

"Yeah, the Eastern APA is over Christmas."

"Should we book you a hotel?"

"No, I'll get one at the last second if I get an interview."

"Do you know where you're applying?"

"Not yet, the ads will be posted soon."

"This is so exciting! I'm fine with moving, but maybe Morrison will want to keep you here," she said.

"It's possible," he said. Nothing was impossible with God, he thought, even that.

THIRTY-SEVEN

I T was raining heavily when he ducked under the Porters' Lodge. He
had never been to St Anne's, so he had left the flat early, allowing
himself time to get lost, and although he didn't get turned around on
the way there, the college was much farther up Woodstock than he had
imagined. As a visitor, its being so far removed from the city center gave
it the charming feeling of an oasis, although there was an unmistakable
atmosphere of isolation, which very well might for those who worked
and studied there feel like being stationed at a wilderness fort that had
been abandoned by its army.

The door to the college opened, and Morrison came out with an
umbrella.

"Ah, I see you've found us," he said. "Apologies for the rain, do come
in. Is this your first time to the college?"

"Yes, it is," he said.

"Well, this way down the hall is a place to leave your coat." He put his
jacket on the rack.

"Right. Have you eaten?"

"No, not yet."

"Lunch is being served, if you're interested."

"That sounds good, thank you," he said.

They walked down the corridor to the hall. There was a buffet line at
the window. They filled their plates, and sat down on the benches.

"Much different from Christ Church, I imagine," Morrison said.

"That's true. But I actually prefer this," he said.

"Yes, me too. It's quiet out here."

They chatted about Oxford philosophy, about the years of Anscombe,
and Foot, and Murdoch. There were stories about Ryle and Strawson and
Austin. Williams and Dummett too.

"I'm looking for someone to help with the copy-editing at *Brain*," Morrison said. When Morrison mentioned *Brain*, he remembered that nothing had ever come of the job Klaus had originally mentioned at *Philosophy Today in Europe*. There was no reason not to apply to this simply because it hadn't worked out before.

"Sounds very interesting. I'll be sure to apply. Thanks for telling me," he said.

"Why don't we get a coffee in the SCR, assuming you have the time," Morrison said.

"That sounds good. Thank you."

The Senior Common Room was empty. "How do you take your coffee?"

"Black," he said.

They sat down in their chairs.

"I understand you're having a supervision issue."

"Yes."

"And you're looking for a new supervisor?"

"Yes."

"And Klaus knows this?"

"He does."

"If you don't mind my asking, what's the issue exactly?" He thought about the talk at the Strawson Room with Dowell and Quiller, the Canada conference, the Carrell volume, and the night at the SCR with Zoe. There was no need to mention all that.

"The DGS told me that Klaus had lied to me in the course of her inquiring into what the issue was in our supervision."

Morrison shifted. "I see. Well, that's a shame. I'd prefer not to hear the details of that, though I can understand why that would be unsettling for you. So, a change is necessary," he said.

"I think so."

"Well, that shouldn't be hard to arrange. Are you familiar with the paperwork?"

"I am," he said. "In fact, I have it right here," he said. He took the papers out.

"Well-prepared, I see!"

"Are you potentially open to taking me on as a student?"

"I'm afraid not. Your work sounds incredibly fascinating, but it's not my area. I'm already stretched thin as it is, with the students I have. But I could suggest some names," he said.

"Okay, that would be great."

"Try George Adamson. He did work on Hegel mostly. He used to be at Trinity. He's emeritus now. Feel free to tell George I've spoken to you," Morrison said.

"Thank you. I appreciate this," he said.

"Oh, you're welcome. Frankly, it's my pleasure. It sounds like a change could do you some good. I'm sorry to hear you've had trouble. George should be up to take you on, I think."

When he got home, Alison looked anxious, but when she saw his smile, she relaxed slightly. "I'm happy you're home. I wanted to tell you that you got a note from Quiller. I saw it because your laptop was open."

"Do you know when he sent it?"

"It was right around when you left to see Morrison," she said. "How'd it go?"

"Pretty well," he said taking a seat at his desk. "Morrison can't take me on, which is disappointing, but he gave me the name of somebody who will."

"Who?"

"Sorry, one second. Let me see the note." He read it and laughed.

"What's so funny?"

"Quiller and Klaus are really falling apart. Quiller says that at this point in my course, it would be too late to arrange a change of supervision, so he's advising me to work it out with Klaus. I just had lunch with Morrison, who told me it would be easy to arrange a change."

"So Quiller's lying?"

"Yeah."

"Who's the other guy?"

"George Adamson. I've heard of him. Never met him. He's retired now."

"Retired? Won't that mean he won't want to help you on the job market and all that other stuff?"

"Possibly. But right now, I can't worry about that. I have to find a way just to get out of here with the degree."

"True. You know, it could be good having an old guy. Maybe he won't care about all this other stuff that Klaus does."

"Hopefully," he said. "I'm going to send him a note."

She came up behind him and put her arms around his neck. "I hope this works," she said.

"Me too. Oh! I almost forgot," he said turning to her.

"What?"

"Don't let me forget that Routledge event tomorrow. The publisher is hosting an event where you can pitch book ideas to their editors. I'm going to check it out."

"You have a book idea?"

"For people at my stage, they're expecting your idea to be a version of your thesis. Since it's basically done, I may as well put it out there and see if there's any interest."

"What time?"

"Two," he said.

"Oh, that's perfect. I'm supposed to meet Janna at three. Where is it? I can meet you there when I'm done."

"It's at the Radcliffe, the building right next to the Faculty."

He sent a reply to Quiller, and then walked to the window and looked at the stars. For now, there was nothing more to do until they heard from Adamson.

THIRTY-EIGHT

HERE was a possibility of snow again in the evening. This afternoon, however, was clear. Clear but cold. He took off his gloves, and smoked a cigarette near the fountain outside the Faculty of Philosophy. The water sculpture directed his thought to the fountain at Tom. He reminded himself to look up more about Mercury sometime soon, maybe tonight when he was home.

A group of fellow philosophy graduate students entered the courtyard from Woodstock and were passing by.

"Hey," one of them said.

He nodded hello, "Luke."

Luke stopped to chat. "What are you doing today?"

"Having a cigarette." He pointed over to the other building. "Routledge is putting on some event this afternoon. Thought I'd check it out in a few minutes," he said.

"Really? Very interesting. I didn't hear about it," Luke said.

"Want to come?"

"I'd love to, but we have seminar. More Rawls," he said.

"Yes, there's always more Rawls," he laughed.

"Tell me about it," Luke chuckled. "Well, good luck. Maybe you'll land a contract. I've heard of stories like that." Luke turned around and walked into the Faculty building with his friends.

In the lobby of the other building was a sign directing everyone interested in attending the event upstairs. Upstairs, a woman from Routledge was seated at a table. There weren't as many people as he'd expected. Maybe a dozen or so. He walked up to the table.

"Hi," he said.

The woman looked up. "Yes?"

"Uh, I'm here to discuss a potential book idea."

She looked at a list. "Is your name here?"

"No. I just heard about the event, and thought I'd stop in."

"So, nobody from your Faculty has contacted us in advance?"

"No."

"What Faculty are you with?"

"Philosophy," he said.

"I see," she said flatly. Evidently, formally the event was open, but really one was supposed to show up only if one's supervisor had first contacted the people at Routledge. He sighed, and took a seat on a couch. He'd stay out of the cold for a bit before heading home.

While he was staring out the window, a man took a seat next to him on the couch. He was middle-aged with slicked back hair. Judging by his sharp suit, he was with Routledge. He didn't say anything to the man, since he didn't want to be a bother.

After a couple minutes, the man put his cellphone down and turned to him.

"Are you here to see someone from Routledge?"

"Uh, well, yes. I am." He put out his hand, and gave his name.

"Billy, Billy Luce," the man said. "I'm a Philosophy Editor at Routledge. What's your area of humanities?"

"Philosophy," he said.

Billy's eyes lit up. "Really? Ah, excellent! Are you a BPhil or DPhil?"

"DPhil."

"What are you working on?"

"Phenomenology," he said.

"Phenomenology! One of my personal favorite areas of Continental philosophy. Do you work with Thomas Quiller?"

"No, Klaus Carman."

"Ah, yes, I know Klaus. He published a book with us fairly recently." Billy paused. "He took a while to finish it," Billy said laughing. "But that's okay. We try to be patient at Routledge."

"Tell me about your work," the editor said. He told him the basics.

"You know, this is just fantastic. We've been looking to commission somebody to write an introduction to this part of the field for a long time. Want to do it?"

He was stunned. "Well, uh, yes of course. I'd be thrilled." The idea of writing the book was simultaneously exhilarating and terrifying. He was concerned that he might fail.

"Great. Let me take your information. Here's my card. Send me a proposal when you're ready, and I'll be in touch." Luce checked his watch. "I'm sorry, I have to go. Very nice meeting you."

"Likewise," he said, shaking Luce's hand.

He looked down at the notes he'd prepared for his book pitch. He would forget about that now. What a turn of events, he thought. He'd come here hoping to have a few minutes with an editor about turning his dissertation into a monograph, and instead an editor had just offered him the opportunity to write the introduction to his entire field. Alison wouldn't believe it. He stood from the couch, walked down the stairs, stepped into the courtyard, and entered the Faculty building. He went up the stairs to the first floor, and examined the portraits of some of the famous Oxford philosophers. It was not an aspiration of his to have his portrait join theirs one day. He simply was ecstatic to now have a way to write something free of interference and control. For the first time since his first weeks here, he again felt like transferring had been worth it.

When he reached the roundabout on Cornmarket, he decided to check his mail at the college. There wasn't anything important in his pidge. He stepped onto Tom Quad and lit a cigarette. He coughed badly, but it didn't matter. Given today's development with Routledge, nothing could disturb or worry him. He looked at the fountain and recalled what he knew. Mercury was another name for Hermes. He tried calling to mind as much of the Roman and Greek pantheon as he could. He wondered why, when he was young, his favorite god had always been Poseidon. Maybe it was his love of the sea. He put out the cigarette and walked through Tom Gate. Across the street was the old graduate apartment. He looked up at his old window. The light was on. He wondered who was living there now. As he was imagining the view that he used to enjoy of the college gardens, a young woman approached the college. She was wearing black designer jeans and a crimson jacket. Her long dark brown hair was blowing in the wind, when her intense green eyes locked on him.

She didn't appear lost, so she wasn't a tourist, who might be contemplating asking him for directions. She could be a student, but he hadn't seen her at the college before, and they were out of term anyway. Before he could leave, she walked up to him.

"Yes?"

She smiled softly. "You think a lot about Mercury, do you?"

He was silent.

She spoke slowly, "You're right. This is just like that night. She's not the only one who can."

He was silent still.

"Were you going to forget to look it up tonight like you told yourself you would earlier?" She smiled. "Well, looking up the name of Mercury won't get you far for what you want to know. You want something deeper anyway."

She laughed and pointed to Wren's tower above them, "You know the story about the Tower. They were building a Tower to heaven." She nodded over to the fountain, "Mystery Babylon is still here. It's all around us. You just need the language to see it." He turned around to see whether the porters were listening to her also. They were busy with some tourists. One of the porters looked at him.

"Need something?"

"No, I just . . . "

The porter waited.

"Have you seen . . . " When he turned around to say something to her, she was already gone.

He started for home. At the train station, he went inside and bought two coffees. When he stepped inside the flat, Alison was in the bedroom.

"You're home!"

"I'm home," he said.

"ASDA arrived. I'll put everything away soon," she said. "Oh, you got coffee."

She walked up to him and kissed him. "Sorry about the change of plans. We lost track of time, and by the time I realized I was late, I figured you would have headed home anyway." For a second, he didn't know what she meant, then he remembered her plans to meet Janna today. She had never shown up after the Routledge book event, but in his excitement, he'd forgotten their plans to meet. Now he was only more distracted after the visitor at Tom Gate.

"Is something wrong? Don't be angry," she said.

"I'm not angry. It's fine that you didn't show up. I forgot about our plans anyway. Sorry," he said. He sat down on the bed.

"So, how did it go?"

"I got a contract."

"What? That's amazing! What happened? Tell me everything!" He told her about Luce.

She clapped her hands in excitement. "This is perfect."

"Yeah," he said.

"What's wrong then?"

"I never told you. This night in London . . . "

"Night in London?"

"Yeah. When I was still here alone. It was before your visit."

Alison looked worried.

"A young woman had been at the pub there. Today on the way home, I stopped at the college. There was a woman . . . "

"The same one? That would be a weird coincidence."

"No, they were different women. I mean, they looked different. But they were identical . . . "

"What happened?"

"She mentioned the statue at the fountain."

"Ugh! The statue! You're obsessed with that thing," she said laughing.

"I don't know why. There's something strange about it."

"What?"

"I don't know. I have to look it up."

He thought for a minute. A tower to heaven. That must be the Tower of Babel from Genesis. He thought more about it. God confounded the languages so that the people could not conspire together against him. Well, that was it. The other name for Mercury is Hermes. Hermes is said to be the messenger god. That was the root of the term hermeneutics, the art of interpretation, the emphasis on language. So, Mercury fountain was really an allusion to the Tower of Babel when God confounded the languages. Mercury, also known as Hermes, was another name for Cush, the kin of Nimrod. What had always baffled him as an entirely arbitrary choice for the fountain's figure now made sense. It was a perfect inversion of what most would think the statue was. He laughed. Here was a famous Oxford college supposedly named in honor of Jesus Christ that places a statue in its main quad commemorating mankind's attempt to dethrone God. It was Mystery Babylon, an open rebellion, just like the one in Genesis eleven, but one very few recognized for what it was. The tourists were oblivious to the esotericism. So were the students, even most of the college dons. There was a core group who understood, and everyone else was in the dark. He wondered if Klaus himself knew that the college statue was an allusion to the Tower of Babel. Certainly, Quiller would.

"Look at this," he said to Alison. He did a search.

"What?"

He pointed to the screen. "Mercury is the Roman name for Hermes. Hermes was the messenger god. That's where we get the name for hermeneutics, which is the art of interpretation. Well, look, another name for Hermes is Cush. Cush was the father of Nimrod."

She stared at him.

"Nimrod led the rebellion against God described in Genesis. They built the Tower of Babel, and God destroyed it, and then divided the speech of man into multiple languages. Hence the need for interpretation, since humanity no longer shared one common tongue. So, in Oxford's largest quadrangle is a statue commemorating Nimrod's rebellion against God, and the dividing of man's speech into the languages because of it. Mystery Babylon, the secret mystery religion. It's Christ Church to the public, but it's truly governed by the spirit of antichrist. They can put it right in our faces knowing nobody will ever understand."

Thirty-nine

B ECAUSE the final weeks of summer had been so eventful, when
Michaelmas term came, he found himself waiting to see what
the results would be. To be sure, there were many moving parts,
and they were connected. After having submitted the book proposal to
Routledge, Luce had replied saying he would be in touch with a contract
shortly. The change of supervision paperwork had been submitted successfully, so now Adamson was his new supervisor. He'd written Morrison
thanking him, and Morrison had seemed pleased. The first meeting with
Adamson had gone well enough. His new supervisor had understood
the outlines of his research, he would supply a letter of recommendation for this season's philosophy job market, he would secure an external examiner for the viva, and he had agreed to set a viva date for early
next calendar year. That only left the confirmation of status as the final
hurdle before reaching the viva itself. Quiller had contacted him about
it, saying that Hodges wouldn't be present for the meeting. He wasn't
worried, since a one-on-one with Quiller would give him the chance to
read Klaus's handler one more time before the viva. He had enrolled in
the Faculty's Placement Scheme, and soon he would begin sending out
applications for jobs at various universities. In a few weeks, he would
present his writing sample for the job market at the Placement Scheme.
Everyone had a don who commented on the paper, and Quiller would be
his, which meant another opportunity to sense what was in store for the
viva. As for this week, it would be a busy one, then. Today there was the
first Placement Scheme meeting. Tomorrow was the first in a series of
Isaiah Berlin Lectures he was meaning to attend. And on Friday was the
confirmation meeting. If things went smoothly over the coming weeks,
he would pass the confirmation examination, he would present his writing sample at the Placement Scheme after which Quiller would be forced

to write him a letter of recommendation for the job market, he would set a date for the viva, and then he would submit his job applications. He might not have the book contract secured in time to mention the contract in his applications, but that was fine, since at least he'd have the viva date set, which meant he could tell selection committees he was poised to take his degree. By then, the term would be over, and he could head back to the States with Alison for Christmas and enjoy a break before he returned to Oxford for the viva. Of course, it was unlikely that everything would go smoothly. There were bound to be some issues. But there was a roadmap forward.

He checked the time and realized it was time to walk to the Faculty for the Placement meeting. When he arrived, there were ten of them. He'd met all the other students before elsewhere. A few of them he knew well. The Placement Director, Ellie Stock, entered the room and everyone fell silent.

"Hello, hello," she said, taking a seat at the head of the table. "I will keep our first meeting today as brief as possible. Before I lay out the details and take any questions, why don't we do introductions." They went around the room stating their names and area of expertise.

"Great, fabulous. Now, here's a sheet with all the major milestones. You must pay attention to these dates. Questions?" Others had questions about the writing sample, about letters of recommendation, and about interviews.

"Mock job talks will start next week. If you are interested in giving one, confirm with me. I already have a list. You should have been assigned a Faculty respondent as well. It's important your paper is polished, because your Faculty respondent will be writing you a letter, so you want to make sure your work is strong, so you give your letter writer something good to work with. Any other questions?"

There was silence.

"Good. Well, that'll do it for the details. As you may have heard, my time as Placement Director comes to an end this term. You should meet the new Placement Director, since he will be responsible for helping you moving forward after this term. There's a seminar about to come in here, so let's go down the hall, where you can talk to him." They all stood up and went down the hall. The room was cramped, and the room was short on chairs, but they were able to fit.

A few minutes later, he walked in.

Ellie turned to the group. "This is Jim," she said. Jim McCoughlin was an American, a recent hire from New York University. The room was excited, because he was famous, and the fact he had agreed to serve as Placement Director meant that everyone knew they'd be able to exploit his connections in the States to their advantage. He ran his hand through his gray hair. "Sorry I'm late everyone. Ellie, is there anything I need to tell them that you haven't yet mentioned?"

"I don't think so. Does anyone have any questions for Jim?" Somebody asked a question about letters of recommendation. The British tended to be more tepid in their rhetoric, something that might form the impression in the mind of an American reader that the recommender was less enthusiastic about the candidate than was truly the case.

"Yes, that can be an issue. It's true that American letters tend to be very gushy, whereas British ones are not. But when a search committee in America sees your letters are coming from Oxford, they will be aware of that. I don't think it's a cause for concern."

Ellie looked at the group. "Remember the deadline for getting your letters to us, if you want the Placement Scheme to vet them. You were supposed to have contacted your letter writers two weeks ago."

One of the students, Alex, one of Klaus's students, was startled.

"Two weeks ago? I haven't contacted my letter writers yet," Alex said. The room laughed.

"*Jesus Christ*, Alex," Ellie said shaking her head incredulously.

The blasphemy was so breezy, it stunned him. He looked around the room, but nobody else seemed to think twice about Ellie's curse. It was so strange, he thought. Somebody like Ellie, a senior professor here in the Faculty, could openly take the Lord's name in vain, and nobody cared. In fact, if he made a comment about it now, or mentioned it to others later, they would find it weird that he thought it was an issue. There was so much discussion about harassment and abuse and hostile work environment. So much rhetoric about diversity and inclusion. And yet, blaspheming Christ didn't even register on the radar. It was perfectly acceptable. The entire presupposition of his profession, and the norms themselves that governed it, was openly antichrist, he saw. He sighed.

Jim looked at him, "Is something wrong?"

He looked at Jim, then to Alex. "I wouldn't worry about your letters, Alex. They're meaningless anyway. In fact, it's probably better that you haven't yet defended your thesis or published anything, because then your letter writers can say whatever they want about your work without selection committees being able to compare the letter to your record."

Alex smiled and another student, Kevin, burst out into laughter, incredulous that he would have said aloud what everyone knew but wasn't supposed to say. He looked over at Jim whose jaw was clenched in anger. Jim looked to Ellie who herself looked away.

After an awkward silence, Jim spoke. "Well, if there aren't any more questions for now, why don't we conclude?" he asked the room. Nobody said anything, and the meeting adjourned.

As he was walking down the stairs, Kevin and Alex caught up to him.

"Dude, I can't believe you said that to McCoughlin. Unbelievable. He didn't know what to say," Kevin said smiling. Alex patted him on the back.

"I missed the deadline for contacting my letter writers because Klaus didn't say anything about it," Alex explained.

"I know," he said.

"I heard you switched supervisors."

"I did."

"To whom?"

"Adamson."

"Adamson? Interesting. He's emeritus now, isn't he?"

"Yeah."

"I've been thinking of making a change too. I don't know if I can work with Klaus anymore. He never reads my work. I go months without seeing him. Was it like that for you?"

"Yep," he said.

They stopped in front of the fountain.

"We should all get lunch sometime," Kevin said.

"That sounds good," he said. They all shook hands and went their separate ways.

The next evening came, which meant it was time for the Berlin lecture. He stood from his desk, and kissed Alison, who was drawing in bed.

"I love you," he said.

"I love you too," she said. "How long will it be?"

"Lecture is a couple hours. I'll come straight home. So, I'll be back by eight."

"Where is it again?"

"The T.S. Eliot Theatre at Merton. Right down the street from Christ Church."

"Okay, sounds good," she said.

When he got there, it wasn't as crowded as he expected it would be. Hodges, Wallace, and Brown were there, along with a few other Faculty with interests in the philosophy of science and Kant. Mostly, though, it was all students. Morrison walked in, and he was going to say hello, but Morrison took a seat without looking his way. Manan was sitting up front. A man took the floor. There were some words said about the history of the Isaiah Berlin Lectures, then some more words about this year's speaker, then clapping. The speaker took the lectern.

"Good evening. I'm so honored to be here in Oxford for this wonderful opportunity to discuss the history behind the notion of scientific philosophy, which, as we'll see over the coming weeks, raises perennial questions about the very relationship between science and philosophy, fundamental questions about what they are, and how in turn they relate to one another. In some ways, I can't think of a more fitting place to do so, with the birth of the Royal Society being here and in London. It was the revolution in modern science, as you know, that forced philosophy to begin radically reconceiving so much of what we had taken for granted about the human condition and the nature of reality. And as many of you probably know, my own thinking on these matters over the years has been heavily indebted to both Kuhn and Kant. Over the course of the next few weeks, I want to work through the development in our scientific understandings of time and space. The idea behind doing so is that it might provide an illuminating lens through which we can appreciate the nature of conceptual change in both science and philosophy. What results, I think, is a conception of transhistorical, but not ahistorical, scientific rationality. Tonight, I want to examine Kant's handling of the questions of freedom and morality within the context of the problem of causality and determinism. That will set the stage for our later discussion of Kant's conception of space and time in the B deduction of the *Critique of Pure Reason*. As many of you no doubt know, the scientific climate of Kant's day is essential to understanding his own project, his Copernican Revolution, as it were. We'll look at Newton, of course, and eventually we'll also turn to Einstein's Theories of Special and General Relativity. I will only be able to allude to it in passing tonight, but essential to the story I want to tell is the Michelson-Morley Experiment." There were handouts going around.

"If you look at the handout, you'll see the plan. After talking about Kant tonight, we'll turn next to Schelling's *Naturphilosophie*. Then we'll turn to the question of psychologism in Helmholtz and symbolism in

Cassirer. Then it'll be back to Kant, but this time with Einstein, not New-ton, as providing our scientific understanding of space-time. Then we'll turn to Kuhn."

His attention turned away from the speaker. The Michelson-Morley Experiment, if memory served, had shown there was no ether. But it had also shown that the earth was motionless. It was that apparent result that had led Einstein to develop his view of relativity. He laughed. The speaker would probably never mention the quotation from Tesla that came to mind: "Today's scientists have substituted mathematics for experiments, and they wander off through equation after equation, and eventually build a structure which has no relation to reality." Here were some of the brightest scientific and philosophical minds in the world all assembled in one place, and the unspoken admission was that none of them truly knew what space and time were, or what gravity was. He thought it was funny how the public believed in what it called science, when the very ones who most closely studied the historical progression of modern scientific development expressed complete bafflement in the face of questions the public thought had been answered. There was a deep irony in these lec-tures being held in the venue they were. Society, after all, was a wasteland.

FORTY

THE weeks unfurled, and things became clearer. He still had not yet heard from Luce. Luce would have contacted Quiller and Klaus about the book, and they would have suggested Luce squash it. Until he heard officially one way or the other from Luce, however, he would hold out hope. The confirmation had gone according to plan. Quiller had commended him for addressing the secondary literature, but now the problem was that the thesis wasn't digging sufficiently deeply into the primary texts in the fashion that a DPhil thesis should. It was all about finding the right balance, Quiller had said with a smile. In any case, he'd passed the confirmation, which meant that he would at least force a viva. There was still the issue of settling on the external examiner, but really that was irrelevant anyway, since in reality whether he would pass or not would come down to Quiller's decision.

That was why today was so important, he thought, as he looked out the seminar window. It was his turn to deliver his writing sample to the Placement Scheme. Stock and McCoughlin were there, along with Alex and Kevin and the others. Everyone was waiting on Quiller.

The door opened. "My apologies everyone. I got tied up in tutorial," Quiller said, taking his seat.

"Okay, great. Let's get started." Ellie looked at him. "Over to you."

"Thanks very much, Prof Stock. And thanks very much for everyone taking the time to be here. And thank you Prof Quiller for serving as my Faculty respondent. I look forward to receiving your feedback." He read the paper, and it went well. This paper, one on art, was much less controversial than the one he'd read at the Strawson Room. It was interesting, and something that wouldn't threaten anyone's personal convictions or ideology. Quiller made a couple points about places in which he might cite something relevant from the secondary literature, but there were no major criticisms. One of the other students asked a question about Manet and modernism, the ensuing exchange was fruitful, and everyone seemed pleased.

"Well, thank you very much for today's talk," Ellie said. They all clapped. He stood and was about to meet up with Alex and Kevin, since they'd developed the habit of going to lunch together after meetings.

Ellie looked at him. "Could you stay behind for just a second?"

"Uh, sure," he said. Alex and Kevin looked at him. "We'll see you at the restaurant," Kevin said.

The door closed and it was just Ellie and him.

"The DGS contacted me." He waited for her to continue.

"She tells me that there's an issue with the thesis." He still waited.

"The word-count. A DPhil is supposed to be capped at eighty thousand words. You're at a hundred thousand. She's told me to tell you to contact her so you can talk about it."

"Okay. I've never heard of anyone having a problem with words-counts. Is this something coming out of my confirmation examination?"

"I can't say. You'll have to talk to her," Ellie said.

"Okay."

"There's another thing."

"Yes?"

"Your supervisor's letter."

"Yes?"

"It's unusable."

"What? What do you mean?"

"The letter's confidential, obviously, so I can't show you. But it's not something you want a selection committee to see. If you have other letters, you'll want to use those. Who is writing for you?"

"My old supervisor Carrell said he'd write. I thought Adamson would, but evidently that's now out. Maybe William Maddow at Sussex would. Or maybe Gardner. He's at Sussex too. He gave me his business card last year after a talk at the Strawson Room."

"That's all good, but do you have anyone here in Oxford who would write? Given the theological bent of your work, what about Eliot Wood? He's at Christ Church. Do you know him?"

"Yes, I know Eliot. He's familiar with my work. I'll ask him," he said. "What about Quiller? He's my Faculty respondent. He's also going to be the internal examiner. Isn't it customary for whoever's in that role to also write?"

"It is," she said.

"Should I ask him?"

"It couldn't hurt," she said.

"Okay, I'll ask Quiller and Wood. If nobody from Oxford writes, I'll use all external letters. That might make sense anyway, since I already have a number of publications. It's probably less important at this stage to have people commenting on my thesis than it is external experts talking about my publications."

"That's true. But somebody is going to have to say something about the thesis. Selection committees will be expecting that," she said.

"Okay, I'll talk to the DGS."

"Good luck," she said.

At home, Alison was waiting. "How'd it go?"

"The talk?"

"Yeah!"

"Talk was fine. Quiller couldn't find any major criticisms. Others seemed to like it."

"What's wrong?"

He sighed. "There's a problem. Or problems."

"What?"

His mind drifted to the night the change of supervision paperwork had been successfully filed, and Adamson had officially taken over. Alison had baked Adamson cookies, and Alison and he had gone out for drinks to celebrate. She'd taken a photo. At the time, he remembered looking at the photo and seeing that his face was filled with dread, even though he thought he had felt relieved. Thinking more about it now, it seemed that he had always known that the change of supervision would be a dead end. There was no getting around Quiller and Klaus.

"Stock told me that the letter from Adamson is a dud. I'm lucky she told me, or else I would have sent it out," he said.

"What? Why would he agree to write you a letter and then do that?"

"Sabotage."

"Quiller and Klaus?"

"Who else?"

"So what are you going to do? I thought you needed a letter from a supervisor."

"I do. My file without it will look weird. It's a kiss of death," he said.

"What are you going to do?"

"Stock said to ask Wood. Quiller's supposed to write as well, since he's my Faculty respondent and my internal examiner. But he hasn't offered to yet. He'll probably say no, and even if he says yes, the letter won't be any better than Adamson's, since Quiller's the one who told Adamson to trash me anyway. These letters are all stupid anyway, honey. They can say whatever they want in them, or not. All the decisions are made off the record anyway."

"What about Maddow or that other guy you met last year?"

"Gardner?"

"Yeah, Gardner."

"I'll contact him. I have enough people to scrape together letters, it's just unlikely any will be coming from Oxford."

"What about Carrell?"

"He said he'll write."

"Did you ask him about Maureen and the volume?"

"No, haven't mentioned it."

"Has he?"

"No."

"Did you tell him about Klaus?"

"Yeah."

"What did he say?"

"He said he couldn't wrap his mind around the evil at Oxford."

"So, he's on our side? That's good at least," she smiled.

He sat down at his desk and opened his laptop and began typing.

"Who are you writing?"

"The DGS."

Alison was alarmed. "The DGS? I thought we were done with her. The change of supervision paperwork went through."

"That's the other problem. They're saying my thesis is too long."

"Too long?"

"There's an eighty-thousand word-limit on DPhil theses. I'm at one hundred thousand."

"Okay, so trim it."

"I can't. They know that. If I trim it, I'll have to eliminate material that's essential to anticipating the objections they know I know are coming from Quiller. If I don't revise it, I can't submit it, but if I shorten it to submit it, then they'll just criticize it for whatever I cut out."

She put her head in her hands, "Why are they doing this to us?"

"There's a system. There's a way of doing things. You either do it that way, or you don't. I didn't play along, so now they're getting rid of me."

"I trust you, I just don't want to see you destroy everything you have. What about the Routledge book? Can't you just find a way to give Quiller and Klaus what they want in the thesis, so they leave you alone?"

"No, they know about the Routledge thing. That's just incentivized them to block the thesis. If I can't get the DPhil, Routledge won't offer the contact, or if they do, they'll later rescind it. There's no way forward without the DPhil."

"Nobody here in Oxford is going to help us. How are you going to do it alone?"

"I'm not," he smiled.

"Well, you know what I mean," she said.

"The Proverbs say, 'Be not envious against evil men, neither desire to be with them.' I'm glad they don't like me. I'm glad I don't belong. This entire place is run by the intelligence services anyway. You think the reason I'm the only person in my program without a letter from his supervisor is because my work is so unworthy? I'm being targeted."

"Intelligence services?"

"Yes, you see that the academics here are a fraud. It's all an institutional façade for what's really going on here. They know I know that, and they're angry, so they're going to try to get rid of me."

"Don't tell anyone about the intelligence services or the Mystery Babylon stuff."

"Or what? They'll call me crazy? I know. All the people who have no idea how the world really works think anyone who tells them how it works is crazy. I don't need to be understood. I'll do whatever it takes to do what God wants me to do, even if that means working alone," he said.

"But Quiller . . . "

"Quiller is a liar and a coward. He's just a dork who was bad at sports as a kid, and now he's a sadistic psychopath getting back at the world. Only losers serve Satan. I'm not worried about him. I don't have to have everything figured out. I just have to obey God. So long as I don't lust after evil things, they can't control me. If I have no desire for anything but the will of God, they have no power over me, because they have nothing to offer me. And if everything good is a gift from God, then they have no control over it, and if something I want doesn't come, it will come later on God's time. And if it never does, then I know it wasn't God's will anyway. It all comes down to mastering oneself. Nobody else can interfere with that. That's the stronghold, that's the fortress, that's making God my tower."

He turned his attention to the note he would send to the DGS. A few minutes after sending it, he received a reply from her.

"I'm meeting her at All Souls tomorrow at two. Want to watch a movie or something?"

"Tomorrow maybe, but not tonight, I'm tired. I'm going to go to bed." She crawled into bed silently and turned out the lights. He sat in the stillness for an indefinite period, then went out to the street and stood under the lamps that were obscuring the stars. He took a lap around the block, but when walking felt pointless, he came back inside, where he fell asleep on the couch.

The next day, he felt nervous walking through the gate to All Souls, but this time there was no issue.

"I remember you," the porter said, tipping his hat.

"How are you?"

"Quite fine. And you?"

"I'll manage," he said. "I'm off to the same place as before," he said, pointing to the office on the quad.

"Good luck," the porter said.

Inside, the atmosphere had shifted. The DGS was not hostile toward him, but she was very nervous. It felt as if someone was in the room telling her what to say, but it was only them.

"I've been made aware there is an issue with the word-count for your thesis," she began. He waited for her to continue.

"You can't submit it until it's under eighty thousand words," she said.

"Who complained? Adamson had said it should be fine."

The DGS was quiet.

"You can't tell me?"

She stared straight ahead. So it was Quiller. The DGS couldn't say it was him, since that would show malice on Quiller's part before the viva. If Quiller's bias was exposed, he would have grounds to petition for a different internal examiner.

"You know, I spoke to Eliot Wood about this issue back in the summer."

"You did?"

"I did."

"What was his recommendation?"

"He said that he'd never heard of the word-count for a DPhil thesis presenting an issue. Usually the problem with a student is getting him to write more, not less."

She chuckled. "That's true," she said.

"Anyway, he told me that footnotes aren't counted. I could rework the thesis to move some of the material into the notes."

She rubbed her chin. "That might work. Let me ask."

"I don't understand. You're the DGS. It's your decision. Who do you have to ask?"

"Please, don't make this more difficult than it already is. I will get back to you," she said.

"Okay, thanks." He stood to leave.

"There are people here who respect what you're doing, you know. I wish you success. But it will be hard. I'm sorry," she said.

He walked onto the High, and took a seat under the Almond tree. He wondered what the Magnolia across from the bar in Texas looked like right now. Maybe its leaves were rustling in the wind, or maybe it was basking in the sun. He lit a cigarette, hung his head, and stared at his shoes.

The decision took longer than he expected. A week later, the DGS wrote him. The footnotes were not a way forward. They would count toward the count. Quiller had seen the plan. If he were allowed to address all the potential objections in the notes, it would free up the space in the body to write whatever else he wanted. Then during the viva, he could point to the notes, and say that he had answers to the objections. By saying the footnotes would count toward the count, he didn't have space to address the objections, and he still had to trim the main body anyway. The entire situation was contrary to University regulation and all informal precedent, but it didn't matter. Quiller could do as he pleased, and everyone knew it. The less he communicated over email, the better, he thought, so he grabbed his jacket, and decided to leave.

"Where are you going?" Alison asked.

"I'm going to talk to Stock."

"The Placement Director? What happened?"

"The DGS says I can't do footnotes."

She shook her head. "What? That's absurd."

"I know. It's supposed to be. That's what makes it so much fun for them," he laughed.

"Okay, be careful. Do you want dinner when you're back?"

"Sure. I love you."

"I love you too."

He walked down Hollywell to Magdalen. The deer weren't out. He made his way through the cloisters, till he found Stock's office. It was unlikely she'd be in, but it was worth a shot. He knocked.

"Come in." He opened the door.

"You," she said smiling.

"Me," he said.

She gestured toward the chair. "Well, have a seat. What brings you here?"

"I've had a chat with the DGS about the thesis. Footnotes are not an option. I'll have to cut the thesis substantially, I'm afraid."

"I see. Did she give a reason?"

"No, not really."

"I've been in my office all afternoon. I'm usually not here. You're lucky to catch me. Why don't you come with me to the SCR?"

They left the office, walked through the cloisters, and took a flight of stairs up to the SCR. There were some dons inside, but he didn't care if they heard whatever she had to say.

They sat down in a corner.

"Okay, so I think I see where things stand with the thesis. Is Quiller still due to examine it?"

"Yes."

"And the letters?"

"Gardner and Maddow both said yes. With Carrell, that means I have three."

"What about from here?"

"Wood said he didn't know my work well enough. Quiller said the same thing."

"Okay, well not having any home letters will be a problem."

"I know."

"I didn't know Klaus and Quiller were this close," she said. He told her about Luce and the Routledge book.

"Okay, well this all makes sense now. So, it's professional jealousy with them?"

"Something like that."

"Here's what I propose. Shorten the thesis as much as you can. I will talk to the DGS about getting you a modest extension. But don't abuse it. Keep everything that's already been published in the thesis. It's imperative you don't cut any of that. I will speak to Harcourt about finding you another internal examiner. Quiller should not be acting as your examiner after everything that happened with Klaus and the supervision. I'll be in touch."

"Thank you," he said.

"You're welcome," she said. He was about to leave when she looked at him.

"What?"

"I should tell you something," she said.

"What?"

"When Klaus was up for his review a couple years ago, a number of us didn't want to keep him. He barely passed. He said he was working on a book that would be submitted to the publisher soon. We're all still waiting."

He nodded and left.

Things were moving very fast, but that was understandable. When he opened the door to the flat, Alison was in the kitchen. She turned to him. "How'd it go?"

"I think we have it," he said.

"Really? Tell me."

"Stock told me that Quiller and Klaus are jealous. That's huge for her to say."

"Okay, but what about the viva?"

"She's going to ask Harcourt to pull Quiller from the viva. Everyone knows he has a conflict of interest because of Klaus."

"Oh, that's amazing. And the letters?"

"I told her that I'm going to make do with what I have. No other option, really."

"What about the word-count?"

"She said that she's going to talk to the DGS about it. It'll be tight, but I'll get a bit of breathing room," he said.

That night, he got an email from Stock, saying that she's written Harcourt about the internal examiner and the DGS about the word-count extension. He lit a cigarette and smiled. He wasn't in the catbird seat at all, but he was surviving. That was good enough.

The end of term came. The day before they were leaving for Texas, Stock wrote again. Harcourt had agreed that Quiller should recuse himself. They would find a new internal examiner at the recommendation of Morrison. He was surprised to see Morrison involved, but no matter. The external examiner would come at the recommendation of Adamson. The word-count extension was approved, and while it was a modest one, it would be enough to allow him to keep all the published material, and incorporate enough material to address the objections he knew were coming in the viva. Things were delicate, but they were shaping up. He could send out his job applications with his set of external letters, he could tell selection committees he was about to set a viva date, and, above all, Quiller had been formally removed from the viva process. Once he heard from Adamson with an external examiner, things would be set. Quiller would still be lurking in the shadows, of course, but the fact that he had been removed from the viva was a serious blow to Quiller's credibility. It would make Quiller angry, but that was fine. People made mistakes when they were angry. Maybe Quiller would.

"Are you packed?"

"Yeah, sweetie. Are you?"

"I'm going to finish tonight," she said.

"It's going to be good to get back to the States," he said.

"Yeah, I guess," she said.

"What's wrong?"

"I'm just sad," she said.

"Why?"

She was quiet. He knew it wasn't the circumstances she had hoped for. They were supposed to be celebrating some new job he was about to land. He would be lucky to hear anything at all from a university.

The next day, they stood on the curb at the airport waiting for their ride. Even though it was mild by Texas standards, they were in shirts, since it was much warmer here than it was in Oxford.

"I never thought I'd be in a t-shirt in winter here," she said.

"I know. We're like those British tourists everyone laughs at who are in t-shirts in fifty-degree weather," he laughed.

"Oh, there she is," Alison said as her mom pulled up to the curb. Linda jumped out of the car.

"There you are! It's so good to see you, sweetie," she said, hugging Alison. He put the luggage in the trunk.

"How was your flight?"

"Long," Alison said.

"Well, it's okay if you're too tired, but Daddy and I thought it would be nice to go out to dinner."

"Where's Dad?"

"He's at work finishing something. He said he'll meet us at the house," Linda said.

Alison took the front passenger seat. He took the seat behind her.

After she was done merging onto the highway, Linda glanced over at Alison. "So how are you, guys?"

"We're doing fine, Mom," Alison said.

"Daddy and I will have to come for a visit soon," she said.

"We're going to be leaving soon, Mom. He's applying for jobs this year. His viva is going to be in a few months," Alison said.

"Jobs? Already?"

"It's been over two years, Mom," she said.

"Oh, I know, I just can't believe how fast it's all gone. Daddy won't believe it, either." He looked at Alison's face in the side view mirror. He could see that she saw there was no point trying to tell Linda everything that was going on in Oxford. Alison sighed.

Linda furrowed her brow. "Is something wrong, honey?"

"No, Mom," she said.

"You don't have to be angry with me," Linda said.

"I'm not, Mom. It's just that we're under a lot of stress right now."

"Stress? Why? I thought everything's going well over there," Linda said.

Alison looked back over the seat at him. "Do you want to tell her for me?"

"Sure. I had to change my supervisor. I have a new supervisor, but his letter isn't going to be useful for me on the job market. So I'm applying handicapped. The thesis is ready, but there are people there attacking it, so it looks like the viva is shaping up to be very difficult."

Linda was quiet.

"Mom?"

"Sorry, what honey?"

"We just told you what's going on at Oxford."

"I'm so sorry. I don't mean to be rude. I was distracted by the road. What's going on?"

Alison sighed. "Never mind. We'll tell, Dad," she said. "It's an academic thing, anyway. Maybe he'll have some advice." He looked up at the sun, as they winded down the highway. He didn't have the heart to tell Alison not to hold her breath.

At the house, Stuart's car was parked in the garage. They came inside, and brought the luggage up to Alison's old room. When they came downstairs to the kitchen, Stuart was talking to Linda.

"Hi, Dad," she said.

"Good to see you," he said, hugging her.

He shook hands with Stuart.

"Daddy and I were just discussing where we should go for dinner tonight. How about Natural Foods?"

"Sounds good," Alison said.

They all got in Stuart's car. He didn't pay attention to the small talk on the way over. At the restaurant, he stood next to Alison, and held her hand while looking at the menu.

"I love you," she said.

"Love you too," he said, squeezing her hand. They placed their order, grabbed their drinks, and took a seat outside under the heater.

"This is so nice," Linda said. "We're so happy to have you back!"

"It's nice to be back," he said.

Stuart turned to Alison, "Have you found a job over there?"

"No, Dad."

"Are you looking?"

"There doesn't seem to be any point. We're probably leaving soon."

"Leaving soon?"

"Yeah, I'm done with my thesis. I'm defending it in a few months."

"Already? That seems a little fast."

"The DPhil is designed to be two years. I'm right on schedule," he said.

"Well, what are you going to do after?"

"That depends. I'm applying for jobs right now."

"Where?"

"Everywhere." He listed a dozen schools off the top of his head. "The last time I checked, I think it was twenty-five applications."

"What about a postdoc?"

"It's not like that in philosophy, Dad. There are hardly any philosophy jobs. It's not like physics."

"I said a postdoc, though."

"Same thing, Dad."

"Isn't your supervisor arranging for something?"

Alison sighed.

"What's the matter? That's a fair question," Stuart said.

He looked at Stuart and said nothing. It was tedious watching Stuart play dumb.

"Dad, his supervisor lied to him. We had to make a change. Now he doesn't really have a supervisor."

"Well, that's unwise. You're not going to get a job without a supervisor who supports your work," Stuart said.

"I know," he said. "You know I know that."

Stuart smirked slightly. It was quiet for a few seconds.

Linda cleared her throat. "Seen any good movies lately?"

He turned to Alison. "I think we have. Why don't you tell them about the Johnny Gosch documentary we saw?" He looked right at Stuart.

"Oh, yeah, that was unbelievable." Alison turned to Linda. "Do you guys know the story about Johnny Gosch? It was a really famous case back in the eighties. He was kidnapped."

"I don't remember that, no," Linda said looking at Alison. Linda turned to Stuart. "Do you remember the story, honey?"

Stuart was staring off into space. When he collected himself, he addressed the table.

"Anyone need any salt or pepper? I'll be right back," Stuart said. He stood up and walked inside.

"It's a very important documentary, Linda. You know, when I was growing up, I remember all the milk carton ads about missing kids, and how all the parents told us not to go anywhere with strangers. At the time I thought it was hysteria, but now that I'm older, and know what I know now, I can see why people were so concerned. It turns out that whoever took Gosch was probably involved in some sort of organized pedophile ring. You and Stuart should watch it," he said.

Linda was silent. A few moments later, Stuart returned to the table.

Linda put her hand on Stuart's arm, "How's your sandwich, honey?"

"It's good," Stuart said chewing.

Alison looked away from her parents. "They've always ignored me," she said.

"We have not," Linda said.

"Oh, so now you magically can hear me again," Alison said.

"Alison, please don't yell at your mother," Stuart said.

"I'm not yelling," she said.

"Don't argue with me. This is supposed to be a nice dinner," Stuart said.

"She's not arguing with you Stuart. She's simply pointing out that you asked a question, and she tried to answer, and then you didn't listen. You asked whether we'd seen any movies. Alison had a recommendation. I think you should watch it," he said.

"This is between us and Alison," Stuart said.

"I agree. That means it's between you and me, too. I'm her husband, and I don't want you talking to her that way anymore. Do you understand?"

Stuart stood up from the table. "I'm not going to take this," he said. He stormed out of the restaurant and walked to the car trunk where he stood pouting.

"Let me go talk to Daddy," Linda said. "You should apologize," she said.

Alison was incredulous. "Apologize? For what? He should apologize to us. You always defend him no matter what, Mom."

"Why don't we go home?"

"Don't worry. We had plans anyway. I'm waiting to hear from Enrique and Kelsie," Alison said.

When Stuart and Linda had left, Alison turned to him.

"I'm sorry."

"I'm sorry. They're your parents."

"I know. But you have to deal with them too."

"It's okay." From a certain perspective, the dinner had been a disaster. But it had been revealing. For one thing, Stuart hadn't wanted to discuss the Gosch story. That told him everything he had to know about Stuart.

"At least we'll be in California soon," she said smiling.

"Yes, that will be nice," he said. When they were there, he'd have to talk to his dad about all this.

FORTY-ONE

I T was happening. Every graduate student's nightmare scenario. The job interviews had all been issued, and he was left without one. He recalled the night at the campus pub when Mick had shown up drunk, and urinated against the tree. At the time, he had empathized with Mick's frustration, even if a case could have been made that Mick was simply reaping what he'd sown. Everyone had heard the horror stories about the academic job market, and had taken the risk. What made his predicament so frustrating, and different, he thought, is that he was being shut out despite having everything that others could only dream of. He was at the best philosophy program in the world. He already had publications in journals. On paper, he was the ideal candidate. But it wasn't at all about what was on the paper, as he knew. All that really counted was what was "off the page." He had not played the game, so now he would be made to pay.

He sighed and closed his laptop. He turned to Alison who was sitting on her childhood bed.

"So that's it?"

"That's it. At least for this year."

"Not even a single interview. Unbelievable. I can't believe they're doing this," she said.

"I know. I'm sorry."

"It's okay."

He hung his head. A tear came down his face.

"Don't cry. Please don't cry," she said. "I hate seeing you sad." She stood up and hugged him. "What's wrong?"

"I'm not crying about the stupid job. You know I don't need one. I'm just sad that everything's so upside down. I wanted to build something with you, and they're taking it all away. I'm sorry."

She looked at him and smiled. "It's okay. We still have each other. That's all that matters. I'm going to run to Walgreens. I'll be back soon," she said.

A couple minutes later, he saw the headlights turn on, and the car drive away. He went down the stairs and out to the driveway. He lit a cigarette, and looked at the park across the street where they'd shot hoops when they'd first gotten engaged.

He heard the door open and close behind him. It was Stuart and Linda. They walked over to him.

"We just wanted to say we're sorry," Linda said.

"Sorry?"

Stuart looked at him. "About the job market. There's nothing to be ashamed about. Sometimes even good candidates don't get anything."

Alison had not mentioned anything to them, and neither had he. Stuart was flaunting the fact he had knowledge he simultaneously had pretended not to have. So, this was the ritual hazing. Stuart and Linda would pretend to be sympathetic over his turmoil, when really it was just a way of bringing up his failure. At the same time, they could pretend the failure was benign, as if there weren't flagrant problems at Oxford contributing to what otherwise could have been a successful year on the job market. Now here they were, having waited for Alison to leave before rubbing salt in the wound.

"You should talk to your supervisor about what you can do to improve the work. Sometimes I have students who don't take feedback well. Part of graduate school is learning to take criticism," Stuart said.

"Yes."

"If you go back to your supervisor and apologize, maybe you'll have better luck on the market next year," Stuart said. There it was again. Stuart commenting on a situation that he previously had been pretending not to know anything about.

"Have you considered talking to Carrell? I'm sure he would help," Stuart said.

"No, I haven't talked to Carrell much. He did say he couldn't wrap his mind around the evil at Oxford."

Stuart looked at him and said nothing.

"We just wanted to say that we're sure Alison will understand. She won't think less of you just because you didn't get a job," Linda said. "You're still pretty young, so you still have time to do all that stuff that comes with having a job and money," she said.

Linda walked inside.

Stuart turned to him and narrowed his eyes. "Good, now you listen to me. I want to make myself clear. I don't like you, and you know I don't like you. But because I care about Alison and her future, I'm going to give you a piece of real advice."

He didn't bother pointing out the lie, that Stuart didn't really care about his daughter. He held his tongue, waiting for Stuart to continue.

"I know all about the theology dinners you've been attending at Oxford. Maybe you're put off by it, but that's how it works. People on the outside think getting into Oxford will make you a success. No, it's about what you do when you get there that makes the difference."

There was a pause.

"When I was at M.I.T., I had a choice to make. To have a career doing what I do, others have to know they can count on you. They have to have assurances that you're willing to do what it takes. I was married with a kid on the way, so I did what it took. If you want things to go anywhere, you have to join the club. That means doing what you're told, and that means doing something on videotape. If you're not compromising, no one is going to help you."

He could see Stuart was expecting a response.

"Some guys cheat on their wives, others end up doing other things. It's up to you to decide what it'll take. I did what it took. The ball is in your court to decide whether you're willing to do the same. Till then, don't expect a job." Stuart smirked and walked inside.

The funny thing about the situation, he thought, is that Stuart truly believed he would be dumb enough to tell Alison what had just been said. The point of the conversation wasn't to help her—of course not. The entire point of the conversation was to get him to run off to Alison and try to explain what her dad had just said. When he did, naturally Alison would be incredulous, at which point she'd confront her dad about it. Stuart and Linda would deny having said what he had, accuse him of lying or being crazy, and then leverage it against him, by trying to guilt trip Alison for being torn over whom to believe. He looked at the house and the cars. Everything Stuart thought that he had was really nothing. Being part of the club wasn't worth it.

He lit another cigarette and was about to head in when Alison pulled the car in. She opened the car door happily.

When she came up to him, she could feel something was wrong.

"What is it?"

"Your parents."

"What?"

"Did you tell them about the job market?"

"No."

"Okay, well they just told me not to be down about getting shut out."

"So?"

"So how do they know? I thought your dad supposedly has his head in the clouds and doesn't know anything about what's been going on in Oxford."

"Well, I'm sure my mom said something."

"Okay, then what did she say?"

"I don't know."

"Well, according to your dad, I should say I'm sorry to Klaus to see if he'll take me back."

"What? He said that?"

"Yeah, just now."

"I don't know. Let's just forget about it."

"He knows that's what you'll say."

"Don't get angry at me. What do you want me to do? You're the one that made the decision to piss off Quiller and Klaus."

"So you agree with your dad, then? I should say I'm sorry to little Klaus? Klaus can sit there and wipe his ass with every imaginable university regulation on the books, lie to me, sabotage my research, and everyone sits there and watches it happen, then tells me to go say I'm sorry?"

"That's not what I'm saying," she said.

"So, what are you saying?"

"I don't know. Let's just forget about it for now. We'll worry about it when we're back in Oxford."

"Wrong. I will worry about it back in Oxford."

"Yes, you're right. I'm just along for the ride," she said. She walked in and closed the door. He coughed, then lit another cigarette.

FORTY-TWO

E remembered someone somewhere having told him that San Francisco was a place where the sun was always shining in one's eyes. It was counterintuitive, since the city was renowned for its fog. But here in the Sunset District, he finally understood. It did feel like no matter which direction one walked, or where one stood, the sun was in his eyes. The fact nothing had happened during the remaining stay in Texas had been a relief. But the underlying anxiousness had not abated. He could feel that something was coming. It was now their last day here in California, and tomorrow it would be back to Oxford. His mother and Alison had spent the trip doing the best they could to tap dance around his professional woes, which only made the problems more obvious. He'd tried telling his mom about Klaus and Quiller, but she gave him that face she did when she was trying to tell someone she'd heard enough. The fact that he wasn't getting interviews, as far as his mother was concerned, was his fault. He had known the rules, he'd broken them, and now he was getting what he'd asked for. It didn't matter if Quiller and Klaus were liars, or if they were cruel, or if his work was being unfairly marginalized. All that mattered was the norms of social existence, and Quiller and Klaus had those on their side. His dad had tried talking about it in front of Alison and his mom, but that had only made his mom more resolute in her decision to ignore the situation. The fact that his aunt and uncle were on the trip didn't help, either. Criminal intrigue and Oxford secret societies were something they would find titillating if they were watching a movie, but they had no interest in discussing that here in this instance, since it would force them to accept such things were real. He laughed, as he took a drag. It was so easy to control people, he thought. The wicked men who ruled the world knew this, too, which is why they exploited it to such great effect.

He walked into the rental. Everyone was in the living room.

"You got an email," Alison said.

"From whom?"

"Beth."

"Beth?"

"Yeah."

"Oh, boy," he said. He sat down knowing it would be bad. He opened the screen.

> Happy belated Christmas,
>> I hope you and Alison had a lovely day.
>> Quick question: I am currently drafting my tutorials for the coming couple of terms, and I want to be prepared to teach Merleau-Ponty in case I am approached (I will have to teach up to 8 tutorials per week during my lectureship and I want to make sure to have each author ready to go, even though it is likely I will only have to teach two or three). So, I wanted to ask you, would you recommend sticking to the Phenomenology of Perception in Merleau-Ponty tutorials? It seems that the exam questions tend to be geared towards that text so I'm guessing that's the way to go. I was thinking of dividing the sessions up into; say the themes of phenomenology, the body, sexuality and language. Do you think that sounds like a reasonable structure? If you have any advice, I'd be most welcome!
>> I hope the final stages of your thesis have been going well.
>> All the best and happy new year!
>> Beth

He slammed the laptop shut. Alison was on the couch next to his mother. "What did it say?"

"You wouldn't believe it."

His dad opened the screen. "Let me see." His dad read for a few seconds then said in disgust, "Oh, you're kidding me? This is pathetic." Alison walked over and read also.

"I'm sorry," she said.

His aunt and uncle were quiet. Finally, his mom spoke. "What does it say?"

His dad was livid. "Regina, you can't believe the crap your son has to put up with. Read the email, Son," he said. He read the email to the room.

His mom said nothing.

His dad was incredulous. "Isn't that unbelievable?"

His mom seemed unpersuaded. "It's a work email. She has a question."

Alison got angry. "No, it's more than that. Beth is taunting him. He applied for the same job. She's trying to brag about getting the job."

His aunt and uncle were interested.

Uncle Shannon spoke, "You applied for the same job?"

"I did."

His uncle turned to the aunt. "That's pretty low," he said.

Aunt Laurie turned to her sister. "Yeah, Regina, if someone did that to me, I would be super pissed."

His dad interjected, "It's worse than that. She's deliberately acting like she doesn't know how to do the job, as a way of provoking him into saying she doesn't deserve it. It came from Quiller and Klaus."

Alison looked surprised, "You think they'd have her write that?"

"Oh yeah. They're taunting him."

She thought about it. "Well, it makes sense. They were on the search committee."

Aunt Laurie opened her mouth. "You mean they're the ones who hired Beth?"

"Yeah," he said looking at his aunt.

"Oh, Regina, that is so obvious," Laurie said laughing.

"It was Klaus, Quiller, and Harcourt on the committee. They didn't even interview me, but they gave Beth the job, now she's emailing me over Christmas to remind me."

His mom said nothing.

"Boy, I don't know. If somebody did that to me, I don't know how I'd keep my cool. So that's what it's like in Oxford? You should write something back to her," Uncle Shannon said.

"I know I wouldn't be nice," Aunt Laurie chuckled.

"Yeah, you know, it's really messed up for her to be cruel like that. You should say something," Alison said.

"You've been putting up with this long enough, Son. Why don't you just put Beth and her little handlers in their place," his dad said.

He sighed. Nobody understood. The torment came from the spiritual trial. Quiller and Klaus knew this. They knew that he would know they were the ones who told Beth to write him. His family saw it too. Quiller and Klaus also knew that the normal human reaction would be to get upset at having somebody like Beth taunt him like that. His family was upset, and they weren't the ones being taunted. Quiller and Klaus also knew that if he responded with anything less than perfect kindness to Beth, that would be used as an excuse to say he was being rude. Beth would play dumb, deny that she had meant to provoke him. She might even suggest that it was a testament to his arrogance that he would think that he was important enough to be singled out for ulterior motives on her part. Of course, that would contradict the entire premise of the email, which openly assumed his opinion was worth consulting. But the fact that Beth would be able to openly contradict herself like that, while accusing him of being unreasonable, was precisely what would make it so delicious for her handlers. The entire thing was a taunt. The words from Romans came to him, "If thine enemy be hungry, give him bread to eat; and if he be thirsty, give him water to drink: For thou shalt heap coals of fire upon his head, and the Lord shall reward thee." He drafted a note congratulating her on the new post, and saying he would be happy to discuss the tutorials when he had returned to Oxford. He sent it, then read it to the room.

Everyone was quiet. He went outside for a cigarette. A few minutes later, his dad came outside.

"I'm sorry," his dad said.

"For what?"

"For encouraging you to send a bad email back to her. I'm glad you didn't. You were right. Quiller and Klaus wanted you to stoop to her level."

"I know."

"So what's really going on back there? I can tell the stress they have you under. I know you're not a pussy, so it must be bad."

He explained everything. The blackmail parties at Wood's, the women they'd tried throwing at him, the underwear in the apartment, the Dutch woman in London, the woman outside Tom Gate, the footnotes, the book contract with Routledge, and the meetings with Stock and the DGS.

"You know Rothschild is there," his dad said.

He sighed exasperatedly.

"I'm sorry, Son, I know you know that," his dad said laughing. "So they're going to flunk the viva?"

"Probably."

"Then what?"

"Depends whether I fight it or not."

"Say you do."

"Then they'll escalate it."

"Kill you?"

"If they think they have to."

"Yeah, I know. What about Howdy Doody? He still playing dumb?"

"Worse. He's now openly mocking me about it. He said I should go back and work with Klaus."

"That little freak really said that?"

"Yep."

"Does Alison know he's in on it too?"

"No, she doesn't see it."

"I don't know what to tell you, Son." They laughed.

"Don't worry about it, Dad. I'll figure it out. Everything's bullshit anyway. You know that."

His dad laughed. "I know. Keep me updated on what happens." They hugged.

His dad looked at him seriously in a way he hadn't in years. "Look at me, Son." He looked at his dad, even though tears were starting to come out.

"Don't be embarrassed," his dad said. "You're doing the right thing. That's why they hate you." His dad paused. "Guys like Quiller and Klaus and Stuart and Carrell are pussies. You'll run them off the field. Just be patient. They're going to torture you because that's what they like to do. They're freaks," his dad said.

"You don't know the half of it, Dad. I tried talking to Stuart about Johnny Gosch."

"Let me guess? He stared straight ahead and pretended not to hear anything, right?"

"Yep."

"See, I know, Son. I know all the bullshit. That's what they tell you to do when you have a security clearance, and you're in a social situation and you're not allowed to talk about something. I've known Stuart was a weirdo since the day he was pissed when Mom tried to get Alison to show everyone her artwork."

"I know."

"It doesn't matter if nobody else understands. You do."

"I know."

"I'm sorry, Dad."

"For what? You don't have to apologize."

"For bringing all this turmoil into your life."

"Hey, don't apologize for that. You think I want a son like your friends? They're not men, Son. You're a man. I don't have a problem helping you navigate what comes up."

"Thanks." They hugged again.

FORTY-THREE

THE stage was set. He had his examiners, and the viva was set for February. An advertisement would appear shortly in the *Oxford Gazette*. Whether anyone would show up remained to be seen. It was the New Year, and he would not dwell on all the shenanigans that had transpired over the preceding months. What mattered now was finishing.

"Honey, it's done."

Alison ran into the room. "Really?"

"Yeah, just heard from the internal examiner. The viva's confirmed for February."

"Who is she again?"

"Patricia Anderson. She's friends with Morrison."

"And the external?"

"She's in London. Adamson suggested her. Phyllis Gaskin. Never heard of her. She went to Oxford years ago. I guess it doesn't really matter who the examiners are. They're going to do whatever Quiller says anyway. But I'll try my best."

"I'm so proud of you," she said, kissing him.

"Thanks. I'm sorry it's been so hard to get here," he said.

"That's okay."

"Oh, I almost forgot. There was a job posting for something in Canada. Nothing will probably come of it like the others, but I figured I'd send in an application to see what happens."

"Did you hear about it through the Placement Scheme?"

"No, online."

"Where in Canada?"

"New Brunswick. It's on the East Coast. It gets really, really cold there," he laughed.

"We're used to that now!"

She walked into the kitchen, poured some water, and came back into the bedroom.

"Where in the world is Billy?"

"No idea. He's probably going to wait to see what happens with the viva," he said.

"I'm so tired of waiting."

"Me too," he said.

The rest of January went by without event. February came, and he decided to go to the college. François was stationed in his customary place, working at Tom Gate.

"Hello, friend," François said.

"Hello, how's it going?"

"Good. And you?"

"Good. I have a viva next month."

"Well, good luck," François said smiling.

There wasn't any mail in his pidge. He stepped outside, lit a cigarette, and walked through the quad. He was in the mood to see the Deer Park. The fastest way would be through the exit on Peck Quad. He passed the library and looked at Kilcannon. It had been months since he'd seen Klaus in person. Odds were that Klaus would be in London, he thought. At Peck Quad he lit another cigarette and sat on the Library steps. In the middle of the quad, the flagpole was flying the rainbow flag. He sighed. Even here it was inescapable. The logic behind the movement was totalitarian. It wasn't about tolerance. It was about compliance. In time, anyone who disagreed with anything placed under the banner would be shunned from society. That was what had already happened at the élite academic institutions, which had been captured. He laughed to himself. Here was an Oxford college named after Jesus Christ that now flew a flag representing everything that was contrary to his teachings about men and women and sexual morality. For him, it wasn't even so much the transgender agenda, which denied the reality of biological sex, or the homosexuality, which ran contrary to nature and Scripture. It was the fact that the entire movement was a flagrant rebellion against God and God's authority. It was all about putting man in God's place, liberating man from the commandments of God. It was not even a radical political agenda, as the public was led to believe. At its heart was an esoteric mystery religion that was all about inverting reality. By the time most people began realizing this, he thought, it would likely be too late. By then the sinister forces he knew were behind the agenda would be well entrenched. The censorship would be rampant. The corporations would be on board. Freedom would be snuffed out, in the name of tolerance, of course. It was an odd thing he had noticed for years. The same people who considered something a "conspiracy theory" would later be the ones to blindly accept what they had previously said was impossible or inconceivable. If, for instance, he had told people twenty years ago that a man in a dress would be able to force everybody to pretend he was a woman, he would have been accused of paranoia. Now those same people who had thought such a thing was impossible were beginning gladly to accept it. They did so, he knew, because their only standard of reality was the herd, what everyone else thought was normal based on what their screens told them. Then again, it was not so surprising that a place that had Mercury in one quad would fly the rainbow flag in the other quad. If the rainbow was a sign of God's covenant with mankind after the flood, then of course the enemies of God would adopt the rainbow as their own. It was a sick joke most people would never understand.

He left the college and began walking to the Deer Park. The deer were beautiful. For them, nothing changed. The schemes and affairs of men were nothing to them. There was something refreshing about that. He laughed to himself, as his thoughts turned again to the flag in Peck Quad. How far we have fallen, he thought. C.S. Lewis had been here at Magdalen. There was no way Lewis would have tolerated the insanity of a man in a dress pretending to be a woman, or two men pretending to be married, or drag queens reading to children in libraries. In Lewis's day, perversion like that was illegal, and those who persisted in it, were referred for psychiatric treatment. Now the mentally ill were in charge, and everyone was being inducted into a collective madness. He tried enjoying the deer, but something was stirring within him. He walked down Cornmarket and entered a store. He bought a sign and a sharpie. He knew what he would write.

Alison sent him a text, asking whether he would be home soon. He put his phone away in his pocket, and walked to Peck Quad. Before he placed the sign at the base of the flag, he checked the sign again for any typos. It looked fine. He read it silently,

> Know ye not that the unrighteous shall not inherit the kingdom of God? Be not deceived: neither fornicators, nor idolaters, nor adulterers, nor effeminate, nor abusers of themselves with mankind, Nor thieves, nor covetous, nor drunkards, nor revilers, nor extortioners, shall inherit the kingdom of God. And such were

some of you: but ye are washed, but ye are sanctified, but ye are
justified in the name of the Lord Jesus, and by the Spirit of our
God (1 Cor. 6:9-11).

There was no need to add anything else. He would let the Scripture
speak for itself. That way, when those at the college who inevitably would
throw a fit did so, it would be clear to everyone that they were arguing
with God, not with him. The word of God is like a two-edged sword, he
thought, cutting to the heart. He put the sign down and walked home.

Walking home to Cripley, he knew he had crossed the Rubicon.
There was no going back. He felt at peace with the decision. He knew
nobody else in Oxford was ever going to do what he just had. Nobody
would speak out against what was happening. He would be the one to
do it, then.

There were those words from the Old Testament that came to mind.
It was Isaiah, he thought, although he wasn't sure. "I heard the voice of
the Lord, saying, Whom shall I send, and who will go for us? Then said I,
Here am I; send me." Oxford was a microcosm of the world. Some people
studied the word of God, others mocked it, but nobody simply obeyed it.
Even if he were the only one, he would obey.

FORTY-FOUR

A WEEK passed. Alison was out with a friend, and there was nothing to do, so he decided to take a walk along the Isis. On the way home, he'd stop at the college.

The sun was out, which was compensation for the cold. Time was strange, he thought. In the moment, time could dilate, and a minute, or an hour, or a day, could feel like an eternity. It had felt that way for months, when he had been here alone without Alison. Then time had slowed again once they had returned together and all the gamesmanship with Quiller and the network had begun in earnest. Really, when he thought about it, his entire time in Oxford had all been about waiting. Waiting on an email, waiting on a meeting, waiting on a decision, waiting, waiting, waiting. And now, after so much waiting, it felt like everything had been an instant. He knew it had nearly been three years, three very long years, and yet there on the river, it all in a way felt like it had been nothing. It was the ephemerality of time, he thought, the fact that everything was always already passing away.

When he got to Folly Bridge, he saw two swans. He stopped and walked down to the water, and sat on the grass. As difficult as the network had made his life here, there were many things he would miss about this place. He sighed. "Goodbye, swans," he said.

At the college, he checked the mail. Nothing again. He stepped outside, lit a cigarette, and walked to Peck. Three male students were in a group talking near the flagpole. He walked over.

They looked at him. "Hi, guys, sorry to interrupt. I just wanted to ask you something."

"Sure."

"What do you guys think about sin?"

They laughed. "Sin? What do you mean?"

"I mean, in general, do you guys believe there's sin? I ask because I'm a graduate student here, and I wonder how the younger students are thinking." He pointed up at the rainbow flag.

One of them spoke, "Well, I believe in moral right and wrong. I don't know about sin, though. That's a very theological way of looking at it," he said.

He smiled at the student. "We're at Christ Church, aren't we?" They all laughed, seeing the irony of the secularist mentality that was taken to be normal, even here.

Another student spoke, "I believe in God. But the Bible is wrong about a lot of things. Look at Genesis, for example. Evolution disproves that."

"Well, before we get to Genesis, I want to stick with the first question. The issue of sin. Do you guys think there's such a thing as sexual morality?"

They laughed. The other student spoke, "I mean, rape and things like that are wrong. But I can't say sex outside marriage is wrong, because that would make me a hypocrite."

He held up his hand with his wedding ring. "I understand. I was guilty of fornication at one point," he said. "You know, if you question that flag," he said pointing behind them, "people call that hate or bigotry. But it isn't. It's not about singling out homosexuality. Adultery and fornication and pornography are wrong too," he said.

The first student sighed. "Yeah, porn is so addictive. We all watch it, but sometimes I feel guilty. I've tried quitting, but I can't."

The other student was about to say something, when there was shouting coming from the library. "Excuse me! Excuse me! Who do you think you are? This is our home. Get out! Get out!" At first, they tried to ignore the shouting, but when it became apparent that the screaming was directed at him, they turned to face the library.

"That's right! You can't ignore me. Who do you think you are?" He recognized the young woman. She was one of the students who was friends with Lavinia, the students who had been posing for photos in the college calendar. She walked up to them and got in his face.

"You need to leave right now, or I'm going to call the police," she said.

"The police? What are you talking about? We were just talking," he said.

She looked at them, and they all nodded.

"You need to leave," she said looking at him.

"Why?"

"Because you're not welcome here." He realized that she assumed he was not a Member.

"I'm a Member." He wouldn't yet mention he was reading for the DPhil.

"Let me see your Bod card," she demanded.

"Well, frankly, I don't think it's your place to demand to see my Bod card, but since I know if I don't show it to you, you'll wrongly assume I was lying and that I'm not really a Member, here you go," he said, pulling his University card from his wallet.

"I'm a Member of the House. Faculty of Philosophy. I'm reading for a DPhil."

She shoved the card back in his hand.

"I'm going to get the porters," she said.

"For what?"

"For causing a disturbance," she said. He looked at the other students who laughed.

"I'm very sorry, but if anyone's causing a disturbance, I think it's you. We were over here minding our own business, when you suddenly barged out of the library, shouted at us from the steps, charged over here, and demanded to see my Bod card. Now that you're wrong, and you know I'm a Member, you're continuing to interrupt us. How about you go back inside?"

Before he knew it, somebody was tapping him on the shoulder. He turned to see the very tall man, another student who was friends with Lavinia. It was the drag queen.

"Excuse me, you have been asked to leave," the drag queen said.

"So?"

"You're making us feel unsafe," he said.

"Unsafe? You don't even know me," he said.

"Molly's asked you to leave. So have I."

"Who cares? Who are you people? We were having a conversation. You intruded."

A crowd had now assembled, and the porters were there.

Molly turned to them. "We've asked him to leave repeatedly, but he refuses. He's going ballistic," she said.

"That's not true," one of the students he'd been talking to said. "He's been very polite. You hassled him." Molly shot the student a death stare.

One of the porters walked up to him. "I'm sorry, sir, it's time to go."

"No, I'm afraid it isn't. I'm a Member of the college, and I'm reading for a DPhil. I have a right to be here, and I won't leave simply because some random undergraduate student I've never met before wants me to go. I have done nothing wrong."

"Don't force us to call the police," the porter said again.

Just then, François approached.

"Hi, François."

"Hello," he said. "What's the trouble?"

"These two students," he pointed to Molly and the drag queen, "have told me to leave because I'm making them feel unsafe. I haven't done anything, so I don't want to leave. You've known me for over two years now. You know who I am."

François looked at the other porters. "I've never had a problem with him. He's incredibly polite. If he wants to stay, he's free to stay." François and the other porters left.

More of the students he recognized from the college calendar had joined the mob. They were yelling and cursing. Some were even trying to pull on him. Out of the corner of his eye, he saw a college official storming up toward them all. He had never met the man, but he knew it was the Junior Censor.

"What's this all about?" The Censor walked up to him. "You've been asked to leave. It's time for you to go."

"Excuse me. Why don't you disperse the mob? The porters just said I can stay. I haven't done anything wrong."

The drag queen turned to the Censor, "He's a bigot. He's full of hate. He's harming us!"

"I know, I'm sorry," the Censor said. The Censor looked at him coldly. "This is your final warning. You must leave now, or I will call the police."

"Okay, if I leave now, am I allowed back into my own college tomorrow? Or only when Molly and this guy aren't within fifty feet of me? I mean, c'mon, this is insanity."

"Let me see your Bod card," the Censor said.

"She already did the same thing. I'm a Member," he said. He handed the Censor his card.

"Reading for the DPhil? Could have fooled me. Well, surely you should have something more productive to do with your time. Why don't you leave the quad and get some work done?"

"My viva is next week, as it happens."

The Censor turned around and left.

He nodded to the three students with whom he'd been chatting. "Well, that was interesting." They all laughed. "See you guys around," he said.

When he got onto the street, he lit a cigarette. He had felt a cloud of rage swirling around him in Peck, a thick heat. Now outside, the oppression was gone. He walked home in the same the way he had come. When he reached the river, the swans had gone.

At his desk, he opened his laptop and sent a note to the Dean, the Censor, Wood, and another senior theologian at the college. It would be important to have a contemporaneous note on the record of what had really just happened in Peck. Molly, the drag queen, and her other Piers Gaveston friends were sure to lie.

FORTY-FIVE

E heard the door open. He knew she would be upset when she found out. He didn't want to talk about it, but he knew they must.

"Hi," Alison said.

"Hi," he said. There was silence.

"I have to tell you something. There's an article that appeared in the paper about me today."

"I know. I saw it." He walked into the bedroom and looked at the article. He began reading sections of it aloud in a mocking voice.

> The JCR LGBTQ+ Welfare Officer told Cherwell that the graduate student in question had also been 'preaching homophobic messages and disturbing students who live in Peck.' She added, 'On Tuesday during the afternoon, he approached many individuals and was very threatening towards them. The porters had to remove him, after our Junior Censor came down to have a word, in which the individual in question was very verbally abusive, homophobic, sexist, and ableist.'

"It's all a lie. I wasn't preaching. And even if I were preaching, what's wrong with that? They're preaching with their stupid, giant flag waving in everyone's faces. They run the college, and now you can see they run the newspaper too. They get to tell everyone else what to believe, while simultaneously pretending to be the victims? And if anyone opposes them, they attack. I wasn't threatening anybody. François came over and said I could stay. You know François. The Censor immediately sided with the mob."

He waited for her to say something. She didn't. "Listen to this nonsense," he said.

> The Censors of the College are now involved in an investigation into the matter. She said, 'I am pursuing a course of action with the Censors, so I am grateful our Censors have understood the gravitas of the situation, and the need to ensure the safety of Christ Church students and visitors in the future, which is why this is being dealt with in the hopes of making Christ Church a healthier, safer place to live!'

"See, there you go. The Censors are going to investigate me over nothing. And why is she working with them? She's only a student! She shouldn't have any hand in an investigation or a disciplinary proceeding. And in any case, she's the one who started the whole problem anyway, and now she gets to run into the press and lie about me? This is defamation."

He continued reading in his sardonic newscaster voice,

> Students have made an impassioned and united response to his actions. She explained, 'On Wednesday, the college community, including governing body, tutors and members of the Cathedral, met with students from the GCR and JCR to take a photo in solidarity with the LGBTQ+ community.'

He paused. "Do you know about the college photo?"

"What photo?"

"Look." He opened a file from his college email that had been sent to the JCR and GCR.

"They sent this out over the college email to everyone yesterday. I've now officially been marked with clown world's scarlet letter. Look at these people," he said. In the photo was a group of about three dozen students and staff gathered around the flagpole in Peck. In the middle were the three accusers from the paper holding the sign he'd left with the Scripture from Paul.

"Notice anything?"

"What?"

"Wood and Klaus are right there. They're piling on now, because they know if they make me a pariah at the college and smear me in the press, it'll be easier to wash their hands of me with the viva."

He wasn't at all surprised Klaus would do what he was doing. For Klaus, after all, this was an irresistible opportunity to drive in the dagger. It was a premature celebration, of course, but Klaus would not realize that until it was too late. As for Wood, in a way perhaps he wasn't so surprised over Wood being there too, given what he'd seen at the male theology dinners.

He shook his head and kept reading,

> A second year Christ Church student, also drew attention to how the community has come together. She told Cherwell that although what he did 'was a hate crime,' the majority of the student body and senior staff have been amazing in supporting the community, which has made me feel a lot safer in college. 'It's good to know Christ Church supports its LGBTQ+ community and wants to stand in solidarity with it. Christ Church is no place for homophobia or discrimination and I certainly won't stand for it! I want to feel safe when I hold hands with my girlfriend and I don't want to worry about this person bringing violence to the situation.'

He threw up his hands in disbelief. "This supposed witness wasn't even there at Peck! She's just made everything up! I looked it up earlier today. It's defamation *per se* to falsely accuse someone of committing a crime that carries a jail sentence. Here in the UK, a hate crime can carry a jail sentence. For her to say I committed a hate crime is defamation. Same thing about the bit about me and the violence. I wasn't violent at all. This is all preposterous. Quiller and Klaus are just weaponizing something that was totally innocuous, in order to weave a narrative to destroy me professionally. They couldn't get me to do anything wrong with all their taunts and provocations, I've made it to the viva, and so they've now decided to resort to fabricating a controversy."

He was nearing the end of the article,

> Another student who confronted him on Tuesday, told the paper that he initially tried 'to explain to him that his homophobic message was disturbing and harmful' but that it 'was not possible to reason with him.' Moskovitz said that after 'several attempts by college staff, leading to increased verbal aggression and the use of ableist slurs,' the graduate student eventually departed. Moskovitz also stated that the turnout for the photo 'was amazing, with many members of staff attending. This serves to show everyone that there is solidarity in Christ Church, and for the LGBTQ members of Christ Church that they are not alone.' But he did add that this incident served as 'a reminder for why we need the flag,' saying, 'When I look at the flag now, I feel less safe knowing that such bigotry exists so close to my home.'

He laughed bitterly.

"So now the words of the Apostle Paul are homophobia, according to some drag queen, who evidently runs the college. And this deviant, who not long ago would have been arrested by the vice squad for public indecency, can now publicly impugn my character and mental health, as if we're all supposed to rely on the word of a drag queen? According to the drag queen, it was impossible to reason with me. Breath-taking! But people like it this way, I guess. They all worship their little flag. It's a death cult."

He drew a breath and coughed.

"You need to stop smoking," Alison said.

"Eh, what's the point? At this rate they're going to be forced to suicide me soon, anyway," he said.

She was quiet. "Let me read you the last part," he said.

> Prof Koby Bruce, the Junior Censor at Christ Church, who asked him to leave the scene, told Cherwell, 'Maybe the big achievement is just that we've been able to get this all to stop and as a community move on.'

"Of course, this isn't over. The Censor is just saying so for the press. This isn't over at all. It's just beginning. They're going to crucify me. Well, not really. Everything is so abstract and mediocre in clown world that even the persecution itself is comical."

Alison sighed deeply. "Why did you do this? You gave them what they wanted! We were so close. The viva's next week."

"I did it because nobody else would. And this is why. Look at what they're already doing to me. It's a take-over. The words of the Bible are now 'hate speech'? Maybe most people don't care right now, but it's only going to get worse, and nobody will be immune. I'm just the canary in the mine shaft. I told you the spirit of wickedness that rules this place. Well, look at their reaction to a simple Scripture. I simply drew what I knew was lurking out of the shadows."

The room was silent.

"So, what? Now you're angry with me, because Klaus got a drag queen and some other liars who all belong to some stupid, perverted secret society to smear me in the press? What was I supposed to do? Somebody had to do something," he said.

Alison sighed, threw up her arms, and plopped down into the bed pillows. "Why can't you just be like everyone else?"

The moon was out, he saw through the window. There was no point in talking, so he would leave for a walk. He had to think about what was coming next.

Outside, he lit a cigarette. It had been a while since he'd walked on Port Meadow, especially at night, so he would go there. He began piecing things together as he walked along the river. Given the photo that had been taken in Peck Quad, the network was out for a scalp. He had been getting slandered around college by word of mouth, with a campaign of whispers consisting of false accusations: "hate crime," "threatening," "aggressive," "unreasonable," and "violent." Now, they had also gone to the press, even though all of that couldn't be further from the truth. He thought about it. The reality was that the police might be summoned to investigate. At the very least, the Censors would want to see him. At first, they would be cryptic about the precise rationale for the meeting and its purpose, but he knew it would be a disciplinary proceeding. If he wasn't careful and simply went to it, he would trigger an administrative process that couldn't be stopped. Before he knew it, he would be sent down. When he was home, he would review the Blue Book and familiarize himself with the college's disciplinary procedures against students who were the subject of a complaint from other students. He sighed. It was going to be a nightmare. There was, though, a silver-lining. If Quiller and Klaus were truly confident about the looming viva, there would be no need to attack him like this. They were projecting strength, but it was rooted in weakness. He would focus on the viva, and take care of this later.

A few days later, the email he was expecting came. It was the Junior Censor.

> I would like to see you, along with Professors Jepson and Simp-
> son, in the Junior Censor's Office—atop Tom 8—on Wednesday
> 24th February at 4 o'clock. This is a matter of some urgency.

He had consulted the Blue Book. The first step in a disciplinary proceeding was a meeting with the Junior Censor and the Tutor for Graduates. If they decided further action was merited, they would refer a recommendation to the Senior Censor. At that point, he could be punished with any number of sanctions, including even possible expulsion. This, then, was the initial meeting upon which the Junior Censor and Tutor for Graduates would draft up their referral to the Senior Censor. The fact the Junior Censor wasn't being honest about the nature of the meeting was a red flag. Most people would go to the meeting naively, and before they knew it, they would be suspended or expelled.

He would keep his reply short.

> I'm afraid I'm unable to meet Wednesday on this short notice. We'll have to reschedule for sometime next week.

The response came that same afternoon.

> We're all busy people, and this meeting cannot possibly be postponed any further. Please come to the Junior Censor's Office (atop Tom 8) at 12 on Monday (29th February): this meeting is your college priority.

He had bought himself a week. He could deal with the viva tomorrow. What he really needed, though, was a lawyer. The timetable was tight, but if he hurried, he might be able to secure legal counsel to help him review the situation and advise him how to proceed before the meeting. An idea came to him. He would write Ben. Somebody here in Oxford or London had handled his divorce. Maybe, then, Ben's lawyer would know somebody who could help. He sent an email, linking the newspaper article, and explaining that the Censors wanted to meet him. He was seeking a lawyer, and he needed one fast.

He lit a cigarette, and also sent a note to the Censor. In the most recent note, the Censor had copied in his college advisor, Simpson. That had been a clear escalation. Now they were resorting to sheer intimidation. His response note held his ground.

> Many thanks for rescheduling the meeting. Since you've suggested that it is an urgent matter, could you tell me what exactly you wish to discuss on Monday, and why the Tutor for Graduates and my college advisor have been invited? It's emotionally distressing to be called in like this without any explanation of what to expect, or what I might do to prepare.

The response from the Censor was swift. The irritation suggested the Censor felt he was losing his grip on the situation. That was good.

> I think you know full well; your own behaviour has caused people emotional distress, and that is what we wish to discuss with you.

So, his intuition had been correct. This clearly was a disciplinary hearing. And it was a stitch-up. The Junior Censor, who himself had been at the quad the day of the incident, knew all of the allegations were false. And yet, he was acting as if they were true. His college advisor, Simpson, who should have by now contacted him to hear his side of things, hadn't said a word. Now Simpson was instead slated to attend the meeting. Somebody had given them all their marching orders. They had been told to get rid of him.

FORTY-SIX

H E took a deep breath. The moment had come. He had to put away thoughts of the skirmishing back at the college over Peck Quad. What mattered was the viva. He walked up to the room, and knocked on the door. Anderson opened the door.

"Come in, please," she said.

His external examiner, Gaskin, was sitting at the table and stood. She had a stern look on her face. That alone may not have been cause for concern, but the rest of the situation was. To begin with, there wasn't a single other person in attendance. From what he had heard, it was customary for one's supervisor to be there, along with other faculty who worked in one's area. Then of course there should be other students from one's Faculty, and of course one's friends. Nobody was there, because everybody knew what was coming. The fact that he had just been smeared in the paper didn't help, either. People were afraid to be seen associating with him. He was a pariah. The network was probably surprised he'd even shown up for the viva. The photo that had been circulated over the college email, then the article in the press, and then the exchange with the Junior Censor, had been intended to send a clear message that things had run their course. Fighting it was futile, they wanted him to believe. He knew that's what they wanted him to think, so here he was for his viva, even if it was going to be a sham. He was not going to hand them a defeat. He would make them work for what they wanted.

"Please, have a seat. We'll ask you some questions after you have first summarized the results of your thesis. If we run long, we might break. Then we'll reconvene."

He summarized the chapters of the thesis, explaining how they fit together, and how each contributed something to the overall claim of the thesis. When he was finished, the examiners asked him some basic questions about the second chapter. Then they turned their attention to the third chapter, the one he'd read in the Strawson Room and presented in Canada. The questioning was hostile and dismissive throughout. He went through the motions, doing his best to remain patient and polite no matter how abusive or derogatory his examiners became. After an hour, they could not get an outburst.

"We have run long. Why don't we take a ten-minute break?" Anderson said.

"Okay, is it okay if I run downstairs to get a coffee?"

"That's fine."

In line, he reflected on the state of affairs. As he stood here, his examiners would be busy contacting Quiller and Klaus for further instructions about how to handle the remainder of the viva. They hadn't scored any major hits, the work was holding up well, and he had kept his composure. He didn't know how long they would want to continue, but they had already reached the upper threshold of what was customary. If they went much longer, that would be irregular.

He entered the examination room and sat down.

"Would you like to talk about the other chapters? We've only discussed chapters two and three so far," he said.

"We will get to those later. We're still unclear what precisely the claim of chapter three is supposed to be," Gaskin hissed. Chapter three was the chapter he'd read in the Strawson Room, the one that had triggered Klaus, Quiller, and Dowell. Quiller was having the examiners ask all the questions he'd not asked during the seminar. It was cowardly, but expected from him.

"Please explain the claim again," Anderson said.

He rehearsed the argument again. When he finished, they didn't know how to object. Finally forced to turn to another chapter, they moved to chapter five, the art chapter that he'd read at the Placement Scheme. First there was an objection based on something from Hegel. That was coming from Adamson, the Hegelian, obviously. He almost laughed. What an experience, he thought. Sitting for a sham viva receiving objections from one's own supervisor, who wasn't even here. It continued like this, and before he knew it, the viva had gone on for over three hours. Sensing that the stich-up was embarrassingly obvious, Anderson tried to recover.

"Well, uh, I'm sorry this has gone on so for long, but we just wanted to be thorough."

"Okay, but we still haven't discussed three other whole chapters of the thesis. We spent almost the whole time on the reduction chapter."

"That's fine. It doesn't matter. We have the information we need. This concludes the viva."

He had been told it was typical for the examiners to let the student know the result, especially if it were positive. He imagined others at their viva, their friends and family and colleagues coming up to hug and shake hands. There would be celebratory food and drinks and photos. Not here. The room was empty, and there was nobody to congratulate him. Everybody knew what was coming.

"Thank you for your time," he said.

He shook Anderson's hand. He put out his hand to Gaskin, who ignored it.

He got outside and called Alison.

"How'd it go?"

"Terrible. Something's wrong. It was irregular."

"Irregular?"

"Yes, irregular."

"What do you mean?"

"I don't want to get into all the details. It went twice as long as it was supposed to, they never let me discuss over half the thesis, and at the end of it, my external examiner wouldn't even shake my hand. Nobody else showed up, either. They're going to flunk it."

"I'm sorry. Let's talk about it when I'm home."

On the way home, he stopped in Tesco and bought a giant shrimp party platter that was used for special occasions. He knew it was somewhat self-indulgent of him, but he thought it would be grimly amusing to eat the party shrimp all alone back at the house. When he let himself in, Alison was out. He lit a cigarette, lied down on the bed, and began eating the shrimp.

Later, the door opened. Alison came to the foot of the bed.

"Shrimp? You ate all those?"

"There are a few left. Want one?"

"No, thanks."

She sat down on the bed and put her head in her hands.

"So what are we going to do now?"

"About the viva or the *Cherwell* thing at the college?"

"Both."

"I'm going to file a complaint about the viva. I'm looking for a lawyer to help with the college."

"Where are you going to find a lawyer?"

"I emailed Ben. His divorce lawyer is going to contact me."

"I don't trust Ben."

"Doesn't matter. We have no other option. Do you know a lawyer here?"

She crawled into bed, and put her head on his chest.

"I'm sorry," he said.

"It's okay," she said.

FORTY-SEVEN

"DAD?"

"Yeah."

"I have a problem over here."

"Do you need me to come over?"

"Yes, I think that will help. I need a lawyer."

"Okay, Uncle Shannon and Aunt Laurie are still visiting here, but Mom can drive me up to SFO now. I'll let you know when I have the flight details."

"I'm sorry."

"Don't be. It's not your fault," his dad said.

When he had the flight details, the next day he took the train to Paddington. From there, he caught the train to Heathrow. The flight arrived and eventually his dad came into the lobby.

"You're wearing a suit," his dad said.

"Yeah, I was thinking we might have to stop in London. But there's no point now," he said.

"You found a lawyer?"

"Yeah, a solicitor they call it. I found him through somebody I know in Oxford."

"Okay, good."

"We need to hurry. He's due over at the house in a few hours. Alison's going to be there, too, to meet him." He grabbed his dad's bag and led him to the tube. They bought tickets and got on the train. On the way, he updated his dad about everything, about the photo sent over the college email, the article in the paper, and the irregular viva.

His dad looked out the window. "Well, they're really making their push, aren't they?"

"Yep."

"I don't know what they're doing. Everything you're telling me is so illegal. The lawyer is going to have a field day with this," his dad said.

He sighed. "We'll see."

At the Oxford station, they walked through the crowd.

His dad looked confused. "Where are we going? Don't we need a cab?"

"No, Dad, Alison and I live right around the corner. We're walking."

They got to the house and opened the door.

"We're here," he said. There was no answer. "I guess Alison's out," he said. He set the luggage in the living room.

"We only have one bedroom. You're going to have to sleep on the couch, unless you want to get a hotel."

"That's fine. I don't care."

They sat down. An hour passed, and the door opened and closed. There were footsteps in the kitchen. A few minutes later, Alison came into the living room. His dad stood up and smiled.

"Come here," he said with his arms open. She walked over, and he hugged her.

"This is so weird," he said. "I never thought I'd be out in Oxford having to talk to a lawyer."

"Speaking of which," he said looking at Alison and his dad, "Dave should be here any minute."

Alison looked at him. "Who is this guy again?"

"He was Ben's solicitor."

"That's all you know?"

"Yeah, for now. We'll have a chance to meet him. At this point, I just need somebody to help me fend off the Junior Censor. Once that's done, we can worry about the article in the paper. It should be easy to remove. It's blatant defamation. I can't believe they were dumb enough to print it."

Alison walked to the window and opened the curtain. "I think it's him. A car pulled up." They waited in the room, and there was a knock at the door.

"I'll get it," he said. He opened the door.

"Hello, is this 1A Cripley?"

"Indeed, it is."

"Then you must be—"

"Indeed, I am. You must be Dave. Please, come in. My wife and my dad are in the living room."

He led the solicitor into the living room and did the introductions.

Alison sat on the chair, with the solicitor and his dad next to one another on the couch.

"Ben has told me a little bit about your situation, and I've reviewed the exchange you've had with the Junior Censor. It's incredible. I've never seen anything like it. The college is clearly harassing you. And the article is very shoddy."

His dad asked, "So what do we do?"

"The first thing is to handle the Censor. It's imperative you don't go to any meeting. It's a set-up. When people find themselves in situations like these, they make the mistake of disappearing. Don't do that. Stay as active as possible. Be at college, go to events, see people. It's very important that you establish a public presence, so they can't spin a narrative about you in your absence."

"Yes," he said.

His dad spoke, "The article mentions a hate crime. Are the police going to come?"

The solicitor leaned back. "It's certainly possible. They're laying the predicate for it. My guess is that if you don't go to the meeting, they might refer the incident to the police. Or at least, they want you to think that's what they'll do. But no matter what, you mustn't go to the meeting. These sorts of procedures are notorious for violating natural justice, sometimes even their own regulations. If they want you gone, they'll get rid of you. You might be able to sue later, but they won't care, because they'll have gotten what they want, which is you out the door."

"Yes," he said.

"If the police come, don't speak to them. Tell them to call me. Do you have my card?"

"No," he said.

"Here. Take it."

Alison was worried. "What about the viva?"

The solicitor turned to him. "The viva?"

He had printed out a copy of the photo from Peck. He handed it to the solicitor. "See the people circled?"

"Yes. Who are they?"

"The three in the middle are the false accusers from the paper. They're students at the college. The other two are professors. One's a big theologian, the other is my former doctoral supervisor."

The solicitor examined the picture and laughed. "The professors, they're settling old scores with you?"

"Exactly." He looked at the solicitor. "I had my viva recently, and it went terribly. It was irregular. My guess is that they wanted to smear me in the press ahead of time, so that when they try to can the work, they figure nobody will want to help me."

"Yes, classic character assassination. Have you heard of Biderman's Coercion Chart? They have you at humiliation and degradation," the solicitor said. "Have you filed a complaint about the viva?"

"I have."

"Good. When will you get the result?"

"I don't know. I could see it going either way. They might want to make me suffer by waiting. On the other hand, they might be so eager to fail me that they'll tell me as soon as possible."

"When they send the result, forward it to me," the solicitor said. "I also need all your emails you've exchanged with anyone here at Oxford that's at all relevant to the incident at the college and to the viva. We're going to have to find a barrister."

His dad looked confused. "A barrister?"

The solicitor explained the British system.

"I'll search for a barrister. In the meantime, play everything cool. I will give you the language to use with the Censor. With any luck, they'll begin to suspect you have counsel, and they'll back off. I read the correspondence. Brilliant work, by the way. You really have him off balance," the solicitor said laughing.

"Thanks."

He walked the solicitor to the door with his dad.

His dad looked at Dave. "Are we going to sue?"

"One step at a time," the solicitor said. "But yes, you have a clear case. What the college is doing right now is egregious. Flagrant discrimination and harassment. There are obvious free speech and religious freedom issues here, too. Then you toss in the viva. At some point, we'll want to go to the press. *The Guardian* or *The Telegraph* will eat this up."

There was silence.

The solicitor smiled. "You want to ask how much we're talking?"

His dad laughed, "The money is not important. But, yes, if Alison and him could get a nest egg out of this, that would make their lives easier."

The solicitor's eyes were twinkling. "I've worked cases similar to this. Workplace harassment, discrimination. With the defamation and all the rest of it, this is much bigger. Those went for three or four million." He checked his watch. "I'm sorry, I have to go. Great meeting you all. Stay strong," he said. They were about to let him out the door when he turned around.

"You know, you've heard about what happened to Wesley?"

He knew. As a young theologian, John Wesley had been the recipient of terrible mockery and ridicule while a student at Christ Church. His Holy Club had won him no friends at the college. In a note to his father, Wesley had said of his experience, "Till he be thus condemned, no man is in a state of salvation."

"Yes, I know about what happened to Wesley. I suppose it means I'm now in good company," he said to Dave. "Blessed are those who are persecuted for righteousness' sake, right?"

"Indeed, ol' chap," Dave said.

The door closed behind the solicitor, and his dad turned to him.

"Do you think we can trust him?"

"I guess we'll find out," he said.

That night, he reviewed the language from Dave for the Censor. He read it to Alison and his dad, then sent it.

> As regards the meeting which you have called for Monday, I must say that I am still somewhat confused as to why the meeting is taking place. I previously asked what this meeting was about and received a most cryptic reply from you.
>
> Would you please let me know in detail what the purpose of this meeting is and if I am suspected of having done something wrong; precisely what breach of regulations I am suspected of having committed? Until I've been given this information, I must respectfully inform you that I don't feel comfortable in attending.

In the morning, the Censor replied.

> My reply was not remotely cryptic; the tutor for graduates and I wish to talk to you about your disruptive behaviour in college the week before last, including our encounter. We want to hear your account of what you had set out to achieve, and to discuss the repercussions it has had within college: you have upset a lot of people and we wish to know why.

Dave gave him another note to send. He sent it.

> As regards the meeting which you have called for today I am still no better informed as to why the meeting has been called. I

previously asked what this meeting was about and asked you to let me know in detail what the purpose of this meeting is and if I am suspected of having done something wrong; precisely what breach of regulations I am suspected of having committed. You have not done so. All you have done is to make 3 very vague and unspecified allegations of behaviour that I have allegedly indulged in namely;

(i) '...your own behaviour has caused people emotional your disruptive behaviour in college the week before last..'

(iii) '...including our encounter...'

Until I've been given this specific information along with any evidence supporting such allegations I must respectfully inform you that I do not think that it is appropriate for me to be attending any meeting with you in your capacity as Junior Censor and with others.

He got a call. It was Dave.

"Ten minutes before the meeting today, write to them, and say you're unable to attend. Don't go. Tell me what they say. I'll be in touch tonight."

"Okay."

Ten minutes before the meeting, he sent an email saying he would not be able to make it. Shortly after the meeting was to have begun, the Censor wrote again.

I find your emails curt and rude, and your discourtesy to me and the Tutor for Graduates - expecting you for a meeting today at 12, to which you didn't bother to turn up - unforgivable; to send an email eight minutes before such a meeting is poor behaviour by any standards.

As for your pretence not to know what I mean by the emotional distress you have caused, I am simply flabbergasted. Your language to me on the one occasion I have met you, was particularly insensitive, to say the least, and I find it hard to believe you are unaware of this.

That night, the call from the solicitor was short.

"Brilliant, you did great. They don't know what to do. By now, they must suspect you have legal counsel. Let me know if you hear anything from the Faculty about your complaint regarding the irregular viva. We'll talk next week."

"Wait."

"Yeah?"

"I have a question."

"Okay."

"Next week I have a collections' meeting."

"What's that?'

"Once a year graduate students report to the Dean for a review of their academic progress. My college advisor and the Tutor for Graduates will be there."

"Oh, that's perfect."

"I just play it cool and don't mention anything, right?"

"You're a natural at this! I don't have to tell you anything. Exactly. Force them to do everything in writing. Don't mention the meeting or the viva. If they bring it up, fine. But tell them you want everything in writing. Call me when you're finished with it."

He got off the phone and went into the living room where Alison and his dad were sitting in silence.

"This is great," he said.

His dad spoke, "What is?"

"Dave said they're trapped. I'll go to the collections' meeting, and see how they want to play it."

Alison looked upset. "I don't know."

"What?"

"What about the article?"

"What about it?"

"Why aren't we taking it down?"

"That comes later. There's no way to force the paper to take it down until we've forced the college to back off."

"I don't know. Something doesn't feel right."

"Well, what do you want? There's nothing else for me to do."

"Don't be angry at me."

"I'm not," he said.

The meeting arrived.

"Just wait right here," he told his dad. He took a drag of his cigarette, and put it out.

"Here in the quad?"

"Yeah. I'm going in there," he said, pointing at the Deanery.

"Be careful," his dad said.

"I'll be fine."

He knocked on the door and the Dean's assistant opened.

"I'm here for my collections meeting."

"Yes, of course. You're next. Please wait here while they finish with the current appointment."

He stepped inside and took a seat in the foyer. After a few minutes, the other student emerged from the room. It was his turn. He stood up, and took a breath.

He walked into the room. The Dean was seated next to Simpson, his college advisor. The other man, whom he didn't recognize, must be Jepson, the Tutor for Graduates.

Simpson, whose thick mustache made him resemble a walrus, was wearing the same red sweater as Quiller. Perhaps it was nothing, simply a result of both men, who were about the same age, having the identical taste in outdated sweaters. And perhaps they both happened to prefer the sweater in the same shade of red. *Perhaps*—there was always a perhaps available, if the mind was willing to indulge in doubt. If one did, it would open unto innumerable interpretations of the situation or event in question, thereby obscuring everything in a fog of indeterminateness. This, of course, was precisely the resulting atmosphere in which men like Quiller and Simpson operated. It was all psychology. They knew most people would succumb to the *perhaps*, would choose to deny what they saw all because they did not want to see it. Here was a very clear, albeit apparently bizarrely banal, example of such an instance. Two men routinely wear the identical red sweater—perhaps it's a coincidence. Of course, it wasn't, but most people would never notice it, and even among those who did, they would quickly convince themselves that what they thought they had seen was really nothing. Or, if they couldn't shake the sense that it wasn't a mere coincidence, they would pacify themselves by believing that it didn't matter, in order to justify not thinking about it. Quiller and Simpson relished this—they enjoyed flaunting something they knew everyone would ignore. It didn't matter if it were trivial, in a way that made it more amusing. It was their way of laughing, of showing everyone their scorn for those who were too stupid or weak to see the obvious. This, he realized, is what such a life became for people like Quiller and Simpson, one big practical joke, in which they thumbed their noses at the very same people they despised for being too stupid to know it. If one were the type to ask why they would go to such lengths to mock people by wearing a red sweater, one would never understand, and one was exactly the sort of person who fell victim to the perhaps, the sort of person whom Quiller and Simpson thought they had reason to loathe. The point wasn't the sweater itself, but what it showed, that Quiller and Simpson were part of something others weren't, that they didn't hide it, and that they didn't have to hide it because those who weren't a part of it were the ones who could be shown they weren't a part of it and yet still not see that's what they were being shown. In short, here in Oxford, even a stupid, obnoxious, everyday red sweater could mean something.

The Dean, Junior Censor, and Tutor for Graduates would be expecting him to be intimidated. It was important to show that he wasn't. He strode up to the table, and without sitting down, put out his hand to the Tutor for Graduates.

"You must be Jepson," he said smiling.

"Uh, yes, yes I am," Jepson said. Jepson shook his hand while still seated.

The Dean looked at him, "Please, have a seat."

"Thanks," he said. He stood for a few more seconds, then sat down. He turned to his college advisor. "Prof Simpson," he said nodding.

"Hi," Simpson said. The Dean was about to say something, but before the Dean could, he held a stare at Simpson.

"Nice sweater. It looks a lot like Prof Quiller's. You two shop together?" Simpson didn't know what to say. The other two chuckled uncomfortably.

Jepson cleared his throat to speak, "We've reviewed your file. You're starting your third year here. Any issues you would like to raise?"

"No," he said.

Jepson smiled. "You should be nearing completion, is that right?"

"Yes. Or, at least I hope so. I had my viva last week. My understanding is that Prof Simpson, as my college advisor, should know about that," he said.

Simpson cleared his throat. "Uh, um, yes. I saw the advertisement in the *Gazette*."

"I'm sorry you weren't able to make it," he said.

"Yes, me too. I'm sorry. I was in tutorial," Simpson said.

Jepson interjected, "Okay, anything else?" They were waiting for him to raise the issue of the incident in Peck and the meeting he'd been fending off.

"Well, I should mention something about the viva. According to the Faculty of Philosophy Graduate Handbook, one is instructed to file a complaint immediately if there's any suggestion that the viva may have been irregular. I think that it was irregular, so I've written the Chair of the Faculty and the DGS. The Handbook says that my college advisor should be made aware also, and since Prof Simpson is also at the Faculty of Philosophy, I figured it makes particular sense to inform you all about the complaint here."

The Dean spoke, "I'm very sorry to hear about the issue with the viva." The Dean turned to Simpson. "Prof Simpson, as the student's college advisor, you should look into the complaint."

There was silence. The three of them were waiting for him to mention Peck Quad. When they saw that he wasn't going to do so, the Dean spoke. "Well, that'll be it for now. Again, sorry to hear about the viva, but we'll straighten that out," he said, looking at Simpson. He and Simpson stood up, and walked out to Tom Quad.

"Good luck," Simpson said, looking over his shoulder.

"Thanks."

Simpson walked off toward Kilcannon.

"How'd it go?" He turned around to find his dad.

"They're hurting badly, Dad," he said. "The Dean told Simpson to investigate the viva."

"Who's Simpson?"

"My college advisor. He's at the Faculty too. He's friends with Klaus. The guy you saw me just walk out of the meeting with."

"Okay, I'll try to remember his name. What about the newspaper article and the *Cherwell* meeting?"

"Never came up."

"It never came up?"

"No. They wanted me to bring it up, so I didn't. I'll force them into email," he said.

"Oh, this is so good," his dad said.

That night, he told Alison about the collections' meeting.

"Okay, great. But where's Dave? He said he would call tonight."

"I left a voicemail and told him nobody mentioned Peck at the collections' meeting. There's nothing for him to do at this point."

"What about the article? Everyone's reading it. I don't want my family to see it," she said.

He looked at his dad. He knew his dad wanted to tell Alison that Stuart should be the one over here helping, since Stuart was the academic. There was also Linda, who herself had been a lawyer. The fact that Stuart and Linda were conspicuously absent was revealing.

A few days later, another email came from the college, this time from an assistant in the Censors' Office.

The Junior Censor, Dr Koby Bruce, and the Tutor for Graduates, Professor Edward Jepson, summon you to an official meeting in the Junior Censor's Office at 12 on Monday, 7th March. You have ignored previous requests to attend meetings; there have been serious complaints about your recent behavior in Peckwater Quad and a disturbance you caused to a junior member of the college outside a night club. These are serious matters which need to be addressed.

He read the email aloud in the living room.

Alison was worried. "What other disturbance? At a night club?"

"Yeah."

"What?"

His memory turned to the night last month when he had been walking home. Outside one of the neighborhood night clubs had been a long queue. One of the girls in the line, who was a Member of the college, had recognized him. He'd stopped to talk. Now it came together. She had been a friend of Lavinia's, one of the students from the college calendar. That meant she was friends also with the false accusers in the paper. She must have filed a complaint, too.

"These people are insane," his dad said. "You can't even go outside anymore?"

"It just keeps getting worse," Alison said, shaking her head.

He again used the language from the solicitor.

I am writing in response to the e-mail received from Rebecca Varlé at the Censor's office summoning me to '...an official meeting.' and your e-mail earlier last week replying to mine. I must respectfully point out that it is simply not true that I have ignored previous requests to attend meetings.

I have responded to all your e-mails requesting my attendance politely and respectfully. However, by contrast, despite my repeated requests, you have still not explained properly why this meeting is being called.

I have repeatedly asked you to let me know in detail what the purpose of this meeting is and if I am accused of having done something wrong; precisely what breach of regulations I am alleged to have committed. To date you have still not provided this information. All you have done in your various e-mails is to make very vague and unspecified allegations of behaviour (adding more examples with each further e-mail as we have corresponded) that I have allegedly indulged in namely;

(i) '...I think you know full well; your own behaviour has caused people emotional
distress...'

(ii) '...your disruptive behaviour in college the week before last...'

(iii) '...including our encounter...'

(iv) '...language to me on the one occasion I have met you was particularly insensitive, to say the least...'

(v) '...there have been serious complaints about your recent behaviour in Peckwater Quad...'

(vi) '...and a disturbance you caused to a junior member of the college outside a night club...'

(vii) '...these are serious matters which need to be addressed...'

It is thus quite clear that I am being accused by you of having already committed serious breaches of regulations and this meeting is not for a fire-side chat but is part of some form of disciplinary process that you are conducting.

But the really odd thing is that when I had my third-year Graduate Student Collections meeting last week with the Dean on 29 February 2016, my college advisor Professor Jepson and Professor Simpson; none of them said anything about any alleged misbehaviour on my part.

I am of course most anxious to comply with regulations but before I attend any 'official meeting' would you please let me know in writing the following:

1. By what specific regulation or power you are purporting to summon me to this official meeting?

2. What specific regulation or regulations I am accused of having breached?

3. The full evidence that is relied upon in support of the accusations made against me.

Until I've been given this specific information along with the evidence supporting such allegations I must respectfully inform you that I do not think that it is appropriate for me to be attending any meeting with you in your capacity as Junior Censor and with others.

The next day, the response came from the Censor himself.

I have had more than enough of your pedantic prevarications; I will take up your persistent rudeness and high-handedness with the Dean and the Senior Censor.

The solicitor called.

"So, what does this all mean?"

His solicitor laughed. "It means they gave up! They have nothing. Worry now about the viva. Once that's fixed, we'll take care of the article online. It's almost time to go to the press with this. I suggest *The Telegraph*."

"Okay."

"How's the family holding up?"

"My dad is frantic. My wife is stressed. I don't know how much longer they can take it, Dave."

"The dons are going to try to sweat you out. You have to be prepared."

"I am."

"Okay, good. Look, I think I've found a barrister. His name's Patrick Newman, QC. Top-notch guy working in the education sector. He's seen this before. He just won an appellate decision to challenge the academic immunity clause. I think he'll be interested in your case. It's exactly what he's been looking for. I'll let you know when we have a meeting set."

"Sounds good." He hung up.

FORTY-EIGHT

HEY looked up at the imposing building. The blustery winds coming from the Thames were chilling them to the bone.

"Is this it?"

"Yeah, 33 KBW."

"I still can't believe I'm doing this."

"What?"

"Walking around Oxford and London dealing with lawyers. I don't know how this is taking so long. Quiller and Klaus and the others should have already been fired for what they've done. It's so obvious. I'm starting to wonder whether the UK even has a legal system."

He looked at his dad before they opened the door. "Well, if this doesn't work, then at least you know there's nothing we could have done. Inner Temple Garden is where the top barristers in London are. This used to be Knights Templar."

They entered the foyer where an assistant introduced herself. She led them upstairs to a conference room. Dave was already seated, holding a huge binder with a case number on the cover.

"Hi, guys, have a seat. Patrick and his clerks will be here any minute." They sat down.

Five minutes later, Patrick came in.

He stood to shake Patrick's hand.

"Thanks for coming. I've been very busy, but I've been able to review the outlines of your situation. Dave has told me about it." He waited for Patrick to continue.

"I think the first thing you should know is that the academic immunity clause is very strong. Although I've recently won a decision at the appellate level allowing me to challenge it, until it has been settled at the High Court, universities in the interim will continue using it to their advantage. I'm afraid there's not much of a legal remedy for you at present."

His dad almost jumped out of his seat. Dave was shocked.

Dave said to Patrick, "But on the phone, you said this was egregious . . . "

Patrick looked at all three of them. "I'm very sorry. I don't mean to suggest I'm not sympathetic to your client's predicament. It's just that proving conspiracy is very difficult."

Patrick looked at him directly, but he said nothing. There was no point getting into it, since obviously the QC wasn't anyone to rely on. When the meeting was over, the QC walked his dad and him out.

"I'll be in touch. If you want, your solicitor can draft a letter in consultation with my office, which we can send into Oxford. My understanding is that you're entitled an academic hearing, if you do indeed file an appeal. I would be happy to represent you at the proceedings."

"Thanks."

"All right, have a good evening." They all shook hands.

When they got to the street, his dad turned to him. "I don't get it. Patrick is acting like there's nothing he can do. This is all such obvious illegality. Send a letter? What's that going to do?"

He sighed. "Dad, I know it's all shadow boxing. But there's no other way. I'm just going to play along, and wait them out. We'll have Dave and Patrick send the letter, then I'll file the appeal. In the meantime, I'll work on trying to get the article taken down. At least the Censor disappeared."

When they got to Paddington, they realized they'd missed the last train to Oxford. They would have to take a cab, which would be expensive. Patrick would have known they were about to miss the train. He didn't tell his dad what Patrick had done, since his dad was already overwhelmed. When they pulled up to the flat two hours later, he realized that neither of them had said a word the entire drive. The lights were off. Alison must have already gone to bed.

FORTY-NINE

I T would get worse before it could get better. From Alison's perspective, which was understandable, things appeared only to be getting worse with no sign of improving. He read the email from Carrell aloud to her and his dad in the living room.

> This is astonishing, and astonishingly awful, news. I never expected that they would take their animus toward you to these extremes. My first question is: is there anyone there on the faculty whom you can trust? I ask, because if your appeal is not successful (as I suspect it will not be), then if you hope to proceed to 'do something' to fix up what you have written so far so as to re-submit it for the PhD, you need to be able to talk with someone who can shepherd it through that process, lest the same thing be repeated. I ask also because you seem to suggest that you don't want to go ahead with the book project until you have exhausted every avenue to get the PhD from Oxford. I think that's the right way to go, but it will require the advice there of someone you can trust.
>
> Beyond that, I am just too far away from the scene there and its protocols to judge whether their way of assessing a 'series of essays' thesis is particularly unfair in this case. It seems to be, but I also don't know what the relation between the formal 'regulations' governing such a thesis (which you seem to have met), the viva evaluation, and the evaluation of the content of the essays themselves. Given these three only partially overlapping evaluation points, there seems to be plenty of room for them to say: well, you passed this part or that part but not the other part so you don't pass. That seems to be the tenor of the Ridiculous Report itself. Is it supposed to be a report on the Viva, or on the Thesis itself?

In any case, it sounds like they treated you unfairly during the Viva, and that they read the thesis with a jaundiced eye. The real question is: why?

Since I think on substantive matters you have pointed out real failings in their readings (basically, they don't know the context of the 'new' phenomenology in which you are writing -- and, generally, are unfamiliar with the history of this strand of continental philosophy), they have seized upon formal problems (relation to secondary texts; loose connection between the essays; etc) to make their points. But again the question looms: why have they taken such a stance?

It appears to me that they have done so because of the tone of your writing. You have indeed imbibed the spirit of Kierkegaard, who engages in argument, to be sure, but also is strongly polemical. Like his, your writing is confrontational, and I believe that the animus directed at you by the faculty derives from that. I suppose this stems from your own sense of yourself as (like Kierkegaard) a 'Christian philosopher' in a context where the reigning assumptions in philosophy are (in your terms) 'atheist' (and for SK, 'Christendom' might as well be atheist). Faculty members of philosophy departments do not take kindly to students who dismiss broad swaths of the discipline as "vanity." You really have to make a very very strong case to use such language in the polemical way that you do. In their minds (again, my guess is) they feel that the bar is far higher for someone who wants to go in for such polemics, and that you have not cleared that bar. I am not judging whether they are right or wrong in this; this is just my best guess about how things have gotten to this point.

The parallels with SK and the Corsair Affair are not to be missed. My guess is that, if your appeal is unsuccessful, the only way forward would be to revise the thesis to remove the polemical and rhetorical aspects and tighten up the connections between the chapters.

In any case, this is really disappointing behavior on their part and a real mess for you. I obviously don't have any real advice; I'm just too far away from the whole thing. But I'm happy to be a sounding board for you as things go forward. You have taken a stand, in the thesis, on something that is deeply meaningful to you. You will have to be the judge of which aspects of it are indispensable and which are not

He stood in silence.

"Son, I'm going to be honest with you. At this point, I have absolutely no idea what's going on anymore. I've been here for over a month and the article in the paper is still not down, the lawyers are messing around, there's too many regulations and rules for me to remember, and there's too many names to keep track of. All I know is that nothing's happening, and it's absurd. Tell me what Carrell is saying."

He looked at Alison. "Do you want me to tell you what it says, or what it really means?"

"What it really means," she said.

"It's like the Beth email over Christmas, only slightly more subtle. It's a taunt."

"But it sounds like he's sympathetic," she said.

"I thought you wanted to hear what it really said."

"I do, but that doesn't mean I can't have an opinion," she said. "Carrell said they're acting out of animus. That the examiners don't know what they're talking about, that it was all biased."

"So? And what did he offer to do?"

His dad spoke up, "Nothing."

"Exactly. It's just a c-y-a note. He knows Quiller and Klaus blew their cover. Now that they flunked the viva, it's too obvious, and Carrell can't be tied to it. So he's going to send me some note pretending to be sorry, but not doing anything about it. It's all shadow boxing."

Alison looked at him. "What's the Corsair Affair?"

"Kierkegaard got slandered and mocked in the press back in Copenhagen. Carrell's saying what they're doing to me here in the papers is the same."

"Well, that's good. He's saying you're like Kierkegaard."

"I know, that's part of the taunting. He wants me to try to equate myself with Kierkegaard, so that everyone can say I have delusions of grandeur."

"But he just said it himself."

"That's what makes it such sport! He can say it and pretend to mean it, but if I tell anyone that, it's proof I'm insane."

"I don't know. Maybe you're being too sensitive," she said. "I think he wants to help, but he can't."

"What about the appeal, then?"

"The appeal?"

"Yeah, he said he doubts it will succeed."

"He's just being honest."

"Why shouldn't it succeed? I have a clear-cut case. What they've done is absurd."

"He doesn't want to give you false hope."

"No, he's rubbing it in. By saying the appeal won't succeed, he wants me to argue with him. He wants me to challenge how in the world he could think that. Then, he can turn around and claim that I'm being unfair to him, and that I'm exhibiting all the personality traits I've been accused of, so maybe it turns out that he was wrong about me. If I tell him that he doesn't mean what he says, and he's not really interested in helping, then he'll say I'm paranoid. So no matter what I do, he can say I deserve what I'm getting."

"I don't know, maybe you're overthinking it."

"What about Maureen?"

"I don't know."

"He wants me to ask about the volume, so he can give me the bad news that I'm no longer involved with it. If I was still going to be working on it, Maureen and Carrell would be talking about it with me. Why would it just disappear?"

"That's just life."

"Okay, what about Luce? You used to ask me where Routledge was. Now you don't ask. So that book has disappeared too. Why? Carrell mentions that one."

His dad stood up. "I'm so sick of these people. They're freaks. They enjoy torturing people. I'm going to take a walk. The next time you talk to Dave, tell him you want the letter sent soon. I'm tired of waiting."

"I know, Dad. It'll go out next week," he said.

He lit a cigarette and laughed. After almost three years here, his examiners had decided that his DPhil wasn't worthy of even a master's degree. It was the worst result possible. Somehow the GSC had approved the recommendation. All he could do now was file an academic appeal with the Proctors' Office.

He turned to Alison. He smiled. "Who's the Proctor?"

"You know I don't remember."

"So, here we are. I told you they would flunk it. Just picture Klaus laughing in London right now at a Rothschild robe party."

The phone rang. He stepped outside to talk to Dave.

"Yeah?"

"I'm looking over the paperwork," Dave said.

"Yeah?"

"There's no signatures or date."

"So?"

"That's a problem for them. There's nothing official, if it's not signed and dated properly. That's just another irregularity. Patrick agrees. We're drafting the letter. It'll be ready next week."

"Okay. You need to hurry. My family has about had enough."

"I know. Almost there." There was a silence.

"Did you hear from your old supervisor in Texas? Carrell? Is he going to help?"

"Heard from him today. He's not going to do anything. He's working with them."

"How do you know?"

"I know, Dave. I wouldn't have made it this far, if I didn't see something that obvious."

"Okay, well, we'll move on. There will be other options."

He was quiet.

"Hello? Are you there?"

"I'm here, Dave. I was just thinking about how amusing it is to watch men try to outsmart God. But that's the irrationality and stupidity of evil. They can spin their stories, tell their lies, hide behind their system, but it won't matter. I know people think I'm crazy, and they think it's over, but I'm going to get the DPhil. The Routledge book, too."

"That's the spirit, mate. You're Captain America." They laughed, and hung up.

FIFTY

H E had died to the world. Or, more precisely, he had been shunned by it. The isolation wasn't the painful part. It was the ceaseless attacks, the strain of knowing that those who hated him here in Oxford and elsewhere were busy devising new ways to attack him. Alison had left to see a friend in the town center, and his dad had gone for a walk somewhere. He lied in bed, and stared out the window. He cleared his mind.

He tried to retrieve the words he felt he had to hear. At first, he was dry, and he heard nothing. Then, there was a flood, and the words began echoing through his heart.

His eyes closed. "*Thou shalt stretch forth thine hand against the wrath of mine enemies, and thy right hand shall save me . . .*" He opened his eyes, then closed them again. "*. . . Keep me safe, Lord, from the hands of the wicked; protect me from the violent, who devise ways to trip my feet . . .*" He sighed, "*For strangers rise up against me, and ruthless men seek my life.*" He sighed again, more deeply, "*Deliver me, O my God, from the hand of the wicked, from the grasp of the unjust and ruthless.*" Tears came down his face, "*I was pushed so hard I was falling, but the Lord helped me.*" He sighed, opened his eyes, and stood from the bed, "*Rescue me, O Lord, from evil men. Protect me from men of violence.*"

He sat at the edge of the bed, and forgot about everything outside the room. He would be content alone with God.

FIFTY-ONE

" CALL me if you hear anything," the solicitor said.

"Will do," he said.

The letter from Dave and Patrick had been sent. There had been discussion about to whom exactly to address the letter, and after weighing the options, they settled on a philosophy professor, Phil Childress, who in his capacity as a member of the Faculty of Philosophy Graduate Studies Committee had voted to confirm the examiners' recommendation to fail the thesis. The trouble for Childress is that in the course of a conversation they had in person, Childress had let it slip out that the GSC had taken the decision of failing the thesis without having actually seen the examiners' report. They had rubber-stamped something without even knowing what they were stamping. Worse yet, the paperwork hadn't been signed or dated, and the result was communicated by a Faculty secretary over email, rather than from the Exam Schools. He was still waiting for the decision to arrive by post at his college address, even though it should have arrived weeks ago. Everything about the process, from the viva itself, to the result, to the way the result had been communicated, was irregular, and absurdly so.

He checked for mail in his pidge, then walked over to the college's graduate computing lab. He logged into his email. There was a pit in his stomach. Childress had responded.

> "University IT policy forbids me from opening any attachments from unknown senders."

He laughed, and called the solicitor.

"Did you see the email?"

"Yes, absolutely extraordinary. They're desperate. I will be sending you the language. Send it as soon as you have it."

"Will do." When the language from the solicitor came, he sent it to Childress.

> Dear Prof Childress,
>> Many thanks for your reply.
>> For ease of reference, the letter from my lawyers enclosed in the original email has also been delivered by hand to your post at your college.
>> University IT policy will not prevent you from reading the hard copy.

There was no response from Childress that day. Or the next. Or the day after that. In addition to Childress, the Chair of the Faculty and the DGS had received the letter. So, too, had the other professors on the GSC. At the college, the Dean, the Tutor for Graduates, and his college advisor has received copies of the letter also. Nobody had been expecting a letter from a QC threatening to take the viva decision to the High Court. They were likely panicking, with no idea about what to do. He lit a cigarette and smiled.

"Want to go for a stretch?"

"Sure, Son. There's nothing else to do here but walk," his dad said.

They got onto the street, where it was sunny and comfortable.

His dad broke the silence. "When do you think they'll reply?"

"No idea. Imagine the turmoil right now. You're talking about a dozen people receiving a letter from a QC. They know this will be in the press soon. They just got caught with their hands in the cookie jar. It's like Dave said, they're going to be pirates slashing to get on the lifeboat. We'll just sit back and let them fight each other."

"Shouldn't we take it to the Oxford legal team? What if the professor dorks just bury it?"

"They can't do that. It's a letter from a QC. They can't ignore a letter from a QC."

"I don't know, Son. Everything's such a joke. I can see them never responding."

"Okay, well, if they don't respond, we'll deal with it."

"I can't be here forever. My passport is going to expire in a few months."

"I know."

"Should we go through the college? Dave said it's good to be seen," his dad said.

"Sure. Good idea. Let's go take a look."

François tipped his cap at Tom Gate. They stood in the quad for a while.

"Look at all the tourists here," his dad said, shaking his head. "Do you think they have any idea how phony this place is? I feel like going up to them and telling them it's all a fraud." They both laughed.

"Come on, let's go."

When they passed the Deanery, Simpson was coming from Kilcannon.

"Don't say anything. Keep walking, and I'll wait behind here. I'm going to talk to him," he said.

His dad passed Simpson, and Simpson approached.

"Prof Simpson," he said. His college advisor was looking at the ground, but there was no way for him to pretend he didn't hear his name being called. Simpson looked up frantically.

"Yes?"

"Did you get the letter?"

"The letter?"

"Yes, the letter. Mr Patrick Newman, QC, wrote to you about the irregular viva you never investigated, you know, the one the Dean asked you to look into during my collections' meeting. You wished me good luck about it a few weeks ago. Have you talked to the DGS or the Chair of the Faculty about the original complaint, or now the letter?"

Simpson was angry. His college advisor stepped up to him.

"It is not for you to tell us what to do," Simpson said through clenched teeth.

"You're right. The rules do," he said.

Simpson stared at him, then walked away.

He caught up to his dad in Peck Quad.

"What did the dork say?"

"He doesn't know what to do. He pretended not to know about the letter."

His dad scoffed, "Are you kidding me? I'm tired of waiting. Let's go see the legal department. Why don't we just schedule something with the Chancellor?"

"We have to wait."

"Why?"

"If we take this to the wrong people too soon, they'll kill us."

His dad looked at him. The people here were so pathetic that it was easy to forget they could be seriously dangerous. They passed the Rhodes statue.

"Think about Bill Clinton walking around here," his dad laughed. "What a joke."

The High was crowded with tourists. Soon, he thought, the Almond tree would be in bloom. He would have to remember to come see it with Alison.

He stopped into a shop for cigarettes. He knew his dad wanted to tell him to quit, but because of all the stress, his dad was giving him a pass.

He lit a cigarette and started coughing. "I know, I know," he said.

"I'm just worried about you, that's all," his dad said.

"Come on, let's get out of here," he said.

They passed the entrance to the Covered Market. Out of the corner of his eye, he noticed a man charging through the crowd from inside towards the street. A few feet past the entrance to the Market, he heard footsteps. The man shoved him hard in the back, knocking him off his feet and nearly down to the ground. The man walked a few feet past him, then spun around and began shouting in his face: "F— you! F— you! F— you!" He had never seen the man. He walked by the man, who continued hurling insults. He wasn't sure where his dad was. He turned around to see two other men stepping onto the sidewalk from the street. They joined the first man, forming something of a skirmish line. Then two more men came out from the Covered Market joining the others. His dad walked up to him. "Come on, let's go now." The entire episode was synthetic, too theatrical. They looked back to see a crowd had gathered, stunned by what they had seen. The men who had materialized from nowhere all darted into the Covered Market and disappeared.

At the corner, he looked at his dad. "You know what that was, right?"

His dad looked at him, "Set-up."

"Yep. They already have the homophobia narrative going. They figured they'd try to get the Islamophobia narrative going too. Imagine the headline now: 'Crazed, Bible-Thumping Oxford Graduate Student Attacks Muslims.'" He laughed bitterly.

His dad was visibly shaken. When they were off the High, he leaned up against a wall. His dad might cry. It wasn't physical fear, just the accumulated stress that had been building for weeks.

"I'm sorry, Dad," he said.

"It's fine, Son."

"At least we know they can't answer the letter," he said laughing.

"They're pinned. I'm telling you, don't be surprised if they never respond."

"Well, now when you go home, you'll be able to tell everyone that you got to experience some Oxford street theater. Did they really think we'd take the bait?"

"They must have thought it was worth a shot. People do dumb things under stress. They must have thought we were close to breaking and would get violent."

"Come on, let's go home."

"I don't want to go for a walk again for a while," his dad said.

"Me neither."

FIFTY-TWO

THE waiting continued, and nothing happened. Nobody had answered the letter. The Chair of the Faculty, Harcourt, had said he should file an appeal with the Proctors. He would do so eventually, but now it appeared only to be a trap. One of the Proctors' assistants had told him in a meeting that there would be no academic appeal hearing. When he showed the University regulations showing he was entitled to one, it didn't make a difference. The University's own rules were being suspended, even in the office responsible for enforcing and upholding them. The newspaper article was still up. He'd written to the editors about it, but they hadn't replied. People would stare at him at college, and everybody at the Faculty ignored him when he came to the building. It had been months since he'd heard from Adamson who'd simply vanished. Worst of all, the lawyers had disappeared also. The solicitor had told him to forget about damages. There wasn't going to be a harassment or discrimination suit. The solicitor had said he was working on the academic appeal, but it was looking increasingly likely that he'd have to be the one to do it himself. He sighed as the words flooded over him, "I am forgotten as a dead man out of mind. I am like a broken vessel. For I have heard the slander of many. Fear was on every side. While they took counsel together against me, they devised to take away my life." The system had been shut down on him, and everyone within it was waiting him out. The message was he should give up and leave because struggling was pointless. His dad was disconsolate, and Alison was hospitalized from the stress. The people doing this had no remorse. He knew they were prepared to kill him, if they thought they must.

"Can we go to the legal department now?"

"Won't matter, Dad. They've shut everything down. The network is working, and everyone knows to stay out of the way. A letter from a QC sits there for months? Unbelievable."

"Don't you have that thing to go to today?"

"Yeah."

"Want me to come?"

"You can't come inside. But if you want to wait outside, that's fine."

"Okay, let me grab my jacket."

They got outside.

His dad looked at him. "Which way?"

"Let's walk through Port Meadow."

"So, what's the plan?"

"The usual. Dave said to stay visible, so I'm going to the event."

"Are you going to say anything there?"

"I don't know yet. I'll play it by ear."

"Then what?"

"Then tonight, I'll go to the event at the college."

"Are you sure? What if it's a trap?"

"No option. I have to go."

They walked the rest of the way to the Faculty in silence. When they got to the building, he told his dad he'd be back soon.

"Be careful," his dad said. "I'll be waiting here."

He nodded and walked into Lecture Room 2. The room was full with other philosophy DPhil students. He took a seat in the back by the window. A few minutes later, Morrison and two other professors walked in.

Morrison cleared his throat and the room fell silent.

"Good afternoon, everyone. Thank you for attending this year's Publishing Workshop. The purpose of today's meeting is for you to be given an opportunity to ask questions about how to go about publishing your research. This might include journal articles, or it might include publishing a monograph, which, typically, will be a revised and expanded version of your thesis. The point of philosophical research is knowledge, of course, but there are practical and professional considerations at play too, so we will answer any questions you might have about that aspect of things."

The two other professors gave brief presentations outlining the viva process, and explaining various ways to rework thesis material into publishable articles or a monograph. They opened the floor for questions. A number of students had questions about whether they should publish or not while still graduate students. The consensus was that they should, because it was increasingly difficult to land a job without publications. A number of other students had questions about whether it was better to publish articles or a monograph. The consensus was that it was hard to say. It depended on one's specific situation.

He raised his hand. Morrison pointed at him.

"Yes, thanks. I think my question is simple. My understanding is that according to the Faculty Handbook, the criterion for a successful thesis is that it contains at least ten thousand words of publishable material."

Morrison spoke, "Yes, that's correct."

"Okay. So, my question is, and I apologize if this sounds rather bizarre, but I thought I might ask nonetheless: if something is published, does that mean it's publishable?"

The room burst into laughter. It was an absurd notion, the idea that something could be published and yet not also be publishable. If something were actual, it was by definition possible. If something was published, it thereby had demonstrated it was publishable. The entire presupposition of today's workshop was that the exceedingly vast majority of DPhil theses were not yet ready to be published. The point of the workshop, after all, was to tell students how to rework and improve thesis material, in order to publish it eventually. If one had already published material in the thesis, that would be extraordinary.

Morrison flushed.

He pressed on, "I mean, I guess what I'm asking is whether it's necessary to have published material in the thesis to pass?"

One of the other professors spoke, "No, not at all. That's not the expectation. It's quite rare to have published material in the thesis."

"I see. How rare exactly? I mean, surely some theses have one article, right?"

"Yes, that would not be unheard of. But, still, it's rare."

"How about three publications?"

"I've not heard of that before. It's not impossible, I suppose. But it's certainly not the expectation." The room laughed.

He turned to Morrison. "Okay, so hypothetically, if somebody were to submit a thesis that contained three publications, would that be good enough to pass? Published means publishable, no?" The room fell silent, as the other students realized that he must be the one everyone had been hearing about, the one whose thesis had been flunked, despite all of its publications. The room turned its attention to Morrison to see how he'd respond.

"Well, as silly as it sounds, for the purposes of the examination, something's being published does not mean it's publishable." The room began laughing again.

"Hear me out, hear me out," Morrison said. "It's a bit like Mill's principle of..."

His thought drifted away, as Morrison droned on. There was no point in listening. It was all just great swelling words of emptiness anyway. Morrison, who had arranged for Anderson to be his internal examiner, evidently didn't care that his thesis had been flunked. Whether or not Morrison had meant to set him up didn't matter. In any case, Morrison wasn't going to do anything to address the situation.

The workshop concluded, and he went outside.

"How'd it go?"

"Depends how you look at it. It was surreal, as usual. According to Morrison now, something already being published doesn't mean it's publishable. The room got a kick out of that one."

"What's the point of even having a Publishing Workshop, then?"

"There isn't one. Now everyone sees that. It's a fraud."

They turned to walk to Woodstock, when he startled. Klaus was coming. His dad and he continued walking toward the street. His former supervisor's red scarf was blowing in the wind, with his hands buried in his coat. As they passed the fountain, Klaus was poised to charge into him. At the very last second, Klaus swerved, his shoulder nearly brushing up against his. He kept walking, and didn't look back at Klaus. His dad spun around, and then turned to him.

"Who was that weirdo? He almost ran into you."

"That was Klaus."

"*That* was *Klaus*?"

"Yep."

"Boy, what a freak. I was wondering who the angry guy storming up to us was. He almost bumped into you. Good thing I didn't know it was him. I would have clothes-lined him."

When they turned onto Woodstock, he muttered, "Oh, boy, here we go again."

"What now?"

"It's fine. Don't say anything. Just wait."

The Chair of the Faculty approached them. The Chair stopped.

"Hello," the Chair said.

"Hello."

They were quiet for a few seconds.

"Is there going to be any formal reply from the University to the letter? We've been waiting for a while now."

"As I said before, you should take it to the Proctors."

"We will, but before we do, we must insist we believe it would be premature to do so without a formal reply from the University."

"Again, all I can say is take it to the Proctors." The Chair began to leave.

"One more thing."

"Yes?"

"What about the job? I didn't even get an interview."

The Chair studied him. "I'm not at liberty to discuss the details of a search. However, I can say that you were in my personal top seven. You'd have to speak to Quiller and Klaus about their lists. Now excuse me, please, I have a GSC meeting."

His dad looked at him. "What does that mean?"

"We'll take it to the Proctors. No other option. They're not going to answer the letter."

"What about tonight?"

"It'll be fine."

A few hours later, he got to the college just as the sun dipped below the horizon. It was twilight hour, and as much as he'd come to loathe the place, the quad's beauty was undeniable. Even Cush himself looked serene in the dusk. He walked into the event which was full. People had wine, and the mood was jovial. He scanned the room and spotted the Dean.

He walked up to the Dean.

"Hello," he said.

"Hello, how are you?"

"I'm good. Do you have a moment to talk about the viva?"

"Not here. But feel free to schedule an appointment with my assistant."

"And the letter?"

The Dean looked at him blankly. Somebody else approached the Dean, and the two began a conversation. He walked away and took a spot against the wall.

A few minutes later, one of the Dean's assistants clinked a glass.

"Excuse me everyone, as much as I'm loath to disrupt the festivities, some announcements are necessary." Another man from the Development Office took the floor.

"Congratulations to you all. It's quite an accomplishment to take a degree from Oxford, and it's our pleasure here at the House to host you tonight to recognize that accomplishment. As sorry as we'll be to see you leave, remember that being a Member is a lifelong journey. You are always welcome back, and we will watch your progress with great pride." The man paused and looked at him.

"Of course, this is also a fundraising event, which means I'm obliged to tell you that you should support the House financially." The room laughed. "I want you all to know, no matter where you go, we will find you. We have an international network, and we're everywhere, so we'll find you." The room laughed. The public meaning was that they were relentless in their fundraising efforts; the real meaning was directed at him. There was no hiding. There was no moving on. No matter where he went, the network causing him problems here and now would reach wherever he thought he might go to avoid them and attempt to start over. He sighed.

On the walk home, he stopped for a cigarette outside one of his favorite coffee shops. He stood on the corner, and watched the people. He thought about leaving, but lit another cigarette. He coughed for a while, but he didn't care.

"Hey." It was Luke from the Philosophy Faculty on his bike. "Love the look, man," Luke said.

"Huh?"

"All denim," Luke said.

He was in jeans, and he'd thrown on a jean jacket without thinking about it. It wasn't meant to be a fashion statement, but evidently Luke thought it was.

"Oh, thanks."

"How's it going?"

He stared into the distance, took a drag, and looked at Luke.

"It's a bit like being in the middle of a Stanley Kubrick movie. At this point, I may as well be Bill Harper and you Nick Nightingale," he said.

Luke looked at him uncomfortably, said nothing, and rode away.

FIFTY-THREE

THE term ended. Summer came. There had been no response to the letter. The article was still online. He hadn't heard from anyone. His Faculty supervisor, his college advisor, the Chair of the Faculty, the DGS, the Tutor for Graduates, Manan, Joseph, and Ben—they were all gone. Everyone had vanished. Alison would be out of the hospital tomorrow. Soon his dad's passport would expire, and he would have to leave. It would be time to file the academic appeal with the Proctors and see what happened. It was clear he was on his own. Patrick had disappeared months ago. Dave only checked in sporadically.

His phone rang. As it happened, it was Dave.

"How's it going?"

"Good."

"I'm sorry I've been so busy the last couple months. Now that it's summer, I'll have more time."

"Okay."

"Could you remind me of the deadline to file the academic appeal?"

"August."

"Okay, we'll be working on that."

"Sounds good."

"Okay, chat later."

His dad came into the room.

"Was that the solicitor?"

"Yeah."

"What'd he say?"

"Nothing. He's stalling."

"He's not working on the appeal?"

"No, he just says he is. They want me to think it's getting done so that I won't work on it myself. Then at the last second, I'll find out the appeal won't be ready, and I'll miss the deadline."

"What are you going to do?"

"I'll let them think their plan is working, and then file the appeal on my own the day before the deadline."

"What about the academic hearing?"

"Not happening."

"But the regulations say you're entitled to one."

"There's no rules here, Dad. You know that."

His dad sighed. "Well, I'm running out of time."

"It's fine, Dad. I won't need you here to file the appeal."

He sat down at his desk and checked his email.

"Well, well, well. Isn't that something."

"What?"

"It's Luce from Routledge. They're offering me a contract for the book."

His dad jumped in the air. "That's fantastic. Ah, hah! I knew we'd get these guys." His dad's face turned solemn. "What? What's wrong?"

"You don't understand. It's a sham."

"What do you mean?"

"It's just another ritual."

"I don't get it."

"Luce doesn't have an excuse not to offer me the contract. It looks weird that he disappeared. So they're tying up a loose end. Since I'm fighting the viva and we sent the lawyers' letter in, they don't want Rout-ledge getting dragged into it. Easiest thing to do is offer me the contract to dissolve the problem, then later void the contract, or claim the book is not publishable. They'll just do the same thing with the book that they're doing now with the thesis."

His dad thought about it. "I see your point. So what are you going to do?"

"Play along. I'll sign the contract, and then worry later about forcing them to publish the book."

He was quiet for a second. "Watch this."

He picked up his phone and rang Dave.

"Dave, you won't believe it. I have just absolutely fantastic news. I've just heard from the editor at Routledge. Remember him? Well out of the blue he wrote to me today to offer a contract." There was a pause. "Yes, let's be in touch." He hung up.

"See?"

"What?"

"Dave didn't know what to say. Hardly a word. He's not enthused. He doesn't say anything about how we can use this development to our advantage with the viva. He's acting like it didn't even happen. Because he knows too. It's just theater." He sighed.

"Is Alison back tomorrow?"

"Yeah."

"I'm sorry for what's being done to you two."

"It's okay."

"Where's Stuart and Linda?"

"Pretending everything's normal. I got an email a few days ago from Linda. A nice picture of Stuart at some conference winning an award." He laughed.

"These people are sick. Their daughter is in the hospital, and their son-in-law is being persecuted, and they act like nothing's going on?"

"Yep."

"You know, Son, the thing that bothers me is that it can be so obvious and everyone pretends not to see. You think Stuart and Carrell have talked?"

"Probably. But even if not, they both know what they're doing. I'll worry about it when I get back to Texas."

FIFTY-FOUR

TOMORROW his dad would leave Oxford, and this was their last walk together. The sun was out, and there were sunbathers in the University Parks. They took a seat on a bench at the pond.

"I'm sorry, Son."

"Why?"

"I failed."

"How?"

"I thought I could fix it. I've been here for months, and nothing's fixed. God has humbled me."

"Me too."

"Where's the solicitor? The appeal is due in two weeks."

"He said he'll be calling today."

"Are you and Alison going to be okay when I'm gone?"

"Yeah."

"I know she didn't like me here. I'm sorry for causing trouble."

"It's fine. One day she'll see why you came here. It's just hard for her."

"Do you think she'll ever figure out what's going on with Stuart?"

"I don't know. Maybe."

"I don't know how you do it, Son, dealing with all the people in your profession. It would have driven me crazy."

He laughed. "Well, you know, Dad, they're trying their best to do it to me."

"Are you sure I should go? I'm worried about your safety."

"You have to go. Staying here wouldn't matter. If they want to do something, they'll do something. Nothing to stop it."

The phone rang. "Must be Dave." He stood up and started walking, as he answered.

"Hi."

"Hi, how's it going?"

"A little concerned about the timetable, Dave. Two weeks till the deadline for the appeal."

"Yes, well, I've been speaking to the Oxford legal team." He put his hand over the receiver and told his dad. His dad's eyes widened.

He waited for Dave to continue.

"They want to know about Adamson."

"That guy? He's been gone for months."

"They say that you didn't pay your University fees, and that's why Adamson stopped supervising you. When you pay, Adamson will resume his duties."

"I paid the fees. I showed you the payment records. That's not why Adamson disappeared. You know that. Besides, I'll be gone in two weeks back to the States. I don't need a supervisor here anymore."

There was a pause.

"Okay, I'll follow-up with the legal people about the fees." Dave paused. "You've had depression issues in the past?"

"In the past."

"This has been a very stressful time . . . "

"I'm fine."

"As your lawyer, I wouldn't want to see you . . . "

"I'm not going to kill myself. I intend to submit the appeal, return to the States, and write the Routledge book. I'll do that whether or not I ever get the DPhil."

Dave sighed. "I see. Okay, let me see what I can do." They hung up.

"What happened?"

"They told Dave to give me the death threat. They're trying to set up a suicide narrative. You know, the unstable, distraught student who couldn't accept failure."

"What are you going to do?"

"Exactly what I told Dave. I'll file the appeal, go back to Texas and write the book, and worry about the DPhil when I'm there."

They walked more through the Parks. He stopped.

His dad looked at him. "What is it?"

The words addressed him, "For the weapons of our warfare are not carnal, but mighty through God to the pulling down of strong holds. Casting down imaginations, and every high thing that exalts itself against the knowledge of God, and bringing into captivity every thought to the obedience of Christ."

He turned to his dad. "I'm going to tear it all down." The phone rang again.

"You're sure you're not depressed? You can be honest with me," Dave said.

His dad looked at him, "What's going on?"

He held his hand over the receiver. "They have Dave on speaker phone with everyone. They're trying the suicide thing again."

He took his hand off the receiver.

"You know I don't lie, Dave. If I were a liar, I'd fit in here with everyone else, and my life would not have been made miserable by them. So, to answer your question again, no, I'm not depressed. And I'm certainly not suicidal. I'm going to file the appeal, and there's nothing anyone can do to stop me. I have to say I'm flattered nobody there even bothered trying bribery."

Dave chuckled, then there was a silence.

Dave spoke, "Okay, well you'll have to make a very strong case in your appeal. I don't know if it will be successful."

"I don't think you understand. I don't care anymore. I'm going to submit the appeal, and that's it. It's not my responsibility to persuade everyone to accept the obvious. The truth has been self-evident to everyone for a long time, and I don't have to pretend that it isn't. It's up to each person to make a decision for himself as to whether he wants to live up to the University regulations and statutes. I can't force anyone to do that. When we're all at the White Throne Judgment, none of this will matter."

There was a very long silence.

"Okay." Dave hung up.

FIFTY-FIVE

H IS dad was gone home. With his dad having left, things were lonely. Alison had not yet come back from the hospital, as originally expected. As he walked down the High, he realized that they've never come to see the Almond tree in bloom. He sat down on the bench. He couldn't walk anymore, with the tears clouding his vision. He lit a cigarette. When the hacking stopped, he took a breath, and stared up into the sky. It was gray, but he knew the sun was up there somewhere. He sat on the bench till dusk. He walked out to the river and sat on a bench there.

He knew he had already made it further than anyone could possibly have imagined. "*Keep me from the snares which they have laid for me, and the gins of the workers of iniquity. Let the wicked fall into their own nets, whilst that I withal escape.*" The fact that the appeal would be filed, and stood any chance of success, however remote, was a miracle. "*If it had not been the Lord who was on our side, when men rose up against us, then they had swallowed us up quick. When their wrath was kindled against us, then the waters had overwhelmed us, the stream had gone over our soul. Then the proud waters had gone over our soul. Blessed be the Lord, who hath not given us as a prey to their teeth. Our soul is escaped as a bird out of the snare of the fowlers. The snare is broken, and we are escaped. Our help is in the name of the Lord, who made heaven and earth.*" He thought about the birds in Paris. Only God had been here. And that was sufficient. "*It is better to trust in the Lord than to put confidence in man.*" He knew everything he had once desired was only death. "*I will walk before the Lord in the land of the living.*"

The others who hated him did so, because they knew he had contemplated doing the unforgivable. He had contemplated treason, by considering dying to the world. They knew they should also, but they were still unwilling. They would hate him more if he made the leap. *"I became also a reproach unto them. When they looked upon me, they shook their heads."* He looked up at the sky. *"Thy mercy is great above the heavens, and thy truth reacheth unto the clouds."* The words flooded over him. *"Be thou exalted, O God, above the heavens, and thy glory above all the earth. That thy beloved may be delivered. Save with thy right hand, and answer me."* The moon, he saw, rises with no eye to the schemes of men. It just was. *"Who will bring me into the strong city? Who will lead me into Edom? Wilt not thou, O God, who hast cast us off? and wilt not thou, O God, go forth with our hosts? Give us help from trouble. For vain is the help of man. Through God we shall do valiantly, for he it is that shall tread down our enemies."* They would not quit. And he was only enraging them by daring to file the appeal. *"They gather themselves together against the soul of the righteous, and condemn the innocent blood."* They thought he was alone. *"For mine enemies speak against me, and they that lay wait for my soul take counsel together, Saying, God hath forsaken him: persecute and take him; for there is none to deliver him."* They were trying to break him. *"I am weary of my crying. My throat is dried. Mine eyes fail while I wait for my God. They that hate me without a cause are more than the hairs of my head. They that would destroy me, being my enemies wrongfully, are mighty."* The next part of the verse cut him to his heart. *"O God, thou know my foolishness, and my sins are not hid from thee."* It didn't matter if others thought he was a religious zealot. It didn't matter if he were being persecuted for his faith. Something was still not right within him. He had not fully surrendered. A great fear overtook him. He knew God would take him soon, if he did not repent. He knew he would deserve it. He could feel that he had been withholding something from God. He was still hiding. *"If that evil servant shall say in his heart, My lord delayeth his coming . . . The lord of that servant shall come in a day when he looketh not for him, and in an hour he is not aware of, and shall cut him asunder, and appoint him his portion with the hypocrites. There shall be weeping and gnashing of teeth."* He knew he must become truly simple. Any residual guile must cease. *"Verily I say unto you, Whosoever shall not receive the kingdom of God as a little child, he shall not enter therein."* He had not abandoned himself. He was not yet a son of God. As much as he hated the world, and as much as those who loved the world hated him, he was still a man of the world too. He would not fear the persecution. He would stop managing it. He would let go. Nothing he was enduring was unintelligible. This simply was the gate to eternal life, he thought. The words of Peter came to him, *"Beloved, do not be surprised at the fiery trial when it comes upon you to test you, as though something strange were happening to you. But rejoice insofar as you share Christ's sufferings, that you may also rejoice and be glad when his glory is revealed. If you are insulted for the name of Christ, you are blessed, because the Spirit of glory and of God rests upon you."* Christ was suffering in the garden, and yet he was asleep. He could not deny Christ any longer.

When he got home, he kneeled on the bedroom floor. He was still. He went into a place within himself he'd never been to before, a hidden chamber of the heart he had not known till then existed. It had been locked shut, and now it was open. God pierced him, and there was no shadow of turning inside him. Just fullness. Search me, O God, and know my heart. Try me, and know my thoughts. And see if there be any wicked way in me, and lead me in the way everlasting.

FIFTY-SIX

THE appeal was filed that morning. Dave was now frantic, and wanted to speak to him. He had been correct. Nobody thought the appeal could appear so suddenly, as if from nowhere. They had all thought he'd miss the deadline. He turned to Alison. "You talk to him," he said passing her the phone. "I'll finish packing when I'm back. I'm going to take a walk."

Ben had asked to meet him at the college. The stated reason was that Ben wanted to see him before he left, but that wasn't it. Ben had been told to see whether he could extract anything relevant about the appeal and the rest of it.

They met at the Broad Walk.

Ben smiled and shook his hand. "How are you, buddy?"

"I'm doing well. Why don't we take a loop around the Meadow?"

"Sounds great. What a beautiful day."

They walked in silence for a while.

"So how are thing with the viva?"

"I filed the appeal this morning."

"I hope it's successful."

"Me too. In any case, I always have the Routledge book." He could see Ben was surprised. Ben hadn't known.

"The book?"

"Yeah, Billy Luce at Routledge has contracted me to write an intro."

"Wow, so you're like the man now."

"I guess so. It certainly shows the absurdity of the viva result. It's fine, though. I accept everything. It's the will of God."

Ben looked at him. "Speaking of which, I have something I want to talk to you about. I think I met someone."

"Yeah?"

"Yeah, her name's Christine."

"She's a student here?"

"Yeah." Ben took a breath. "You see, well, we have been seeing each other. And, well, you know how it is, I was weak."

"I see."

"I feel terribly about it. I know we're not supposed to." He could see Ben smiling at the memory of it, even though he was saying he regretted it. He was the Romans wretch, the man who said he wanted to be righteous, but really did not yet want to be, and felt guilty that he didn't yet want to be free of his sin.

"Well, it happens. I used to be a fornicator. But when you repent and are born again, those sins stop."

Ben got defensive. "Well, yes, I repented of it. It's like 1 John 1:9 says."

"I don't think that's what the Scriptures mean by repentance. Repentance doesn't mean an ongoing cycle of saying you're sorry for your sin. It means a change of heart. It's a rebirth and a renewal. When that happens, the old man dies, and the past deeds of the flesh are put to death. You won't be fornicating anymore."

Ben was irritated. "I don't want to be rude, but I don't appreciate someone saying I'm not really a Christian."

"I'm saying that the Scriptures say there are deeds that will bar you from the kingdom. Fornication is one of them. So is adultery. And drunkenness. And greed. And lying. There's a whole list of things in the Scripture I left at Peck Quad that's caused such a stir."

"But there's grace," Ben said.

"Grace is the power of God. It doesn't forgive you of ongoing sin, it enables you to walk in holiness. Grace doesn't lower the bar, it raises it."

Ben looked at him and intoned, "Yes, but we must not forget, 'Not of works, lest any man should boast.'"

"I don't think the verse from Ephesians means what you suggest. Deeds are imperative to salvation. Christ himself in John says that we'll all be judged according to our deeds. In any case, what about belief itself? According to your theology, one still must believe in order to be saved. So, you can't escape works. Even belief is a work. One must choose to believe. That's a deed."

"Well, I don't want to argue. I was just saying that I'm struggling with this. I really want to keep seeing her," Ben continued. Ben was right in a way. There was no point in arguing. Ben knew the truth, but he didn't want to accept it. He would hide behind all the theology and doctrines of men, in order to placate himself, and to justify his lifestyle to himself. That's what he'd learned from being here. Theology was an intellectual excuse for the theologians' disobedience.

When he finished talking to Ben, he cut across the High Street. Outside Jesus College, he bumped into Dowell. Dowell was shocked to see him.

"Uh, hi," Dowell said.

"Hello, Mike," he said.

"What are you doing?"

"Out for a walk. Last one. Alison and I leave for the States tomorrow." He waited to see whether Mike would mention the viva or the smear campaign.

They stood and stared at each other in silence for a while. Mike smiled, and then his eyes narrowed. Klaus's friend had decided to remove the mask.

"How many times do you think you've been warned?"

"At least twice. Maybe three times."

"This is your final one. You know what happens."

"See you around, Mike. Good luck here. I'm sure Quiller and Klaus are going to love having you as a colleague. Big things ahead for you guys in the Strawson Room."

Mike stared.

"All good things, Mike," he said before walking on.

FIFTY-SEVEN

EXAS was just how he remembered it. Life there had gone on unchanged, as if he had never left for Oxford. Now that he was back, it was as if Oxford were nothing. Place was strange like that. No matter where one went, one was only passing through. What had begun as a fairy tale adventure abroad had become an odyssey simply to return. Now that he had, he realized things had never been an odyssey, either. Everything was really just a pilgrimage, even if everybody else didn't want to see that they were only passing through, too.

In the first month here, things had become clearer. Or, rather, what had always been clear to him was now becoming self-evident. Carrell had vanished. There was no word from Maureen. Carrell and the others would try to block the Routledge book as they had the viva. Stuart and Linda were still playing dumb. Even the result he had received yesterday from the Proctors' Office hadn't led Stuart to say a word. Contrary to everyone's expectations, the Senior Proctor had upheld his appeal by voiding the viva. He had read the letter aloud to Alison in her childhood bedroom.

> I write concerning the complaint you submitted to the Proctors regarding your examination for the DPhil in Philosophy. I am partially upholding your complaint, and directing that your first examination be voided, on the grounds of procedural irregularity, as set out in paragraphs 2 to 4 below.
>
> The result was not properly confirmed by the Graduate Studies Committee before it was notified to you. Whilst it is highly unusual for a board of graduate studies to disagree with the recommendations made by doctoral examiners, and your result was subsequently endorsed by the board, those recommendations should be scrutinized and either endorsed or questioned by the board before the result is finalized and communicated to

the student. The outcome of the DPhil examination is a decision of the board, not the examiners . . .

I am instructing that your first DPhil examination be voided, and that two new examiners be appointed to examine your thesis. For the avoidance of any appearance of bias, I am also instructing that both of these examiners should be external examiners . . .

In order to proceed, you ought to have a new supervisor within the University's policy, or at least an internal co-supervisor in addition to Mr Adamson. It is entirely possible for you to have a nominal internal supervisor in the Faculty, and an external (either to the Faculty or University) co-supervisor expert in your field, if there is no appropriate person in the Faculty. You may wish to discuss with your supervisor(s) the appointment of appropriate new examiners, and whether you wish to make any changes to your thesis before submission. Please discuss your supervision arrangements with the Director of Graduate Studies in Philosophy . . .

Your viva voce examination need not necessarily take place in Oxford. The University requires you be physical present with at least one examiner. If travel to Oxford is prohibitively expensive (for example, if you are residing in the United States) and at least one of your examiners is also a resident in the US, then the Faculty should look kindly on a request for your to be examined in a facility which is convenient to you both and which meets the University's requirements for an examination to take place over video-conference . . .

A Completion of Procedures letter will be issued fourteen calendar days after the date of this letter unless a request for reconsideration or clarification has been submitted, in which case the Completion of Procedures of letter will be issued with either a) my determination not to issue clarification or reconsider the case, (b) the clarification of the decision or (c) the decision following reconsideration.

Yours sincerely . . .

The night of the decision, he sat at the dinner table, waiting for Stuart to say something. They ate the salads. Then the main dish. Then the dessert. Dinner passed, and Stuart said nothing. He wondered whether Alison understood what was going on, but he doubted she did. She was so elated to see the appeal succeed that she was oblivious to anything else. He didn't want to tell her that even if he did get the DPhil, which now seemed likely, he would nevertheless be blackballed out here in Texas.

The smear campaign was still going, the gossip had traveled far and wide, and he had no support of any kind from anyone at Oxford. He would work on the book, and then he would have to push it through just as he was doing with the thesis now. But even if he were successful in publishing the book, it would be ignored. He would still be blackballed. That's how the network operated. He had sighed at the dinner table.

Linda had turned to him with a puzzled look on her face. "Is something wrong?"

"No, Linda."

He had bit his tongue at dinner, because he had known things would be relatively better soon. Tomorrow they would be moving into their own place. Alison has asked what he was looking for. His only desires, he had said, were that the place be in a neighborhood good for walks, and that it have a window with a nice view for writing. They'd found a place fitting the description, a small apartment in an old building nestled in a historic neighborhood lined with oaks and ivy.

Standing in the lot now, he looked at the building. The time for memory was past. It was time to move forward. Or at least to try.

Alison walked up behind him, and wrapped her arms around his waist. "Emerson," she said. "That's a good street name for you, my little writer," she said.

His memory turned to a moment outside a coffee shop here in the neighborhood. At the time, his second publication had just appeared in print, and his friends, or those he had thought were his friends, had learned of it. He had stepped outside for a cigarette. Clara followed him and sat down next to him. She nodded her head in the direction of Mick, who was sitting inside. "Mick told me about the new paper." She paused. "He says you're a very good writer," she said. He knew what she meant. He had a gift, the others were envious, and he was only asking for trouble by reminding them of the fact. He knew she wanted to leave Paul for him, but she was too afraid, since she saw that he was on the verge of social suicide. When Mick and David and Cody and the others had ostracized him, she would be left without any friends in town if she made the decision to be with him. He wanted to tell her that he had no intention of being with her, anyway. She thought they were similar, but they weren't. She was in love with the idea of him, not him.

Stuart and he took the couch up the stairs and put it in the living room. Linda was already inside. Alison came in behind them.

"Wow, this is a small place," Stuart said. He turned from Stuart, and looked out the window where he would put his desk. The leaves were rustling in the wind.

"I like it, Dad," she said.

"Well, I guess it's something all right for being temporary," Stuart said. Of course, Stuart knew that things were only beginning, and that living like this would not be temporary at all. But if he said that to Stuart, Stuart would play dumb, and everyone would get angry at him, and leap to Stuart's defense. He said nothing.

Stuart walked out with Alison to the parking lot. Linda walked up to him, and put her arms around his elbow.

"You should write a book about everything that happened in Oxford," she said.

He studied Linda. There were many things he could say. Anything he said would just be stating the obvious. Sometimes, as he knew, words were useless since there was no point in speaking. He could point out that none of what had happened in Oxford would have happened if Stuart and she had stepped in to intercede. He could point out that everything that happened there was not over, and that he would be living with the fallout for years. He could point out that Alison didn't deserve to be punished the way she was being punished. He could point out that his dad shouldn't have had to spend six months on a couch fighting against criminality that Linda had ignored but was now suddenly pretending to care about. He could say many things. But there was no point. It was a taunt. Linda wanted him to say all these things.

"Maybe one day."

The next morning, he was at the writing desk. Alison put her chin on his shoulder and kissed his neck. "I have to go to work. I'll see you tonight. I love you." They kissed.

"I love you, too," he said.

"What are you going to do today?"

"Write," he said. She smiled and kissed him again. The door closed behind her.

He opened the Book, and read the page.

> He that hath an ear, let him hear what the Spirit saith. To him that overcometh will I give to eat of the hidden manna, and will give him a white stone, and in the stone a new name written, which no man knoweth saving he that receiveth it.

He leafed through the Book, and read another page.

> A wise man scaleth the city of the mighty, and casteth down the
> strength of the confidence thereof.

He put the Book down on his desk.

If he were smoking still, he would have lit a cigarette. He looked out
his window into the yard below. He had spent three years at the most élite
college of the world's most prestigious university. He had walked the halls
of Wolsey, Wren, and Locke, of Auden, Carroll, and Rawls, of Penn, Eden,
and Gladstone, attended the dinners, met the future politicians, argued
with the eminent philosophers, sat at the feet of the distinguished theologians. Having seen the pinnacle of its institutional power and prestige,
he had confirmed what he'd suspected about the world since childhood.
The world was a lie. The pious theologians were part of a homosexual
blackmail ring, the philosophers did not love wisdom, only their careers,
tomorrow's statesmen were shallow and mediocre, while most of the others were all there simply to party and be able to brag about it later. A
night at a college garden party with British Royalty, or a masked ball at a
Rothschild mansion, were not nearly worth the price of his soul. Frankly,
everything driving the others he had met there repulsed him. The money,
and the power, and the sex, were nothing to him. As for those who suc-
cumbed to the temptation, who were taken in by the allure of the illusion,
these men of the world were condemned to strive inevitably in vain for
what they had been promised they could become. It was a pathetic delu-
sion, as he had seen. He shook his head and smiled.

Only Christ is King.